DAVID ESTES
& GD PENMAN

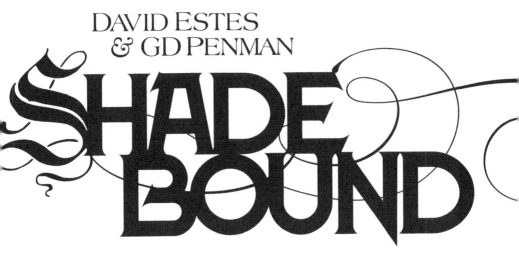

SHADE BOUND

THE LAST KING

BOOK ONE

Wraithmarked
CREATIVE

Editor: Taya Latham
Cover Illustration: Anastasia Bulgakova
Cover Design and Interior Layout: STK·Kreations
Art Direction: Bryce O'Connor

Trade paperback ISBN: 978-1-955252-48-5
Ebook ISBN: 978-1-955252-32-4

Worldwide Rights
1st Edition

Published by Wraithmarked Creative, LLC
www.wraithmarked.com

For Emma,
stop complaining I never dedicated a book to you.
— GD Penman

TRUTH TOLD BY CANDLELIGHT

Arancia, Regola Dei Cerva 94

In the dark of the night, a child was crowning.

The village of Sheepshank appeared on no maps and was snared by no roads. The villagers, if pressed, could tell you they lived in the Kingdom of Espher, though if you asked for the name of their king, you'd be liable to come back with no answer. The reach of sovereigns and divine authority did not stretch so far. Kings of old were recounted in tales by the hearth, but with no more sense of reality than the tales of Greenteeth, Ultimo Re, or Aceta Madre in her poison dell.

With no kings, no gods, and no masters, the place locals called Sheepshank may sound an idyll, but there is no place in the world free from oppression, and for the shepherds and farmers, fear was the forest.

The Selvaggia stretched deep and dark across the northeast of Espher and beyond, dense and overgrown, tall and prone to creaking out grand operas when the northern winds swept down.

The sheep for which the village was named were Agrantine Blacks, more goat or vale than the puff-balls of wool you'd find in the lowlands, with horns that could stick a shepherd's gut if he was fool enough to crop them when he should have coaxed. If they went wandering onto the steppes to the north, a shepherd would give chase for days and nights. Lynx, wolf, and carrion crane would give a Sheepshank shepherd no worry at all. Yet if a sheep went wandering under the canopy of the Selvaggia, it was gone. Such was their fear of the place.

For generations beyond count, the family in the rosemary-thatched cottage were born, lived, and died in Sheepshank. Grandmothers, mothers, and sisters were in attendance on that night, despite the lateness of the hour. Every one of them roused and ready. A kettle boiled water from the well. Old dresses had been torn to rags. All was ready and all was going well.

To city-born folk, screaming, sobbing, and wailing might have meant different, but farmers knew how meat was butchered and lambing happened. This was Nella's first child, always the hardest. Her own grandmother's pressing hands had assured them the babe was coming right. All that was left was to be there. Cool hands on frenzied skin. Comforting gibberish whispered in her ear. Firelight and cold winds sweeping in through the gaps in the shutters.

Nella's whole body became an instrument of pain. She bucked and she bowed as the waves of it shook her. The comforting hands became shackles to hold her down, to keep her legs spread though she desperately wanted to clamp them shut against the burning.

She cursed every woman that held her, called them every foul thing she knew, and not a one of them flinched or blinked. The old ones even gave toothless grins at her loathing. They'd all been in her place. If they hadn't, she wouldn't be there at all.

When her daughter slipped free of her, she was too numb to even hear her babe cry. She heard nothing at all. Nella's head fell back on a bundled blanket and she dragged in the first breath she could remember taking all night. The air tasted of salt and iron. The heat she'd found unbearable a moment before was now a comfort. She came back to herself and held out her arms for the baby.

It did not come.

The women stood huddled around the child, and even her own mother drifted away from Nella's side to go and peer down at the bundle among them. The baby did not cry. Bloodless and aching, Nella tried to haul herself up. Her racked body betrayed her, she slipped back, she could not see.

The muttering and whispering from the old mothers were so low that the fire's crackle drowned them out. Nella could not hear them over the hammering of her heart. Her baby. Something was wrong with her baby.

She let out a cry of pain. All the pain she'd swallowed down and pretended not to feel because it would be worth it to hold her baby in her arms came back to her. Sobs racked her as the contractions had moments before.

All at once, eyes turned back to the mother, all comfort flowed back into her and as tears flooded out, the baby, her baby, was pressed onto her bare chest. It was warm. She'd thought her baby dead and cold, but even through the tears she could see the infant move. Blinking the tears away, she saw her daughter for the first time. A full head of dark fuzz that would grow to be curls like hers. Wide eyes. Olive skin. Her daughter lived, but she did not cry.

Bruise-colored lips puckered and worked as an aunt's hands cupped the babe's head and brought them to Nella's breast, but still there was no sound. No sound from anyone at all. The silence lay heavy over them.

Sheepshank was home to simple folk, and when simple folk had no answer to the why of something, they feared it. Already in the rear quarters of the rosemary-thatched cottage, whispers were spreading. A silent babe was not right. There was no ministry to the souls of Sheepshank, but some things were still known and passed down. Parent to child. Warnings dressed as stories. Fear dressed as whimsy.

From some auntie's bundle of prized possessions, a feast-day candle was fetched out, already melted to a nub. They lit it from an ember and carried it to mother and child where they lay.

Even when the babe was plucked from her mother's teat, she didn't weep. Her mouth worked, her eyes opened, but still the baby did not cry out. The candle was held beside her, and her shadows counted.

A shade had no flesh of its own, but it hungered for form. This much every child could tell you. Why mushroom circles were to be walked around not trod through. Why the old fields where battles were fought lay fallow and the gravestones standing in the wild places of the world were to be left in peace. Only the wise knew that when a shade took a body and hid within, it would still cast a shadow of its own. If the baby had been taken by a shade, the candle's light would reveal it.

Pried from Nella's grasp, the newborn showed no need for the support of the hands that held her. Slick from the womb, she should have had no more strength than a bowl of water to hold itself upright, yet this babe turned its head from side to side, blinking those wide eyes in wonder at all the gathered women. The whisper again.

"Unnatural."

The candle was held up, just beyond the baby's reach, and all eyes turned to see what was cast. There was the baby's shadow, as it should be. Dark and crisp on the white daub wall. The aunties breathed a sigh of relief. The baby's shadow shivered as the candle flame flickered in the gust.

The candle flame stilled. The shadows did not.

The borders of the shadow were crisp and clean no more. They blurred and twitched. Shapes that had no business dancing on a farmer's wall darted in and out of the baby's body.

Through it all, Nella understood nothing, she looked askance to her mother only to be shushed to silence. She saw only her baby, held up in silhouette. The dancing forms of things that should not be were above her head, out of her sight.

The baby did not have two shadows, like a person taken by a shade in a story. She had dozens. All of them springing to life and fading just as fast. Reaching out from the child then snapping back inside. The auntie who held the baby nearly dropped her on the spot. It was only swift intervention that saw the child nestled back in her mother's arms.

The women took their argument to the hearth. Huddling around the fire's light as though it might protect them from the frightening things beyond their understanding. Nella cared nothing for their whispered debates. She had her baby in her arms once more. She was drunk on the touch of her. With shaking hands, she stroked the slickness of her own body from the baby's hair. So fluffy already, so soft to the touch. "Orsina, I shall call you. My little bear."

Nella's husband Tobia did not come inside the house, because the old mothers had not called for him. Until they knew what was to be done, it was better not to have more voices raised. Truth be told, they knew what had to be done, but none had the courage to do it. Not when they had just seen the shadows dance.

In the end, some small part of the truth had to be portioned out, and so Nella's husband was called to the door. "Something has gone wrong. We need the midwife."

Nella and Tobia were young. They believed whatever the old and wise told them. With only the crescent moon to see by, he set out. Beyond the village walls, the fields stretched out in plateaus. Nothing was allowed to grow tall between the houses and the forest. Nothing that would give succor to any beast of the wild trying to creep in.

These fields were where Tobia toiled most of his days. A river had once run through here, but generations ago some clever man from Covotana had come with tools and books. He'd taught their grandparents how to turn the fields they'd once burned flat and kept fallow into rice paddies.

Here and there, an olive tree still grew between the shelves of earth, but they produced little and their fruits were bitter. Still, they served as markers on Tobia's course through the sucking mud. Even in the dark of the night, this place was so familiar to him that he was not liable to falter, but with dread lodged in his gut, it helped him to have something as solid as bitter olive wood to cling to for comfort.

Selvaggia loomed large on the horizon. A lurking beast growing greater with each step he took towards it. Soon the moon itself seemed to be swallowed down into the dark of the wood, and all Tobia had to guide him on was the starlight.

Even now on the verge of panic, he would not enter the forest. To lose his wife or his child would be the greatest tragedy he could imagine, but there were things in the woods that went beyond the limits of his imagination. Fears he could not name. Nightmares of which he could not dream.

Beneath the reaching boughs, Tobia came to a halt. With shaking hands, he struck sparks to tinder in the vine-wrapped brazier that was now more verdigris than copper. Three times he struck sparks with no luck at all. It was a still night, with no wind to blame, and the moss was dry to the touch. Again and again he struck the little clumps of pyrite together to no avail, until finally they were snatched from his hands.

He nearly lost his footing before he recognized the woman beside him. He had not seen the midwife approach. Her limping steps had broken no twig and rustled no leaf. It was as though she'd sprung up fully formed right by his elbow to tut at him disapprovingly.

"Born on the wrong side of the sheets with no father to teach you how to bang rocks?"

With a twist of her wrists, sparks seemed to shower from the tinder-stones, and the brazier whose light was meant to call her out from the depths of the woods caught aflame. She gave him a moment to speak, and when it became obvious he was too busy tripping over his own words, she filled in the blanks. "They're wanting for me in the village, then?"

"My wife," he blurted. "Our baby."

The old woman's face was impossible to see in the depths of her hood, but when she held out her hands to warm them by the flames, they were weathered and wrinkled, like the skin of a roasted feast-day bird.

"Which be ailing? Mother or babe?"

Tobia's mind froze up. There were things he knew he should not say to the midwife, and they flooded his mouth before he could bite down. He was not to ask her questions about the forest. He was not to ask how she lived, or where she lived. He was never to ask if she lived alone. The moment stretched out, until he realized what she was truly asking.

"Both? They didn't tell me."

Her next tut sounded like a nut being cracked. "Didn't think to be asking, eh? Your wife and your baby and you didn't even think to…"

She moved off, still muttering to herself before he had the time to answer, striding towards the distant watch-fires meant to keep the things of the forest in sight and at bay. Tobia had to jog to keep up with her. The rice fields did not seem to slow her. She moved like an old hand, placing her steps on the hidden stones beneath the surface with an ease Tobia envied.

As they came closer to the light, he saw more of the old woman. The draped shawls he'd taken for black were greens and violets, roughly woven but pristine and vibrant. Her face was still turned from him, as it always had been in childhood's bad dreams. Until the final moments.

The watchman gave no challenge and the packed dirt of the few streets Sheepshank could muster lay empty as the midwife stalked through the village with Tobia still trailing behind. She was a thing of the Selvaggia, but the village had made their peace with her, turning their eyes away in exchange for the care she provided. The only thing from the Selvaggia they wouldn't try to burn on sight. Though the young and foolish might toss rocks at her when she was spotted flitting through the trees.

Tobia followed her all the way to his own home where she was ushered inside and the door slammed shut in his face. This was not a place for fathers. Not yet.

Nella still lay with the babe in her arms, marveling at the cooing and sighing it made. The old mothers had said nothing to her, and would not unless they were forced. It was a terrible thing to lose a child. Why not let her bask in the moments she had?

It took but a moment for the situation to be explained to the midwife, and a moment longer before she laid her hands on Orsina. "That be a good name for this runt. Bears bear burdens well."

No grown man of Sheepshank would have met the midwife's eyes, few of the women either, but Orsina had no fear in her yet.

"All right then, shades, who be riding in this baby?"

There was no reply from the child, though it was clear that a shade rode her even now. Before the midwife's eyes, Orsina's hair was growing longer. She looked a week old already.

"Come now, speak your name, shade. There's few don't know me in these parts. Tell me true and I'll not feed you to Ginny Greenteeth."

This time there was an answer, but it was cacophonic. Voices screeching and screaming to be heard over one another. A legion within.

The midwife rocked back as though she had been struck. Mothers, aunts, and grandmothers quivered in terror. Nella curled around herself. Weeping openly.

They say the touch of cold iron can drive out a shade. That being shown its own reflection can startle it from a body. They say a lot of things, and few of those things are true, but there are some small talismans that can drive a lesser shade away. Mixtures and tinctures made from the mushrooms that grow around shade-circles. Meteoric iron. Things that only the brave or the mad could harvest. The wizened little pouch the midwife drew out from her shawl held some of those things. To the right buyer, that pouch would be worth more than the whole of Sheepshank, not that anyone in the room knew it. She pressed it to the baby's chest.

The copper pots of the house leapt off their hangers to clatter to the hearth. The morning milk soured. Every horse in Sheepshank woke from torpid dreams to find their manes knotted. Every sleeping woman too, though there were few enough of them on a birthing night.

Roiling shadows burst forth from the child, sweeping out through the house and doing what mischief a thwarted shade would. The sheets on which Nella lay were shredded, the wood of the frame scratched and scored.

All that had been trapped in the baby was forced loose. Old scars opened and bled anew. A tempest of chaos and fluttering shadow danced through the house, overturning and smashing all that could be destroyed. They were worth nothing, in the end, the baubles that were lost, but they were all the young couple had strived to scrape together. All lost.

It ended as swiftly as it had begun. The shutters of the house burst open. The hearth fire died. Every breath was held. In the total darkness, the only sound was the baby's wail. It was done.

The old mothers felt sure things had been set aright. Nella had never understood what was wrong to begin with, only that the pouch now bound to the baby with a deer-leather cord was never to be taken off. Not even when they bathed her.

All the cheer that had been silenced along with Orsina's cries came out in full force. It was early in the morning, but there were few houses that held no cousin or friend to Nella and her kin. The whole village rose early and partook in the celebrations. The rosemary-thatched house filled up. Hands were clapped. Shoulders squeezed. Gifts of cloth and durum flour enough to last weeks or more. Through it all the baby cried, and it was like music to the ears of the old wives, even as the menfolk flinched.

For Tobia, the fear had been replaced with joy. His daughter wasn't even a day old and she'd already been promised an apprenticeship when she came of age. She would never know the toil of the field, cut rot from her feet, or wake with a crooked back. Her fortune had been assured by some accident of birth, and while she'd never be wed and bring a bride-price to her family, it was a small price to pay for such a hope.

Tobia meant to walk the old woman back to the border of the woods, to talk over the details and keep her safe from harm, but she was nowhere to be seen once he was done planting soft kisses on Orsina's and Nella's heads.

At the edge of the village, the watchman saw the brazier by the Selvaggia blink out and settled back into the layered warmth of his cloaks to wait out the night. If he could not see to the edge of the woods, he would not have to know what was there. If he did not see the beasts of the wood, his dreams would not be haunted.

2

A PAIR OF PAIRS

Gemmazione, Regola Dei Cerva 112

When the twin kings sent a summons, there was no polite way to decline unless you were prepared to part ways from your head. For a child of the Volpe line, there were few polite ways to accept, either. To say that the Familia Volpe were pariahs in high society was an understatement of epic proportions. It had been a generation since they had attended a ball in the palace, two since they'd claimed their empty seat in the Teatro Dei Signori. Artemio's father had said that it was the price one paid for being a living descendant of the true king—but only when he was in his cups and sure even the servants couldn't overhear.

The Cerva had ruled for as long as anyone living could remember, and it was in their best interests to maintain the illusion that their line stretched back into antiquity rather than spawning abruptly a century or so before in one bloody night. As a student of history, Artemio was all too aware how often crowns changed hands through such circumstances. It made it difficult to feel much indignance. Luckily, Artemio harbored grudges the way other men ate meals. He had indignance to spare.

Harmony had come begging with him not to go to the palace before the grey light of dawn was even over the city.

She came hammering at his chamber door in the House of Seven Shadows while he was still dressing himself. Of all the skills he had learned since coming to the city to begin his studies, he valued his newfound ability to go from one outfit to another without the involvement of servants to be the most useful. Even if he never graduated, he would not have to suffer the rough hands of a knight of the wardrobe again. It felt like a small victory against Mother each time he fastened a button for himself.

"Let me go in your stead. You are the heir, I am a less valuable hostage." She had started before she even had the blindfold off her eyes.

"Harm," he scoffed, "if they'd wanted a hostage, they would have come in force. Not sent some mongrel servant with an invitation."

She pushed back her shoulders and lifted her chin. The very picture of indignance. "The House would not stand for such a thing."

"The House knows which side its bread is oiled on. What am I to them?" The last pearl button slipped into place in his waistcoat and he moved on to the next layer. "If the court wanted me, Prima Cicogna would hand me over to them wrapped up in a bow."

"Father would—"

He cut her off with a click as his feet slipped into his calfskin boots. "Shout and stomp and do nothing, as he always has."

"Let me come with you at least." She was trying not to let it, but the whine was creeping into her voice. Even at nineteen, his twin would always be the little sister begging for her place in his games.

"No matter your skill with the blade," he was dressed at last, heading for the door and very deliberately leaving his sword belt where it hung on the wall behind her, "you could not fight the whole palace."

"With our talents, together, we could break free if it is a trap."

"And live for a week as outlaws before they caught us, plucking fruit from trees at the side of the road while our lands are razed and hot irons put to Mother? I think not."

She followed him into the hallway, yelped, and darted back in to retrieve the strap of lace she wore over her eyes when visiting here.

Her brother had been bequeathed an ancient gift of their bloodline, just as their father had. Her inheritance had been less arcane. A stocky build. Auburn hair. Ruddy apple cheeks. Just like his. Yet he could walk these fabled halls with his eyes wide open and she could not.

Each corner and doorway was carved with lines to help visitors and servants guide themselves around. Most of the time, Harmony did not rely on them. It had been more than a year since she took up residence in the guest chambers. So long as nothing was left lying in the halls, she could stride about as surely as she did on any cobbled street in Covotana. In her haste, she traced her fingers over the lines now. Leapfrogging from one to the next as her dress ruffled around her with each hasty step.

"Artemio."

She was certain he'd come this way, but now it was as though he had vanished entirely. She tried again.

"Artemio?"

When his hand pressed over her mouth, she almost bit down on him. The bastard. He leaned in close to her ear. "Dear sister, there is nothing you can say or do that will change my mind. If they decide to execute me, I shall come and haunt you immediately so you are the first to know. Could you ask for more?"

She licked his hand and he jerked it away in disgust. She could always reduce him to a child again. If only his appearance reflected that youthful energy. A streak of grey already ran through his hair, and in those moments when she wished to torment him of an evening, she would count the new wrinkles his tuition had provided him in the last week.

"If you die without me there to protect you, I'll kill you." Her slap missed him entirely, which was fortunate, since it had been at face height and he didn't fancy explaining to royalty why he had a palm print on his cheek.

"While the planning is lackluster, I certainly appreciate the sentiment." Artemio chuckled. "Now may I go and see the kings, or do you have further tantrums you wish to throw."

She zeroed in on his voice and managed a halfhearted shove. "Go on, go, see if I care what they do with you."

He wiped her spittle from his palm onto her tresses then jogged out of reach. "I love you too, Harm."

For all of its prominence in the annals of Espher's history, the House of Seven Shadows was far from central within Covotana itself. The city had grown within an ancient caldera, raised up from the surrounding fertile farmlands but constructed within the gentle curve of that bowl. The House of Seven Shadows stood near to the caldera's rim while the palace lay in the center.

Dearly beloved at arm's length.

It was a testament to the fear and respect the people of Espher held in their hearts for the institution that in a place so desperate for every inch of real estate that it had begun to build up into the sky and dig down into the volcanic tunnels below, there was a small park grown up around the House, like it was a country villa.

The downside of which was that there was not a coach to be had without hiking out to the terra-cotta streets beyond the hedges. Artemio grumbled every step of the way, but it was more out of habit than any actual discomfort. The other scions of noble houses complained, so he complained along with them, wondering all the while how many were only complaining because the others did too. Or if any one of them was actually put out by a gentle walk through a park before flagging down a coach.

The driver was a mongrel, pigeon feathers where he should have had hair, face stretching to a beaked point, all clumsily hidden under a hood. If Artemio had any sort of reputation to protect, then he wouldn't have dared to be seen driven by such a thing, but luckily his family's name was lower than dirt so he didn't need to delay.

Artemio had spent little time in the capital throughout his youth. The Volpe presence at social events tended to be limited to quiet meals in dark rooms with many toasts of loyalty to the true king. With entirely too much emphasis given to the word *true*.

Covotana itself eluded his recollection. His memories of the city itself were much like this coach ride. Glimpses of tall white stucco buildings beyond the drapery. Distant sightings of landmarks that his reading of the histories had ingrained in his mind as almost mythical.

The palace lay at the deep center of the city, set back from the crowding buildings in a grand pool of shimmering blue-green water. Limited by its position as an island, it had no option but to grow upwards rather than out. It stretched now into the pale morning sky, tall enough for towers to be seen from out in the fields beyond the city walls. Artemio had come here on his arrival to Covotana as a student to bend his knee and swear his fealty as any noble son must. It was the last invitation he had received.

Theoretically, he should have been in attendance every day at court and at every function in the palace now that he was living in the city, but that rule seemed to have lapsed in his case. The invitations never came, and when all the other students were pouring out into the streets in their finery, he was left to enjoy another day of solitary study or endure another evening of his sister's heckling card games.

After he crossed the bridge over the shimmering water, a servant stood waiting for his arrival in the blue livery of the palace. One of many lingering by the palace steps for guests far more esteemed than he. Still, Artemio couldn't help but feel a sting when he was led not to the entrance of the palace, but rather around the side of a tower to where a servants' entrance lay ajar for him. His father would have thrown a fit at the slight, but he was proud to say he was not his father. Practicality was one of the few virtues fate had granted him, and he was intent on clinging to it for all he was worth.

The palace the nobles walked was all smooth marble and pale statuary. The servants' passages had more practical flagstones. The simple beauty of the white stone that Covotana had been carved from was on display, unobscured by tapestries and paintings. Up the spiral staircase, Artemio counted the turns as they went, habitually. If he had to escape the palace as Harmony feared, it would help to know the way out.

Finally they came out into a solarium, the top of some tower or other. If they'd meant to make him break a sweat, the kings had forgotten how far south the Volpe estates were and how mountainous the region. This was a brisk morning stroll for a country lordling.

It was a rare thing to see both kings in one place at a time. The entire purpose of the confusion surrounding which of the identical brothers had been crowned was to render assassination attempts pointless, yet here they were, sitting side by side in identical gilt robes with identical expressions of identical dull boredom, eating their breakfast from the same table.

There were no servants here, no attendants or guards. It was confusing, to say the least. One of them glanced Artemio's way and he startled into a stiff bow.

"Master Volpe, come and eat with us."

One did not refuse a king, and if he was about to die, then Artemio could see no reason to do so with an empty stomach. He slumped down in the crassly gilded chair across from the shining kings and helped himself to some bread, cured ham, and olives. He bit into one and felt it pop. Fresh as a spring breeze.

If the kings were troubled by his manners, they made no sign of it. Their indifference was immaculately presented, just like every other part of them. Their hair rich and dark, oiled back from their faces so every aquiline detail could be seen. Their countenances pale with powder. Madrigal and Canticle Cerva were barely a decade into their reign, and to Artemio's mind, they were doing all they could to remain a footnote curiosity in the histories still to be written. He did not blame them. Kings who lived interesting lives rarely did so for very long.

When he bit into the bread and found it dry, he leaned over to dip into the kings' shallow bowl of oil before he realized the social suicide that such an act involved. It was too late now, he was committed. He sat back and ate. The oil was good too. Fruity.

Neither king so much as raised an eyebrow. They were very well schooled.

"We have long desired your attendance in court, Master Volpe. The Prima speaks highly of your talents."

Lies compounded with lies. If they'd desired his presence, he would have been invited. If the Prima was fool enough to mention his existence, then it would have been to disparage or make unfavorable comparisons. Whatever her talents in their shared occupation or her actual opinions on his talents, the Prima was an esteemed diplomat.

Still, one did not call a king a liar. "It is a pleasure to be here of course, but I must warn you, if you keep feeding me like this, I may never leave."

That drew out a titter that was rapidly quashed by a glance from the other brother. "We are pleased that you enjoy the fruits of our larders. When matters are more settled, perhaps you could dine with us more… frequently."

An offer like that would have been enough to make most courtiers piss themselves in unbridled delight, but Artemio remained, in his heart of hearts, a pessimist. "Which matters might you mean, your Majesty?"

"Right to the crux of things, Master Volpe?" It was the other king speaking now, though the voice was exactly the same. Cadence, tone, and pitch. That must have been difficult to learn. "I must say your rude manner is… refreshing. Life in the court can be a tapestry of intrigues. It is pleasant to have someone speak so… directly."

"I imagine it must be hard to sit down on even the largest seat in the land with everyone jostling to lick at your backside." The words were out before Artemio even realized it, and then there was no way to snatch them back. Mother had always warned him his tongue would get him killed. He'd never believed her.

For a moment both kings stared at him in stunned silence, then their composure broke. One of them flushed bright red beneath his powder. The other began shaking with restrained laughter. Spittle flying from his lips.

When they stopped, he was probably going to die. So he took the time to help himself to another handful of olives.

The red-faced one continued to shudder, but the one who laughed found his words. "Oh, Master Volpe, you turn virtue to sin. Would that circumstances were different and you might be a presence in court. I wager you'd… shake us free of our webs."

At least one of the twins didn't want him dead, then. Hopefully the one who had the deciding vote. "I am glad that I'm amusing, if nothing else."

The king leaned forward to rest an elbow on the table. "Our hope is that you'll be more than... amusing, Master Volpe. We have a task for you. One suited to your... unique talents. A task that might allow us to restore your proper standing in court, and the Teatro, if it were to be accomplished."

It would have to be an impossible chore to overturn the grievous sin of his birth. Some diplomatic post so onerous that it would leave him dead or a worthless husk. Nothing less would be sufficient. Of course, declining a king's polite request would leave him in much the same sorry state. "Whatever you desire of me, I am yours to command. How may I be of service?"

The kings both interrupted their hilarity with a synchronized smile. That was downright unsettling. "You will doubtless have heard some rumors of the recent... troubles befalling Espher?"

Artemio settled back in his seat. "Nothing."

"You are trying to tell us you know nothing of what has been happening?" The red-faced one, rapidly fading back to white, raised an eyebrow. "Nothing of the... rumors?"

"I regret to tell you that I study and I sleep. On the rare occasion when I'm feeling particularly raucous, I play a game of cards with my sister, who lives just as lively a social life. To hear rumors, somebody would need to speak to me."

This time there was no laughter, just a sigh. "What we tell you in this room... it is for your ears alone."

"Of course, your Majesty. As I said, I have nobody to tell, even if I had the foolishness to betray your trust." He'd tell Harmony of course. His life would be intolerable until he did, but they didn't need to know that.

Both kings leaned back in their seats. "There has been a series of... deaths. Esteemed members of our court are dying. At first the incidents were isolated, now they have become a pattern. Fourteen of the highest-born in the land... gone before their time."

"I suppose we do not have the good fortune of witnesses?" Despite himself, Artemio could feel himself getting caught up. For all of his natural restraint, he had a penchant for puzzles.

"Not a one. Neither the families nor our own agents have been able to explain how these assassins gained entry to the… locked chambers where these killings took place."

"Your agents?" Artemio wasn't the first to be hauled into some dark corner of the palace and given this impossible task. "Might I ask why you are replacing those agents with someone as… untried as I am?"

"Noble scions of the grand Familia of Espher. Chosen for their fitness… sharp minds, to a man."

The other king chimed in, "The latest victims of the conspiracy."

There was the painful end of the arrangement, showing up at last. He was being offered up like a sacrificial lamb to whichever murderers were slaughtering their way through the nobility of Espher this week. His heritage made him more than expendable. Either he solved the problem or he died—it was win-win for the Cerva kings.

Artemio licked the last of the oil from his lips, then nodded. "I shall need the full compliance of the noble houses that I visit. No doors slammed in my face because of my name."

"Of course." The king gave him an indulgent smile. "You shall have our… writ to serve as your seal and ambassador."

Artemio braced himself. "I'll need honesty from you too."

That brought both of their smug smiles to a frosty halt. "Beg pardon?"

"I'll need to know the truth if I'm to make sense of this." Artemio set his elbows on the table and met the kings' glowering head-on. "I have no care what version of the tale is told in rumors and history when the task is completed. But to succeed, I shall need an honest accounting. Not the prim and pretty version you've doled out to your dead helpers."

Tight-lipped, the closer king replied, "The castellan has all of the information your… predecessors have gathered."

"Carefully trimmed and annotated," Artemio snapped back. It was like he was trying to get himself killed.

With a great show of rolling his eyes, the king who had laughed leaned back in his seat. "What secret is it that you believe we are... keeping from you?"

The other was less indulgent. "And what... rank arrogance makes you think you can make demands of your sovereign?"

Artemio had no good answer for the second question, so he focused on the first. "I ask you only this, your Majesty. Who benefits from these deaths?"

"Who benefits when the greatest lords of Espher falter and the bold flinch at their own shadows? Nobody benefits... It is an affront to all people."

All people of Espher at least. The Agrantine Empire would love to see their northern neighbor weakened, and there were countless neighboring kingdoms that would delight in her noble houses falling into disarray. Even if individual houses were not weakened, the handover of leadership from one generation to the next was always a time of turmoil. Not to mention the complex and myriad grudges, feuds, and factions at work among the nobility of Espher even at the best of times.

Once upon a time, Artemio had been visiting the farmlands around Villa Volpe when a plough stuck on a rock in the field. Oxen and men united to free it—not Father, of course, but all the lesser men. In the end, the stone was overturned and a whole nest of vipers had sprung loose from beneath, setting every farmer and bull running for their lives. This was what he was being asked to willingly step into. He would not do so blindfolded. "In that case, my last question is this: Why have you decided to entrust me with this task?"

Both kings' eyes narrowed. "Is this your admission of being... unworthy of such trust?"

"You clearly recognize I am as loyal as any man in your court or I would not be here at all. But I could not help but notice that you have no guards in here. And given that my invitation was delivered there, you know well that I study at the House of Seven Shadows." It was bright in the solarium, with cunning mirrors driving sunlight down onto them from all angles. Even so, he was certain he could see the kings' eyes drift towards the shadows he cast. "If you truly have no clue as to who your mystery assassin is, how could you have known that you did not just invite him to breakfast with you?"

The kings glanced at each other, then the more antagonistic of the pair seemed to deflate a little. "We regret to be the bearers of such news, but it seems your father has not thought to write to you in his grief… The latest victim of this plague of assassins, almost a week ago, was Contessa Loretta Volpe."

He was beyond suspicion because his own mother had been a victim. That made perfect sense. Yet for some reason, Artemio's mind could not leap forward to the next logical step in the puzzle. He sat in silence, his carefully schooled expression betraying nothing, the wheels of his mind spinning without progress. Mother was dead.

It was no surprise to him that Father had not troubled to write to him informing him of this fact. That neglect was the one constant Artemio clung to as his heart froze to ice within him. Father's indifference to his children could always be relied on.

Artemio was going to have to share this news with Harmony. He was going to have to take her aside in some private room and tell her Mother died a week ago. Assassinated. He would have to watch her face crumple and her sorrow overtake her. She would weep and sob while he was powerless to take any part of her pain away. Somehow she would find a way to blame herself. It would be her fault for coming away to the city. It would be her fault she was not there, in the locked chamber where her mother had expired.

The indignance Artemio always had to spare flared to life, cutting through the numb silence. His mother was dead for no good reason but some political game. He drew in a deep breath. "Thank you for taking time out of your busy day to inform me of this, your Majesty. I shall collect the information from your castellan and begin my inquest immediately."

"Our thanks to you… Master Volpe."

Artemio rose and was already striding towards the door with purpose when the other king called out behind him, "Happy hunting."

Artemio bit down on his retort and left.

3

RIDE OF THE OLD MAIDS

Brina, Regola Dei Cerva 102

The girls of Sheepshank would not play with Orsina. It was well known that she was to be apprenticed, that she did not need to learn how to work the olive groves, the durum fields, or the rice paddies, but in this she was not unique. Jealous children did not throw stones at the smith's son or the weaver's daughters. The shepherds got no dirty looks when they walked the market, nor did their sons, or their sons' sons. So it could not be simple jealousy that made Orsina a pariah.

She was not the prettiest little girl in the village, this much was true. Her wide eyes had not yet settled in her face, giving a hint of the frog to her countenance. With no work but the keeping of the house, she often wandered bored and came home muddy. Her curls fell thick about her face, and her mother had to cut mats from them more than once when the girl had gone chasing through bushes in pursuit of rabbits.

Both children and parents hated her because she knew things she should not know. When they lay on beds of flattened durum after harvest looking up at the stars, the children would play at naming the constellations. Orsina knew their real names. It spoiled the game.

When Chiarina's parents were arguing and she came to play with red-rimmed eyes, the other girls tried to give her comfort. The same soft assurances children everywhere gave to assuage feelings of guilt for the bickering of adults. Orsina took her assurances too far. Of course it was not Chiarina's fault her father had kissed the blacksmith's wife.

Chiarina's father had two black eyes the next day and slept in the chicken house the rest of that season. Chiarina was forbidden from playing with Orsina ever again. Where Chiarina went, the rest of the girls followed.

The boys would still play with her for a time. She was as rough and tumble as the rest of them, and they were less inclined to periods of introspection or chatter. It was with them the rabbit chases began. With them she learned to climb a tree and rain overripened olives to burst on her pursuers when a game turned to a scuffle.

So while her parents worked the fields by day, she was not entirely alone in the world. Just distant. By night, they were as warm to her as they could bring themselves to be, but with every word they spoke there was a lingering disappointment.

She was not as they had been, she was not as they had expected. Quick to answer back and stubborn as a mule. Sins compounded by the fact that once her father's temper had cooled and he asked around, the little girl was always proven right and Tobia wrong.

Even her mother caught herself watching the child not as a mother should, but as the hunter eyes a wild boar, always waiting for the pleasant demeanor to drop and the goring beast within to reveal itself. She had not forgotten the night of Orsina's birth, and while the old mothers would not speak to her of it beyond none-too-subtle checks that the girl still wore the medicine pouch about her neck, she remembered some part of their whispers.

Always at the back of her parents' minds remained the indisputable fact that someday she would walk off into the woods, never to return, and the inevitability of that future hung over them all, tainting whatever joy they could find with each other.

All these mounting sorrows came to a head on the morning of the funeral.

Old Mother Perlita had been dying for as long as most folk in Sheepshank had been alive. If it was not her dreadful cough this week, it was her aching gut the next. Cataracts milked up her eyes, wrinkles and warts covered her skin, her back bent until she was almost doubled over. She had not two of her own teeth left, but her tongue had never lost any of its edge, even in her last day. It seemed to most folk that she would outlive Sheepshank itself, and there were none left who could remember when she'd been born or which family she'd birthed, so everyone shared out care of her as evenly as they could. She had been tucked up under her blankets by a well-stocked fire one night and was cold and empty when the dawn came.

This far north, frost would come to lie on the ground through the Brina season's mornings, and once in a moon the rains would turn to sleet. Snow did not come to Espher even this far north, but that did not mean it felt no sting in winter. There were no crops to tend, and the sheep, if they could be convinced, would stay close to the town so as to have ready access to the hay and chaff laid down for them. It made the ground hard to dig through, so all the men had to take turns with sickle, hoe, spade, and pick to open out a grave beyond the village walls.

There was no holy man to say words, but stories were shared. Memories of the woman she'd been. The time she chased a full-grown Smith Segno up a tree with an olive-wood switch after he spoke ill of her béchamel. The time she cared for Mother Velia all through the sweating sickness, even though everyone else was afraid to come into the house. When Orsina stepped forward from beside her parents, everyone thought they were in for a heartwarming tale.

"She isn't gone." Orsina's little voice sent out a ripple of confusion. Death might have been strange to a child in the city, but to a country girl, it was as common as the mud on her feet. It was not possible that she did not understand what had happened. That was when the little girl pointed, not to the grave but to the side of the gathered people. "She's still here. Why are you ignoring her?"

Nella snatched for Orsina, but the little girl darted out of her reach.

"Why are you ignoring her? She's screaming? Why isn't anyone listening to her?"

There was a chill in the air and cloaks were wrapped tight around everyone who could afford them, but still a shiver ran through the people of Sheepshank. Tobia had a hand over his mouth to contain his bark of fury. Nella's perfect oval face that so many women envied was flushed with shame. Still Orsina danced ahead of her grasping hands. "She's right there! Why are you all ignoring her? She's right there!"

The social graces of Sheepshank were very different than in the city. When everyone has a hand in raising a child, everyone feels some sense of duty to them. It should have come as no surprise that one of the other farmers grabbed Orsina by the scruff of her neck.

She had never been a willful child, for all that she knew and said things she shouldn't, and any grown man laying hands on her should have been enough to still her, but in her hysterical state she didn't even notice his broad hands. He gave a fierce tug to put a halt to her cries and ripped the back of her dress right open. The hand-me-down cloth, stitched and restitched into so many different combinations through the years, was a mass of hidden seams. They opened up to the bottom of her shoulder blades, and the deer-leather strap of the medicine bag had only a moment to choke her before it snapped in two.

Free of his grip, she ran forward to the empty space where she insisted Old Mother Perlita stood. Her arms outstretched for the same halfhearted embrace the old woman had granted every child in the village when they met her. She was a hard woman to please, but she was kind to the little ones. That was another story they could have told about her, if her burial had not been interrupted so rudely.

Orsina fell through the empty air, all the way to her knees without the old woman's presence there to support her. She looked around in confusion. All the world had said things were one way, and her own senses had told her they were lying. Now even her senses betrayed her. "What?"

Nella and the ham-fisted farmer were both still hot on her heels, but now that it seemed her outburst was done, they paused, sheepish and painfully aware of the eyes of the whole village upon them.

The little girl in her ripped dress rose back to her feet and turned to face the furious crowd. Tears pooled beneath her wide eyes. "Mama?"

Like a thunderclap the cold wind swept out through the crowd, strong enough to throw back hoods and make the children stagger back a step into their mother's embrace.

Orsina had been almost upright before the impact. The force of it seemed to double her over. The bare stretch of her spine surged upwards in a painful arch, stretching youthful skin until it paled to white. A noise eked out of her, a strangled cry of pain cut through with a guttural wail. Two voices crying out together.

"You killed me."

Orsina's sobs could be heard clearly, but the louder voice coming through her throat was unmistakable. A voice the whole village had heard their whole life. A voice they'd never thought to hear again.

"You think I didn't see you slip powders in my wine, no? Poisoning me. Tired of taking care of me? All my years wiping arses and darning socks, and when I needed you, it was too much work."

Perlita took a step forward, dragging Orsina along like a rag doll. The cold wind whipped out from her, scattering the crowd back. Nella and the farmer caught each other's hands, but they did not run, they stood their ground, for the girl. Nella found her courage through willful ignorance as she always had. "Orsina, my love, what are you saying?"

Tresses that had covered her face were flung back. The girl's head snapped up with a crunch of bones. Her milky eyes fixed on her mother, seeing nothing. "Poison in my wine. Just a little medicine for the aches, no? Liars all. Murderers all."

The farmer knew what he was seeing, even if Nella would deny it. He bellowed the word like a talisman against his mounting terror. "Shade!"

Funereal rites and propriety scattered in the chill wind. Children screamed as their parents snatched them up and ran.

"Murderers!" Perlita's scream swept after them with the force of a blow. All her confusion and rage unleashed now she had some anchor to the world of the living. Every step she took twisted Orsina's body further out of shape. Old bones stretching young meat. Life sapping away from the little girl with every moment, bringing her closer and closer to being the haggard old woman who now rode her flesh.

Tobia pushed against the tide of running farmers and shepherds, friends and family all. He searched the boot-churned earth for the midwife's pouch. A knee caught him in the side of the head and set him sprawling. He crawled towards his daughter. Dizzied but still searching.

Nella reached out to the thing that her daughter had become. "Orsina!"

A burst of wind struck the girl's mother down to her knees. Frost rimed her lashes as she wept. The midwife's bag was lying untouched underneath her. Panic and denial gave away to memory. The winds that blew through the cottage in the fearful silent hour of waiting for the midwife. The whispered demand that the baby never be parted from the medicine bag. Nella seized it and rushed towards Orsina once more.

The howling winds grew stronger with each passing moment. Perlita's wrath was stoking itself to new heights. The wind did not slap Nella down this time, it lifted her off her feet and flung her to the graveside.

Pouch and contents tumbled from her grasp as she screamed through the air. Untethered, the dried herbs, fungus, and rusty shards came raining down. Tobia's eyes followed his wife as she fell, he saw it all and he knew despair. Always the fear had remained. Always they had known their peace would come to an end, but never had they considered it might end like this. He whimpered, "Not like this."

Grass tore up from the ground. Wooden grave markers half gone to rot with age snapped apart. The farmer who'd stood his ground beside Nella had broken and run, only to be struck down with the same fierce winds that had launched her across the boneyard.

Through the tempest, Tobia could see the rest of Sheepshank fleeing to safety. The coffin of Old Mother Perlita had overturned, and her bloating corpse tumbled out by Nella's side. They'd broken her back to get her to lie straight, and now her corpse flopped at the waist like a crippled scarecrow in the wind.

Only one person stood against the fury of the winds, forgotten by the villagers. The midwife strode through the wind with a hand held to the level of her eyes. As splinters and mud spattered off her cloak, she took them in stride.

"A tantrum won't bring you back, you daft old baggage."

Orsina froze in place, head swinging from side to side like a startled mare.

"Stop your nonsense now, Perlita. Go take your rest. You had time enough. More days than most be getting."

Orsina's jaw clicked open, tendons distending. "They poisoned me. Killed me."

"They gave you the medicine I mixed for you. Because you were hurting. Would you rather have been hurting?" The old woman had to shout to be heard over the wind.

Locking eyes, Orsina scuttled closer. The eye of the storm moving with her. Pushing her father and mother to their knees. "It wasn't my time. It isn't fair."

"Fair? When's life or death ever been fair, Perlita? You're old enough to know better."

The two old women stood face-to-face now, nose to crooked nose. The freezing storm dropped. Splinters rained down. Tobia breathed a sigh of relief. At last it was over.

Orsina's blind eyes narrowed. "*No.*"

The midwife caught hold of Orsina's face, palms flat against her cheeks as the wind began to howl. The winds that had not touched the old woman before buffeted her now. Only her grip on the girl kept her in place. She had to scream now to be heard, her ancient voice cracking. "Hear me now, child. Perlita be dead and gone. All you've got in you now is an echo. A shadow. A shade. It has no hold on this world. It's got no brain to think. You can push her out."

Perlita howled, a sickly wet sound, and the wind threw back the midwife's cloak and shawls, scattering them across the ground and leaving her bare to the chill in her patchwork dress.

"You can beat her, little one. She is weak and this is your world, not hers. Your body, not hers." The midwife drew Orsina closer, straining as the girl's bones twisted about beneath her skin. "Push her out, little one. Feel her inside, feel the places where she is holding. She's barely even a shade. Just a memory. One little push is all it will take."

Tears froze on Orsina's face, and even as they watched, her body changed still. It was past her shoulders now. Yet it was her voice that whimpered out, "It hurts."

"It only hurts until it is over, little one." The midwife's sour face cracked into a smile. "Now push."

The wind stopped and started in stutters. Orsina's body lurched. "She is *mine*."

"She belongs to herself. And you, dead or not, you've sense enough not to cross a witch, don't you, Perlita?"

Orsina's spine snapped straight and the scream she let out was entirely human and wretched to hear. "Get her out. Out. Get out!"

Perlita did not want to go. She had clung to her mortal life for decades beyond memory. Even when her body faltered and failed, she had refused to move on. Even when everyone she had ever loved went into the ground, she lived on. She had more practice at staying alive than anyone in Sheepshank still living, but she was at a disadvantage. This was enemy territory. The echo of the woman who had been was surrounded on all sides by the hostility of the one she had invaded. A shade could not feel. The pain of the body meant nothing to Perlita, for she had no flesh of her own, but the life that was contained within that flesh, it could sustain her.

She had been fading since she died. Less and less of who she was remained. All the memories she'd clung to were abandoning her. The bright, the sweet, the dark, and the sour; they all blurred to grey as she faded from the world. With the font of this child's life to drink from, she could hold out a little longer. She had her very existence to fight for, but it still was not enough.

Orsina pushed her out.

With one final shudder, the girl's eyes washed back to their natural brown and she toppled limp into the midwife's arms. The cold wind was gone. The shade destroyed.

Nella did not stir at the graveside. Tobia scrambled forward to reach for his daughter, only to catch the old midwife's stare and stumble to a halt.

The girl could barely stand after the racking she had just suffered. Bruises surrounded her every joint. Yet somehow this old woman had the strength to hold her up. "Fetch out anything you want the little one to have of you. Leave it by the pyre this night. She moves to the forest now."

"What? No? You can't." Even now Tobia's mind had not caught up to current events. He was still living in the morning when the high-noon sun was risen. "She isn't of age to apprentice yet."

The midwife held Orsina close. The girl's spindly limbs barely thinner than her own. "Look around, lackwit. There'll be no life for her here. Not after this. You want her to burn? You want them to burn you out while you sleep? Frightened fools love their fire."

This was all happening too fast for Tobia. He was a man accustomed to a very different pace of life, where the slow curve of the sun across the sky was his only deadline. If Nella was here, she would have been able to speak. To say some clever thing to keep their daughter safe and well, but Nella was still unmoving by the graveside. So deathly still that it sent a shot of terror through him, and he rushed over to cradle her in his arms.

When he looked up, the midwife and his daughter were gone.

The old woman had not waited to see if Orsina's mother lived, so she could not tell the girl when Orsina finally woke. It was a cowardly thing, but one did not live in the Selvaggia without a healthy fear and a streak of practicality. Either Nella lived, and she'd be another hook dragging the child back to the danger of Sheepshank, or she'd died, in which case she'd be a crushing weight on Orsina's conscience.

Sometimes, not knowing was better.

4

OATH OF A RAT

Gemmazione, Regola Dei Cerva 112

The castellan led Artemio through a fresh set of unmarked passages and spiral staircases until they emerged ever so briefly in the public part of the palace. Stepping out from behind a tapestry, the castellan struck a frantic pace to bring the young guest to one of the guest rooms unseen, and Artemio had to jog to keep up, even though it felt somewhat sacrilegious to be running in the palace. Mother would have had his head.

Once more, the workings of his mind seemed to seize up at the thought of his mother. A key was pressed into his hand, and the castellan stood watch in the hallway as Artemio slipped inside to the stuffy silence of the room that had been designated for his predecessors in this thankless task.

The bed was missing the down mattress, and there were some rust colored marks on the flagstones below that explained precisely why. This was not only the depository of all the information that the Cerva had collected about their mysterious assassins, it was also the scene of one of the crimes.

Whoever had slaughtered the man lying sleeping in his bed had left the papers undisturbed. Or had removed any incriminating information with more subtlety than the stains Artemio now spotted on the drapes and ceiling would suggest they possessed.

To lose so much blood, the man must have been torn limb from limb. Artemio had another brief flash of his mother's face. Was this how she'd died? Shredded by some impossible assassin. Body parts scattered. The mind he had always been so proud of betrayed him now. The patterns in the blood told him a gruesome story, and his imagination overlaid it on his parents' bedchamber.

He had to confront this horror if he meant to go on, but he meant to do so on his own terms. There was still blank paper aplenty in this room, and he would not be able to read any of many stacks filled with notes until he had cleared this miasma from his own mind. On the paper before him, he scribbled: *Contessa Loretta Volpe. Who? How? Why?*

Neither of the first two questions had answers, or even the hope of answers, at this moment in time. He would have to read through the reports his father had forwarded to the kings—added to the pile of mail by the door to this chamber sometime before his arrival—and the descriptions of the previous murders.

Who did it benefit for Mother to die? If it had been his father, then there would at least have been some logic to it. Were some foreign power at work to destabilize the current dynasty, then it made perfect sense to remove Father. Without the House of Cerva, many would default to following the Volpe, and even if his power could not be assured in the long term, Father would still serve as a stabilizing influence when a provocateur would want chaos.

Beside the word *why*, Artemio wrote down *Count Cleto Volpe*. Despite their vociferous differences of opinion, it was well known among those who hung on such rumors that the Volpe marriage had been a love match, and that they still shared their bedchambers even now after all these years. If she had been slain in her bed, as so many others seemed to have been, then it was plausible the assassins had meant to slay her husband instead.

She had no standing or position outside of their household and targeting her to distract Father with grief would be ill advised. It may have distracted him from the everyday running of his estates, but only because he was devoting every waking moment to destroying whichever enemy had struck at him. Artemio could not conceive of a conspiracy that could so cunningly navigate every other aspect of a plan yet be fool enough to light a fire under Cleto Volpe. It had to be an accident.

The door creaked open. Artemio had been given the castellan's key, and he had locked up behind him. Perhaps he was going to learn the secret of how the assassin killed people in locked rooms faster than he had anticipated.

If they meant to take him as easily as the simpering courtiers who'd come before, the assassins were in for a rude awakening. Cleto Volpe may have been a known danger to their plans, but Artemio had done well to keep his own presence and capabilities well hidden from the world at large. Even the House of Seven Shadows did not yet know his limits.

The curtains in the chambers were drawn, the fireplace unlit. Only the candelabra above illuminated the space. Any shade could have put the candles out, yet in times of crisis, it was always going to be to Bisnonno Fiore that Artemio reached. His great-grandfather had once been a king, and his death had been brief but brutal. Such things gave power to a shade.

The familial connection had made it all too easy to convince Fiore that Artemio was the best match for him, yet even as he fluttered on the edge of fading away, the old shade took convincing to drink his fair measure of the younger generation's life to sustain himself.

This time he got only a sip. A single ruddy hair on Artemio's head turned white. Artemio did not need Fiore to ride him, only for him to pass through the room. The dead king's touch spread chill throughout Artemio, but it was a small price to pay.

With only a brief shudder of effort as the cold wind tore through the room, every candle snuffed out. Wax spattered down around Artemio in a rain, but he felt nothing. Fiore departed just as swiftly as he came. Had he a mind left, it would have rebelled at visiting the palace where he had been murdered.

The figure now silhouetted in the doorway was not a striking figure. Indeed, Artemio could think of few figures less imposing than the tiny woman who shuffled inside, tutting at the dust and the darkness. She wore a servant's simple garb, her back was bowed, and there was the unmistakable swish of a tail over the flagstones behind her. A mongrel.

She made her way across the room with practiced ease, sidestepping furniture until she reached the fireplace, tinderbox and tapers on the mantel. That was where Artemio caught her, hand brushing beneath her furred chin to lock around her throat. "How did you get through that door?"

His grip on the sides of her neck was tight enough to show his strength, without pinching the airway she needed to reply. At first she made nothing but a strangled squeak of terror. "What?!"

"How did you come by a key to this chamber when the castellan gave the only copy to me?"

She croaked out. "I'm the maid?"

He shook her then, and her shawl fell back, exposing the extent of her depraved mutation. Buck teeth protruded over her lips. Thick black hairs marred her olive skin. Her ears had grown huge and rounded. Mongrelized with a mouse, or more likely a rat. Disgusting. It took a force of will not to toss her away and wipe his hands. Instead, he had to move closer, growling in her ear, "You have keys to every room in the palace?"

"Yes, my lord. I mean. No, my lord." She was quivering within his grasp. "Master of the Chambers has the wing keys. Hands them out with his orders."

Artemio pushed her away and swiped his palms down his trousers. He could still feel the hair prickling at them. "This chamber is not to be touched, or cleaned, or serviced. Make that clear to your Master of Chambers. If he asks why, direct him to the castellan."

"Yes, my lord. I'm sorry, my lord."

She made a break for the door now that his hands were no longer on her, but already, his mind was spinning with possibilities. He put his foot down on the hem of her skirts, inadvertently nipping her tail. She jerked to a halt. "Who pays you?"

"My lord? The Master of Coin gives us our pay once every…"

"Don't pretend that you don't know what I'm asking you."

She was the very picture of wide-eyed innocence, but for her verminous countenance. "My lord?"

"There's lace on your shawl, girl. I felt it. A chambermaid doesn't make lace money. Give me the name of the generous patron who lines your pockets and sent you here this day."

Her eyes darted from side to side, innocence beginning to evaporate as she sought an escape route and found none. "I don't know what you could mean, my lord."

Those who bound themselves to shades were made sensitive to certain connections by their exposure to the unseen world. When creatures shared their life with each other as mongrels did with their bond-beasts, it was invisible to the naked eye, but all too obvious to a student of the House of Seven Shadows.

Artemio's hand darted out and squeezed. To a bystander, he would seem to be molesting some poor maid, and in all likelihood, they would have looked away. She was just a servant, after all. Yet it was not the flesh of her breasts he had crushed inside his hand, but the rodent nestled between them. It let out a terrible shriek and struggled in his grasp, but it could not bite him through the embroidered surface of her blouse, while he could crush it with a twist of his fist.

The maid wailed. "Please, my lord. Please don't hurt her."

"Tell me what I want to know, and there need be no more hurt this day."

"They'd kill me, lord." She was still shaking as she spoke. It gave her voice a vibrating timbre. "If they found out I've told on them."

"Then we must endeavor to ensure they do not find that out. Now, give me the name."

As it turned out, it was not a name, but a who's-who of Covotana's high society. Every one of them was curious as to who the kings might rope in next to continue the fruitless shadow war, so at the first mention of a visitor to the solarium this day, a half dozen missives had arrived at the girl's boarding.

Where most of the palace servants might find some small patronage from curious courtiers, this mousy-girl had instead accepted every offer that came her way. She hadn't the wit to realize it, but this left her in a very precarious situation.

A single patron could have protected her if it came out that she had been passing information, or at least provided her with some pension after her flogging on their behalf. But should the time come that she was exposed while on a dozen payrolls, her lack of loyalty was liable to be considered reason enough to abandon her to the wolves.

When Artemio took the time to explain this to her, it was not out of kindness, but cruelty. He needed for her to understand just how easily her life could end, even if he released his grip on the rat he'd plucked from her blouse.

"When the truth comes out, you shall have no friends in high places to keep you from the headsman. Rather you will have secured for yourself more powerful and numerous enemies than any one person could hope to cultivate in a lifetime of wickedness."

"Nobody is going to know, you said." Somewhere in his litany of veiled threats, tears had welled up in the eyes of the maid. If she couldn't school her emotions for the breadth of a single conversation, it was frankly amazing she hadn't been caught out yet.

He began to second-guess his own decision. "Nothing in this life is free. I will not share your secret with the world, but in exchange, I expect you to share the world's secrets with me. Not only do I wish to know everything you are telling your patrons, I want to know everything they are telling you. There is treachery afoot in the palace, and I mean to root it out by whatever means are necessary."

She blinked the tears away. Eyes glinting once more. "So you'll be employing my services too, my lord?"

Artemio could feel the bait being laid, but he allowed it. "So long as our arrangement remains confidential, I shall keep your secret."

"Might you be paying, my lord?" There was a hint of a cheeky smirk there. A glint of buck teeth. "To ensure my loyalty? The going rate is…"

The smile Artemio returned her was pure condescension. "Your loyalty to me is already ensured. After all, I hold the other half of your soul in my hand."

The rat sat passively between Artemio's palms. Pressed, but not crushed. The connection that mongrels shared with the beasts they bonded was not well studied, but the theory was that they had been gifted the lesser part of the talent those who bound shades used to extend their rapidly dwindling years. But without the wit or training to correctly bind themselves to an impresario and share their life span with another human, the mongrels instead found solace in the beasts of the earth. Cutting their own years brutally short by sharing them with a creature that expired all too swiftly.

Artemio tightened his grip. "This little delight shall remain in my care until our task is done, then I shall gladly return her to you."

For a moment it seemed the girl would turn feral. He saw her tense, ready to pounce. He had heard rats could turn vicious when cornered and very briefly regretted that his sword belt was still on its hook back in the House of Seven Shadows. The rat in his hands let out a squeal as he tightened his grip on it, and that snapped her out of it in an instant. "Please, my lord. Please. Don't be hurting us."

"I have no intention of doing anything so crass." Artemio turned his crushing grasp into a gentle stroke down the rat's spine. "Your pet shall remain in my care for so long as my duty continues, and at the end of that duty I shall return her to you, well fed and cared for."

"You can't. None of the others... You can't do this. It ain't right."

"Neither is spying on the people who put a roof over your head. I suppose we are both immoral at heart. Though I have the justification of necessity while you only had avarice."

She reached out towards her rat, as though instinct rather than rational thought guided her. The tears came again, just as ineffective as their first wash over Artemio's sympathies. "You're a monster."

Artemio shrugged. "Show me a man who says there is no monster in him and I'll show you a liar."

In the face of such apathy, there was little the maid could do but obey. She fetched Artemio a storm-lantern and watched as he removed the candle and deposited her rat inside before twisting it shut with wire. Neither girl nor rodent gave much in the way of argument.

He gave her no reassurances from that moment on. Only instructions. "I shall expect to hear from you once every week. If I have not, I shall assume that our arrangement is at an end. If you hear anything pertinent to the assassinations tormenting the court, reach out to me immediately. If you serve me well in this, there may be a place for you in my household, where you might be shielded from the consequences of your foolish overcommitment."

"I wouldn't live under your roof if you paid me." The maid seemed to have some spark left in her, despite Artemio so thoroughly defeating her.

"A free servant, even better." He had settled at his desk and watched her as she lit a taper and the candles above them. She stood staring defiantly at him with those beady little eyes for a long moment before he tutted. "I am certain you have other duties to attend to."

With much stomping of feet and swishing of her tail, she departed. That was one step forward at least. A spy in the palace. Albeit a poorly placed one.

The rat made a little chirp in its lantern, and Artemio peered in at it and sighed. He was aware that if left to their own devices, rats would eat more or less anything they could set their teeth to, but he had no idea what they were meant to eat. A trip to the library would be necessary. Presumably someone throughout all of history had kept one as a pet and had the foresight to leave instruction behind.

He had taken a name for neither the servant or the rodent, and he now wondered if it might have been an oversight. If this investigation stretched on, he could hardly be expected to call the two of them Maid and Rat for weeks on end. A glance around the room furnished him with a solution. Above the bedframe, spattered with blood, was an oil painting of the queen mother, now sadly departed.

"Make yourself comfortable, Daria. We have a long and studious day ahead."

She chirped once more.

"Indeed, my predecessors have left me a mess of ill-filed papers to untangle. How astute of you to notice."

The rat turned around a few times before lying down on the far side of the lantern, facing away from him.

"I have been in the palace for only a morning and I am already reduced to talking to rodents. This does not bode well for my sanity."

When there was no response, he had no more excuse to ignore the work set before him. Starting from the most yellowed-looking vellum, he began to read.

5

CHILDREN OF THE SELVAGGIA

Arancia, Regola Dei Cerva 104

The first year in the deep dark woods was the hardest on Orsina. Or better to say that for the first year in the deep dark woods, Mother Vinegar was the hardest on Orsina.

Neither girl nor crone had spent much time learning the care of others, both having devoted a similar proportion of their lives to mastering solitude, and both had a stubbornness to them that would have made a mule seem pliant. Neither one was willing to give an inch.

The first days, Orsina was in shock. Everything was new, everything was strange. When Mother Vinegar barked a command, she obeyed because she had no clue what else to do, and the old woman was satisfied that everything was as it should be. Then the girl found her footing.

When the morning water needed fetching, she was nowhere to be seen. It was no worry. Mother Vinegar had been fetching her own water long enough. When the herbs needed to be bundled to dry, she was gone. That was no worry either. Clumsy child fingers fumbled knots. No great loss there. Wasn't like there weren't hours enough in the day for doing things before the brat came along.

Beneath the boughs of the Selvaggia, light was a ghost of the world beyond. Green and dappled when it came through, but mostly a forgotten luxury. It was not a forest the way those in the preened parts of Espher would know it. There were no clean pathways, no trimmed grass, the undergrowth reached as high as the lower branches, and to make progress, you either followed the flow of the woods, trailing along the rabbit trails and streams, or you came with a blade and forced the forest to part.

When the sun came down, only those who kept an eye turned to the sky knew it, and even they would have to check twice. Mother Vinegar knew. She could feel the cold creeping in her bones before the sun touched the horizon. The cold was familiar. The other sensation curling up in her stomach was not. It was not fear. Mother Vinegar was the thing other people feared, not subject to its whims herself. But she could recognize that curled chill in her gut as kin to fear, a distant cousin perhaps. Descendant from the same root of dread, but not the flowering stem. The girl. Where was the girl?

Selvaggia was not as dangerous as the people of Sheepshank thought it was. The beasts of the true wild that came roaming through were few and far between. The old shades that gathered in the thicket might have given some shepherd or farmer the scare of their life, but they weren't any danger to them. Not really. To the girl, though, they presented a lethal risk, one that Mother Vinegar, so intent on getting her settled under her own watchful eye, hadn't the chance to warn or ward her against.

A soft woman might have gone running out into the woods to look for her, flapping her arms and fretting. Mother Vinegar sneered instead. If the girl would run off without her leave, then falling to a shade was her just reward. Most of the shades in the forest were weak enough that they'd only manage a sip at her years. Maybe a wrinkle or two would set the girl on the road to behaving herself right. The coil in Vinegar's stomach twisted at the thought of the girl fallen under a briar, shade after shade riding through her, stripping her years away. Still, she didn't go and look. That would be admitting defeat.

When Orsina slipped back into the house an hour after sunset, there was no dinner left for her. The bread crust had been thrown out for the birds, the stew scraped from the kettle. Mother Vinegar sat in her rocking chair, paying her no heed. Not a word was exchanged that night, nor the next day when Orsina took herself out roaming again at the crack of dawn.

Each day the dread coiled, and each night it spun out into rage. Rage that Mother Vinegar swallowed down without a sound. Wouldn't do for the girl to get ideas about attachment. Wouldn't help her to think that the old woman had any love in her heart to share. That was the way folk got broken hearts and bitterness. Any kindness in the girl would be a hole for a shade to climb in through. Better this way, better sour and closed than vulnerable.

The third night the girl came wandering home, Mother Vinegar had a bowl of gnocchi there waiting. Muddy-kneed and wide-eyed, the girl set to it while the old woman used an old deer-bone comb to pick the worst of the thickets from her hair. When it hooked in a tangle, she used the knot of hair to drag Orsina's head back like she was about to string a bow. "No more roaming until your work is done. No more roaming at all until I says so." Mother Vinegar gave the hair another sharp tug. "Understand me, brat?"

For a moment the tension held. Comb, tangle, hair, scalp; all straining at their limit. Orsina's eyes met the old woman's glower. A girl of eight years against all the cruelty the forest could instill in a hag. Orsina's hairs began to ping loose as she added to the strain, giving the old woman a slow nod but no answer.

The next morning, she was home. The next week, they spoke. Small things at first. How a knot should be tied. How much water to add to the pot. Which herb would bring out the poison with the bile. Which bulb would slow the stuttering heart. There were some who'd spend their life learning the secrets Mother Vinegar swatted down like flies and many more who'd die for the lack of that learning. Orsina took it in stride, never showing an interest or a care. Taking on whatever burdens were thrust her way without complaint.

The only time her eyes lit up at all was when Mother Vinegar sat her down in the evening and spoke to her of the shades. Through their wanderings, they crossed paths with plenty of shades through the day, and every time Mother Vinegar behaved as though the words they whispered and the shadows they cast were not there at all.

The old woman's silence infuriated Orsina. She knew the shades saw Mother Vinegar and Mother Vinegar saw the shades. In her deliberate ignorance, Orsina saw the same stubbornness that had let a girl wander the woods unattended. Yet to admit her annoyance would be admitting defeat in this strange game they were playing.

The evening stories were different from what she was used to. In Sheepshank, tales of the shades were rare and spoken in hushed tones for fear of inviting a shade in by naming it. Mother Vinegar spoke of them with the same dull repetition she rattled off the species of birds or the leaves of herbs. She took all the majesty of a hidden world of wonders and made it mundane. A box of tools. All the stories of Orsina's youth withered in her memory, replaced day by day with facts.

Every word that came out of Mother Vinegar was a fact. Solid as stone and unwavering despite any opinions to the contrary. When she told Orsina things that seemed to make no sense, it was as though she could hear the girl's doubt, yet she never corrected herself. Never wavered. Her world was filled with plants that grew to rhythms unseen, seasons that could be predicted by a glimpse of a bird's feathers through the thicket, and those same facts, applied with the regularity of a poultice to draw all wonder from the world.

A month passed before they went to visit Ginny Greenteeth.

A month was long enough for Orsina to truly believe that all the fear-mongering tales she'd heard about the forest were nothing but tales. She was living under the same roof as the Aceta Madre, and the most frightening things about her were the smell and the sharp edge of her tongue. The few animals she had seen roaming the forest were either smaller than her or so afraid that she barely caught a glimpse of them.

The shades were much the same. After being taken by Perlita, Orsina had been dreading every shade she saw. She reared back from them like a startled mare, watching from the corner of her eye as the old woman pretended not to be looking at her with contempt.

"You've a hole in the heart of you. A hollow. Same with all the Shade-bound." It was the first time they'd actually spoken of what Orsina was. Of what had happened to her back in the graveyard. It took the wind out of her. The old woman toddled on as if it was nothing. Just as she always did. Calling back over her shoulder, "That's why a shade can climb in you. That's why they be wanting you. Not a snack, a home."

Like the rabbits and the birds, the shades of the forest scattered ahead of their coming. Glimpses of them through the dappled light, but nothing more. Every one that flitted away made Orsina all the more the fool for fearing, all the weaker for having been taken by some old woman.

Orsina glowered at them. "Why aren't they coming knocking then?"

There was a hint of a smile on Mother Vinegar's face. "You've got the door shut now. Slammed it and pressed up against it. Maybe even put some locks on. There's few enough of them are strong enough to push in when you're holding it shut."

Greenteeth was waiting at the bottom of her pond in the deep woods. A convergence of all the little streams that ran through the forest amidst exposed stones and moss so thick it would have made a better bed than any Orsina had ever lain down in. She had her marching orders from Mother Vinegar before they'd even set out for the pool. She was not to speak. She was not to touch the water. She was not to reach out to the shade beneath the surface in any way. She was to behave as much like a stone standing still and silent in the midst of the woods as she could accomplish, and even then she was to run the moment Mother Vinegar addressed her directly. After a month of naught but the glimmers of ghosts, Orsina was understandably skeptical.

Deep in the murky water, Orsina couldn't even see Greenteeth, but by the prickling of hairs on the back of her neck and the shiver that ran through her, she believed Mother Vinegar's words.

"Off your lazy backside. We're here visiting, Gin."

Orsina startled. After all her talk of shades being mindless, now the old woman was chatting away like the presence beneath the water was an old friend.

"What little mouse comes a-creeping in? Who wanders so far to see Ginevra Greenteeth? What little babe comes to dip their toes in my pond?"

Orsina had almost convinced herself that everything that had happened back by the graveside had been a dream, that she was just a little mad and there was nothing to fear. She wished she was a little mad. A little mad would have been easier.

Orsina heard without hearing. The shade, whispering into her head. She didn't know the voice, but she could taste the mold of old rotten wood and feel the press of drowning water in every word.

"Don't be starting with your nonsense now. You know me, Ginny. And mind your manners, there's no toes for eating, neither."

Orsina's giggles bubbled over and they just wouldn't stop no matter how hard she tried to swallow them down. There was a manic edge to them by the time Mother Vinegar turned to face the girl, moving slowly, like when there was a wild animal she was trying not to startle.

"It's just like in the stories."

The full weight of Ginevra Greenteeth's attention fell on her. Orsina could taste pondweed, her eyes clouded with algae. Until then, she was just catching the edges of the shade's voice, now it thundered inside her.

"What's this little treat you've brought me then?"

Orsina's laughter was strangled by the water she felt bubbling up her throat. Mother Vinegar was glowering at her with enough force to send a grown man running. "Don't you pay her no mind, Gin, this daft thing is just about to get sent home with a flogged arse for talking when she was told not to."

"How could we ignore such an offering. So brimming with life. So rich with it. Come into the pool, my little dove, the water is lovely and cool."

Orsina's feet moved before she had the chance to stop them. Just a step, but wouldn't it be so nice to cool off after a long day walking through these woods. She hadn't had a proper wash since Mother Vinegar took her in. It would be so easy to just slip into the water and… she stopped.

Mother Vinegar had not moved, she had not made a sound, but a memory had caught Orsina instead. Her body doing things she did not want it to do. Her life trickling away. She stopped dead at the memory, then took a step back.

"You have been teaching her well, Madre, but I shall have her yet."

Now Mother Vinegar moved again. Now her hand closed over Orsina's wrist and the flat of her hand skipped off the back of the girl's skull. A crack that could be heard through the woods, louder than the flowing water.

"I've taught her *nothing*."

The shame was good, the flush of heat on her cheeks as she blushed, it reminded her that this was her body, it reminded her of how she felt after Perlita rode her. Shamed, worthless. She would not feel that way again.

This time the pond water washed over her without making it inside. The chill touched her skin, but not her mind. She pushed back. Her arms lifted up, but they didn't need to, it wasn't like there was something real to push back against, no tide to part with a wave. The water ran away from her.

There was a bitter edge to Greenteeth's voice. *"Someone has."*

That was all for the first day, and the second. More than anything else, it felt like Mother Vinegar was testing Orsina's limits. They went to visit, and Mother Vinegar and the thing in the water exchanged stories, but nothing more. Meanwhile, Greenteeth pried at Orsina, trying to worm its way inside her. It never had the same beginner's luck again, and now Orsina understood what they were there for, she pushed back more and more. By the end of their last visit, the shade could barely even be heard above the water.

Walking home from the pond, it was like all the colors were drained from the world. All of the shades, blending away to nothing. Held back by Orsina's will alone. They'd creep back in as the days went by, but now she knew how to push them away. She knew how to close herself to them. The most dangerous thing in the woods became the brambles hanging low from the branches, the odd wild animal roaming through.

By night, the old woman's tales became instruction. She set a stump of candle on the floor between them as it was about to die and had Orsina watch as the last sputters of wax gave birth to a puff of smoke. Mother Vinegar glanced up from darning a shirt's elbow to mutter, "That's your shade. All they are. Here and gone as fast. You stay well clear of the dying and you needn't fear."

Orsina's brows drew down at that. All the other statements of absolute fact she'd sat through from the old woman had some grain of truth, but this made no sense at all. "They aren't, though."

"What's that you say?" Mother Vinegar's eyes narrowed somewhere down in the thicket of wrinkles. "You know better, do you?"

"If they were gone that quick, we'd never see them. They're all over the woods. I see them every day."

The old woman broke her usually impenetrable stare. "Catch a puff of smoke under glass, it'll linger."

"Is that all old Ginny Greenteeth is then?" Orsina skipped right to the point. "Smoke in a glass?"

"Some fires make more smoke. Don't they? Wet leaves. Rotten wood."

"But the smoke doesn't last long enough for folk to write songs about it."

"All right, all right," Mother Vinegar grumbled. "There's things that can be done to stretch them on longer. To keep them going when time should've rubbed them away. Songs and stories, remembering them, that helps them along. Though minding them wrong can twist a shade up something fierce. Make it into something it never was to start. Feeding them too. That's how your kind gird them. Slip them a little life here and there to string them along."

There was a hint of heat in Orsina's voice. "My kind?"

Mother Vinegar's lips pursed. "Hollows. Binders. Necromancers. Your kind."

"So that's what I need to do, is it? Feed them up and keep them like pets? Is that why you've got me chatting to Ginny once a week, you want me to tame her?"

"There's no taming a shade. They're not beasts, they're not people, they're smoke. They're echoes."

"Ginny talks real well for an echo."

"You've learned nothing. All this time and you've learned not a thing."

"How am I meant to learn anything when you don't tell me anything."

"I do. I did. I just did, didn't I."

"Oh, the monster in the pond you've been chatting with for weeks isn't actually talking, you're just imagining it."

"Fool girl. You've been learning your plants. Do you think the umber pitcher would catch flies without nectar in its trap?"

"So what, she isn't really speaking?"

"Anything can make a noise. Do you be thinking mockingbirds are thinking out their answers too? To think you need a head, shades have naught."

The old woman looked to be genuinely incensed. Orsina had been a quick study and wise enough not to argue when she was told things. She'd offered little opportunity for Mother Vinegar's supposedly acid tongue to be used. It was strange enough to her that she was taken aback.

"Why are you so angry about this?"

"Because if you think of them as people, they'll work on you and they'll win you, and you'll die. They've all the time in the world to worm their way in your head if you let them. Don't give them a way in. Don't give an inch. Don't let them fool you, girl. They only need to get past you once and you're done."

Sullen silence settled over Orsina as she bit back every answer that came bubbling up. How could Mother Vinegar be old friends with Ginny Greenteeth and not believe the shade could think? How could she know shades by name, but not think they were any different from a carnivorous plant? Orsina couldn't wrap her head around it, but she still had a healthy fear after all that had happened in her short life. So she took the words as truth, even if her heart called them a lie.

And so the months rolled on.

For all the native aggression of the woods, there were people living within them. To start with, Orsina and Mother Vinegar dwelled within the old stone-built cottage just an hour's hard walk from Sheepshank, halfway between a ruin and a home.

They were not alone. At the farthest northern reach of the Selvaggia, the men of the steppes cut down snow-weighted pines for their spear-shafts, and while their hunters rarely roamed this far afield, with no stars to navigate by, Orsina had already met a half dozen of them in her time.

Steppes men were strange to her eyes, pallid and shorn, stitched into furs and marked with bright inks beneath their skin. She did not fear them, as other girls of Espher surely would have, because by the time they came to her neck of the woods, they were half starved and terrified. It was a coin's toss between whether Mother Vinegar would invite them in for stew or run them off when they got close enough for her to take notice. The beardless ones were more liable to get supper before finding their feet on a northbound trail, but there was no real logic to it.

Beyond those lost souls, and the shades that seemed to fester and multiply beneath the canopy, there was only one person young Orsina saw with any sort of regularity through her youth in the forest.

Kagan.

The first time he came to the mossy heap Mother Vinegar called home, it was so deep into the dead of night that even the old woman, who seemed to thrive on only a few hours a night, had drifted off. Orsina had woken to the sound of the kettle being stirred and the fire stoked, but thought little of it. The old woman kept her own time, sipping soup in the odd hours and fighting the chill of night however she must.

In Sheepshank, Orsina had the comfort of a bed. A little cot tucked away in the corner with a straw mat, but a bed all the same. It was one of the few things she looked back on fondly. Here she slept on the cracked flagstones by the fireplace with a fur wrapped around her to keep the chill of the earth from climbing in while she slept.

A boot nudged her backside, and her eyes popped open. Kagan looked down at her with just as much surprise as she was feeling. The two of them stared at each other for a long moment by the light of the stoked embers.

Orsina's eyes had more or less settled now, and the wild curls of her hair had been bound up in a braid rather than run the risk of catching in the undergrowth. She looked more or less like any girl who spent her days living wild would.

Kagan's eyes were golden by the firelight, vertically slit. He was hairless. Horny scales had risen up out of the skin along his brow-line, and there was a dusting of flatter ones elsewhere. A ridge of them across the top of his bare head. A tracery of them along his jawline, thickening up towards ears that had fused back into the sides of his skull. If a man and a lizard had a child together, it would not look like Kagan, but if that child went on and bred only on humans for a few generations, then Kagan would be a good approximation of its grandson. The parts that were man seemed just as foreign to Orsina as the parts that were serpent.

Olive skin, sun-darkened, was the norm in Espher, and Kagan's was within a few shades of that, but his features could not be more different. A wide squared jaw, hawkish nose, and heavy bags under almond-shaped eyes marked him as a foreigner as surely as the reptilian traits marked him as alien in other ways.

His voice was what really startled Orsina. Deep and resonant, she could feel the bass of it in her bones. "Why's there a kid on your floor?"

Somewhere out of sight, Mother Vinegar was banging through her herb cabinets. "Apprentices that do their chores get to sleep through the night. Leave the brat be."

"Apprentice? Didn't think witching was the kind of job you could teach." He crouched down beside her, the soft leathers he wore folding without a sound. "Is she treating you right, kid? Are you learning how to bitch out a man for getting cut and then charge him a whole side of boar to stitch him up?"

"You think my words are no more than a dog's barking. No wonder you never pay them any heed, eh? I tell you time and again…"

"Just because they're down doesn't mean they're done fighting. See, I do listen."

Mother Vinegar snarled, "If you really listened, you'd have fewer scars, eh?"

"And you'd have less bacon."

In their years together, Orsina had heard many strange sounds from the old woman. Croaks and snorts. Groans and grunts. This was the first time she heard Mother Vinegar laugh. Whatever remnants of sleep still clung to her were brushed away by her surprise, and she popped upright to see if her ears were deceiving her.

The cackle was gone and the usual sour expression back on Mother Vinegar's face by the time Orsina saw her, but by then it was too late. There could be no doubt of what she had just heard.

The girl's mouth opened and the first thought in her head sprang right out. "What are you?"

Kagan threw back his head and laughed, jagged teeth all on display. "I'm a hunter, girl. A tracker. Best that there is. What are you when you aren't a footstool?"

She scrambled to her feet, furs still wrapped around her, and he had to stand himself or risk being knocked off balance. "Mother Vinegar says I'm going to be a witch. An even better witch than her."

"She said that?" He glanced up at Mother Vinegar, smirking. "Did she?"

"The brat's talking out her rear end. Ignore her."

Orsina shrugged. "She didn't say it, but she thinks it really hard."

"I couldn't have been cursed with a more worthless apprentice, slovenly, foul-tempered, stench-riddled…" The old woman trailed off.

Orsina had a smug little smirk on her face. "She thinks it."

When their eyes met, Kagan recoiled.

He'd always thought the dire repercussions of meeting eyes with a witch were just talk. In all his dealings with Mother Vinegar, they'd behaved perfectly normally and he'd felt nothing like this. His own magic, fragile as it was after all these years away from home, felt like it was being strangled.

He was afraid of this child all of a sudden. So he did what he'd always done when he was afraid. He stepped forward and offered her his hand. "I'm Kagan."

She eyed his hand with suspicion for a moment. Spotting the claws protruding beyond his fingerless gloves. With a shrug, she took hold. "Orsina."

"Pleasure to meet you."

Their introduction was cut short as Mother Vinegar barged through with the kettle full of boiling water. "If you're both done flapping your lips, we've work to do. Since you're up, girl, fetch me out the bone needles and some clean rags."

"Yes, Mother."

For all of Mother Vinegar's clucking about the girl, there was no denying her apprentice sprang into action when asked. Kagan couldn't have made sense of how the old woman filed her belongings away in little cubbyholes around the cottage, but the girl knew her way around everything well enough that she didn't even need light to fetch out the suede-wrapped needles.

Kagan was stripped to the waist by the time she returned and laid out in front of the fire. He'd been so glib before that Orsina hadn't even realized how badly he was hurt. There were gashes notched across his ribs, not a boar's goring tusks, but the claws of something bigger. Thick scales ran down the length of his spine and over his shoulders, but his flanks seemed to be exposed and human.

Curiosity got the better of her, and she crept closer to the man. "What did that to you?"

Mother Vinegar cut Kagan off before he could even start. "Rest your rump here, girl. You'll be the one making these stitches when I'm gone, eh?"

Kagan twisted his head to the side to see them. "Planning on going somewhere?"

Mother Vinegar hissed at him, and he turned back around rapidly. It was a bad idea to antagonize your surgeon. "Some folk have the decency to age, eh?"

When she jabbed the needle into his side, Kagan didn't flinch. Orsina supposed if he could hop around and make jokes while he had the flesh carved away from his bones, a little more pain wouldn't trouble him.

Orsina leaned in as close as she could without blocking the firelight and ran a reverential hand over the scales on the outside of Kagan's arm when she should have been watching Mother Vinegar's industrious stitching. "What is he?"

Kagan lifted his head to answer again, but a tut from Mother Vinegar had him lie back down with a groan. "He be what he says he is. Best tracker in the woods. His people, the Arazi, they can feel what beasts are feeling, think what they're thinking. He can touch souls with a beast, and he uses it to kill them, or worse."

"What's worse than killing?" Orsina had drawn her hand back. Reverence fading all too fast.

"There's folk in the city would love some beast of the wild to keep as a pet. Locked up in a cage all its days when its blood screams at it to run and hunt. There's worse folk yet that'll set beast on beast to watch them fight."

Into the heaped furs, Kagan rumbled, "It's a living."

"It's a monstrous waste of the gift of your blood, and you ought to be ashamed." Mother Vinegar tugged hard on the gut-thread, drawing the wound shut and making Kagan grunt with pain.

Kagan moaned. "Can the girl do the rest?"

"She's had no practice." Even as she said it, she was handing the needle off to Orsina, who looked at its bloodied length with no small amount of horror.

"Can't hurt worse than your gentle touch."

The sad truth was that for all Orsina had heard about the wickedness of this hunter so far, he'd judged her right. She couldn't bring herself to hurt him, even if he was as monstrous as Mother Vinegar said he was. She'd watched her own mother stitching clothes often enough to know how it was done, and for all that skin had its own horrible elasticity, she'd done trickier things at Mother Vinegar's behest before. Reaching into beehives to lift out wax. Skinning rabbits in one tug. Blocking out the voice of Ginny Greenteeth when it called to her across the forest. She distracted herself with chatter.

"Where are you from?"

He grumbled into the furs once more, eventually turning his head enough to say, "I travel where the hunt takes me."

She dipped the needle back into his skin, taking as much care as she could to keep him from harm. "But where did you come from? I've never seen anyone like you before."

This time his grunts and grumbles were the only answer at all. Mother Vinegar sank down by the fire, a cup of some steaming herbal concoction clasped between hands so old they were barely more than bones. "Sore subject, for this one. He's an exile."

This time, Orsina tugged a little harder on the thread. "Are you in exile because of what you do to the animals?"

That drew out a laugh from him at least. "You think the Arazi give a damn how I treat their strays? If you even knew what they do with... If you had any idea the things I hunt in these woods, you'd eat your words. They'd give you nightmares, little girl. Thunder lizards, wyverns, sabre cats. All the things you read about in storybooks. They're real and they'd come eat you up if it weren't for me leading them off, hunting them down, and selling them along."

The next stitch went smoother, and the next. She had found her rhythm. "I don't read stories, and I'm not scared of lynx or lizard."

"No stories?" Kagan looked up at Mother Vinegar with disdain. "What kind of education are you giving this child?"

The old woman drew a long noisy sip from her cup. "She'll be needing her feet on the ground, not her head in the clouds, eh?"

"Childhood without stories." He exhaled heavily. "It's like a bed without a blanket."

"We make do without either here." She slurped once more, then added, "Though the girl will likely want to thank you for that fur she sleeps on."

Orsina let it slip from around her shoulders, then shuddered in the chill. "This was yours?"

He shrugged, tugging one of her stitches back open. "That old bat has sewn me up more often than I can count. Only seems fair to give something in return."

Mother Vinegar leaned a little closer. "Did I hear you rightly when you said you had a side of boar for me this time?"

"Still hanging out in the woods, draining off." He kept trying to turn and see what Orsina was doing, even though it was quite impossible to look at his own back. "Suppose the wyvern didn't have a taste for it. She wanted a bite of me instead."

"You put your beast down before trailing blood to my door, eh?" It was phrased as a question, but it had the weight of a demand.

"Dead. Had a buyer all ready for her too. I just lost some good money."

Orsina closed up the last gash. "Nearly lost more than that."

"True enough." He laughed then winced as it pulled at his stitches. With exaggerated slowness, he rolled over to face Orsina, watching as she wiped his blood off her hands with a tattered scrap of cloth. "My thanks to you."

"Thanks? She doesn't need thanks, she needs that side of pig, eh? You'll take her out to fetch it come dawn before some other beast is off with it."

Orsina took the news without complaint, but Kagan rumbled, "I will, will I?"

"You'll be doing that, and the next time you're passing, you can bring me some more of the blue-green berries from the north woods. The last batch have all dried up over the summer."

Orsina had retrieved the fur and returned to her place by the hearth-stone, settling down to catch what little sleep was left in the night. She didn't lie down yet. Instead, she watched as the serpent-man and the witch sniped back and forth at each other.

"You can use them dried."

"Not if I'm needing the juices."

"And why would anyone be needing the juices?"

"Because nursing babes take just as bad with shaking fever as their mothers, and they haven't the teeth for chewing, eh?"

With a grumble, Kagan settled back down. "You strike a hard bargain. Fine. I'll bring you all I can carry and half the pig."

"You'll bring the whole pig or I'll pull that thread out of you, eh?" She prodded at him with her foot. "Three days you'll be staying here. What use have you for a rotten half pig in three days' time? We'll strip it and hang it, and when you come back around, there'll be tack ready for you."

He didn't agree, but he did lie down and shut up, which the old woman seemed to take as a sign she'd won the argument. With a satisfied little huff, she started ambling, tidying away the mess that his coming had made in the carefully ordered mess she usually cultivated.

This close, Orsina could still smell Kagan's blood. She could hear the soothing rhythm of his breathing, the tempo stuttering when he drew in too deeply and the pain of his wounds troubled him. She didn't mean to care. Mother Vinegar schooled her against it with rigor. It did no good for a witch to care about the folk she tended. It would make her slow to cut away what needed to be cut away. Slow to choose who should live and who should die.

Orsina was a child still, for all the burdens she bore. She could not prune away feelings as soon as they grew. She had no love for this strange creature nestled on himself at the far side of the fire, but she felt some entanglement all the same. She was still trying to pick that feeling apart when sleep took her.

A LEGACY OF FAILURE

Gemmazione, Regola Dei Cerva 112

Noon had passed by without notice, and Artemio was eating into his afternoon classes before he'd even made it out of the first heap of notes. Albano Granchio was the first inquisitor to die, the seventh victim listed chronologically in the rather haphazard timeline Artemio was sketching out. Albano was the third son of that family, talentless and slow-witted as far as his notation indicated, a political appointee to secure that family's loyalty.

Albano's note-taking left much to be desired, and from the many different handwritings on display, it was apparent that he cycled through scribes at the same rate other men changed their shirts. While his timeline of events marked him as the seventh victim by its abrupt termination, a glance at dates and details of decomposition suggested he was actually either the ninth or tenth. Since there was no way to know for certain, Artemio composed his list based on discovery of the bodies rather than the specific dates of the murders. There simply wasn't enough information to do otherwise.

Quirino Cigno assumed the investigation after the Granchio lad proved his incompetence in a rather spectacular fashion, spraying blood all across the patios of his father's townhouse. It was Quirino's blood that stained this very chamber and his diaries that provided Artemio with the wealth of useful knowledge.

While Albano made a note when it was absolutely necessary, and not a moment beforehand, Quirino struck the other extreme. Margin notes proliferated until they were consuming the main text. Which votes were being discussed in the Teatro on the date of the murder, which way the dead men meant to place their vote, what they had been wearing the last time they were seen, friendships they had recently formed. It seemed that while Albano had repeatedly banged his head against the problem of how the murders were being committed, Quirino had skipped forward to consider why.

As a creature of the court, his natural assumption was that the killings were courtly business, diplomacy taken to its sharpest end, and as such, his investigation reflected this. He had an encyclopedic knowledge of the various alliances, factions, friendships, marriages, and snubs he was trying to factor into the killings. Yet for all his efforts, there seemed to be no pattern. No one agenda was being pushed by those who died, nor did their death seem to advance any faction of which Quirino was aware. Which suggested either some conspiracy with an as yet unpredictable agenda or some other motive to the murders.

He'd asked the kings who benefited from these murders, and from their seat within the carefully constructed cocoon of courtly politics designed to hold them at arm's length from the world, they could think of nobody at all. Yet the truth was that these killings were sowing fear among people who had never experienced it in their lives. Even without accounting for the great houses currently rudderless thanks to the death of their patriarch, fear led to chaos.

Any enemy of Espher would benefit when the ruling class was in flux, but so too would any domestic group with an axe to grind. The only thing that kept Artemio convinced this was the work of some foreign power was the method of each murder.

While Albano had politely declined to include the gruesome details in his notation, rendering them nigh on useless, Quirino had provided detailed descriptions of the states in which the bodies were discovered.

Dismembered was one of the first words to jump out at Artemio. *Eviscer-ated* was another. He had to stop and push all thoughts of Mother aside before he could continue. It was bad enough when he was picturing a blade in the dark and a cut throat, but the way these victims had been destroyed was brutal. If he had not taken Quirino at his word regarding blade marks, he would have assumed the injuries described were the work of some wild animal that had been set upon the victims. It was enough to turn his stomach, even before Mother came into the equation.

Whatever other complaints Artemio might have had about the people of Espher, they were not savages. Many of his complaints through the years were that the people of Espher were quite the opposite, too civilized and genteel to survive in the real world where empires rose and fell like pounding waves on the beaches of history. He honestly didn't believe any of the preening peacocks of the court or Teatro had the stomach for this kind of violence. Which left only the enemies of Espher to contend with.

Inevitably, as he tapped at the glass side of Daria's cage, his mind turned to the Agrantine Empire.

Living in the border provinces, they were the threat that haunted every waking hour. The once royal House of Volpe was permitted to retain a standing army, encouraged to, even, yet for some reason the promise of land in the breadbasket of Espher was insufficiently tempting to appeal to any of the young cavaliers on the rise. They would not tarnish their reputations by allying themselves with the Volpes, and as such, a large proportion of the wealth that the fertile land provided to Father was spent hiring mercenaries to guard the border, where the once great Tagliare had now slowed to a much-forded trickle. These mercenaries brought the Volpe reputation into further disrepute, perpetuating the cycle that necessitated them to begin with.

It was not that Agrant had made any overtures to war. There was no massing of troops upon their borders or rumors of marshaling forces elsewhere, but their relationship with Espher had always been complex. Artemio was willing to admit to himself that Father's view on the Agrantine would always be colored by their own family's history with them.

Though the truth would never truly out, Father remained convinced the Agrantine had supported the Cerva coup, in an advisory capacity if not in a material manner. It did not take a wise man to recognize that the relationship between the two countries had warmed considerably since the change in leadership.

They had been far from the brink of war prior to the end of the Volpe reign, but there could be no denying that their southern neighbors received no kindness or concession.

Now trade boomed. Father had to grit his teeth and watch as the Agrantine's dour caravans crossed his land. Scowling out at whitewashed wagons and soberly clothed merchants and muttering that it was unnatural for any man who made his fortune through trade to dress without a hint of pride or flair.

If the Cerva were puppets of Agrant, then these assassinations may have been from some other kingdom attempting to destabilize their grip. If the Cerva were puppets of Agrant, then the assassinations may have been the latter's attempts to weaken the will of the landed gentry and render them more pliable to commands from on high.

More information was required, and Artemio was not liable to find it within these sheaves of paper. More pressingly, his last lesson of the day was with Prima Cicogna, and while the others might have forgiven him an absence in light of his summons to the palace, she most assuredly would not.

Snatching up the rat, he left the room with all due haste, pausing for only a moment at the door. At the price of another minute of his life, Artemio called on Bisnonno Fiore to spy out along the corridor for him.

When the shade rode him, he suffered a doubling of his vision. He saw the corridor outside, empty and silent as it was now. What he needed to know. Cast over the top of it came a vision of the past. Fiore Volpe had walked these halls many times, surrounded by the crowd of courtiers and servants that were any king's due. A living storm of swishing silk and delicate furs that followed him everywhere he went. There was music in the halls. Chatter and song. Sunlight streamed in through windows that were now shuttered. Shades always remembered their lives as brighter than the present, it was part of their nature. Yet there was no denying that this remembered version of the palace was more appealing.

To be insidious was also in a shade's nature. When Artemio allowed one into his mind, it was not always possible afterwards to decipher which memories were his own and which had been introduced to him by his discourteous guest. Was the palace better under the Volpe rule or was this only how Fiore wanted to see it? The worst part was that even the shade itself may not have known the truth of the matter. Emotions colored memories, as did ambitions, passions, prejudice, and simple failure to recall. A beautiful maiden could become a hideous hag in the recollection of one who loathed her. A proud and noble king could become a hunchbacked child-murderer in the memory of his enemies.

It was an unsettling thing to be unsure if a thought was your own, but it was the price those who dallied with shades paid for their power. They walked the blade's edge each time they allowed a shade inside them, not only for the fear that it might break free of control and drink away their life, but also because to be ridden by a shade was to be changed.

Walking in the silent footsteps of his ancestor, Artemio made his way out of the palace, through passages where royal children had once played and even the servants had forgotten. There was no way to sneak from the palace unseen. But by now the crowds of courtiers and their attendants were a heaving, perfumed mass. With a downward glance, it was a simple thing to pass unnoticed among them. He had their look and their mannerisms, even if he'd never lived among them.

Some would call it good breeding. Artemio would not.

With no care for the nature of his driver, he found it to be a simple thing to flag down a mongrel with a hedgehog's spines poking through his hood, and from there onwards to his final lesson of the day.

It was considered extremely uncouth to run within the House of Seven Shadows, but the grounds were fair game for some brisk walking. The whole day had gotten away from Artemio. Mother always complained at the way he lost himself in his books to the exclusion of everything going on around him, and here he was proving her right.

This late in the day, there were other students milling about, lounging on the marble benches by the ponds, conducting illicit romances in plain sight, or simply politicking in this miniaturized version of their social strata. Artemio powered past them all without a backwards glance. He already had a reputation here for his rudeness. Such a thing would barely be noticed by the self-involved scions of the highest houses in the land.

Almost every building in the city was pasted with the same white stucco in emulation of the palace's stonework. The House of Seven Shadows had the actual stone throughout most of its structure. The exception, and Artemio's destination, were the lecture halls, where wood dominated instead.

Every floorboard creaked beneath Artemio's feet as he was forced to walk the length of the hall and assume his seat. Every eye was turned his way except for those of the Prima. She pointedly did not look at him. She cleared her throat after the discordant creaking had stopped and then launched into her speech anew.

"As the most advanced students within this institution, your eyes must now turn towards the future beyond our walls. Less than a year from this very day, you shall form an unbreakable bond with your choice of impresario. Their life shall flow through you as freely as your own, and it is vital that each of you remember that it is no less precious than your own. I do not mean, of course, that your lives are of equal value, rather that what you take from them is still a depletion of your own available resources. If your impresario loses their life, you shall expire with them, so it is a common practice to drink a sip from each glass rather than drink more deeply from one or the other."

There had never been any doubt that Artemio and Harmony were to be paired. It was a matter of long-standing tradition when there were twins. From the moment Artemio had shown the talent, both of them set to preparing themselves for that coming day. Their whole lives, shaped for that single fact.

"It shall feel strange in the beginning to draw upon the reserves of another. You will have to break the habit of a lifetime of solitude. You shall remain here within Septombra until we are assured the correct balance has been achieved."

Coming here and listening to the Prima speak was necessary to avoid any undue attention, but it was also an act of cowardice. Artemio had no idea how Harmony had spent her day, where she had gone after they parted in the morning, or even if she was still within the grounds of the House, but he should have sought her out immediately. He could justify his work in the palace, but not sitting and hearing the same things he had learned from books as a child repeated as if they were some great wisdom. His attention wavered as Prima Cicogna rambled on, "…great advantages are to be found in this fresh-filled font beyond the extension of our own life span. With more cache to spend, we find ourselves in the enviable position of being able to squander a little in the pursuit of education. For instance…"

Two shadows leapt out behind her for an instant before the candelabra snuffed out. The windows lining the hall shuddered. Papers ruffled as wind tore through the halls.

Artemio was lifted from his bench by an impact from below and flung into the aisle. Compared with what a bound shade could really do, it was a love-tap.

There was widespread tittering among the other students. All too happy to see someone else drawing the Prima's polite wrath.

Artemio made a show of getting up off the floor and rubbing his backside. "My apologies, Prima, it seems that in my lateness I accidentally sat in the place of the whipping boy."

Cicogna rolled her eyes at his indignance. "I suppose you have some reason for your tardiness? Something in your private affairs that is infinitely more important than the uninterrupted education of you and your fellows?"

For the second time in the day, his mouth ran away from him. Speaking the truth when it had no right to. "My mother died."

The tittering stopped. The Prima's grim disciplinarian smile faded. "That is a great shame, my dear. The Contessa was admired by many."

A long silence lingered over the hall until finally he asked, "Might I be excused?"

It would have been quite impossible for her to refuse after making such a faux pas. "Of course."

Artemio left the lecture with an even greater sense of urgency than he had arrived with. Once he was certain he could not be heard, he broke into a jog.

If he had kept his mouth shut, the rumor mill would have had nothing at all to feed upon. If he'd kept his mouth shut, he wouldn't have to race the story of his mother's death back to Harmony. Even now he had no idea what to tell her, but given the alternative of her learning through the network of whisperers she seemed so attuned to, he had no option but to speak directly as swiftly as possible.

Starting with the suite of rooms that had been turned over to her on arrival in the House, Artemio began his hunt. It was not safe to turn his shade loose here as he had Bisnonno in the palace. There were too many others at large, and the six for which the place was named were all too willing to prey on their weaker kin.

Yet there was still much that these lingering specters had to offer when it came to information. They were beneath notice to the students when they were seeking partnership, but only a fool would overlook them entirely.

The open-air gymnasium was built back towards the rear of the gardens, as far from the general populace of the city as possible. It was not that the clatter of blades would disturb them, but rather that when their blood was heated, some of the younger students would lose their composure. Losing control of a bound shade could be dangerous.

For now, at least, there were no ghosts there that Artemio did not bring with him. Just his sister, moving through the motions of her drills, dressed in a man's clothing, as she was wont to when she could find some excuse for it.

She wore his sword belt crossed over with her own. They were paired blades, just as they were paired siblings, each the same weight and length, interchangeable tools. She spotted him approaching and let out a cry of relief that she swiftly masked with a joke. "Your head's still on, so they didn't lay you down and lop it off as soon as they saw you. Your neck looks a bit red, did they try to hang you like some common cutpurse instead?"

He glanced around. The pale sand on the ground bore only her footprints. It seemed nobody was spying upon them. "Not yet, but there is still time."

She drew his sword and tossed it to him. It fell, untouched, to the sand at his feet. "Come spar with me for a bit, maybe I'll save the hangman the effort."

"I'm not in the mood." He bent to pick up the weapon and tidy up after her out of habit. "We need to talk."

"Talk while we spar." She assumed a low guard position. The tip of her blade angled towards his feet. "How often do you leave your sword hanging on the wall these days? It will become as rusty as you."

Reluctantly, he turned until his body was side-on to her. The sword still loose in his hand. "Neither my sword nor my skills are your concern."

"I'd say most things about you are pretty concerning, actually." She feigned an attack, but he was unconvinced.

"I am really in no mood to cross blades with you, figuratively or not. Can we please just talk?" This time there was no feint, he had to sweep his blade up and across his body to deflect her thrust. "Harmony."

"Who is stopping you from talking? I'm all ears, I cannot wait to hear what was so important that you couldn't even send your sister word that all was well."

She swiped at his face, slow enough that he needn't even have parried, but out of habit he did. With a twist of her wrist and a sudden push, she locked their blades together between them. She giggled in his ear. "Rusty."

They were evenly matched, with his natural advantage in weight and reach counterbalanced by the musculature and reflexes she had built through years of training just like this. He could not force her back, but neither was he willing to strike her with his hands. She had no such compunctions. Her slap set his ears ringing and he reeled away. "Harm, there was no time."

"No time to write a note? No time to ask one of the million servants in the palace to carry it to me? All day I have been waiting for the worst. Waiting for word that you were… Have you got a heart, dear brother, or is there naught but ice beneath your breast?"

Her blade danced and darted in the afternoon's hazy light. Flitting like the dragonflies they used to watch over the ponds. She was right enough, he was rusty. He could feel sweat beading on his forehead just from turning aside this little flurry. "They want me to do some work for them."

"Oh I see, you're a big man in court now, that is why you didn't have time to send a note." She countered his clumsy riposte by stepping inside his guard and stomping down onto his instep. He sprang back with a grunt of pain.

He slapped away the next thrust with more force than was entirely necessary. "Will you stop it. There were more pressing concerns than your worrying."

"More pressing concerns?" His eyes tried to track the swishing tip of her sword, but she had always been better, always been faster. Her sword slipped right in past his guard, and the flat tapped the underside of his chin. Perfect and precise. "You prick."

"Mother is dead."

The tip of her sword wobbled, scratching a line across his throat. "What?"

Artemio let his own sword drop to his side. "She died. Quite some time ago. Father didn't bother to inform us."

The sword fell away from his neck. Harmony's hair fell forward over her face. "She's dead?"

"I'm sorry, Harm."

"Sorry? You're an idiot. She can't be dead. Who told you she was dead?

The Cerva? You know they're all liars." Her sword flicked back up again, pointed at his chest again. Wavered. "What did they say, she caught crotch rot off our whoremonger father? You know they're liars, and you swallowed every word they told you."

Artemio took a step back. "She was killed. A hired knife, sent for Father."

She stepped to him again, but her cuts were clumsy, angry. Easy to predict and deflect. "If it was sent for him, he should have been the one to receive it."

That stopped Artemio dead in his tracks. "Harmony."

"Oh don't pretend you've got a sense of propriety," she scoffed. "Nobody hates Father more than you. You practically salivate at the thought of your inheritance."

Artemio wet his lips. "I want nothing from that man."

"See! That isn't what loving sons say about their fathers."

He managed to bat her sword wide and step inside her reach, only to be rewarded with a backhand across the jaw that sent him stumbling.

"Harmony." He wiped the blood from his lip. "You need to stop."

She brought her sword down on him. He only saw the shimmer of it. Death shining blinding bright in the sun.

He could never have brought his sword around to parry. He could never have done anything to save himself if he were alone. But he was never alone.

As the blade came down, Artemio opened and the wind whipped. Artemio could never have turned the blade, but Bisnonno Fiore could.

The old king rode up through Artemio, and the whipping winds he carried with him snatched the rapier from Harmony's hands.

She whispered, "Mother."

He dropped his sword and surged forward to catch her. Artemio wrapped his arms around her as the tears began to flow. He let his own come too.

They stood all alone at the back end of the gardens, crying out their eyes for the one parent who had ever shown them the slightest amount of affection.

7

THE WATERS OF THE WOODS

Arancia, Regola Dei Cerva III

When Orsina followed him into the woods, Kagan made no complaint. The old woman wouldn't let her young apprentice wander the woods if it weren't safe. Neither one of them had too much to say in their first few trips out together—Kagan was used to being alone, Orsina was used to nothing but sniping and rebuttal each time she opened her mouth—but they found their rhythm soon enough.

"Why did you get exiled?"

Kagan bit back his anger. She was a child no matter how much she'd grown since last he saw her. She had the tact of a child. "Crimes."

"What sort of crimes did you do? Did you try to steal a dragon's treasure pile? Did you seduce the dragon-king's mistress?"

He paused mid-step. "Do you even know what *seduce* means?"

"Kissing, right?"

He shrugged. "Close enough."

She caught up to him, close enough to faux-whisper, "So you got exiled for kissing crimes?"

For a long moment, he was silent, then eventually he let out a gruff sigh. "No."

"Did your dragon get exiled too?"

He could feel a headache on the far horizon, creeping closer with every question. "No."

"So you had a dragon?"

"Yes."

She was bouncing as she walked at his elbow. Her braid springing up and down behind her. "What was it like? What are dragons like?"

"Large," he rumbled. Then, realizing it wasn't quite enough, "Reptilian."

"Did you ride your dragon?"

The memory of it ached. The furnace beneath him. The scales shimmering in the sunlight, above the clouds. "Sometimes."

"Did you have a special saddle for it?"

He blinked. "Yes."

"That must have been expensive, all that leatherwork. Back in Sheepshank, they used to say making tackle was the most expensive work they ever got done."

"I don't recall the price."

"Was it a long, long time ago?"

He tried to count back through the years of his exile and realized he had lost count somewhere. "Before you were born."

"So are you really, really old?"

For the first time, he looked put out by a question. "No."

"So you were really young for a dragon-lord?"

"No."

"Were you young when you did your kissing crimes?"

He had slowed to a crawl, head cocked to one side, listening. When he could not sense any sign of his quarry, he answered her. "I was younger, but not young."

"So you were exiled for kissing old people?"

He let out an exasperated groan. "No kissing."

"You were exiled for not kissing?" The snap of her fingers silenced the birds in the trees around them. "You broke off an arranged marriage meant to tie two feuding families together and left the dragon empire on fire in a civil war?"

"I thought the hag didn't tell you stories."

She shrugged. "Doesn't mean I can't tell myself them."

They crossed a stream, she bounding along without a care in the world, he lifting her cautiously to avoid anything that might have been lurking down in the gully. For a few blessed moments, there was silence, then she started up again. "You don't talk much, do you?"

"You do."

"Mother Vinegar says I never stop talking. She says I drive her up the wall."

He raised a scaled brow. "Indeed."

"That's why she said I should go out hunting with you today, so she could get some peace. Which I think is just silly because..."

"Shh."

"...even though I talk a little bit she talks even more. She even talks when she is on her own or she thinks I'm sleeping. I think it is because she's been stuck out here in the..."

Kagan reached back and covered her mouth. She nipped his palm with her teeth, but he did not flinch. This was not their first time playing this game. When she tried to pull back and return to her ceaseless chatter, he pointed the tip of his spear across the clearing.

It was like a waterfowl gone terribly awry. Tall as Kagan at the shoulders, but taller still when it raised up its head at the end of a serpentine neck. There was a shimmer of scales beneath the feathers, an amalgam beast of serpent and bird. Orsina couldn't tear her gaze away from the eyes, turning from the talons and stumpy wings to seek the reflection of the dying day in the golden saucers turned her way.

By all rights it should have run. Yet it stood there, stiff as a petrified log. Orsina had never felt Kagan's power, never even felt the slightest press from him. From what few snippets of the Arazi arts Mother Vinegar had been willing to whisper, she didn't even know if she'd be able to feel him working at all. All she could do was guess that the calm was emanating from Kagan. Sympathetic emotion that flooded the crocorax's head and made it stand perfectly still as he took his aim and threw.

The bird toppled and Kagan released whatever hold he had on it. For the briefest moment, Orsina could feel the shade of the terror-bird in her head. The tangle of instinct and emotion and pain, before it faded away to nothing.

Kagan didn't see his little companion flinch. He was too focused on the hunt, on the prey. He'd crossed the distance to the dying bird and hauled out his spear before Orsina even saw him moving.

His shoulders strained as he tried to lift the bird whole. "Now I remember why I bring you along, so you can carry things."

She was back at his side and grinning, pushing all thoughts of what she'd just felt aside. "Aw, is the big chicken too heavy for you?"

"Why don't you try to lift her?"

Orsina was nothing if not willing to try new things. She got both shoulders under the bird's long neck and managed to stand upright. Blood ran down into her hair. "I've got my end."

"Ah yes. The head is the heavy part, isn't it. Giant brain. Crocos are known to be so clever."

Orsina blew her blood-slicked curls away from her face. "Smart enough to hunt in packs."

Kagan drew a great knife, the blade as wide as Orsina's palm, and set to work splitting the head from the body. "Not this one. She's a straggler from off the steppes."

"What could scare a terror-bird all the way down here?" The head came away, and the rest of the body toppled to the side with a crunch of foliage.

"Nothing. Even a wyvern would leave them in peace. Too much trouble. That's how you know this one wasn't the sharpest arrow in the quiver. Probably spooked by the sound of its own farts."

With no chance of hauling the beast along whole, Kagan was butchering it in the field. He cocked his head once or twice to sniff, and Orsina, recognizing the motion, had frozen in place expectantly. Each time he shrugged and went back to his work she let out the held breath. The third time, she finally asked him. "Scavengers?"

He scoffed. "The bird's stink should hold them off long enough. Plenty will come pick over the body, but none would risk the claws. If we're quick, we're fine."

With a little spin on the spot, Orsina shucked the crocorax's severed head from off her shoulders to splatter in the bushes. The sudden thump set the birds in the canopy above to flight, but nothing went scurrying away. There were no rats, rabbits, or any of the other little things that filled Mother Vinegar's stewpot to be seen. Maybe the terror-bird really had scared them off.

A giblet hit her in the side of the head. "Are you helping?"

"Keeping watch is helping."

He growled. "We don't need to keep watch. Come help peel the skin away."

She turned to look upon his work and felt her stomach turn. "I do not want to do that."

"Nobody wants to do it." He hauled hard and the whole side of meat was exposed. "But they all want to eat. Do you want to eat?"

She'd turned pale enough that her freckles made an appearance. "Not anymore."

It wasn't often she got to hear anyone laugh these days. So when Kagan's belly laugh rumbled out, she didn't even care that it was at her expense. Her own face cracked into a grin at the sight of him rocking back on his heels.

Later, when she pieced her memory of that day back together, she would wonder if it was all the noise they were making that drew the dragon to them. If it had been the scent of all that blood. If the dragon had been the thing hunting the crocorax all the way from the steppes. If it was just bad luck that their paths had crossed. The last seemed the least likely to her—after so long in Mother Vinegar's tutelage she struggled to believe in coincidence.

The dragon burst out between the trees, knocking oaks aside like they were tinder-wood. It was everything the stories of the great beasts of the

Arazi aeries spoke of and so much more. No story spoke of the waves of heat that washed out ahead of their coming. The furnace dryness that pulsed from their bronzed scales. The sheer insurmountable bulk of a creature so large it almost defied explanation. Orsina's eyes rejected it.

It could not be alive and so massive. It could not move with such sinuous grace and such power as to topple the very woods as it passed through. Not a creature, but a force of nature. A natural disaster on four legs, wings tucked tight to its sides but flexing with each bellow pulse of breath.

She was so busy being in awe of the beast that she could not even see the danger. She did not see the claws, the teeth, the flames coiling between them.

Kagan hit her full-on as the fire leapt out at them, bearing her down to the dirt and rolling off to extinguish what little of the sizzling venom had clung to his cloak. With hands held wide, he called out in the Arazi tongue.

The dragon showed no sign of understanding any more than Orsina did. The great burning eyes narrowed at the sound of a voice and it surged towards them. Even now, in what could have been her final moments, Orsina could not shut up. "Are you planning on lording over this dragon any time soon, dragon-lord!?"

He scooped her up and ran, but it was pointless. There was no tree in the forest that could hold back a dragon. "It does not work that way."

Fire spread in their wake, but still Kagan ran. There was no question that the dragon could overtake them, only a matter of time. When life narrowed to moments, every extra moment that could be squeezed out was a victory. The forest that had become home passed Orsina in a blur. She wrestled to be free of Kagan, to run for herself, but it was no use. She bounced against his shoulder, rattling alongside the spears on his back.

She could see the great beast keeping pace with them, tearing up trees and casting them aside as it went, unflinching, relentless. "We can't outrun it."

"I know." Kagan leapt over a gully that Orsina would not have even seen. Even now he moved through the forest like it was his home.

The dragon didn't need to leap. Its great clawed feet were longer than the gap. It crossed without even noticing.

Orsina was sixteen years old. She had spent most of the time she could remember alone in the most frightening place in the world. She did not need courage. This was where she lived. "Then stop running. Stand and fight."

"I cannot."

She thumped her fists on his back. "You're going to die anyway. Fight it!"

"You are not Arazi. You don't understand." His voice dropped to a rumble, almost impossible to hear. "I will not harm an aslinda-dragon. I will not. There is no greater evil."

Orsina rolled her eyes. "Did nobody teach her that eating people is bad?"

"She is feral. Unbound."

She thumped against his back. "So bind her!"

"I cannot! I am already… I cannot."

The flames burst out from amidst the trees once more. Washing across Orsina's back.

What had run smoothly off the dragon scales on Kagan's flesh clung to her hair, to her clothes. It burned like nothing she'd ever felt. Hotter than the burning sun, hotter than the brightest fire. Kagan dropped her to the dirt once more. Tried to smother the fire in the loose soil and mulch, but each time one part was damped out, another blazed to life.

Orsina could not help but scream. A mindless, animal response to the pain. It wouldn't matter in a moment. The dragon was upon them. Rearing up on its hind legs, balancing with its tail, it stood taller than the great old trees around it. Wings stretched out wide in triumph.

"Not like this." Orsina hissed.

Ginny Greenteeth swept into her. Not just a welcomed guest, but demanded. Commanded.

Orsina's eyes brimmed over with stagnant water. Her body, scorched and stung by the dragon's fire, was swept clean of every ember as the flood came pouring forth. Pondweed coiled out of her hair. Silt and mud oozed from between her lips to dribble to the leaves below.

Kagan did not know the voice that came bubbling out.

"The water is lovely, deep, and cool."

As the dragon gnashed down at her, Orsina did not flinch.

"Deep enough to drown a fool."

Kagan cried out as she was swallowed down whole, but he was not surprised. No matter what witchery the girl had at her beck and call, she was only human. Nothing human could withstand a dragon. Nothing in the world could withstand a dragon.

It had been a long time coming, but Kagan had always known he would meet his end by dragon's fire. He drew himself back up to his feet to face it with some dignity. All these long years in exile had been lived in the memory of this moment, standing proudly before a dragon awaiting the death he was due. It was almost a relief to have come full circle. As if fate had circled close once before, but now the orbit was ended. He held up his arms and accepted his death.

It did not come.

The dragon's jaws snapped open, the magmatic glow of its innards washing out over the dim forest floor, but the fire did not come. A great ugly gout of steam rolled out, reeking of rot and ruin, but flaming death did not. Whether Kagan or the dragon was more surprised by this was impossible to say.

Something deeper than sense drew him forward. Some instinct that mattered more to the Arazi than self-preservation. The dragon's serpentine neck bunched and coiled as it tried to regurgitate whatever morsel was blocking the flow of flame, and without thinking, Kagan reached out to stroke along its scales and offer comfort. He had not thought he would ever touch dragon scale again. When the sharp edges bit into his palm, he bore it with all due reverence. It felt like home.

The dragon began to back away, as though the knot in its throat was a fixed location that it could simply move around. Mud burst forth from its mouth with every heaving breath. There was no question of the fire within it being quenched, such a thing could not be done, but for all its power and majesty, it was still alive. It still needed to breathe.

Over and over it retched and retched, bringing up mud, tangled pond-weed, and water, endless slopping waves of stagnant water. The clawed feet, so steady beneath it just a moment ago, splayed in the churned mud as it struggled for air. Kagan did not even know he was screaming.

"Stop it! Stop! Orsina! You must stop. You are killing her!"

If the girl could hear him from inside the great burning heart of the beast, he could not say. Even if she could, what did words matter to Ginny Greenteeth who rode her. The dragon stumbled, the low rumble of her furnace heart faltering and spluttering as she drowned.

Kagan's voice had given out by the time the dragon died, just as the dim light was failing. It felt like hours had passed since the ordeal began, but time had lost its meaning. When the time finally came, he felt it more than he saw it. Not only was the presence of the beast in his mind gone in an instant, so too went the heat.

When it died, it ceased to be a dragon. To all outward appearances, nothing had changed, but to Kagan and his kind, the change was obvious. He moved from the paralysis of the horror he had witnessed back to the practicality of a huntsman as he rose, drawing his blade. Feeling along the soft underbelly of the dragon until he could feel the lump. Slicing between the scales cleanly, without tears blurring his vision. He had none left to cry. Orsina slipped out in a shower of blood and pond filth and lay there in the mud for a long moment.

There were no rites for dead dragons among the Arazi, but when the unbound died, they were carried as high up into the mountains as they could be borne and laid out for the sky to take them. She'd done the most wicked thing that could be done, but she'd done it to save him.

Orsina was not one of his people, but she had died so that he might live. He felt the same stab of duty and obligation as if she were kin. He looked down at her, curled about herself like the very first time he'd met her, sleeping on the floor of the witch's cottage. Just a child.

Her constant tangled mess of hair splayed about her now, twice the

length it had been before he'd seen fire scorch it away. He reached out to
brush it from her cheek and then snatched his hand back. She was still
warm. For all the mud and stagnant water clinging to her ragged clothes,
she still felt alive. The last heat of the dragon, perhaps. He pricked her
cheek with his claw and she flinched away.

Alive. Impossibly alive. She stirred beneath his hands like she was
having a bad dream. He could not believe it.

"Orsina."

She did not answer. The constant prattle of her voice did not come.
The protestations at being woken. The bitching and the moaning. None
of it. He shook her. "Orsina!"

There were a dozen different ways that she could be dying, and after
fishing the clot of mud and slime from her mouth to be sure she was
breathing, he could think of a cure to not one of them. Mother Vinegar
would have all the answers.

Meat, dragon, and sorrow forgotten, he scooped her up.

Reeking of dragon, blood, and venom, there was no beast in the Selvaggia fool enough to test him that day, and he cast aside all stealth in his
hurry. The low-hanging brambles skittered over his thick skin, scratching
at the places where he was the most human and passing over the rest
without a mark.

He had never moved so fleetly through the Selvaggia in all his years
there, and he would never run that way again. Heart in his mouth, terror
at his heels. He had known fear. He was born to fear and knew it like an
old lover, but he had never felt this way before. As though he had something left to lose.

The door to the old rickety cottage was knocked clean off its hinges
as he barreled in, and the old woman had a dagger out of her apron and
pointed before either one of them saw the other. Orsina hung limp between
them for just an instant before Mother Vinegar was swept up in the same
frantic motion that had carried him this far.

She was borne down onto the furs by the fire, Mother Vinegar hissing and cursing all the way. Her withered fingers darting about so fast and sure that Kagan couldn't follow their motions. "You damned fool. You stupid, blithering, wretched imbecile."

Kagan drew back, but he had no words to defend himself. "There was no way I could have known. There was no way anyone could have known a dragon would come to these woods. Do you think I'd be here if I'd known that…"

Mother Vinegar didn't even hear him as she drew the scorched cloth away from the strips of old scarred skin where the dragon's fire had eaten into the girl. "…moronic things to do, letting the girl go roaming all by herself when you knew she wasn't ready yet. You knew she wasn't. She shouldn't have been out the doors without a watcher. She shouldn't have had a minute to be tempted. You daft old hag, you've gone soft."

"She did it for… It was for me. She saved us both." He shuddered at the memory of the girl's voice, half Orsina, half Ginny Greenteeth. "She did a terrible thing, but it was for the right reasons."

"A year of her gone for naught." Mother Vinegar let out a groan as she worked her way down the girl, checking her over. "Ugh. Hair for miles. Burns healed rough with no poultice. Teats fit to bursting on her."

Kagan averted his eyes as the prodding went lower. "She's a dragon-slayer now. My people will want her blood. Espher too, though they'll draw it slower."

Finally it was enough to make the old witch take notice. "What's that, now?"

"The aslinda-dragon." He said it slow, like she was a startled mare. "She killed it."

The old woman scoffed. "What shite you talk, boy. There's no dragons in these woods."

The day caught up to him in a rush. The pointlessness of the argument. The ache in his legs. He sank to the floor with a huff. "Not anymore. A feral was breathing fire a few miles north before it crossed her."

Old as Mother Vinegar was, her eyes were still shrewd. Narrowed as she examined his face. "A dragon? Not a wyvern, not a…" She trailed off with a sigh. "You'd know best I suppose."

He pressed the heels of his hands into his eyes, like he could push the images away somewhere to the back of his head where he didn't have to watch them replayed. "It… it swallowed her down and she…"

Mother Vinegar cut him off with a sharp laugh. "She stuck in its craw, same as she does in mine. I can just see it now."

When Kagan looked up in surprise, the old woman held up the ruins of Orsina's garb. "She's a year on, but her cloak still has the burns, tooth-cuts, and slobber." She sighed and looked down at Orsina, lying still as the dead. "You stupid, stupid girl."

With laborious effort, Kagan made his way back to his feet and hauled the door back into place. "What was she meant to do, die?"

When he looked back, the old woman was wrapping her apprentice up in furs with her eyes pressed shut. "Better she had."

Each step seemed to drain his strength more and more. It was a wonder he could even stand, let alone plod back to fall beside the fire with a groan. It was not hot enough. It was never hot enough here in the forest. Even an inch from the flame he could feel the cold and the damp encroaching. He missed feeling the fire inside him. Feeling the life of the dragon he'd pinned his heart to flowing back and forth between them without halt. Too many years, he'd been cold. Today was the closest he'd come to warmth and it had almost killed him. "What can we do for her?"

"Do for her? Nothing. She's done for herself." The old woman flopped down right alongside Kagan, rustling in her apron for a briarwood pipe and the twist of foul black-spiced pig-tail tobacco she favored. "There'll be no coming back from this. It's beyond my skill."

He closed his eyes. It was what Kagan had expected to hear, but he still regretted hearing it. "So she's going to die, after all that?"

"Die? I wish the world was so kindly. No boy. She'll live. Our little bear will live. The burns healed fast with a shade sucking her dry, bruises and bites too. The rest is exhaustion. She gave too much. A year or more.

Gone like that." She snatched a burning stick from the fire and lit her pipe. "She'll live the rest of her life knowing how that felt. Knowing all that power was there at her beck and call, and all it would cost her was a little bit of herself."

She blew out a long plume of green smoke.

"She'll live, but she'll regret every minute of it."

Kagan was about to say he didn't see how bad that could be, then he remembered what it felt like to fly. To know he'd never fly again. "It was my fault. If I'd wondered for just a bit longer what could have chased a crocorax down. If I'd gone up and looked for smoke. If I'd…"

"No point in all that now." She held out the pipe to him, and he drew in an aching lungful of the foul smoke, regretting the decision the minute he made it. "You said yourself, nobody could have known. Nobody could've expected. What's done is done. But you're not done doing."

The old woman's voice grew fainter, softer. Whether it was exhaustion overtaking Kagan or the old woman taking care not to wake her ward, he couldn't say. "She'll need a teacher. Now that she's tasted it. There'll be no keeping her out of their business."

He glanced sideways at her. The light dimming. "She's got you."

"Me?" She let out a bitter bark of laughter. "I've had sense enough through all my years to keep the shades out. Nothing I can teach her."

Kagan feigned amazement. "By the burned god, did Mother Vinegar just admit she couldn't do something?"

She whacked him with the back of her hand as he chuckled. "You're not so big I can't put you over my knee for a paddling, boy."

The laughter trailed off. "So where's she going then?"

The old woman sighed so long Kagan feared she might deflate entirely. "Covotana. Nest of weasels that it is, they're still the only folk with a school for her kind."

"Long walk." Orsina looked so small now she was sleeping. Out in the woods, she'd strode like a giant, but here he'd always see the little girl.

"Aye, well, good thing she's young and you're used to it."

It took him a moment to register her words. "Me? You want me to take her? You think I hide in the woods for the fun? They'll gut me, skin me, and sell me as a rug."

She shrugged. "Pull your hood up."

"Pull my... They kill my people on sight." The growl was back in his voice now he'd found some anger to hold on to. "I'll be strung up from a tree."

"Good reason to get away from the woods then."

He was almost roaring. "You cannot seriously be asking me to..."

"Asking? Boy, when have I ever asked a thing. I'm telling." She snapped around to glower at him. All the weight of her years bearing down on him in that one stare. "That girl is going to wake up, and you're going to walk her out of these woods, and we're never going to see hide nor hair of her again, all because you couldn't see a dragon six feet from your face."

The guilt was an unnecessary twist of the knife, but Mother Vinegar had never been one to use a half dose when there was enough for the full one.

"You just said..."

She snapped. "I said you'll take the girl to her teachers and carry a letter along for introductions. You'll do it, and you'll do it without a word of complaint, or I'll be the one with a new rug."

8

SALTING THE CUT

Gemmazione, Regola Dei Cerva 112

T he journey south had always been joyless. A return to the isolation of Father's little rural lordship and all of the rules and strictures that came along with it. In Covotana, they had to conduct themselves impeccably so they did not bring disrepute on their family, but the Cut was another thing entirely. All eyes were upon Artemio and Harmony, day and night. There was no moment when they could breathe easy. No time when Father would not be informed of a single hair out of place.

From the perspective of a grown man, it was obvious to Artemio that his father's omniscience within his domain was greatly exaggerated. Not every peasant was on the man's payroll, except in the most indirect of ways, and not every servant would run off to tell on them the moment they made an uncouth comment or joke in the privacy of their own rooms. Yet the illusion was rooted in reality. Father only needed to catch them acting up once in a blue moon to convince them he could see them all the time.

Artemio still had a switch scar across the back of his left thigh. Small enough that it would never be questioned. Positioned such that nobody in public would ever know of it. Yet when Artemio turned the wrong way at the wrong time, he could feel it pull. So too was Father's attention felt. Absent, except when it was least expected or welcome.

On the subject of unwelcome and unexpected things, here Artemio came, heir to all that he surveyed, master of nothing. Least loved, firstborn son of Count Volpe. At least people had some fondness for Harmony. Her kindness was a well-known temper to her father's and brother's harshness. Her mother had been the one to carry baskets down to the farmers struck destitute by bad harvests come midwinter. Harmony had been the one to toss out copper coins as their carriage rolled through the town. A smile from her got them beds for the night, while a smile from Artemio brought nothing but fearful looks. For the longest time, when he was a young boy, he'd been convinced he was hideous by the reaction of the girls about the villages. That was before he heard the lurid tales of young lordlings running rampant through their own domains. His father hoarded respect like a miser and left only fear for his son.

Their passage took a week and a half, with rare stops to change out horses as they tired. It passed like a dream. The rocking of the carriage on the barely paved roads of the south lulled both the Volpe siblings in and out of consciousness. The land of their childish dreams, the only world they knew, golden farming country that kept bellies filled from there to the steppes. The gold they remembered. The mud and shit seemed to have passed from their recollections somewhere along the line.

It wasn't that either one of them grew homesick. Home was where their parents lived, and nothing short of literal torture made that sound like a more palatable option than anywhere else in the world. It was simply the blindness of familiarity. Before their year in the city, these delightful aromas were the norm, unnoticed. Now that Artemio knew better, he wished he didn't. Knowledge wasn't power, it was suffering. He could have happily gone his whole life not knowing that his little slice of Espher stank of dung.

Most nights they did not stay at an inn or even in the common room that town aldermen set aside for visitors or travelers. They would have had to push to be accommodated, and neither one of the Volpe children had the energy for it. Not when they already knew the trial by fire they would soon have to endure.

When Father was calm, he was a living nightmare to deal with. How he would behave now, with the only person in the world who had seemed to keep him sane and stable gone, neither one of them dared to even guess.

The Cut rang long and dry across the southern border of Espher, and above it on the highest peak to be found in these lowlands, looming like some great dark dicing cube dropped by gaming gods above, was the Osservatore. Home to them both for many years. Though it had never felt so much like home as Artemio's little suite in the House of Seven Shadows had come to.

If their travel had been solely for the stated purpose of mourning, then Artemio doubted either he or his sister could have forced themselves up the steps into the un-liveried carriage. Even the odious drag of duty wouldn't have stirred him were it not for the very specific reward that he meant to reap ahead of time. There was a prize back here in the south he meant to claim before anyone else could take it, one he and Harmony had long plotted to steal out from under their father's nose. Duty forced them to come south now, to weep for their dead, but it was the prize that drove Artemio onwards with a fire in his belly.

Not all memories of his childhood were so bitter as the days he spent under his father's watchful eye. Some were only terrifying, instead of soul-sapping. They rode on past the Volpe family's seat of power, the village, all signs of hearth and home, then headed on along the Cut.

For as long as Espher had been, this southern border had lain here, and while in times of peace and prosperity there was little here but crops and swine, when the drums of war were beating to the south there had been walls and towers. Ruins now, long left to go to dust and desolation, but a common place for a boy who wanted to be out from underfoot to go roaming when he knew he'd be getting a switching regardless of how early he came creeping back.

It was to these dusty relics of a martial past they traveled now. Most were little more than moss-clad heaps of buried stone. Little bumps on the horizon that scarcely warranted note. Their final location was more, and less.

If the young Artemio Volpe had not been so attendant to his history lessons, then he would not have known there was a stricture to the construction of the border watchtowers. If he had not been so neglectful of his other lessons, then he would never have had the opportunity to count out his paces and calculate where the missing tower on the crest should have stood.

Back then, when he'd been barely up to his father's chest, the prospect of exploring some forgotten tower, lost to the ages, had seemed romantic, like he was one of the historians he was forever reading about, uncovering secrets of the past. In reality, it had been thick with spiders and the walls seemed to sweat mud as he dug his way down into a half-collapsed stairwell.

He retraced his steps up the hillside now, the placement still fixed in his memory. The main difference this time was not his longer gait, or the knowledge of what had made his last visit such a font of childhood nightmares, it was Harmony at his side. She caught his elbow when his ankle turned on a buried bit of masonry, she shared a terse smile with him when he felt his nerves beginning to prickle. It had been so long since his last visit to this broken place that he almost felt like it had been a fever dream he was recalling through a haze.

Yet there the hole in the dirt was, down under the roots of an old, bent elm, and here he found his feet carrying him down onto the rot-marked wood that had once been oiled and maintained by knights of the realm, or their squires.

Harmony caught his collar when the step beneath him began to creak alarmingly. "If you fall down and die, I'm going to laugh at your funeral, just so you know."

"Best make sure that I don't fall then." Normally he would have had some witty quip to bat back to her, to keep their minds off the matter at hand, but with Mother's funeral already on his mind, it was difficult to muster any humor about the whole subject.

The last time he had come, there had been excitement bouncing Artemio down each of these steps and he had only a child's weight for them to bear. Now every step was painstakingly applied, a test of strength and of his will to go on. Harmony would never let him live it down if he retreated here on the doorstep of destiny. He would hear about his fear of the dark for each day of the rest of his life.

The air turned from the warmth of the sun-stroked fields to damp mud as they descended, and for a time, Artemio truly doubted himself. He wondered if his childhood adventure had been imagination taking flight. The stairs shone beneath him with a silica wash. Limestone somewhere beyond the dirt was leaking out shimmering stone to encase everything in its crust. Then the air began to dry, and his hair began to crispen. In keeping with the theme of childhood games, Harmony whispered, "Getting warmer."

There were ruined towers all along the crest, but this missing one was at the heart, important enough to be broken down, whether by invaders or those who had abandoned it. Once, there may have been barracks arrayed around it, the tower may have stood broader and prouder, boasting heraldry and artillery, it may have hosted the Shadebound who came to serve here in comfort. There was no way to know now the tower was down and only these foundations remained, sunk deep into the clay-rich earth of the Cut and showing only when the hot days of summer warmed the stone enough to blight the growth of grass above. Here and there on the wood, stone, and leaking mud, orange rust shone out. Iron turned to crumbling nothing. Heat still rising with each step.

Harmony halted at the base of the stairs to try to get a tinder spark to jump into an oil lantern, but Artemio moved on, seeing with things other than his eyes. He could feel the hammer on the anvil. Hear the heaving of the bellows. The heat faded now. Barely an afterthought to the churn of muscle, metal, and motion. His nose filled up with soot and his hands tremored with the impacts.

Down and down into the dark he strode, and the shade beneath the tower lay waiting. Steel thrumming all about it.

There were many things that were taught in the House of Seven Shadows about binding a Shade. About forging a contract that has no loopholes. About a reasonable rate of exchange, life for power, based on

the rarity. For his part, Artemio already had one very advantageous partnership worked out down to the fine details, but it had not been like this.
There had been no approach, no danger, when he met his grandfather's
shade. It had all been arranged for him.

The thing they never taught him in the House of Seven Shadows
was courage. In lecture halls and dusty books, confronting a Shade in its
lair was as simple as walking in, there was no dread, no sizzle as eyelashes
were licked with heat. Apprehension crawled up Artemio's throat as he
went deeper into the ruin, to where the old forge had stood and the old
blacksmith now lingered.

Last time he'd turned back before now. Last time, he'd heard the anvil
thunder. He'd learned much since then, enough that he had to force his
mind open to let the forge spirit in.

His voice came out a croak in the heat. "I'm here to make you an offer."

Some shades held on to a fragment of the mind of the person they
had been. They could not think, but they could communicate in a manner
that made things easier on the Shadebound. Others, like this flagging and
ancient spirit, had lost that mask of humanity.

It was a being of hunger and want. All it had was the heat of its flames,
and all it longed for was fuel to burn. All in all, a very straightforward
transaction. Probably simpler than the arrangements he had made with
Fiore. The only trouble was fixing values. When he fed it a taper of minutes,
it tried to gulp down an hour. When he withdrew to protect his reserves,
it flung out heat and flapped in a tantrum.

There were places where Harmony could not follow him, and as soon
as she realized a shade did lurk in this overgrown mess of a basement and
not just in her brother's imagination, she took to her heels.

Flames flared out from the shadows. Soot lines scorched out where
she would have been. On and on it seemed to go, Artemio's soft voice
mumbling out questions without answer and the roar of the furnace. Each
time the flames flared, she almost leapt in to save him. Every time, she
held herself back from a battle she had no way of influencing, let alone

winning. This was what she feared, more than anything else. Not the dark or the fire or the danger, but standing back helpless, unable to touch a thing while Artemio faced it all himself.

She had known she would feel this way, he had known she would feel this way, but neither one of them would have dared to suggest that she stay behind. No matter what happened, they were in this together. Even when it made her grind her teeth together to keep from crying out.

Slowly, painstakingly, the flares began to slow. Artemio's mumbled words to himself crept to a halt too. The air around them went from scorching, to warm, and finally down to the cool and dank that it should have been from the start.

When Artemio came back to her, he looked ragged and exhausted. There were lines around his eyes that had not been there before, and fresh strands of grey hidden amidst the red of his hair. Yet he was not burned, and he had a smile on his face as he staggered up to her. "You got it?"

His breath smelled of coal dust and iron as he did his perfect impersonation of their father. "The task was accomplished."

She had to half carry and half drag him back up the rotten stairs. Every one of them creaking beneath their feet as the cold that had long been held off them began to creep in. There would be no more children's stories about fairy fire drifting around this old ruin now. No shade haunting it. Not now that it had been taken and tamed and bound. When their skin touched, Artemio felt feverish, but Harmony knew it would not last for long. Just as the chill had not clung to him beyond that first shaking night after Father forced him down into the basement to receive his first Shade.

The carriage driver stared down at them with unabashed interest as they returned, but he was not fool enough to speak. And as glaring as his interest in them was, it was still a footman's interest, not an educated gaze. He did not spot the three shadows that Artemio now cast. Before the sun had even touched on the horizon, they were on their way once more. Trundling back along the road to the only keep in miles.

The Volpe flag hung at half-mast atop the battlements of the Osservatore. The familiar icon of a golden fox above a triple-peaked mountain on a deep red. The less polite sectors of polite society would have said it was a fox driven out into the high hills after its den had been taken, but having seen the twin kings' crown up close, Artemio now recognized it all too clearly in the heraldry. The sigil of his family was a fox above the crown.

Everywhere else Artemio's eyes turned, there was black cloth strung. When Cleto Volpe mourned, the whole land mourned with him or showed merriment at their own peril. Even the guardsmen who halted their carriage wore a black band around their arms to show their own sorrow. Lowborn men his father had hauled up from men at arms to minor knighthoods. The closest the king in exile could muster to a real court.

Artemio drew in a deep exhausted breath, then let all his anger at Father wash away. It would not serve him well in this place. A frown at the wrong time, a word out of place, anything might condemn him and put his mission in jeopardy. He could not risk it. Civility was a mask, but it was armor too. So long as he maintained appearances, his enemies could not work against him openly either. He wondered for a brief moment if this was actually a lesson his Father had been trying to impart to his children through his actions or just a side effect of the razor edge the man lived and thrived on.

It could be read either way, but through all of his life, Artemio had chosen to think the worst of Father. Perhaps now, with the man broken and beaten, he might find some kindness to show to his children. Perhaps the pigs in the pen at the bottom of the hill would take flight.

Through the shrouded halls they followed after the castellan, his red robes dyed quite permanently black. Perhaps the color of death was more apt for a house in perpetual decline. Perhaps the castellan simply did not believe the mourning period would end before he joined the Contessa in the grave.

Father was stationed behind his desk, as he ever was. Like a spider at the heart of some great web. He did not look up from the letter he was writing. "I did not summon you."

How could anyone fail to love a man so abundantly loving to his children.

Artemio was the eldest, therefore the unenviable task of conversation fell to him. "Nor did you inform us of Mother's death. In your silence, we were forced to assume that you had been rendered incapable of scribbling a missive."

"Do not think to lecture me on niceties, boy." Father's eyes flicked up just long enough to impart a withering stare. "You have no standing."

Even after all the hard years of training, Artemio could not bite back his anger. It was a fatal flaw, of that he had no doubt. Already it had brought him within a breath of the headsman too many times. "Ah yes, my intolerable rudeness certainly entitles you not to even tell us our mother is dead."

Harmony stepped in front of her brother and spoke up, as if she might drown Artemio out. "Father, we did not know in what state we would find you. Artemio and I both feared you might be too overwrought to write, and that is why we came. To be here for you in this trying time."

"I do not need you." Cleto returned to his writings. "I do not want you."

Even knowing how stupid it was, Artemio could not let such words pass. "Usually that is the subtext of our conversations, rather than outright stated. Are you certain that you are all right, Father? Your subtlety seems to be slipping."

"Still your viper's tongue before I have it set to an anvil and stilled permanently."

The old man's eyes locked with Artemio's, and the only thing he could see was hate. The only emotion the son was certain the father was truly capable of. The only time he knew Father wasn't performing to elicit the desired response. Good.

He clapped his hands. "And we're on to the usual threats of gruesome violence. You see, Harmony, he is fine. Just the same as always. We were fools to worry for him."

"Will you be silent." Spittle misted out from Cleto's pursed lips. Speckling his precious papers. Perhaps he truly was overwrought. That was the most Artemio had ever gotten out of him. It actually succeeded in shutting him up for a moment.

Harmony hopped into the conversation again before things could go any further downhill. "Whether you have called for us or not, we are here for you, Father. Whatever we can do to ease your suffering, all you need do is ask."

"Then heed my wishes and depart." The cold mask slid right back into place. His attentions turned back to his blotter. "I have no use for children underfoot."

Even if he used the word to be dismissive, it was nice to be acknowledged as Cleto's children at all. Sometimes it had been difficult to draw even that much connection to the man. Admittedly, it just went to prove to Artemio that he would never be seen as anything more than a mewling babe by the man, but it was something.

Something that Harmony was swift to latch onto. "Of course, Father. We do not mean to impose on your time. Now that we can see you are well, we shall depart with all haste."

"My health does not falter. Nor does my focus." The scratching of quill to parchment resumed. "Is that well enough to sate your prying?"

Harmony had always been better than the rest of them at letting Father's words wash over her. Eventually they would erode her stony resolve, but in the short term at least, she could endure. Ignoring the question, she posed on of her own. "Might we spend the night at least? It is a long road from here to Covotana."

"You do not need to tell me, child. I know all too well how far we have fallen from Covotana."

"So supper then?" She gave him a smile. Her mother's smile. Soft as a feather's brush. Barely there if you did not look for it. Cleto looked for it.

He sighed. "If we must proceed with this farce, have the boy keep his lips sealed. I shall suffer no more insult in my own hall."

Artemio opened his mouth, only to slam it shut again as Harmony's heel pressed down into his foot. She answered smoothly for the both of them. "As you wish, Father."

Those magic words did the same trick they always had. Cleto returned to his all-important work, and his children were shuffled out with all haste. This was when Mother would be there. Not to comfort them, never to comfort them, but to reinforce whatever lesson Father had been trying to instill. To use softness and cajoling to convince them their punishment was just and righteous.

Artemio paused there in the hall, waiting to hear the click of heels and the subtle insinuations about keeping his snideness to himself. It did not come.

The weight of the moment, the darkness of the hall: It all seemed to come crashing down on him. He scrabbled for Harmony's hand and discovered to his surprise that it was already held out for him. They did not weep together, for it would displease Father for his children to show weakness, but they clung tightly to each other's hands as they set out towards their old rooms, trailing behind the castellan once more.

Years. It had been years since they'd walked these cold halls, clinging to each other for comfort, yet here they were again. Nothing changing but the drapes. Old instincts came to the fore. To put on a brave face for his sister and make believe that everything was going to be all right. "Nice to see that becoming a widower hasn't made him any less of a bastard."

Harmony managed to twist her strangled laugh into a mortified gasp, even as the castellan's ear pricked up. "Artemio!"

"No, no, I really mean it. Can you imagine what it would have been like if he'd tried to comfort us? If he'd smiled? I would have shit myself on the spot. It would be a sign of the end times."

This time Harmony had to bite her knuckles to keep the laughter contained. She looked at him with pleading eyes. One more push and she'd burst out laughing, and the shade of Mother would burst out the wall, shrieking about decorum.

Artemio wet his lips and let the smirk fade away. "I mean it, I'm glad he hasn't changed at all. At least that means we don't have to worry about him."

She very carefully avoided the true meaning of that statement. That he didn't care if the old bastard lived or died, choosing instead to pretend that Artemio was praising the old man's persistence of character. "He has always been able to take care of himself."

"Were it but a few weeks ago, I'd have said he was able to take care of Mother too, but…"

The castellan turned on him with a gasp of dismay. "My lord!"

For an instant Artemio's mind went blank, then the name sprang up in him. "No need to stand on formality, Cesare, we've known each other too long for that."

"Your poor father has suffered…"

Artemio cut him off with a sneer. "A fraction of what he gladly doles out on others. Yet you expect me to feel even a glimmer of sympathy for the man?"

The castellan rallied admirably with a fresh onslaught. "The Contessa would not stand for you to speak of him so."

"Perhaps if he'd performed his duties as the ward and protector of this household with more vigor, she'd be here to tell me so herself," Artemio snarled.

"How dare you speak of the Count in such…"

The old servant's collar was bunched in his fists, and Artemio could not recall having snatched it. "I dare, my puttering old friend, because unlike you and the other poor souls trapped under his yoke, my fate is not beholden to this crumbling edifice or the monster that dwells at its heart."

Harmony's hand was on his arm. Not nearly as gentle as it appeared. He could feel the strength behind the grip. It brought him back to himself. "I… I'm sorry. The news came as a shock to me. I have not had much success in setting my mind at ease since I heard. You are right enough, Cesare. Harmony. Both of you. I should not speak ill of the man, certainly not under his own roof. He has just lost his wife in the most barbarous way I could imagine."

"As it should be. My lord." Cesare seemed to deflate back down to his usual proportions, all his righteous anger fleeing and propriety stamping it back behind the wall.

Artemio pushed the advantage. "Tell me, Cesare, I know he puts on a mask of strength so that we do not worry…" Harmony made a sound like she had choked. "How has he been sleeping since it happened?"

"Ah, well. Well enough, I suppose." Tight-lipped as always. It seemed every grain of information would have to be extracted manually.

"Which chambers has he taken?"

"The green room on the second story, so at least he does not want for comfort."

There was a lapse for a moment as Artemio tried to consider the best way to phrase his next question. "I wonder if you might do me a favor, Cesare?"

"So long as it please my lord," Now, there was an important caveat. "I am at your disposal."

"We have had no chance to mourn. We only just learned of the tragedy a few days past." Harmony glanced sideways at him as he laid it on thick. "Might we see where it happened?"

"What? My lord, that is… obscene." Cesare had actually flushed beneath the layer of powder he still applied to his face, chasing the fashions of court from decades before. "There is a mausoleum being prepared in the west gardens that shall hold your mother's remains, but I cannot think why you would want to…"

"Because I want to know what happened to her. Not the rumors and lies being spread about court, nor the abridged version that Father would share with us to protect us. I need to know what became of my mother, or I shall know no peace." Artemio forced his voice to crack and tried to conjure a tear. "You can understand that, can't you, Cesare?"

"The investigation…"

Even biting the inside of his cheek had failed to elicit a tear, so Artemio switched to barely contained rage. He didn't even need to fake that. "May never be resolved if this is like any of the other… killings of this sort. I need something now to set my fevered imagination to rest."

"My lord, what remains in their chambers, it would do quite the opposite. I saw… I saw too much when first I heard your father cry out for aid."

"Cesare, you are a loyal man, as good a servant as anyone could ask for, and it is my hope that when the burden of leadership passes to me some distant day in the future, you will still be here to help me shoulder it. Yet for all of that, you are not of our blood. You do not know the burden of our blood, nor the things it allows us to do. If you do not let me into the chamber, then you are taking from me my final chance to speak with my mother." It was a lie, of course. Any echo of the Contessa was long gone by this point. But the common man knew nothing of shadecraft. "Do you understand what you are taking from me with your denial? Would you do that to me?"

The Castellan's objections crumbled in the face of the combination of emotional appeal and threat. "Your sister…"

Artemio lay a comforting hand on the old servant's shoulder. "I would not inflict such sights upon either one of you, my old friend." He gave the shoulder a squeeze, struggling to even find the cadaverous form of the man beneath the layers of padded cloth required to survive in the perpetual chill of the Osservatore. "All I require is for you to unlock the door and depart."

It was clear that Harmony was unhappy to be sent on her merry way, but he thwarted her attempts to nudge him with an arm wrapped around her waist. He leaned in close to hiss in her ear. "You do not want to see what is in that room. You do not want it to be the memory of her that you are left with. Please don't fight me on this."

He had never seen her so pale and wan. Even when she'd been forced to watch his beatings as a child, there had been a flush of anger in her cheeks. Before traveling from Covotana, Artemio had taken her aside and told her as little of the task he had been assigned as was possible, while still conveying to her the dangers involved. She had pried for more, because she was Harmony, and he had tried to keep more from her, because he was her brother and did not want her dreams to be troubled. In the end, her prying had won out more than his caution, of course. Before they had departed Covotana, she had known every detail of the murders, something she was doubtless regretting now, knowing the carnage that had to be hidden behind their parents' bedchamber doors.

As the castellan led her off, taking care not to look back, Artemio steeled himself. In all of his years, this suite of rooms had been forbidden to him, and the prospect of observing the site of his own mother's murder pushed the dread that he felt about stepping through the portal from the dull prickle of a childhood rule about to be defied and into genuine anxiety. Not for the first time, he cursed his own mind. Were he a foolish man, he'd have had nothing to fear from the room ahead. He would have seen the stains or marks, and they would have meant nothing. Even as a man of moderate intellect, he might have been able to simply observe the evidence.

When he stepped into the room, he saw the murder.

The blankets were still in disarray, dragged out into the room and across the flagstones. Father's bare feet could be clearly seen as rusty stains. Artemio clung to the door for a moment, pretending to himself that he was examining it. Noting the key on the inside. The only key to the room. Mother and Father had always gone to bed at the same time, so there was no need for another. It had been one of the few tenets of their marriage, that no matter what troubled one or the other, neither one would lay down to rest until the other was beside them. Or at least, it had been their rule for as long as Artemio still lived here.

As he crept closer, taking careful steps to avoid any hint of blood, more and more of the death revealed itself.

The butchery of it.

Mother's body was blessedly gone, and there were clear signs of where parts of it had been dragged. Where the remains had been small enough to be lifted cleanly away without disturbing that which was around it, there was still the pool and droplet of blood to mark positions.

There was no more time for reluctance or self-pity. If Artemio meant to catch the killer, then he needed to do the very thing he'd been frantically avoiding since first taking on this quest.

He looked at the gore, and he let his mind work backwards through time. Here was the dug-in press of an exposed rib. Here a clump of hair had left a ghost of itself in rust up the post of the bed. With every part in place, he worked backwards, following them through their trajectory, through the frenzied violence, the spatter and the horror, back until the last moment his mother lay alive and breathing, still asleep when the Last King's scythe fell.

The death had been explosive.

There were alchemical concoctions that might take a person apart like this, but they would have left residues and stains of their own. Damage to the mattress, the drapes, the walls. There was no way Father could have emerged unscathed from the indent in his side of the bed if such a thing had been done.

Bisnonno Fiore was ever the easiest for Artemio to call, so he traded away another wrinkle to see through the old echo's eyes. There had been no shade called here. No expression of the power that could be channeled through a practitioner of the art. The old king faded without a second thought.

Two options down, Artemio moved in closer, crouching level with the bed, searching for any signs in the down-stuffed cloth of the mattress for the nature of the force that took his mother apart.

"What the hell are you doing?"

Artemio fought the lightning bolt that shot up his spine telling him to straighten and feel shame. He was too old and too tired of this routine for Father's words to have him running for the nursemaid.

He kept his gaze steady on the topside of the bed and did the math in his head. That gutless bastard castellan must have dropped Harmony at her chamber and then sprinted the length of the Osservatore back to Father's office to tell on him.

Swallowing his distaste, Artemio reminded himself that this conversation did not have to be undertaken at a fraction of the pace of which he was capable. Nightmare that his father was, there was no denying he could make rapid-fire connections with the best of them. "I can't imagine that you thought the crown would allow you to conduct your own witch hunt."

Cleto raised an eyebrow. "You?"

"Who better?" He gestured imperiously to the bloody mess of a room. "Look at all of the lovely motivation I've been given."

Artemio watched his father carefully as the old man spoke. There was no possibility that Cleto would share the details of his own experience or investigation, but the lie he wheeled out would still offer a clue. Like a knight trying to protect a hidden wound, the position of the shield might give it all away. "Mark my words, boy. Those back-birthed brats on the throne are behind it. It's just an excuse to be rid of you when you fail. A clean way to wash their hands of our bloodline."

"I doubt even half the Teatro know who the Volpe are by now. If they strung us up and set us alight in Covotana, the only complaint you'd hear would be about the smell."

"The people remember their true allegiance."

Artemio just let that nonsense hang in the air between them. In his experience, the commoners' allegiance went to whoever kept food in their belly, kept a roof over their head, and whipped them the least. When it came to the noble houses, loyalty was bought for a marginally higher price, but it was still bought. Harmony said Artemio had no romance in his heart. In truth, Artemio had no romance in his head. He had no room for it there since he was using the massive amount of space it apparently occupied for things like thinking.

Apparently enough of his doubt showed on his face to enrage his father once more. Not that the man needed much enraging. "Get out of here. Run yelping like a cur to your masters, if you please, but I'll not tolerate you in this room."

Artemio shrugged. "I was done anyway."

As he passed by the Count, the old man snarled after him. "You never should have come here."

"I go where the crown commands." He paused at the door. "Such is the price of loyalty."

It wasn't a necessary twist of the knife, but he'd be damned if it wasn't the most satisfying thing he'd done in his whole life.

9

WALKING THE MERIDIAN

Brina, Regola Dei Cerva 111

For almost a season, the girl had lain still. Not sleeping. Not waking. Just still. When Mother Vinegar pressed broth to her lips, she would drink it down. When she was hauled about, she would go where she was put. A simple task like splitting wood could be set and she'd move through the motions again and again, but the vital spark that made Orsina herself had been burned away.

Kagan had left to return to his hunting, promising a reappearance by first frost, and Mother Vinegar had not even troubled to look up from her ward to wave him off. He had never seen the old woman so racked with care for another. It troubled him.

When the girl came back, it was in pieces. One day her braying laugh in the silence of the clearing. The next a whispered story of the Graverobber, told to herself, curled up by the fire. With the lack of work, the muscle she'd been building melted away, and the extra year that had been snatched from her filled in the rest with softness in places where before she'd had none. None would say she was pretty, but with those wide bright eyes starting to focus once more, she could at least be called striking without it being a sly jab.

There was no one moment when Mother Vinegar could say for certain the tide had turned and Orsina was washed back to the shore, but sure enough, before the first frost crusted the vines outside, she was talking away again as if there was nothing better in all the world than to flap her lips.

Mother Vinegar took it as a sign. They had not spoken of what Orsina did on that fateful day since her recovery began, but now that the time was fast approaching for the girl to head off, she needed to be told she was going, and why.

"Covotana?"

Mother Vinegar didn't look up from the soup pot. "That's right."

Orsina tried again. "The capital. Covotana?"

"That's the one." The old woman's head bobbed along with the bubbling of the kettle.

Once more with feeling, Orsina said, "You want me to go to…"

"The House of Seven Shadows." Mother Vinegar cut her off. "Best place for you."

Orsina flopped down onto the heaped furs. "But I'm not a… But… what?"

"They've had sense enough to train lowborn like you in the past." Mother Vinegar slopped out their dinner and passed it down. "When they see the depth of your curse, they'll do the same again."

There was a frantic edge to her voice when Orsina asked, "Is this because of what happened with the dragon? Because…"

"You'd do best not to mention that to anyone. Plenty folk would call you a liar, and them that believe you will be out to get something for it." Glancing over at the stricken look on the girl's face, Mother Vinegar did the unthinkable and tried some kindness. "You're not a bad lass. Terrible apprentice. But not bad in the other parts of you. You'd have done well witching, but this thing of yours, this… hollow the shades slip into. It needs dealing with."

"I thought that was why you brought me out here? I thought that was why I've been living in the woods since I was barely old enough to think." Soup set aside, Orsina practically crawled to the old woman. "What was the point of all that if we weren't dealing with it?"

"If you'd have kept your head shut you might have waited out your days in peace, but you had to…"

Twice in her short life, Orsina was facing exile from all she knew. Once had been enough to break Kagan. Once had been enough to leave Mother Vinegar herself so scarred up on the insides that she'd never let anyone close again. There were tears pricking at the girl's eyes. Even with her bad sight and the dim light of the cooking fire, Mother Vinegar could see that another push might have sent the girl tumbling back into the silence and stillness that still haunted the moments she wasn't kept busy. She could see all of that, but she could see the second shadow lingering behind the girl too. The looming darkness of the thing from beneath the pond, always here with her now. Latched into her heart.

"I'm not blaming you for fighting with everything you've got. Nobody could blame you. But you've opened a door now that can't be shut. Old Ginny Greenteeth won't be the worst of them to come knocking. There's older and stronger than her out there. Old enough that they don't need inviting. You need to be taught to ride them, not let them ride you."

The tears had pooled in the girl's eyes, but they weren't falling yet. "And what about you?"

It knocked the old woman off track. "Me?"

"Alone out here in the forest with nobody to take care of you…"

The old hag was still cackling two days later when Kagan arrived.

There was little to pack for the girl. She owned nothing and wanted to owe nothing. Apart from some tack she could justify to herself as the fruit of her own labors and the clothes on her back, which she couldn't leave behind for reasons of dignity, she left her apprenticeship with the witch empty-handed. Overly formal, she even gave a curtsy to the hag before they departed into the southern reach.

"Thank you for all of your help."

Mother Vinegar flinched. She hadn't been able to help at all, just delay the inevitable. That one had barbs to it. The girl would have made a good witch, right enough.

There was no long road for Orsina to meander along towards the horizon. She rounded a corner out of the dell, and she vanished into the trees. Gone from Mother Vinegar's life as fast as she'd arrived. The old woman felt her shoulders slump though she told them to stay up. She felt the tangle in her chest like she'd breathed in cobweb. Kagan didn't help at all, laying a heavy hand on her shoulder and rumbling, "Don't you worry, I'll take good care of her."

Mother Vinegar snorted.

"And I'll take good care of myself too."

"Ain't you I'm worried for." Mother Vinegar brushed him off and ducked back inside her overgrown cottage. "It's everybody else."

Kagan let out a sigh to himself. Everyone in this country was so dramatic. He blamed it on all the Opera.

To her credit, Orsina had continued to travel south through the unfamiliar woods. To her detriment, she'd wandered far from the proper path, trailing along a rabbit run that led to a gully and then a spring. She was almost ready to turn back and look for Kagan when she spotted him out of the corner of her eye. "Damnit, Kagan. I'm going to tie a bell around your neck."

"It isn't my fault you move through the undergrowth with all the grace of a wyvern in heat."

She feigned a retch. "Is that a thing?"

"As far as you know."

She threw a stick at him, but it missed by several feet to bounce off a tree. They both smiled, and then just when Orsina was feeling like herself again for the first time, her smile fractured. This was too much. Too soon. Too like the last time. A tremor ran through her, and she could swear she tasted swamp water on her lips.

Kagan hoisted her off her feet before she knew what was happening. The disorientation of being lifted and spun around over his shoulder combined with the disorientation her own mind was inflicting on her about where and when she was. The forest swirled and she came back to herself. "Hey! I can walk."

He bounced her on his shoulder but didn't put her down. "I can see that from the way you walked in completely the wrong direction."

She hit him on the back. "Well, I've never been this way before."

"Well, then perhaps the person who has been this way should lead?"

She tried to mimic the rumble of his voice. "Well, then perhaps the person who has should put me down and get on with it."

Kagan let out a long rumbling sigh. "It is going to be a long walk."

"So you're my horse now? You're going to carry me the whole way?"

"No." He dumped her into the bushes. "It is going to be a long walk listening to you the whole way."

There was no question that the distance was greater than either one of them had traveled in recent years. Almost a match for Kagan's long slow march of misery down over the steppes in the days following his exile. Yet this time he had more company than bitter memories, and complain as he might, he took no small amusement in the antics of the girl.

Over and over again, he caught a wry laugh halfway up his throat and strangled it. So easily he could forget what she had done? So easily he could set aside the sin and love the sinner? There was nothing worse in all the world than a slayer of dragons, yet he found a smile tugging at his lips each time the girl goaded and badgered him.

When they bedded down around the fire at night, Kagan took the first watch, and he was left alone with his thoughts. They seemed to grow darker as the fire burned lower.

While the sun was still a faint glow on the horizon, he thought of abandoning her. Even if she were not the most grievous of sinners, what was she to him? There was no reason for him to obey the demands of some hag of no consequence, sequestered away in some forest far from anyone who might help him regain his rightful place. The first few miles might have been safe enough, but beyond them came more and more danger. Civilization reared up ahead of them, more fearsome than the dragon that had once pursued them, and while Kagan was an Arazi warrior with fear of no mere man, a group of peasants could bludgeon any great warrior to death whether he was afraid of them or not. There were other forests where he could hunt. The whole of the steppes lay open to him too. There was no reason the girl could not simply wake up and find him gone.

When the only light was the flame flickering between them, he thought of smothering her in her sleep. To abandon her would not ensure her death. The only way to make certain that she paid for what she had done was to slay her himself, and though he could not drown her as she had drowned the poor dragon on the hunt, he could choke the life from her. He could close his hands into a fist about her scrawny neck and squeeze and squeeze until all the evil she'd done washed away.

When the fire was down to embers and it was time to rouse Orsina and restock it, he thought of killing himself. He could not kill her. He had all night to do it, his hands quaked with the anticipation of soft flesh between them, yet he could not kill her. He had affection for her, but that had never stopped him killing before when his honor demanded it. That would have been easy for a master of emotions to push aside. It was not the fear of her looking up at him with betrayal in her eyes as he slaughtered her that stayed his hands. It was the fear of her looking up at him with the eyes of some primordial monster that she had given over her flesh to.

Espher had never been to war with his people, and now that he had seen firsthand what even an untrained manipulator of their magics could do, he feared the outcome such a conflict could bring. Were he still mounted on his dragon, armed and armored—as he was born to be—then he could have stood against this child without doubt as to the outcome. But down here in the dirt alongside her, it became a matter of chance.

She roused at his first touch, as though her long season unmoving had given her all the sleep she'd ever need. She fed the fire, settled into his place, and smiled down at him as he tried to summon up the courage to do what should be done.

He didn't manage on the first night, or on the second. On the third night, they slept huddled together, cowering beneath the lea of a toppled tree's roots as the seasonal rain began to pound and lightning tore great ripples across the sky, cracking "loud as the beating of a dragon's wings." Those whispered words were the first time she heard Kagan willingly speak of dragons since her return to the waking world, though he flinched and turned his face away from her soon after.

In the dead of night, when the thunder rolled her right out of her sleep, Kagan was still staring up at the sky, waiting to see something behind the curtain of cloud. Solemn face illuminated by the lightning's flare. There was a low rumble in his throat, almost too low for human ears to hear. A song.

Come morning he was even more grumpy than before as they stepped out from under the boughs of the Selvaggia and into open country. The rain did not slow, nor did the chill it had settled into their bones show a hint of moving along once they'd set out. The sun never seemed to fully rise that day, masked by the rains, and by midday the dark and the damp began to take their toll on the travelers. In the sky above there was no sun, and in Kagan's heart there was dread.

The smart thing to do would be to find a road and find an inn for the night, give the girl some time to recover. All that time off her feet had left her so breathless after a few hours of walking that she could barely talk at him incessantly anymore. A forced march could kill as surely as dragon fire. He'd seen it. But for every step they strode on closer to her grave, they moved a little farther from his.

By his reckoning, it was three hundred miles to Covotana. A day's travel for a dragon. Two weeks' hard march. She wasn't going to make it. Not like this. If he'd money in his pouch, they might have found a caravan heading south and bought their way on. If he'd a brain in his head, he'd turn around and run in the opposite direction.

When they reached a road, they followed it. He didn't run. She didn't slow, though he could see the weight of the miles on her back.

Even exhausted, she wouldn't shut up. "Is this the way to Covotana?"

"It is a way to Covotana."

She rolled her eyes. "But is it in this direction?"

"This road meets other roads that lead there." Kagan picked up his pace a little. If she had enough breath to pester him, she had enough breath to jog.

She caught up to him in a couple of bounding strides, considered jumping up onto his back the way she used to when she was smaller, then thought better of it. "But this is the right way?"

He cast a long glance her way, then sighed out, "This is the way I am taking us."

"You don't know the way to Covotana." Her brows drew down as she finally voiced the suspicion.

He already had the lie ready on the tip of his tongue. "Everyone knows the way to Covotana. Covotana is south. This road leads west, yet it will meet a road that leads south, so it is the way."

She was scrambling to get far enough ahead of him to get a good look at his face. "Are you sure?"

What was the point in lying to her? It wasn't like she could turn back now. "No."

"You've never been there?" Orsina gaped up at him. As if her more worldly companion had strode the length of the continent before settling on the same overgrown thicket she'd been born to.

"Of course I have not." He scoffed. "I am an exile with no title or allegiance to keep me safe in foreign lands. I'd sooner stick my head in a sack of snakes."

She wrapped her cloaks and shawls around herself a little tighter, not that the drenched cloth was doing much to keep out the cold or the wet. "But you're taking me there?"

"They're your people." He flinched even as he said it. "You'll fit right in."

She gave him a dead-eyed stare. "I'll fit in. In the sack of snakes?"

"You already bite anyone who disagrees with you." She couldn't see him grin, but there was a rumble to his voice that had to be a laugh.

"Hey, I grew out of that!" She was giggling despite her indignance.

"Did you? Or did we just stop disagreeing with you while in biting distance?" As if to prove his point, she kicked at his shins and he had to dance out of reach.

"I was a baby!"

"My scars tell a different tale." He thrust out a finger level with her nose. "Witness this! Witness the breadth. Adult teeth!"

She grabbed at his wrist and mimed a chomp. "One time!"

His own laugh turned to a snarl before it reached his lips and he advanced on her. "One time. Once is all it takes to damn you. One mistake. One sin. Then the rest of your days are forfeit, sure as if you'd been the one to die."

"All right!" Orsina caught hold of his shoulders, a pile of dirt heaping up behind her heels as he kept coming closer. "I get the message! I promise I won't bite you anymore."

If there had been fear in her eyes, he might have been able to do it. He might have been able to absolve his own sin and escaped the doom that awaited him, but even as he loomed over her, a veritable giant in a kingdom of gnats, she was still smiling up at him like he was a friend taking a joke too far. She patted him on the shoulder and his resolve crumbled to dust. "You... you had better not. We are not carrying all this dry meat so you can turn to cannibalism."

"Hey now, that's from Mother Vinegar's private barrel." She turned back to the road with a bounce in her step despite the rain doing its damnedest to wash the smile from her face. "You know her... It's probably human meat."

There was a lull as they trudged ever on, with Kagan still so lost in the swirl of his own thoughts that it didn't cross his troubled mind until too late that something was troubling the girl too. He shook some water free from where it had gathered in the scaled ridge along his brow. "She will be fine on her own. You don't need to worry for the hag. When I get back, I will look in on her. As I used to."

The absurdity of it was enough to yank Orsina out of whatever melancholy had taken hold of her. She blurted out, "What?" before degenerating into a fit of laughter so serious they had to stop walking for her to catch her breath afterwards. "Mother Vinegar is going to outlive all of us. Dragon magic or not. If the skies opened and lightning came down, she'd just scowl at it until it went away. The medicines she makes? None of them do anything; plagues flee because they heard Mother Vinegar is coming."

He didn't smile, but there was a thinning around his scary lips that Orsina had learned meant he was trying not to. It was strange to her, that he'd spend so much of his life trying not to show the joy he was taking in it, but she didn't pry. She didn't even know how to start asking how he'd ended up this way. He grunted. "I take your point. My hope was you'd take some comfort in knowing that what you'd left behind was still there."

She dithered along the road, still caught up in her own story, still oblivious to the grim mood that seemed to be pouring down on her companion with the rain. "If they burned down the whole Selvaggia, she'd be sitting on top of the heap, bossing around whoever came to sweep out the ashes."

Eventually he could take no more of her glibness. "I know nothing of the place I left behind. I hear no word. I see no sign of my people but the rare beast coming down off the steppes."

Orsina stopped in her tracks. This was the closest they'd come yet to discussing… what had happened before. "Which then tries to murder you."

"Or I hunt in turn…"

She opened her mouth, but he held up a hand to her, his head cocked to the side, listening to something she couldn't hear. "Off the road."

She moved without having to be told twice, but she was still her. She couldn't just go in silence. "What? What's happening?"

He flinched as whatever sense let him do his work overwhelmed his composure. "Horses… Run ragged. Quickly, down off the road."

She was already slipping and sliding down the embankment at the side of the road, struggling for balance when he came skating down past her, hooking an arm around her waist and dragging her down into the filth beside him. Pressing her down, pressing the breath out of her before she could complain.

At first it sounded like thunder rolling overhead, and she strained to look up before Kagan caught hold of her head in one clawed hand and dragged her in closer. Eye-to-eye with him, she finally fell silent. The thunder was not overhead, it was in the earth. It was rumbling through the ground. Through her. She could feel it in her bones. The hammering of hooves.

She had only seen the horses of a farming village in her time. Big beasts, but dull and hapless. She would not recognize them in the things that streamed along the road, slick with lather and rain.

Kagan would have known them. Even if they weren't burrowing into his head from their proximity. He'd fought warhorses on the steppe. Even though they fared poorly against draconic cavalry, there was an edge to them he'd found all too familiar. Beasts ridden always at the edge of madness.

The thunder faded. Orsina jerked herself free of his grasp and spat a gob of mud at him, gasping all the way.

He was lost in thought as he crawled past her, back towards the road. They were both coated with mud now on every side. Every fold of their clothes weighted with it. He grumbled under his breath. "Cavaliers at full gallop."

She slugged him in the shoulder the moment she had her feet. "What the hell was that about?!"

"You didn't want to be at their mercy." He dismissed her fury with a wave of his hand. "Not out here with nobody around."

She kicked him. "I'm from Espher, you big slab of stupid!" Another kick. To no noticeable effect. "They're on my side!"

"You're a peasant girl, and they're men of power. They're not on your side. You're their prey."

He could feel it prickling on the back of his neck. Not the chill of the rain or the wind, but the same cold he'd felt permeating the girl when he'd lifted her broken body from the dragon's throat.

"I'm nobody's prey, Kagan."

"They wouldn't know that. They'd ride you down if they were in a hurry, and do much worse if they had the time to spare." When she opened her mouth to object he talked right over her. "You might fight them. You might win. But then you're the mad witch who killed a troop of cavaliers and they send their whole army to put you down."

Even now he could see her trying to string together an argument, but he closed the distance and wiped the mud back from her face, slicking down her hair and stilling her for a moment. "Who we are, what we can do... those things don't matter to the ones who sit on thrones. If you aren't some lord or lady, you aren't a person. You're a problem."

She set her jaw and jerked her head out of his grip. "I don't believe that."

"Believe it or not, they'll kill you all the same." He sighed. "Straightforward or slow. They always get their way."

10

WALTZ OF TEETH

Gemmazione, Regola Dei Cerva 112

The room had been ransacked. Every cupboard pried open. Splayed sooty footprints spilling out from the fireplace where someone had been digging up the flue. The rat-girl didn't even have the courtesy to look embarrassed about what she'd done. "You weren't here."

"The investigation is not always going to place me here at your convenience." Artemio pretended he did not see that she had torn the room apart looking for her damned pet. "You know how to write. Leave a note."

Her eyes darted to the overturned heaps of papers spread across the floor. "Write? How many hours do you think I have in a day?"

"Enough to spy for anyone with a coin purse that jingles." He caught himself before it became a snarl. Anger wouldn't undo what had been done. It wouldn't make her more pliable. She was desperate. He understood desperation all too keenly. He sank back into the chair. "Just… report to me now."

The sloped shoulders tensed up. "Where is she?"

Insolence was not something most of the nobility of Espher would have tolerated. Just imagining what his father would do to a servant who spoke to him in the manner this mongrel used was enough to break a cold sweat on Artemio's forehead. "The rodent traveled with me and ate well on table scraps. I think she may even have gained weight. Now report."

The tension eased a little, but the rat-girl was still looking entirely too stubborn for Artemio's liking when she said. "There's nothing."

"Two weeks I was on the road, and you have nothing to tell me?" He scoffed and turned his attention back to the notes he was attempting to put back in order. "You aren't worth what they pay for you."

She let out a squeak of dismay. "There's all the usual sh… stuff. The Spring Waltz is coming up so rumors are thick as… stuff. Marriage proposals. Broken promises. Lady Cavalla's eldest is pregnant out of wedlock. Nothing to do with this though. Just… nothing."

He let their eyes meet as he rose from his seat and wrapped his cloak around his shoulders. Letting the weight of the situation settle on her just as heavily as the mantle of thick cloth around him before he spoke. "I'm beginning to question your worth."

"You want miracles." She looked genuinely aggrieved. "I'm just a maid."

He waved at the chaos she'd made of this study on his way out. "Then clean this mess up. Maid."

The palace had been his first stop on arrival in town. Needless to say, Harmony was less than delighted to be sent along to the House of Seven Shadows with his luggage, yet there was a limit on how much she could object when he more or less leapt from their moving carriage.

He fully expected to receive an earful from her on his return to the school, but after so long away from his studies, he knew there was no possibility of delaying it any further. Not if he didn't want the outpouring of sympathy from Prima Cicogna and the other staff to abruptly dry up. A death in the family could only be milked for so long. Two weeks was probably close to that limit.

Nothing of the journey back to the House stuck in his memory until he was walking the halls once more and double-guessing his journey. Wondering if he'd been seen. Wondering if he'd been clumsy and painted a target on his own back.

There were two stops to make. One to his own chambers to ensure his property had been returned and to allow Harmony the opportunity to chew him out, then the next to the Prima's offices so he could be chewed out by her for abandoning his studies at a vital juncture. There was no point attempting to avoid either, but at least the promise of the Prima's denigration gave him an excuse to cut his darling sister's complaints short.

By the entrance to his room, there was a small table. Above it hung his cloaks, his sword belt, and Harmony's blindfold. The table was ostensibly there to hold mail delivered by a servant. In all of his time at the House, he could count on one finger all the people who had ever sent him anything.

Those that supported his family's claim to the throne would never be so foolish as to openly send him a letter, and those who did not support his family's claim considered him to be a pariah. Nobody sent him mail except for Mother.

The envelope sitting open on the table was surprising. Harmony sitting beside the table and reading his mail was anything but surprising. "I believe that was addressed to me."

She waved it at him. "It's an invitation."

Artemio hung up his cloak and went to check his chest had been delivered to the right room. He called back over his shoulder, "Oh charming, has some fresh nest of serpents been uncovered that they need a fool to jam his head into?"

"It is an invitation to a ball."

He stuck his head back into the room. "I beg your pardon?"

"You don't even know how to dance." There was a hysterical edge to her laughter.

"I can fumble my way through a waltz." He came back into the room properly as his confusion built. "Did you say I've been invited to a ball? Who would invite me to a ball?!"

"Someone who knows you're in the Cerva's favor."

He tried to snatch the invitation from her hands with no luck. She was quicker and the same length of limb that gave her the advantage in a fight kept it from him. "The invitation is from Lady Anatra. They host the Spring Ball every year. How do you not know this?"

"It never seemed relevant."

"The first social event of the season after everyone holed up at their country estates over the winter emerges, and you don't think it is relevant. I swear you are intent on the family name dying out."

"Oh come on now, it isn't like I ever expected to... dance."

"Well, you will be attending, I hope. If you don't, I might have to murder you."

"If I attend, then everyone will know I have the king's favor. They'll question why. When my investigation becomes public knowledge..."

"That horse is out of the stable and galloping for the horizon, Art. They know. It is known. You wouldn't be invited otherwise."

"You know. I know." He mentally tallied rat-girl but didn't mention her. "Father knows. But this letter was here waiting for us, so Father couldn't have told anyone. News wouldn't have traveled that fast."

"Keep going." Harmony tapped her foot beneath the table. "You'll get there in a minute."

"If a servant was on the payroll of the Anatras, then..."

Harmony let out a little hiss. "A miss on that thrust. Try again."

Artemio's brows furrowed, until enlightenment came like a soap bubble bursting. "The Cerva. The kings."

"Finally." She threw back her head and groaned. "I thought you were meant to be the clever one."

He was pacing back and forth now, brain bubbling back into action, the way that had always annoyed Harmony. "There's no point in having a lightning rod if you don't hoist it up."

Harmony knew her role as a sounding board well. She bounced back the questions that she thought she ought to. "You think they want the assassins to come after you?"

"I think they think I'll be able to fend them off. None of the victims have been Shadebound. Whatever means is being deployed against them, they have not shown any signs of an attempted defense." Even as he said it, his mind continued spinning through the possibilities. "The kings must think it is magic. They must think I can withstand it."

The smile had slipped from her face in the midst of all this pondering. "Or they think it will kill you and get a threat to their throne out of their hair."

He gave her a rueful smile. "It is win-win."

"Not for you."

"No," he said softly. "Not for me."

She shook herself out of it. "So, do you think I could get an invite too?"

"I think if I show up to the social event of the season with my sister as my date, I would deserve to be a social pariah." He grinned back, glad for the change of subject.

The ball was not for a few days, and as usual, Artemio had grossly underestimated his sister's tenacity. While he was trying to catch up on his missed lessons, she was there, demanding to escort him, for his safety. His enemies could be around any corner, why shouldn't she be there?

Her insistent demands switched to pleading by the next day, a recitation of her endless suffering. As if he did not know every part of it like it was his own. As if he had not been her sole confidant through every single one of her many lonely years.

By day three, his betrayal was unforgivable, he should be ashamed of himself, and she had nothing more to say to him. Yet somehow she kept finding her way into his presence to repeat that she had nothing to say to him until finally, inevitably, he gave in. He pinched the bridge of his nose and sighed. "Your invitation is conditional. It is essential you understand that."

She let out a sound akin to the steam whistle on a kettle, then began to babble. "Thank you. Thank you. Thank you. You're the best brother I could ever ask for, and I am ever so very grateful…"

"This is not an excuse for you to indulge your filthy socialization habits. We will be working."

"Of course, oh General my General, I shall march to the beat of your drum. And I shall wear the green dress Mother bought me for my first season in the city, the one I never got the chance to wear. It will be out of fashion of course, but I'd rather save my stipend for more pressing matters. I shall have to get the chest let out a little, and the hips. Perhaps I might get some seed beads sewn on while work is being done on it."

"Harmony, I beg you, focus. We are going into enemy territory. There will be no telling what might happen."

"Perhaps someone will be so taken with my beauty that they'll overlook our blighted name and ask me to dance."

"Harm."

"I shan't be accepting any proposals of course, our arrangement would make that impossible, but it would be so nice to dance just the once."

"Harmony!"

"Yes, brother dearest, light of my life?"

"I need you to teach me how to dance."

"Oh, you really don't know how to… no, of course you don't. Not manly enough, right?"

"Indeed."

"Well, no time like the present. Up you get."

So for the last two days, as some poor seamstress who Harmony had already acquired the details of worked frantically to get her dress ready, the two of them waltzed. Between writing papers, examining reports from the previous murders, discussing potential suspects lurking in Artemio's own extensive notes, and attending lectures, Artemio learned how to perform a clumsy dance. It lacked all the grace he and Harmony shared in the gymnasium, but it would have to be sufficient in the unlikely event that anyone requested he join them on the ballroom floor.

There was no budget for the kind of fashion the rest of the court would be displaying, and there certainly wasn't going to be a bursary offered up by Father for this sort of thing, so they made do, piecing together something that could at least pass for presentable, if a little formal and old-fashioned, for Artemio to wear. It fit with his family's reputation as the old power for him to be a little behind the times, or at least that was how Harmony spun it.

Artemio was even able to convince himself they looked quite striking as they strolled down through the gardens alongside the luminaries of more favored houses to clamber up into the coaches provided by the hosts. There were enough of his fellow scions that he managed to pass invisibly until they were actually inside a coach—then the dream came crashing down all too quickly when some girl looked across at him with patent disgust on her face and asked, "Are you in the right carriage?"

He didn't flinch. "I am. Perhaps you're the one who has lost their way?"

That promptly annihilated any chance at overhearing rumors on the way to the party, so Artemio had to hope that once the guests were more lubricated, he might find some quiet corner to lurk in where everything could be overheard. It wasn't as though he hoped to hear open talk of sedition on the dance floor. Just hints. All he needed was a thread that he might pull on. No matter how tenuous a connection any event or muttered rumor might have, he would chase it down to the ends of the earth. But first he needed that thread.

If an evening of awkward company was all it took to get his investigation moving once more, then he'd tolerate it, just as he had all the years of social isolation that had gone before. He had tried to grant the other riders in the carriage some degree of comfort by looking out of the window, but they had failed to return the favor. Harmony was blushing to the roots of her hair at so much unwanted attention. Looking askance to him, to make it all better. So he turned his scrutiny upon the other passengers with no small amount of malice. If he and his sister were going to be made to feel like some sideshow spectacle, the least he could do was live up to that dubious standard.

The girl who'd spoken up was the first to receive his attentions. Brown hair. Beauty spot high on the cheek. "Vivace Ragna? Your father fought the Agrantine at the Battle of Cestino. He acquitted himself admirably until the countercharge."

He pointedly did not mention that the man broke and ran when the Agrantine heavy cavalry made their assault, collapsing the whole Espher battle line and costing them the day, and the valley. He didn't need to tell her that. She knew, and now she knew that he knew and had the words on the very tip of his tongue. Harmony did not know her military history and had no idea what Artemio was saying, yet her blush had begun to recede. She might not have understood how he had deflated the Ragna girl, but there was a sparkle in her eye now that she realized they were not entirely defenseless.

The boy sitting beside Vivace was unfamiliar. More brown hair. Blue eyes were unusual for Espher outside of the old royal line, but Artemio still couldn't place him. Some minor son of a greater house? Artemio waited. Looking at him. Letting silence fill the carriage until the weight of it grew unbearable. The man extended a hand. "Allegro Anguilla."

Artemio shook the offered hand gratefully. Some degree of politeness wasn't too much to ask for, it seemed. He even granted the boy a genuine smile in thanks for that kindness. "I can't believe we aren't already acquainted. Do you study at the House?"

"Newly arrived from the country. I'm afraid I didn't catch your name."

"Terrible manners. My mother must be turning in her grave." That little mention was enough to make the man seated on the same bench beside Harmony, with his back turned to the two of them, flinch. Every word was calculated. "I am Artemio Volpe."

The color drained from Allegro's face as he hastily withdrew his hand. "Volpe?"

"Exactly." Artemio smiled, turning to the last passenger. "And of course, I'm sure you already know Demetrio Cavalla, or at the very least you must know his sister."

Another flinch, but puzzled expressions from the rest of the carriage. Perhaps rat-girl had some purpose after all, even if it was just to provide him with the ammunition to needle those who looked down on him. "And of course this is my sister, Harmony. I do hope you get the chance to know each other better. Although not as well as you know Demetrio's, of course."

Allegro was still fumbling, trying to get his words together. It was almost terminally ill spoken when he blurted out, "I wasn't aware you were going to be invited."

It wasn't a question, but the question that was on all of their lips was clearly burning bright just under the surface of that fumbled statement. Why had the Anatras invited the Volpe twins? That boded well. It meant his work for the twin kings had not yet become public knowledge, and those who were in the know meant to court his favor quietly. It was advantageous in respect to the assassins—and a terrible impediment otherwise.

Those courting him wanted him isolated so nobody else could attempt to win him over before knowledge of his activities became public, but that left him to fabricate a reason why he was suddenly invited to social events after his long years in the desert. He elected simply to keep his mouth shut and look back out of the window after saying, "Yes, it was a pleasant surprise for us all."

The awkward silence might have come back after that, but now it belonged to Artemio. He could puncture it whenever he pleased. He could spin them whatever tale he wanted or persist in his stubborn silence as it burned each and every one of his fellow noble scions that they were not going to be the most interesting person in the room at the party. As they turned a corner, Harmony's shoulder bumped against him just a little harder than momentum would have necessitated. A glance showed a smile spreading across her face as she basked in the discomfort of her peers.

Artemio was not his father. He did not have to be in control of every situation he was in, but in times of discomfort, he could not deny that there was some part of him that wanted that control, that needed it to feel safe. To keep Harmony safe.

On arrival, the other passengers departed from the carriage with all the haste and grace of a burst dam, scattering off to find their friends, dancing partners, and confidants and spread word of his presence. Perhaps the idea of finding a quiet corner and listening along to the chatter had just been a pleasant dream all along. Only Artemio had manners enough to offer Harmony a hand down the steps.

The Anatra compound within the city was palatial. Giving even the House itself a run for its money in terms of architecture and scale. A sprawling villa across a mixture of larger two-story buildings where the family and guests stayed and a variety of outbuildings to house servants, animals, and whatever else a noble house required. At present, a solid half of those outbuildings seemed to have been converted from their typical purposes into themed bars and kitchens, providing guests with more than they could feasibly eat in a dozen evenings such as this. Every luxury taken to its greatest excess.

The grand courtyard between the buildings was already populated with arriving guests, the carriages having been sent out to fetch them in waves, with the least important arriving first so that the more important could be seen arriving by a greater audience. Between the people towered great white marble statues. Beneath their feet, grand mosaics had been laid out across the space, interspersed with channels of water flowing from one fountain to the next that incautious guests might tread in after sampling the wines brought down into the city from the Anatras' famed vineyards.

Perhaps Artemio's opinions on all of this may have been different if he had grown up among these people. Perhaps he would have considered the evening to be a source of excitement rather than dread. He doubted it. There was a degree of artifice in everything that happened here, from the meeting of glances to the clinking of glasses, that made him feel ill at ease. As though he had not been taught the steps to the dance.

As they strolled down towards the house from where the carriages had abandoned them, creeping ever closer to the growing orchestral groan of music muffled by thick walls, he let his gaze travel not to the far higher walls surrounding the compound, or the artistic displays of gardening that were meant to enrapture guests, but to the people.

The guards almost perfectly concealed by pillars and shrubberies. The servants, pristinely human and practically vibrating with their desire to be perfect. So much importance poured into this one event, all so the rich and wealthy could stand around and talk. As though standing and talking were not freely available on any street in the city. As though the words being spoken here had so much more bearing on the world beyond those high walls than any other traders' haggling.

Harmony seemed entirely lost to the romance of it all, overlooking all of the reality in favor of her dream. She drank in every sight with a desperation that made Artemio heartsick to watch. All of her life she had longed for this, and now she could only have it as a farce so he could scuttle around gathering information. If nobody else offered, then he would have to dance with her at least once tonight. To let her close her eyes and pretend he was someone else and she was living the life she craved.

The life he had taken from her by his very existence. Certainly, she would not have attended the grand balls of Covotana had he not been Shadebound, but out in the country, she could have lived a quiet life, been wed to a man who cared for her more than the stigma of her lineage. She might have found some joy, or at least some peace. Instead, she had made herself a weapon to rust by his side. Well, not tonight.

Artemio stopped and pushed her forward. "Walk down alone. It seems that I cannot escape attention, but you might. Secrete yourself somewhere inside, entice some gentlemen to dance with you. Listen more than you talk. Have a pleasant evening, and I shall pick over it all with you on the ride back to the House."

"And who shall keep you out of trouble?" She gawked back at him, clearly torn between the party and her presumptive duty.

He looked her up and down with an eyebrow cocked. "My apologies, I did not realize you had a sword hidden somewhere in that dress of yours."

Her brows drew down. He shouldn't have poked fun like that if he wanted her to do as he asked. "I…"

"Shall be of much more use to me as a spy if you have not been tarred with the same brush as I." He cut her off with a hand held an inch from her mouth so he did not smudge her makeup. "Now off you go. Have yourself an evening. Come and find me before midnight. Do not do anything untoward."

"Me?" She shivered, though the night held no chill, and when she met his gaze there was wickedness shining out. "Never."

With that pronouncement of his impending doom, she strode off down the path, catching up to some stragglers from one of the other carriages and inserting herself into their conversation with a grace of which he was overwhelmingly envious. So long as she kept her name to herself, this might be something like a pleasant evening for her. A smile played over Artemio's lips for just a moment. He could not enjoy himself, but he might take some vicarious joy in proceedings through her.

Artemio almost called a shade when he felt an arm interlink with his, and he had to swallow down a yelp before he turned to realize who had latched onto him.

"Artemio Volpe, finally coming down from his ivory tower to walk among us mere mortals."

Rosina Aquila. They had shared some classes together before her graduation the previous year, but few words. It had not even crossed his mind that she would be here. Stiffly, he made his greeting. "Rosina, what an honor to walk in with you on my arm."

"Oh, don't worry so, I shan't be trying to ravish you in the bushes. I simply cannot imagine anything worse than having to walk in alone."

She had slipped her hand through his arm and fallen into pace with him so neatly that he could scarcely believe it. So familiar for someone who wouldn't look him in the eye months back. Was her family in the know about the king's favor? Was she simply an opportunist? He remembered to speak just a step too late. "I've no doubt that walking in with me probably comes close."

She laughed as if he'd just told her something hilarious. He definitely hadn't. "All eyes will be on us, I can scarce imagine anything better."

"No eyes on me," he grumbled. "No eyes would be better."

Once again her crystal laugh echoed down to the plaza. Heads began to turn. Even Harmony was giving them a quizzical look, ready to run back to her brother's aid. All as Rosina intended.

He rested his hand on hers where it was pressing into his arm. Very forward. How people would talk. "How have you been, Rosina?"

"Oh, you know." She was trying hard not to crane her head around, but her eyes were flitting about like she was one of the moths beginning to gather around the lantern posts. "Neither good nor bad."

"Are you looking for someone in particular?"

She laughed again, but it had a forced edge to it this time. Clumsier than he'd expected of her. "All this excitement, it turns a girl's head. You know."

"I don't." He tightened his grip on her hand. "I don't know."

She smiled at him again as if his non sequiturs were charming. They were close enough now that Artemio could hear the chatter dying out in a wave as they approached. Where he walked, conversation died. As it always had been. The only difference was that now he was somewhere busy enough that it was noticeable.

The crowd parted around them as Artemio made a beeline for the main house, ignoring all the little diversions that had been set up to amuse and entice the guests. He wasn't running for cover, but there was no denying that his pace was somewhat swift compared with Rosina's preferred stroll. She almost stumbled keeping up with him. "Are you in a hurry to be somewhere?"

"Not at all, but I imagine you want your grand entrance, don't you?" She struggled to keep her eyes on his face for even the long moment she was faking puzzlement. "That was the purpose of this whole exercise. Was it not?"

"My goodness, you would think you didn't want to be seen in my company the way you are behaving." Again, the edge of false joviality to everything she said and did. Smiles that didn't reach her eyes.

"I'd prefer not to be seen at all." Why lie when the truth was so much harder to disprove? "I've no idea why I received an invitation to this evening's festivities, and I'd prefer if the good manners that brought me here didn't cause anyone else any discomfort, as we seem to be doing at the moment."

"Oh, pay them no mind." She leaned in scandalously close. So close that the hard boning under the front of her dress dug into his chest. "They're just jealous."

If he was meant to succumb to her feminine wiles, she was going to have to do something considerably more impressive. He flatly replied. "Jealous."

"Of the special attention you've been receiving."

For a half a moment he thought she meant the attention he was receiving from her, then he realized the significance. "I didn't realize that the... special attention was so widely known."

"Those of us with connections at the palace know." The scandalous lean was meant for whispering in his ear, apparently. "Those of us who should know who is coming and going in the presence of his Majesty."

If that was true, it actually presented an excellent opportunity. If only those with close connections to the palace knew he was heading up the investigation, then any assassination attempts would indicate that one of the high families of Espher was responsible. All he had to do was get through the evening without making a scene and the whole thing might be turned to his advantage.

"Thank you for... clarifying our situation. Shall we head in?"

She smiled. "By all means."

Within the widespread doors of the villa, golden light glimmered. The music rose as they covered the last few feet. Rosina was something of a comfort at his side. The warmth of her tethering him to reality as he looked in on a world he never thought he'd experience. Warm—right up until the moment she channeled a shade and became deathly chill to the touch.

Time seemed to slow as he turned to glance at her. The air around her thickened and rippled as she wove a protective cushion around herself. He clamped his teeth together like he'd been trained, just before the impact knocked him from his feet.

The golden glow. The sky. The mosaic. The golden glow. The sky. The mosaic.

Artemio tumbled end over end before finally rolling back to his feet. His cloak tattered beyond saving. His head, tucked down into his chest by the initial blow, thankfully cushioned from harm.

Even so, he came up dizzy with his two shades whipping around him in a tempest, just begging to be let in. To protect him.

He silenced them with a jerk of his hand. They came when he called. Not when his heart beat too fast.

To buy time to think, he let his mouth run. "That was rude."

A man came bustling out, about five years Artemio's senior. A student of the House who he'd never crossed paths with thanks to that gap in age. Finely dressed, but finely dressed in clothing loose enough to allow him to dance around laterally as well as in a waltz. Fine clothes to fight in. When he shouted, it was for the plaza to hear, not Artemio.

"How dare you lay hand on my fiancée?"

There it was. The reason Rosina had latched on. The excuse to attack him that even he could not deny. All before he'd even stepped into the home of the Anatra family and received their hospitality and protection. It had been slickly executed, well conceived, and it had already failed.

Artemio didn't even trouble himself to look at his assailant, not when he could already make out Harmony elbowing her way through the crowd. She was going to involve herself, and the delicate social mores crystallized around them would shatter and people would die. Harmony most likely among them. He could not let this happen.

A second shadow flitted out from him and Bisnonno Fiore leapt from the solid ground of his being to catch Harmony by the hair. Hissing in her ear, "Stop."

She had never known the old king, but the voice still carried as much command now as it had in life. There were few who still held the old king in regard, but those who did, did so with a feverish passion. Worshiping his memory like he were a deity and pouring all their expectations of the man into the shade. They believed that a true king could stop a man with a word, and so Fiore could. Harmony froze in place.

It cost Artemio the time he needed to strike back at his foe. His own shadows betrayed the shade he'd called, giving false warning to the buffoonish would-be killer that Artemio meant to do him harm.

When the next lash of wind struck out, Artemio deflected it with a flash of fire that chased back along the funnel towards the shade that called it. The fiancé's finely tailored sleeves caught alight before he could loosen his grip on whatever weather shade he'd managed to master. The crowd was not thinning despite the danger. Dinner and a show at the Anatra Spring Ball.

By the time the man had beaten the flames out, Artemio had his next move prepared. "Excuse me, sir, I do not know you. Is this meant to be a challenge?"

Both a goad and a question in one. It had the desired effect. "I walk out to find you caressing my future wife and you think I will let it stand!?"

A dart of air, invisible to the naked eye. Sharp as a razor. Caught in another flare of flame belched out from the forge spirit Artemio had tamed beneath the broken tower on the Cut. It loved to burn more than anything else.

"A duel then?"

"To the death."

Artemio grinned. He had him. "Then might I ask what you mean by calling shades against me? If I am the challenged party, do I not have the choice of weapon?"

The crowd inside had pressed up to the doorway now, nudging Harmony aside and forcing Artemio's challenger out into the evening air. He was a truly unimpressive-looking character. Weak of chin, but hiding it with a whiskery little beard.

With surprise on his side, he might have taken Artemio in the initial rush, but their plan had been too reliant on making announcements to assure the gathered nobles that the murder was justified.

Now he was flustered and red-faced, fumbling at his belt for a rapier. "You'd rather I slit you open then? I have no trouble with slaughtering a cur whichever way it must be done."

This fool wanted it to be theatrical, and who was Artemio to deny a man his dying wish. "If it is my choice, then I choose teeth."

There was a ripple of laughter that the fiancé took to be mockery. He flushed red once more. "I say, choose a weapon or I shall…"

"Teeth. I did not stutter or slur my words. I choose teeth. If you want my blood, then you must taste it." He unfastened his cloak and cast it to the ground. "Come on then, if you have the courage of your convictions. Come and take a bite of me."

Artemio's words silenced any laughter or muttering now. The fiancé took a step towards him and Artemio opened his mouth. Not to speak, but to show he was willing. The man standing against him dithered on the spot. It was one thing to cut a man down or set your shades on him, but actually fighting, like an animal. It was beneath a man of good breeding. Obviously. Artemio could almost see these arguments fluttering around in the fool's head, unvoiced. His mouth flapped. His fists clenched, and to the absolute delight of the crowd, he stomped his foot and spun on his heel. Trailing off as he pushed his way back into the house, "If you aren't going to take this seriously…"

The circus act was completed to everyone's satisfaction. They all had their story to tell when they got home, or to anyone who was out of favor and missed an invite to the big event. Although judging by the heaving bodies within the villa, there couldn't be many of those.

Artemio bent to retrieve his ruined cloak, thought better of it, and then turned the motion into a stilted bow to where Rosina still stood, stunned and silent. She hustled off after her future husband with all haste, assuming she could still face marrying the coward after such a pathetic display.

For a moment, Artemio waited. Waited to see who would break ranks, amble over, and offer him something in the way of congratulations. Who would be the first to publicly out themselves as a friend to him, and by unfortunate extension, his family? As it turned out, nobody.

He stood there until the crowd grew bored and moved back inside. The flow of bodies around him continued. It was as though there had been no attempted murder mere moments before. Polite society at its finest.

Finally, when everyone had shuffled away from the scene, only Harmony was left. His only companion, as she always had been. She mouthed something to him, but with his blood still thumping he didn't have the concentration to decipher it. He waved her away with a smile.

Still she lingered, risking with every moment yet more attention being drawn to her. He'd given her the perfect opportunity to slip inside unseen and unconnected to him, thanks to all of these amateur dramatics, and she was squandering it.

By the same token, he could not follow his instinct and beat an immediate retreat to lick his wounds and ponder over the significance of the botched assault on his person. He could not abandon Harmony here in this den of jackals. No matter how much faith he might have in her abilities. Not when there were some who'd risk so open a move against him, just for existing.

He drew in a deep breath and considered his options. With an even more painfully forced smile, he waved her off again. She went, glancing back at him all the way and bumping right into someone else. She slipped into a conversation from the apology, then headed off with her new friends into the house proper. This was the world she was meant for.

The kings had not realized it when they gave him his task, but the situation really was a win for him however it panned out. If he succeeded and survived, he became the lord he was always meant to be and society would be forced to accept him—and Harmony as part and parcel. But if he failed and died, she would be free. She'd be free of her obligation to him, free to be the person she deserved to be instead of lingering in the periphery of his existence.

At one of the outbuildings, he took an opened but untouched bottle of wine from out of a servant's gloved hand before they could pour it wastefully into a glass for some sycophant. He took a glance at the label before knocking back a mouthful. A 107 red, heavy and full-bodied. Perfect to get angrily drunk with.

If he made it into the house itself, then his safety would be assured by the Anatra family and the laws of hospitality, yet for some reason he could not bring himself to walk through those doors. Part of it was the hope that Harmony might still fulfill her part in the quest if he were not there to interfere, but a part of it, he had to admit, was stubbornness. If he went inside, it would be an admission that he needed the blanket protection afforded to all. Perhaps he did, but announcing it rankled him.

The true assassins had no issue with disrupting the polite rules of society, so it was not as though his life was any safer if he accepted the Anatras' protection for this one night. Not if the secret of his visit with the kings was not out. He would be guarding his back against the waiting knives of everyone with a grudge against his father.

Since the very beginning of this entire mess, Artemio had a plan in his back pocket he had hoped he would never have to resort to—outing himself as the investigator, claiming he was close to a resolution, and then waiting for the inevitable attack to come so he might interrogate his would-be killer. While the methodology of the murders had not yet been established, Artemio still clung to his confidence that his talent with shades would allow him to sidestep the consequences.

The targets were being carefully chosen and selected to avoid those who could channel shades, so it stood to reason that the assassins' choices were being informed by some protection that the Shadebound held against their machinations.

Yet what he had never considered was the situation he was in now—someone entirely ignorant of his current assignment from the throne coming for him with lethal intent. Rosina knew the kings had entertained him, she would have told her fiancé, yet so open a move as this assault could not be the work of the assassins to date. It was too clumsy. They would not have lasted this long if operating with such foolishness. It had to be the work of some other party so fearful of the return of the Volpe family to a position of influence that it was worth feigning ignorance over the king's returning favor, and some small part of their ire at losing them another agent. There would be no shortage of those. Father had seen to that.

Filtering out all of the others who wished him ill before such time as his investigations became public knowledge would be a challenge in itself. Not everyone would be so brash as whoever put Rosina's beau up to his attempt.

So it was that Artemio made his way to the side of the great courtyard between the houses and settled on the edge of a marble flowerpot with his wine bottle in hand. There he sat as the night drew on, watching those grand lords and ladies who insisted on arriving late so their entrance might be observed by as many as possible.

Duchesses and dukes from all corners of the kingdom had gathered here in the city for Gemmazione and would not make their departure until towards the end of the arid summer season. Traveling in the morning and the evening to avoid the worst of the heat to ensure they were back in plenty of time to oversee the labor of their peasantry when the harvest was upon them. Not to help, of course, but to ensure none of them slacked. It was a well-known aphorism among the landed gentry that just as a watched kettle never boiled, an unwatched peasant never worked.

He drank and he scowled and he sneered at anyone fool enough to make eye contact with him. In short, he made a spectacle of himself. An obnoxious display he considered to be both beneath him and necessary. One way or another, he needed to put all of the unrelated threats down. Inside the house, in the swirl of the ball, any number of the noble families might have approached him and made their intentions about his future known. They could have done it in absolute anonymity, winning him over to them without running any risk of political backlash. Out here, they had to be seen to support him.

Not one person had come over to congratulate him when he diffused the duel without bloodshed. Not one had cried out in his defense when a botched attempt was made on his life. The silence had been deafening, and he needed it to end. If even one other family showed an interest in him, then it could be leveraged into protection against the rest. There was a complex web of alliances among the different houses, bound by marriages and common interests, and even the least of them could offer up more protection than his own through the right plucking on that web. Even if they weren't actively trying to protect him, his association with them would suggest that an attempt on his life may be an affront to that family, and since the greater families often used the lesser ones in their thrall as cat-paws in these games, there was no telling how large a sleeping bear might be stirred.

The hours rolled on. Artemio's wine bottle emptied out to bitter dregs and he set it aside. All the aches of his tumble earlier now crept up to haunt him, blending with the strange hollow feeling of trading away fragments of his life to the shades to make his mood even more grim. They were really going to leave him out here to hang.

A servant cautiously approached with another bottle of red balanced carefully on a silver tray, and with nothing else to keep off the evening chill, Artemio reached for it. Upon the tray were notes. A half dozen of them in all. None bearing an official seal, but every one of them indubitably from one of the houses trying to curry his favor moving forward.

The Anatras would be one of the note-scribblers, of course. The invitation to the ball could be denied as a mistake if necessary, and there were always arguments to be made that a party was not complete without some scoundrel causing trouble, allowing for the invitation of said scoundrel without any loss of face. Still, Artemio felt certain they were well connected and conniving enough to be in the know before the Aquilas at least. Or at least cunning enough that they would not have been manipulated into inviting him by some third party without seeing some direct benefit. He could trust in them to be tacitly on his side while offering nothing. That was more or less the reason they had accumulated such wealth, power, and station in the city to begin with. Playing all sides and taking none.

He gathered up the notes from off the tray, after carefully retrieving the wine and giving thanks to the serving boy. Pristinely human in his livery. For a moment the boy dithered on the spot, as though he were waiting for a reply to the bundle of notes, then he leaned in close and whispered, "There is one true king."

It was an innocuous enough statement in most places. Even in Espher it was hardly sedition to claim that but one of the Cerva twins was the true ruler and the other a placeholder. But spoken here, to Artemio, it had a weight to it.

Artemio looked from the servant's solemn face to glance around the courtyard to make sure nobody else was listening in. None of the smattering of nobles passing through would dare to look this way, and they had swerved well clear of this whole side of the courtyard. The servants, though. Some of them were looking over at Artemio with that very same expression on their faces. Somewhere between concern and admiration. He didn't know what to do with that information.

Feeling awkward, he turned back to his notes. He had the list of names he required should his investigation be abruptly cut short. A laundry list of the rich and powerful of Espher, every one of them too cowardly to show open support for him but quite willing to court his favor now they'd found a way around that impediment.

Here was all the effusive praise he'd deserved for resolving the duel without bloodshed, the thanks for attending despite the circumstances, the praise for undertaking so onerous and dangerous a task for kings and country. Every letter written in the same stilted formal speech, the words blending together from one to the next in their oppressive similarity. By the end, he could scarcely recall who had written what. There was no clever cipher or secret message here, just tentative outreach to a potential ally.

Far from where he held court, dancers began to pour out from the main house, the festivities finally raucous enough that they could no longer be contained by walls. The music seemed to follow them out as the servants scattered, and it was enough to make Artemio glance up in confusion before he spotted more musicians tucked away among the shrubs.

No eyes turned his way, but he was most certainly being observed from the periphery of the dancers' vision. It did not matter that they looked half in their cups and lost to the dance, that was a simple lie for the nobility. His continued presence was noted, his refusal of the Anatras' protection mentally filed away, and the notes he had received observed. At this distance, the seals and contents could not be deciphered, only the volume of them.

With a start, Artemio realized this stack of letters might prove more valuable than any number of polite conversations in plain sight. If he had been approached in person, then the parameters of his relationship to each of the other houses would have been clearly defined. But by refusing to commit, the nobles courting him had given him something much more dangerous. The contents of those letters were unknown. The writers unknown, beyond their presence at this very ball. He could be an ally to any house. From the grandest to the smallest.

He went through them again, not actually reading anything, but giving everyone the opportunity to see him reading them. Making sure to smile as he folded each one in turn and tucked it into his jacket.

The imbecile fiancé would be the last attempt on him unrelated to the assassinations. Of that he was certain.

It was more than he could have hoped to achieve when the evening began, and with Harmony off conducting her own investigations in relative anonymity, he considered his time on duty to be officially over. The Anatra cellars were cold and deep, full of wines of such vintage that the kings themselves could scarcely have asked for better. It was time to get back to the serious business of drinking them dry.

11

SHIELD OF VIRTUE

Gemmazione, Regola Dei Cerva 112

The winter rains gave way to spring rains. The difference barely noticeable to two poor travelers on foot. They gave Kagan an excuse to keep his hood up at least. An excuse he had to use more and more often as they moved deeper into inhabited territory. The wild lands of the north gave way to smooth rolling hills of carefully cultivated fields and orchards.

Roads had given them swift passage down to this dangerous place, away from the wild places the civilized feared, but now they led through towns and they were peppered with wagons and carriages and eyes. Always Kagan felt them on him. Not a real awareness like he felt from the horses, but an imagining that lay as heavy on him as the load on his back.

The girl could no longer be called a girl, in all honesty. She was a grown woman now thanks to the years that the day they did not speak of had taken from her. He'd hoped the harshness of the road might have thinned her back down to a girlish shape, but as her muscles grew taut and her belt buckle tightened, it only emphasized how much she'd changed. He did not care for it. Still, he could not deny that Orsina's old fire was still within this new shape.

Kagan truly believed the strain of travel might have killed the girl, yet here she was, still bounding along at his side, keeping to his pace despite his longer stride, and carrying enough breath to chatter on throughout the day despite it all. Even the rain seemed to stop troubling her after the first week while it still sank into him until he felt like his muscles were cold blubber. Everything they saw had to be observed, commented on, explained. He found himself tiring long before she did.

The only solace of her constant chatter was that he did not need to keep such careful watch through the day. If a rider was approaching, she'd have twenty questions about it before they were close enough to see. If there was a walled town up ahead, she'd be asking about the flags flapping on its ramparts. He couldn't have asked for a better scout.

Towns, they skirted around, but travelers they could no longer afford to avoid if they meant to make any progress. Oxen drew carts at half the pace a man could walk. Trains of farmers heading to market turned the paved stretches between the fields into vast dawdling social gatherings despite the inclement weather. Kagan's hood stayed up.

Those nights when they could, they'd taken shelter in outhouses and barns, unnoticed and leaving before dawn so the owners could make no complaint. The few times they'd been spotted by ill luck, Kagan had been forced to slink back into the shadows and let Orsina do the talking. That she was so young and guileless paid dividends. Nobody believed she could be doing anything untoward, and the story of their trek to the city—once carefully stripped of its reason—was a familiar one.

Kagan used her as a shield through all their long walk south, resenting her chatter but dreading its end too. He had not meant to become attached to this girl. He had not meant to care for her like she was his own. Every day, he was forced to remind himself that she was a monster, a slayer, the most wicked of all who walked the earth, but so far from home he found even that fundamental truth seemed weaker. The dull pain he felt when he looked at her was less about her sin and more about the day when he would turn back north and never see her again.

That day crept closer with every step.

Where there were more people, Kagan lost more control of their situation. When they got close enough to see the rise to Covotana, the roads

had grown dense and packed. They could not skirt around the crowd. There
was no escape. They moved with the farmers and traders. Orsina drifted
away from him and back as they shuffled along with all the other peasantry,
and for the first time Kagan was forced to really contend with how far
he had fallen from grace. In any Arazi settlement, this crowd would have
parted for him, flung themselves in the ditch to make way for a man of
his stature, just as these people would part for a cavalier on horseback. He
tugged his hood lower over his face and thanked the skies for foul weather.

Eyes everywhere. Eyes on him, studying him from behind bow-slits on
guard towers. Eyes of farmers, wide and fearful of his size. Of merchants,
taking measure of his clothes, his worth. One wrong step and he could
die here. All it would take was for one of them to draw attention and he
was doomed.

He nearly did their work for him when a soft hand closed around
his claws. He almost leapt away before he realized it was Orsina. "Nearly
through."

The low rumble of his laugh started in his chest before he caught it.
She was comforting him. He was delivering her into some nightmare life
of servitude to the necromancers of Espher, and she was trying to calm
him like a spooked wyvern.

Unchallenged, they moved beneath the walls of the city. An impossible show of overconfidence, or perhaps just a necessity with so many
bodies moving through the pinch of the gates. If all were stopped and
questioned, crops would rot in the wagons and the tail of the queue would
expire of old age.

When they stepped out into Covotana, it was all the two of them
could do to keep from gaping. Neither one had seen a city like this before.
For all that he was worldly, Kagan had never dared approach any town
in Espher, and there was nowhere beyond the steppes like this. There was
nothing like this anywhere else in the world.

White plaster and marble statuary rose up from terra-cotta streets.
Water flowed everywhere, from fountains, from rooftops, through gut-

ters, fresh and bright even as all the mud of the road was tracked in. At the center of it all, the palace rose like a shining pinnacle of achievement, impossible for the younger kingdoms and empires of the world to match.

It was easy to forget how long Espher had stood. While the Arazi still painted their faces with the blood of their kin and rode wyverns across the wild north, brawling in tribes, squabbling over who got to gnaw the bones of their hunts, Espher had built a tower into the sky. The foundations had been laid before the first dragon was tamed, but more than that, what had been built atop those foundations had stood unchanged through all the generations that followed.

There was beauty here in the city. Not the natural beauty that Kagan held above all others, but something close. Something human but rebuilt and grown over so many times that the artifice had been worn away. Until the city had become a natural place that change washed over. A mountain made by hand.

Away from the crowd, Kagan suddenly found himself lost with no sign of a landmark or star to guide him. It fell to Orsina to lead him by the hand once more, and she did, through markets packed to bursting and streets of houses stacked atop one another until they blocked out the sky, until the bowl of the city became the whole world and even sound could not escape it. Voices echoing back and forth until Kagan became convinced this was the necromancy he'd always been warned the Espher practiced. The voices of those long gone, still echoing.

To cross the distance of the city on the open road would have taken them a few hours at most. Through the tangled warren of streets, parks, dead ends, twists, and turns, it took them the rest of the day and into the evening before the House of Seven Shadows even came into sight.

Of all the sights Orsina had relentlessly described as they made their way through the city, this was perhaps the least striking. She said nothing at all once she realized which building they were looking up at, and as they approached the gates, and the servant standing waiting by those gates, it seemed her voice had failed her entirely.

Kagan had seen fear take men's voices like that before, but he'd never expected it of the girl who faced down a dragon empty-handed. He reached down and caught her hand. "You don't need to go any farther. There will be other ways to manage your... problem."

She shook her head and forced a smile. "This is where I'm meant to be."

"Where you want to be is where you're meant to be."

"I get what you're doing, and I appreciate it, but..." She stared up at the building beyond the gardens, looming low against the night sky but casting such a long shadow he worried she might drown in it. "There's no way out of this. I am still going to be what I am. Whether I'm here or anywhere else."

He let her hand go and approached the servant on sentry duty, letter brandished. If she meant to move fast and leave her fears behind her, he would not stand in her way. Even if their haste brought parting ever closer.

Some sort of relay began as they watched, one servant running the letter to another farther into the grounds, on and on, all the way up to the House itself, where a blindfolded servant in plain dark grey livery came to carry it away. Time ticked by. Kagan was painfully aware of the girl standing shaking at his side. Of the servant, studying his face, his hands. Eyes pressing at him again. He could not wait to be free of this beautiful city and all its inquisitive citizens.

When someone came from the house, it was the Prima herself. A stately woman garbed in the same greys as the servants, severe, with her hair drawn back into a high, artful mound of curls. A servant walked along the side of the path, holding out a parasol to keep the rain from touching her.

Until the final moment, the Prima's face was that of every other noble Kagan had ever met, and he was ready to snatch up Orsina and run, but as the Prima stepped into the light of the street lanterns, a thin-lipped smile appeared. "You have chosen a most fortuitous night to arrive in our company. We have more students absent than present. Attending the Spring Ball."

She held up the letter and addressed Orsina. "You are spoken of very highly. Your skill as a binder of shades has been compared here to some of the finest students of this great institution. The only question I have is who, exactly, this Aceta Madre actually is."

Kagan and Orsina glanced at each other in confusion. "I was to be her apprentice…"

"Yes, I have heard all about what a swift study you are, I just do not know who you studied under." Prima Cicogna flapped the letter out like a courtesan's fan. "She writes to me as a peer, yet I have not a clue as to her education, lineage, or indeed your own provenance."

Orsina frowned. "I'm from the Selvaggia, I mean, Sheepshank."

When that did nothing to illuminate the teacher, Kagan added in his bass rumble, "At the foot of the steppes."

That only seemed to exasperate the Prima more. "But what line were you born of, child? Who were the shade binders of your family?"

"What?" Orsina cocked her head to one side, as though the odd-shaped thought might fit in better at a different angle. "They were farmers?"

The Prima let out a titter. "You surely jest. Both of them?" She leaned in closer, speaking softer. "Listen to me, child, this is a place of learning, not a place of judgment. If you were born on the wrong side of the sheets…"

"I wasn't!" Orsina bleated in surprise, head snapping around to Kagan. "Was I?"

He shrugged helplessly.

"My dear child, the binding of shades is a hereditary blessing passed down through the noble families of Espher. A gift from our ancestors. Farmers do not receive that gift."

Kagan shrugged again when no answer was forthcoming. "She's got it."

"Worry not, my dear." The Prima placed a comforting hand on Orsina's shoulder, then lifted it clear when she felt how crusted the girl's cloak actually was. "This is far from the first time in the history of this institution that we have encountered a student of unclear provenance. We shall simply fabricate some lesser-known House for you until such time as you are wed into a greater one."

Once more Kagan found himself growling involuntarily. "Wed?"

The Prima held up her hands with a light laugh. "Or adopted, if that is the course that she chooses to take. If she has the capabilities this letter claims, there shall be an abundance of noble houses desperate to make her theirs. I should not worry."

Orsina had been so thrown by everything she'd faced so far, the fire at her core seemed to have been tamped down. With the challenge hidden in the Prima's words, Kagan saw it flare back to life. "I do."

"Well, my dear, why don't you allow me to be the judge of that. Come inside and we shall test you as all our new students are tried." She moved to put an arm around Orsina's shoulders, then thought better of it. Calling back over her shoulder as she headed back up to the House, "Your servant may depart, if he too is so confident in your talent."

Kagan could still feel the weight of all the city's eyes upon him. He needed to be gone from this place as fast as his legs could carry him. Crouching down until he was nose-to-nose with Orsina, he rumbled, "Take care of yourself, girl."

She lunged for him, and he fully expected the usual slug in the shoulder before her attack resolved itself into a hug. "You too."

The bounce was back in her step when she set off after the Prima. Diving headfirst into the long shadow of the House. Kagan watched her for longer than he meant to. Planning all the while to turn and leave. Telling himself it was foolish to be hung up on sentiment. That sentiment would get him killed, standing around just to watch the girl go.

He dragged himself off into the night streets the moment she was out of sight. Moving just a little faster than was advisable after so long standing still. It was like passing through a dense forest, or the tunnels in which they sometimes found basilisk burrowed into chalky hills. Kagan hated it, but he pressed on all the same. The long curving road where the House of Seven Shadows had nestled gave way to the warren and then to what Kagan would have called a real city, the slums. The size that had made him stand out so badly among farmers and traders kept him safe here. Eyes peered out of the shadows, but they passed over him smooth as the rainwater.

He'd be marching all through the night to get clear of the city gates come dawn, but it would be worthwhile to be out into air untainted by the breath of a hundred others. He was so caught up in his mad dash for freedom that he scarcely noticed the guardsmen closing off every entrance to the square where he'd stumbled until he'd almost reached their line. "Dragon-lord. What brings you to our city in the dead of night?"

Kagan backed away slow, hands lifted up from his sides so even in the dim light they could see he had no weapons. Or at least none in hand. "I've no dragon, my friends, and my business was just that. Business. Had a delivery to make."

The guard who was speaking stepped out of line, closing in on Kagan. Confident with his men at his back. "Spying are you?"

"No, sir." Kagan stared down at the man's feet. He'd met plenty of men like this through his years. All noise and swagger, just desperate to swing their petty power around and get the respect they had in no way earned but were entirely convinced they deserved. "Just passing through, sir."

The man was close enough that even over the city's background chatter, Kagan could actually hear him smile. "That's just what the last spy said too."

Kagan had judged him wrong. "Shit."

Kagan was sluggish from all his days on the road. His hunting instincts turned to mush with inaction. His fist caught the guard under the chin and lifted him clean off his feet.

There was no point in running when every exit was blocked, all he'd do would be to burn through the precious little strength he had left. Instead, he put his head down and charged the closest line of guards. All he had to do was break through and run. If this was all the personal crusade of one unconscious guard intent on aggrandizing himself at the expense of others, he'd be able to stroll right out of the city.

Clubs swung down to meet him. Hammering into his broad back. Knocking him to his knees. Human bones would have broken under the cudgels. He was made of sterner stuff.

Roaring, he came up into their legs and bowled them over. Still they were swinging, raining down blow after blow. He did not stop. He did not flinch.

The slap of boots on the paved road warned him that the other guardsmen were closing in. Kagan had to push through now or they were going to take him. He had never been captured, except when he handed himself over for the judgment of his kinfolk. He had never been tortured, for it had never been necessary. All of these things he knew of only from stories. Stories he had no desire to live out.

Up on his feet, his legs coiled beneath him, ready to leap and bound free of the tangle of bodies and bludgeons. That was when the closest guards leapt on his back and carried him down to meet the ground once more. Feet and clubs. Pain digging down through all the layers of ridged bone and scaled skin, until finally, blessedly, Kagan felt nothing more.

12

TRIAL BY ORDEAL

If she looked back, she would break and run. All of her life was there behind her. Everything she knew and loved. Even if she wanted to, she could not think about it. There were tests ahead, and not just the ones this old woman had planned. It felt like the two of them were speaking in a different language from each other. Even though they used the same words, the same inflections, everything meant something different.

When the woman the servants called "Prima" asked about family, it was like she was one of the shepherds trying to work out what Orsina's wool would be worth at market. When she asked about the journey, she had expected a list of towns, inns, and houses where Orsina had been made a guest. Not stories of rain and forests and sleeping in barns. Despite her age, the Prima's face bore few of the marks of time. Yet every time Orsina answered one of her questions as fully and politely as she could, a little wrinkle appeared between the old woman's eyes. She was getting it all wrong somehow. Her answers grew shorter and shorter, until she was barely saying enough to answer at all. Always Mother Vinegar had told her she talked too much, now she was paying the price. What would happen when they rejected her? Could she find her way back to the forest? Would the shades devour her as Mother Vinegar had said?

She was shaken from her reverie at the sight of the entrance ahead. Everywhere in the city there had been the same pale wood, yellow-orange even in the dim light that filtered down from on high. Yet these looming doors would not have looked out of place in the deep forest. Soot-blackened and solid and, above all, old.

The whole building felt old to Orsina, old the way the Selvaggia had, or more properly, old the way Ginny Greenteeth had. She stopped for a moment on the threshold. The House felt more solid than all the rest of the city. More real. The Prima was saying something, but Orsina couldn't hear her over the echoing presence of the building before her.

"Sorry, what was that?"

The same sly smile that had appeared on the Prima's face down by the gates was back. "Is something occupying your thoughts, girl?"

Orsina blushed. "I'm sorry. I didn't mean to get distracted. It is just. The building is…"

"Six

of power are bound within. That is what gives our House its name. The natural shadow is cast by the building itself, but the other six, they fill this place as they would a shade binder." The Prima leaned in closer, her gaze scraping over Orsina's face for any hint or clue. "Do you hear them, girl? Do they call to you?"

The first test came so swiftly that Orsina might not have even noticed it if not for the pressure of the Prima's stare. She closed her eyes for a moment, wondering if she'd be turned away before she even got inside, then decided on honesty. She shook her head. "No. I can feel… something. But I don't hear them."

All the Prima said in return was, "Curious."

The servant who had accompanied them all the way along the path with his parasol held high over them, his back getting drenched by the rain, was holding a long silk handkerchief out to her, but the Prima placed a hand on his wrist. "I don't believe that will be necessary."

He frowned under his own blindfold, but quietly obeyed, folding the handkerchief back up and tucking it back onto a shelf by the door. The Prima beckoned Orsina forward.

When she stepped over the threshold, it was like she'd stepped into a bubble of silence. All the chatter of the living fell away. She hadn't even realized how much it was weighing on her until it was gone. She smiled at the Prima and was quietly thrilled to receive one in return. "Those who lack our gift find themselves overwhelmed by the shades that reside here. The visions that are presented to them are... unsettling. Many lose their minds. Yet here you stand unbent and unbroken."

"So you believe me now?"

"My dear girl, I had no doubts." Once more the Prima reached out as if to put an arm around Orsina then rethought it. "This is simply the procedure our new students must pass through."

Orsina's brows furrowed. "What if I'd heard them?"

"Then, my dear, you would have been on par with the vast majority of the students when they first arrive, untrained and unprepared for the challenges this place brings. If you could hear their voices, then you would still be vulnerable to them." They moved through the atrium and into the main part of the building, layers upon layers of balconies lining the floors above them while the central fountain cast a cloud of mist up towards the grand skylight atop the House. "From your mistress's letter, I am to understand you have been taught to ward off such intrusions. I am pleased to find there was no exaggeration."

"Mother Vinegar wouldn't..." Orsina paused, trying desperately to reframe her usual expletive-riddled descriptions of the old woman as something that someone polite could swallow. "Getting praise from her is like wringing oil from an olive pip."

Another thin-lipped smile. Like Orsina had let her down again but she was too polite to say anything. "Charming."

They moved on through the mists and down into a stairwell, rounding a wood-paneled corner and unveiling just how little of the House could be seen from the surface. Just as there were tiered balconies stretching up to the roof of the building above, so too were there layers upon layers down here beneath the ground, carved into the bubbled volcanic earth and polished with centuries of footsteps until they were as smooth as marble, illuminated by a massive chandelier dangling down in a mirrored position to the fountain above.

Orsina could not help but move over to the edge and look down. As above, so below. At the bottom of the building was a midnight-dark pool where the skylight had been on the roof of the building above. She jumped when the Prima spoke at her shoulder.

"Residential suites are in the upper building, as are the halls where our theoretical lectures are conducted, but the practical exercises are best unobserved by outsiders." She smiled at Orsina's wide-eyed expression. "It is here that you will meet your real teachers. The six shades bound here are as different from one another as they are powerful. As you learn to master them, so too shall you master your own gifts."

It felt like something was expected of her, so Orsina did her best to sound confident, even as she came to realize just how thoroughly she was out of her depth. "Sounds easy enough."

"Spoken with all the vigor and ignorance of youth. Do you know how many of our students graduate each year as masters? I can count them upon my own two hands this year." The Prima strode off, shaking her head, and Orsina had to hustle after her or risk being left behind. "The majority of my students shall leave with little more control of their gifts than you have already exhibited in resisting the call of the shades."

They rounded the corner at the end of the row and descended another stairwell, this one turning away from that central chamber and out along a corridor that could more rightly be called a tunnel. A tunnel carved through the solid stone in a perfect circle. Still the Prima chattered on as if there were nothing unusual about any of it. "It is… a disappointment to me, but far from a surprise. Make no mistake, your gift may be an innate birthright of those who should rule, but that does not mean the path to control of it will be as simple. It requires work. Real, hard work. Something I find the spoiled children of the great houses often flinch from. It is my hope that your unique circumstances might provide you with some measure of impetus."

Orsina forced herself to ask, even though she could feel shame prickling at her cheeks. "Impetus?"

The Prima tittered. "Drive, my dear. Ambition. The desire to succeed and the will to pursue it. It is my hope that you are ready and willing to put in the work required to make something of yourself."

Every step they took seemed to draw sweat to Orsina's brow now. As though they had been walking for hours instead of minutes. Some of it was the ever-climbing temperature, but most of it was the effort she had to exert just to hold back the pressure that seemed to have encircled her head. "Prima, where are we going?"

"You, my dear? You are going for a bath. While I am going to try to find something that will fit you among the clothing that has been abandoned here through the years." She sighed and stopped dead. Spinning on a heel to face Orsina again for the first time since they'd delved beneath the earth. "If you wish to be accepted as a student in this institution, then you must appear to belong here. Your manners, your... brackish speech, these things we can train you out of, and they can be masked in the short term by isolation and silence, but your presentation, your dress, and your... aroma... must be addressed at once."

A splash of mud on her skirts had never troubled Orsina, but even she had to admit that her traveling clothes were in a fairly foul state after almost a full season on the road. "I've smelled better."

The tight-lipped smile returned once more. "One can only hope."

There were dozens of doors on either side of the passage, every one of them unmarked but for the trail of wax from the candles burning on their lintels. How anyone navigated around the House of Seven Shadows was entirely beyond Orsina. At the end of the line, she was ushered through to another chamber of that same smooth black stone where the heat was almost unbearable and more steam filled the air, leaving her almost blind but for the circular golden glow of candles somewhere farther in. "I assume that you can bathe without assistance?"

"There are folk who can't?!" Orsina's jaw dropped.

"You would be surprised, my dear girl." The door creaked shut, swollen with all the moisture in the air. "I shall return shortly."

Then Orsina was alone with her thoughts. For the first time in as long as she could remember, she was alone. No strangers. No Mother Vinegar. No Kagan. Nobody but her. Her and the ache in her head. It must have been the steam, doing something to her head. Making it feel like some great beast was stepping on her skull. The only way out was through. She took careful steps forward into the steam, feeling her way with her boot-caps.

The bath sloped up out of the floor in a smooth curve, completely unlike the tin baths that she'd seen back in Sheepshank. She could barely understand what she was feeling until her knees collided with the side and she dipped her hands into the water standing in wait for her.

She leapt back with a cry, the heels of her palms already blossoming with blisters. The bathwater was scalding hot.

A simple mistake, exacerbated by the fog and her own muggy head. She grit her teeth through the pain and moved on. She'd had worse. Feeling around the room, she tried to find some font of cold water so she could bring the heat down and came up with nothing. She returned to the bath at the center of the room and felt around its sides, its upper edges. There had be a way to make it safe for human use. They wouldn't just have a pool of scalding water down here with no purpose.

Orsina's eyes narrowed. The Prima had not said there was a single test before she'd be accepted as a student. She'd said tests. Plural. Once more she held out her hands towards the water, but this time, with painstaking effort, she crept backwards inside her own mind, inside her own space, withdrawing enough that whatever else might dwell here could be heard.

"What little babe comes to dip their toes in my pond?"

Ginny Greenteeth was there in an instant, pressing to get in again. To finish what it had started.

Orsina slammed her walls back up so fast she almost missed the whispers echoing all around her. If she had thought that the Selvaggia was dense with shades, it could not compare to this place. A whole city thrived and died on the doorstep of the House of Seven Shadows, and every dying soul was beckoned here by the gathered shade binders, whether on purpose as a part of their training, or as the natural result of any vacuum. Those that were bound and used served their purposes, those that did not, lingered. A cacophony of shades. More than Orsina had even known existed. They clamored outside of her defenses, desperate and fading. The Prima had promised her six shades, not six thousand. Six, no matter how powerful, might have been managed, but as it stood, Orsina would not even be able to hear them.

Still, she felt more certain than ever that the water in this bath was kept to its scalding heat by some bound shade, and that mastering it was the key to this test. She was shaking. Whether from the effort of holding all the shades at bay, or the shock of hearing Greenteeth's voice scraping over the inside of her skull again. The shaking would not stop despite the blazing heat of the room. It would not stop no matter how sternly Orsina impersonated Mother Vinegar's voice to herself, commanding an end to, "All that silliness, eh?"

How long would it take the Prima to fetch her some clothes? That was the deadline on this puzzle. Orsina forced down her defenses and immediately tasted pond water. Like Greenteeth had never left. She spat a mouthful of it up into the scalding bath with a whimper. "Go away. I don't want you."

"How could we ignore such an offering? Come back to my pool, the water is lovely and cool."

Orsina grit her teeth and pushed against the intruding shade, pushed the way she had when old dead Perlita had lodged in her head by the graveside. It was enough to knock Greenteeth loose. If only for a moment. Enough that Orsina could reach out desperately for whatever else there was to find. Swarms of shades rushed in only to be batted aside; there was something bigger here. Something with enough life within it to burn this hot. The thing that had been crushing her head like a nut between stones since the moment she stepped foot in the House. She reached and she reached, and she could taste the brimstone of the shade. It was down beneath her feet, lurking in some hidden darkness beneath the foundations of this place. Down so far that even the many strata of floors down here couldn't come close to breaching it. In the heart of the dead volcano below the city. She coughed up another mouthful of swamp water.

"Just a touch more, my little dove. Just a drop. For all the help we gave you. For all the times we didn't drown you in your sleep. A little gift."

"Shut up," Orsina growled down into the water. "I'm not trying to talk to you."

"The old spent cinder down beneath won't talk to you, it's sleeping. I'm here for you. I can give you what you need. All I ask in return is…"

Orsina had to drag her voice back down from a bellow. Wouldn't do for the Prima to hear her talking to herself. "Everything. That's all you ask for. Everything. I'm not falling for it again. You'd drain me dry without a second thought. You're a monster."

"When you drink, are you a monster for slaking your thirst?" Orsina actually preferred when Greenteeth tried on her condescension rather than this wheedling. It set her teeth on edge.

This close to the water, the rising steam was reddening Orsina's skin, but she would not flinch. "Nobody dies when I drink."

"When you eat. A belly full of meat. You say there's no death?"

"You took more than I was willing to give." It sounded stupid even to Orsina's own ears. Like a child bleating that the world wasn't fair. Wasn't it true of every shade that they'd take all you let them? The only thing Mother Vinegar had drilled into her about them from the start was that they'd drain anyone dry given the chance. It was the one truly reliable thing about them.

"Could you make this water cold?"

Greenteeth surged right in against the barriers. *"My waters are lovely and cool."* Orsina could feel them. Lapping at her toes. Creeping up her shins with a tickle.

From dry lips, she whispered, "What's the cost?"

There was movement all around her. The steam rolled and rippled as the shade she'd carried with her all the way from the deep forest swished back and forth around the bath. Studying it.

"One hour of your time."

"A minute."

The full weight of Greenteeth's wrath struck her then, like dropping to the bottom of a chill lake from standing safely on the shore. Sudden. Shocking. Not enough to break through. Not nearly enough, especially when Orsina was already bracing for it. Greenteeth strained and pushed and lashed out with all the power it had at its disposal, then finally, it folded.

"A minute then."

It was harder than it should have been to let her walls down again. Hard to trust—not in the shade, which was treacherous and mindless by nature—but in herself. Hard to believe she would not be overwhelmed as she had been before. It was like stepping from a clifftop and hoping that before she hit the ground she would remember how to fly. She did it all the same.

The water was cold when Greenteeth dragged her hands down into it. Chill as the deep pool in the deep forest, so deep and dark you could sink down into it and never return to the surface, bones tangled down in the weeds. But the heat crept back. *"What is this trickery?"*

Orsina grinned, even as swamp water washed out between her teeth. Gurgling, she laughed. "One minute, Ginny Greenteeth, and not a second more."

The water cooled, then heated, then cooled then heated. Over and over the two shades struggled with it. Competing to assert their nature on the pool of otherwise inert liquid. With all of its attention turned to the battle it took little more than a nudge for Orsina to dislodge Greenteeth from where it was nestled inside her.

The water pulsed from hot to cold, hot to cold, but now both sides in the clash were tiring. It could not reach the deep-water chill or the roiling heat that both sides were reaching for. Orsina stripped out of her clothes, ignoring the crack of sweat and mud as she pulled them away. She did not look at herself, because every time she'd caught a glimpse of her own body since the last time Greenteeth rode her, she could not shake the feeling that it was not hers. Scrambling into the bath as fast as she could, she set to scrubbing. The water was hotter than she'd like, but it did not scald her now. It was the work of a few vigorous minutes until she felt like the worst of the filth was gone, and she was doing her best to untangle her hair when the door creaked back open.

The Prima stood framed in the doorway with that same thin-lipped smile fading from her face. In one had she held a bar of soap, in the other, a dress worth more than the village Orsina had grown up in. "You…"

Orsina turned to look at her but said nothing. The steam that had filled the air was all but gone now, hanging in the vaulted ceiling like a cloud overhead, but doing nothing to obstruct their view of each other. The Prima crept closer, under the guise of passing the bar of soap. Her eyes were unfocused, her mind traveling elsewhere.

Eventually, with that same fine line between her brows, she took her place behind Orsina and began washing her hair, as though she were a servant. Orsina had not had her hair washed for her since she was barely old enough to walk. The experience was unsettling. When the Prima spoke, it was soft. "The purpose of this exercise is to teach our new students how little they know. To show them that shades can affect the world in ways they do not need to understand to respect. I have never seen any student… brute-force their way to success in this exercise."

Orsina ducked her chin down to her chest. Shame flushing her cheeks as much as the rising heat. She felt every bit the scolded child. Her voice was like that of a child when she spoke. Small. Scared. "I didn't know what you wanted me to do."

The long silence that followed as the Prima worked soap suds into her hair was agony. But when the Prima spoke, it was not to condemn her. "What you have done here is impressive." Orsina let out the breath she had been holding. Fresh ripples ran across the surface of the bathwater.

The Prima tightened her grip in the girl's hair. "But it was also terribly dangerous. I can see now why you were sent to us. You must not spend your life so… frivolously. To cool bathwater, it is beneath a shade binder to use their gifts for such things."

Orsina had tears in her eyes when she twisted around in the bath, her soaped hair falling limply from the Prima's hands. "It was a test to see if I could stay and learn here. That didn't seem like a waste. That seemed like the most important thing I'd ever done."

"And there it is, the drive." The Prima's face betrayed nothing. But the line between her brows was gone when she reached out and turned Orsina away once more. Resuming her work loosening the tangle of the girl's hair, she said, "You must understand that there is a degree of risk involved here, for myself as well as you. If the families of the other students learned that someone born to less-than-noble parentage were being trained here, it might do irreparable harm to the reputation of this institution. I needed to know if you would be worth that danger."

Orsina spoke up with more confidence than she felt. "And?"

"You are."

13

THE BLADE DANCER

Gemmazione, Regola Dei Cerva 112

It seemed that the taste of corpses would never be washed from Artemio's mouth, no matter how many bottles of wine he had rat-girl fetch up from the palace cellars. He had stopped drinking for brief periods since the attempt on his life, but they had become briefer with each passing day.

The time it took him to attend to his remaining lessons at the House before scurrying back to this crusted den of papers and misery. The time it took him to visit with the families of those he was meant to be avenging. They were universally bewildered by the killings, and if there were some pattern to the dead, then it evaded Artemio as much as it did those who were left to bury the remains.

Those nobles who had discovered the body became hysterical trying to describe the states of their loved ones. Some children looked like a shade had drunk their years since a parent's death a few months past. It was the luxury of the powerful and the comfortable to fall apart when the world went awry. The servants were able to walk him through the shuttered rooms. Lift aside the veils and show him where the bodies were buried. They were the ones to offer up diaries and schedules for cross-examination until Artemio felt like he knew these dead people better than they knew themselves.

The wine helped all of this along, of course. It helped to make the rough edges of each story smoother, the tears more forgettable. It helped him to pretend that the pieces of his puzzle were not pieces of flesh and blood.

"Can't you just stop?"

He was startled out of his reading and drinking when the maid said it. Not so much by the words, but by the tone. The sympathy. He was holding her life hostage and she felt sorry for him. That was a grim indictment of his progress. "No. I can't."

She crept a little closer, tail swishing nervously at the back of her skirts. "It's making you miserable."

"Yes." He sank back in his seat swirling the dregs of the latest glass. "It is."

"You aren't going to find anything. None of the others found anything. All they did was try and then die."

"And I'm sure you'd much prefer I live a long and happy life."

"If you die, I don't…" She sank down onto the seat opposite him. It was far from acceptable behavior for a servant, but their relationship was as far from acceptable as it was possible to be, short of him announcing his intentions to court her before the kings. He barely even noticed. "I don't know what will happen to me."

"Ah yes, my charming little hostage. It would seem that our futures are both tied to my success, long life, and prosperity. Perhaps encouraging me to abandon my post is not in your best interests after all."

She looked affronted, as much as it was possible for someone with the face of a rodent to look affronted. "I wasn't… you're just so… sad."

"An unknown conspiracy of such deftness that it has evaded every hint of pursuit has murdered my mother, along with a whole host of other moderately innocent people." He knocked back the last of the wine and groaned. "I just wasted a fair part of my very limited time left among the living interviewing all the miserable families of all those miserable dead people only to discover they knew nothing more than I do. I need… I need a change."

He hefted himself to his feet and swayed a little. "I need to stop chasing my tail. There is nothing in the old notes or in any of the fresh ones I have scribed for my impending replacement. Even Harmony's extensive spying at the ball turned up nothing of use. I must move forward."

She had startled to her feet too. As if she was going to catch him when he fell. He didn't fall. "What are you going to do?"

A smile found its way onto his face for the first time in days. "I am going to find the one who benefits."

She trailed after him as he snatched up his sword belt and cloak from where he'd cast them aside. "And… what do you want me to do?"

He snapped his fingers at her. "You're going to find out who is engaged to marry Rosina Aquila so I can visit him in his home and beat him to death."

"What?"

"Well, perhaps not to death. Perhaps he will tell me what I want to know while he still has teeth." He paused at the door, turning his head to listen for anyone passing in the hallway. "Get me the name, if you would be so kind. The people at the ball were too polite to mention him after his embarrassment."

When he emerged onto the streets of Covotana, he was startled to meet the dawn. He had been reading and drinking and banging his head against a stone wall all night through, yet exhaustion did not find him. Perhaps it was the wine, perhaps it was his newfound resolve. Either one could have explained away the fire in his belly.

He flagged down a carriage and headed straight for the southern edge of the city. To do what he should have done from the very beginning.

There were few embassies in Covotana, and those that were there could not stand the test of time. There was no place within the ancient city for foreign architecture, and anything outsiders had built was subtly replaced not long after they had vacated the premises.

Only this one embassy stood in Covotana now, a stark, low-slung building without pretension among the bristling gaudiness of the many countinghouses and mercantile guilds that populated this quarter of the city. As much a place of worship as a place of political business.

Within the outer walls of the embassy, before the building could be reached, there was a flat square of green grass, trimmed meticulously short by one of the acolytes who had gathered here in the years since its founding. Not a courtyard like one of the noble houses. Not a flower garden or a miniature farm as most of the merchants would have installed. Just this simple, unostentatious square that said as much as any amount of statuary. In a city where every inch was filled to the walls with life, this space was one of deliberate emptiness.

The gates of the embassy were never closed. The Agrantine welcomed one and all to come and bear witness to the show Artemio was lucky enough to catch the tail end of that morning.

He heard it before he saw it. The singing of the blade through the air. This was not the kind of swordplay that you found in Espher, where the martial arts had given away in recent centuries to reliance upon shade binding. Nor was it the kind of swordplay that showed up on any battlefield throughout history by Artemio's humble reckoning. The only place in all the world that this dance with the blade could be seen was here in this little square of grass, every morning, just after dawn.

There were some things in life that even Artemio had the good manners to stand back and let happen. Things that were too beautiful to spoil for the sake of his convenience.

Ambassador Modesta was a common sight in court. Not particularly beloved by anyone—it was not politically expedient to be seen as a friend to the great beast stirring to the south—but indubitably influential all the same. Yet those who had seen her garbed in the corsetry and dresses of an Espheran noblewoman had not truly seen her. Here she was as she should be. Her shaved head glistening with sweat. Her simple tunic tucked at her belt to keep her legs free for the motions of this dance.

As she was a common sight in court, Artemio had never met her, and as first impressions went, it was difficult to beat the sight of her moving through her training routine. The Agrantine Empire boasted no magic of its own, yet through strength of arms alone, it had gathered together the warring kingdoms of the south, who were in receipt of such gifts from their gods, under one banner all the same.

To a student of history, it seemed unprecedented. Artemio had never been able to make sense of it except by excusing the conquered as lesser kingdoms with lesser magics than Espher could bring to bear. Seeing Modesta move, he understood that he had been wrong. This was the Agrantine magic. This was the power that let them move the proverbial mountains and best people who had ruled for centuries.

Wind parted on the blade's edge, and it sang. A thrumming note Artemio could feel in his teeth. Just a single, simple cut, sword spinning up from her hip to point to the sky above, and already he could see the precision of each movement. Artemio was not the most gifted of swordsmen, but he had been trained by better and had watched those with both the skill and the talent learn how to use the lethal tool that hung from every nobleman's belt. They flowed like water from move to move, from parry to thrust to riposte.

This was nothing like that.

The sword seemed a living thing in her hands, twisting and spinning and cutting the air with a whine. Arcing and flashing all around her as it seemed Modesta barely moved at all. Gliding gracefully through her own motions as the blade did all of the work.

It was almost impossible to follow everything she did. Every part of her was in motion, and every time he thought he could predict which way the sword would turn next, he was surprised. Glancing away to the awestruck peasantry and then back again, Artemio realized that his own training with the sword was making the display harder to follow rather than easier. He was looking for specific movements. The high guard, the lunge, the graceful footwork of an expert duelist, and none of them were there—or rather, they were there, but subsumed into other motions. There were no moves in her routine, there was only one, from start to finish, without thought, hesitation, or pause. Just relentless progress. Breath drawn in, violence exploding out. Step by step, breath by breath, every movement measured and lethal and perfect.

This was what his father had feared.

At the end of the display, there was a gentle patter of applause from the gathered crowd. Nobody could say that the common folk of Covotana did not appreciate free entertainment, even when they had to crawl out of their beds in the early hours to see it. At first Artemio almost snorted at the sight of a street vendor with a portable cart offering thimblefuls of coffee, but then he thought better of it and bought a shot before strolling through the gates.

Modesta had settled herself on a bench at the far end of the green to oil her steel. In the south it would have been quite unremarkable, but here it was set apart by the blade, much thicker than the sharpened needles that duelists and bravos loved to whip about, and sharpened on both sides for cutting. She looked up from her work at his approach. "Have you come to spar with me?"

He let out a nervous chuckle despite himself. "I suspect it would be a very short bout."

"Not at all, Lord Volpe. I hear that you acquit yourself well when pushed. Did you come here for me to push you?" Her mimicry of the Espheran language was flawless and unaccented, but the insistence on ending every utterance with a question marked her as Agrantine. It was considered politeness there to never fully close a conversation. Something to do with their faith. Everything down there seemed to be something to do with their faith, but Artemio had never quite been able to decipher the complex philosophy that guided them.

"I've been pushed enough for one lifetime." With a grimace, and no invitation, he seated himself beside her. "I'm here to do a little poking and prodding of my own."

"I am married to the Eternal Emperor for as long as I serve as his envoy." She leaned in close enough that the smell of her fresh sweat washed over him. "You understand that this means I have sworn a vow of chastity?"

"No. I…" He had his hands up and a blush spreading across his cheeks before he even realized what he was doing. She was good. "You're playing with me."

"This is the way I find the men of the north prefer to speak." She smiled at him. Open and pleasant. If she was faking her amusement and her kindness towards him, he didn't know that it would be better than genuine mockery. "Would you rather that I am blunt?"

He lowered his hands carefully and blew out a breath. "If you'd be so kind."

"Then might I ask, if you do not wish to spar or romance me as those who came before you did, what brings you so early in the morning to my little slice of paradise upon the earth?" She turned her attention back to the sword. Carefully buffing the unmarred blade with her oilcloth.

Artemio wondered if his reputation as a social bludgeon preceded him, or if his clumsy way with words was known only to those who'd suffered through it. "You know about the killings. The assassinations of Espher's nobility."

"It would be difficult indeed to miss such momentous events in this great city." She didn't even bother to look up from her work as she acknowledged it. "Do you imagine there are any who dwell in the shadow of the court who know nothing of it?"

In for a penny, in for a crown. "Who do you believe is responsible?"

She looked up at him then, a brow raised. She didn't shave those off, it seemed. "Are you the one who has been tasked with discovering such things?"

He met her gaze with the beginnings of a smile that he had to blame on the wine. He definitely didn't enjoy this verbal fencing in normal circumstances. "Are you trying to evade the question?"

"Would the situation not have to be dire indeed before the son of the old fox turned to Agrant for aid?" she asked him in return. The endless questions.

"I am not my father, I do not have his… prejudice against your people." Artemio caught himself answering her distractions instead of staying on target. "More importantly, I'm not here because I'm out of options. I'm here because I recognize that you are a valuable source of information that I may not be privy to."

She smiled more widely at him, and for a moment he was struck by just how pretty she was. Were she blessed with a head of hair instead of a warrior's harsh shave, then half the nobles of Covotana would have been tripping over themselves to test her vows. "What could possibly have come to my ears that does not reach those of the kings' most beloved servant?"

"You have news from your own kingdom. News from beyond our borders." He leaned in a little closer as he said, "News from those factions within the kingdom that would see the Cerva line ended."

She laughed, and it had a richness to it like fine wine. He hadn't believed that the Agrant had any soul in them at all, yet here she was, bubbling over with humanity. It was a fine trick. "You cannot believe that your father speaks to us?"

"I'd rather you didn't speak of him, either." He flicked away that distraction with the same disdain as the last. "Who do you believe is responsible for the killings? You must have an idea."

"Is this the moment when you would expect the villainous Agrantine to throw up their hands and admit culpability? To claim the blood of your people is upon our hands and that your hunt is ended?" She brandished her sword for a moment, before slipping it silently back into its scabbard.

He sighed. "If you'd be so kind, it would save me a lot of running around."

"Would that I could end your efforts so easily." She settled back and crossed her legs. It felt vaguely scandalous to Artemio that she did not have on skirts, and he could see the muscles of her legs shift. "Alas, it was not I, it was not my people. Did you hope that it was?"

"It would have tied things up in a neat little bow."

"You say you do not share in your father's prejudice against us, yet we are the only foreign power you attempt to lay blame at the feet of?" Her smile began to slip, back to the stern woman of iron he had seen going through a blade-dance on his arrival.

He decided to go with what felt natural and replied glibly, "You're the most convenient, right here on my doorstep. It would have taken a long time to ride all the way to foreign courts just to accuse them of murder."

She arched her brow once more. "And do you not think that such a visit might have ended in your own demise?"

She had a fair point. It wasn't like he was going to kick in the doors of the dragon-lords and accuse them of exploding Espher's citizenry. "A distinct possibility."

"Yet you did not think that strutting up to me upon my sovereign soil, while I have a blade in my hands, might provoke the same violence?"

His heart skipped a beat, but he kept his smile steady. "Well, that was a distinct possibility too, but I feel protected by the chain of reason that would follow." He interlaced his fingers on his lap. Nowhere near reaching for his sword. "If I were killed, my killer would be assumed guilty of the crimes I'm investigating. Since you deny all involvement and enjoy a privileged position in our court, I'm probably safe."

"You do not think your people would hold me responsible for the terrible sparring accident that took your life?" Her accent slipped into a mockery of the cliché of the mindless Espheran noblewoman. "How was I to know that you would be so clumsy with the sword on your hip?"

"If you meant to kill me, you would have done it at the start when I first asked." He leaned back against the ivy-clad wall. "Now you're just posturing."

"And why could I not have chosen this moment to be insulted by your words?"

"You forget that I watched your little dance before we started talking." He nodded out at the grass. "Elegance and efficiency. To kill me now is neither elegant nor efficient."

She seemed to weigh his words for a moment, then nodded. As if she agreed with his reasoning, and if she had not, then she would have drawn her blade. Maybe she really would have.

"I do not know who is behind your assassinations, beyond the fact that neither I nor the emperor has sanctioned them." She leaned in closer once more. He could feel the heat still radiating from her. "Do you believe that every attempted coup within your borders is supported by Agrant?"

"The last one was."

"Do you not mean to say, allegedly?" She smiled. A little secret smile, just for the two of them. They both knew the truth, yet she'd never speak it. Nobody ever would.

"Come now, Ambassador, it is just the two of us. Even now you can't admit it?"

"Alas, I was not yet in this role at the time, and my predecessor passed away before conveying any details of plots to usurp thrones. Perhaps the Cerva have better records?" It was hard not to read her smile as an act of cruelty now, given her words. "Does it sting your pride to serve them?"

"Does it sting yours to serve your emperor?" he snapped back, just a little too quickly. "Everyone serves somebody. Even kings are beholden to the lords that keep them propped up. That's the contract of living with other people. Sometimes you have to do things for them in exchange for what they do for you."

She scoffed. "And what do your kings do for you?"

"Pave the roads. Protect the borders…" She was not rolling her eyes, because that would have been rude, but she was looking away from him, like he was embarrassing himself. "Did you mean what they have done for me personally? They grant me the authority I require to go about my business. They gave me breakfast once?"

"Nothing more than table scraps to bring a dog to heel. This is how cheaply the son of the old fox is bought?"

"Now this conversation is finally becoming interesting." A grin spread across Artemio's face. "Why exactly are you trying to drive a wedge between me and the kings?"

She did a very good impersonation of being appalled. "I cannot comprehend why there is not a chasm between you already, with all things considered. You must know of what happened to your predecessors by now. Why do you risk your life in the service of these men?"

It was the first time anyone had ever asked him so bluntly, and he found himself surprised that he was sure of the answer. "I serve Espher."

"Duty?"

"Whoever sits the throne." Artemio looked back out across the grass, out through the gate, to the hustle of common people with no idea of the lofty matters being discussed in spitting distance of them. "This land is mine and I will do what I must for her."

"Then I believe we understand each other at last." The ambassador placed her hand upon his knee. Improper by the standards of both their societies, but it took only a glance at her solemn face to know that this was not flirtation, but camaraderie. "We are both creatures of duty, bound to onerous tasks. If I should come across anything that would help you in yours, might I invite you to share a meal with me and discuss it in private?"

"That would be ideal. Thank you so much, Ambassador." Artemio's social calendar was really filling up. Between assassination attempts at balls and death threats with an ambassador, soon he wouldn't have time to play cards with his sister anymore. He rose to his feet and gave as gracious a bow as he could muster.

She stopped him with a raised hand. "Before you go, might I ask one more question for my own curiosity?"

He was feeling generous after her kind offer. "By all means."

"Why did you come to me?"

"Well, I thought that was obvious." He laughed, "I suspect you, Ambassador. You have motive. When Espher falters, Agrant benefits."

She seemed delighted all over again at his honesty. "Yet now you take me at my word?"

"As you said, you're a creature of duty. You'll say or do whatever benefits Agrant, regardless of how it grates on your conscience. I cannot trust a word you say to me, unless I am certain that telling me the truth is to your advantage." He completed his bow uninterrupted this time. "I was just here to learn which lies you would tell."

For a moment it seemed she might actually be speechless, but she recovered fast. "It has been a pleasure to make your acquaintance, Artemio Volpe. I hope you find what you are seeking. Would you take such a benediction from me?"

With a laugh, he strode towards the bustle of the city. "I'll take whatever I can get at this point."

"May the emperor's good fortune follow you as you speak with the dragon-lord's representative in the palace dungeons." He could hear the smirk in her voice.

If she saw his step falter, she was too polite to comment.

14

WITHIN THE COCOON

Gemmazione, Regola Dei Cerva 112

Harmony looked the peasant girl stuffed into a fancy dress up and down with dismay written all over her face. "What am I meant to do with that?"

"*That* is going to slap the teeth out your head if you call her *that* again."

The Prima held up a hand to stop the ensuing sniping. "Harmony, it has come to my attention that you are lacking in activities to pursue due to your unique social situation."

Through gritted teeth she answered, "Yes, Prima."

"As such, my dear girl, it occurred to me that you might be the perfect person to undertake a certain task for me. One I would consider a personal favor."

Harmony wet her lips. Being owed a personal favor from the Prima was not something to be sniffed at. "How can I be of assistance, Prima?"

"This charming young woman is Orsina Aceta, a scion of a small house from the northern reach who has exhibited some talent in the arts we study here." The girl gave Harmony a sullen stare. Belying all the sweet lies the Prima was spinning about her. "Despite her good breeding and natural charm, I am afraid that country living has left her somewhat bereft of the education in elocution and manners that most families would bestow upon their young. My desire is for you to remedy this situation with all haste. Make her as... acceptable as is possible in your time together."

Harmony's mouth fell open. "You expect me to believe she is the daughter of some country noble?"

The Prima gave her a tight-lipped smile. "I expect that after your careful tutelage, everyone else will believe it. Yes, my dear girl."

Harmony opened and closed her mouth a few times as her brain tried to work through the problem with which she was presented. "And if I refuse?"

The Prima pouted. "Well, then we shall both be very disappointed."

Orsina spoke from behind her in a bitter monotone. "Yes. Please. Teach me how to be just like you."

Harmony sniggered, despite herself. There was no way she was going to turn the Prima down. So she might as well find her amusement somewhere. "All right, I'll do what I can with her, but if she still acts like she was born in a pigsty by the end of it, it isn't my fault. Some things can't be fixed."

Orsina restrained herself from leaping at Harmony without any intervention from the Prima this time around, but it was clear from the narrowing of her eyes that she was just waiting for her opportunity to get the other girl alone.

"Then I shall leave the two of you to devise a curriculum of studies. I'm afraid that young Orsina shall be attending classes throughout most of the day soon enough, but come evening she will be all yours, in perpetuity."

The Prima was already heading for the door of the suite when Harmony called after her. "Does she know how to play cards, at least?"

Orsina's voice was just a little above a growl. "Ask her for yourself?"

The Prima smiled at them as she eased out of the room, as if the two of them were going to be fast friends and not pull each other's hair out within a few minutes.

Blowing out a breath, Harmony turned to Orsina. "Well, can you?"

"No."

Harmony clapped her hands together. "Great, I'll finally have someone I can beat."

In the ensuing hour, she beat Orsina soundly. Round after round. Until it seemed like Orsina simply couldn't grasp the game at all. Eventually she tossed her cards down and grumbled, "You're cheating."

Harmony laughed out loud. "Just because you don't understand the game doesn't mean I'm cheating."

"Every time, you've got good cards. Every time." She kicked the leg of the table as she tried to cross her legs in the voluminous skirts. "How am I meant to win if I've got bad cards and you've got good ones?"

Harmony was genuinely confused. "I... don't always have good cards?"

"But you bid in every time." Orsina jerked her chin at the heap of polished pebbles between them.

"Yes." Harmony spoke slowly, like she was dealing with a child or imbecile. "Because that is the nature of the game."

Orsina threw up her hands. "But why would you bid if you've got bad cards?"

The confusion suddenly made sense to Harmony, and she had to restrain herself from laughing. "Because you don't need good cards to win. You just need the other person to fold."

For a moment, Orsina sat gobsmacked before she finally whimpered out, "You're lying?"

"That is the challenge of the game." Harmony let a little of her amusement slip into her speech now, making it sound like she was just delighted that Orsina had worked it out. "You are not playing against the draw of the cards. You are playing against the other players."

Orsina blinked hard. "I didn't know you were meant to lie."

Harmony scooped up the stack of cards and shuffled them once more. "Another round?"

Orsina's brows had drawn down. "Is it all lies?"

"Whatever do you mean?"

"Everything you're meant to be teaching me. It is all just lying, isn't it?" She glared up at Harmony with genuine anger on her face. The sort of thing that a noble-born girl would never let anyone see. "Not just the big lie, that I'm some noble, but all the rest of it. All the way down. Even just talking like this is all... lies."

"Politeness requires some omission, certainly." This was unfamiliar philosophical territory for Harmony, like asking a fish to describe water. "If a friend does not look good in her dress, I would not inform her of that until she was in a position to change it."

"Not just that, all of it. There's no honesty in anything. The Prima doesn't believe in most of the things she's saying. She just says them because she's meant to, or because it might make other people do what she wants."

"We do not accuse our betters of telling us things that are not true." Harmony repeated her mother's words verbatim without even realizing it. "It isn't polite."

"You all even lie about lying."

Harmony's ire was finally up enough that she raised her voice. "Well, excuse me for spending my whole afternoon trying to help you deceive the entirety of the courts of Espher."

Orsina took a deep breath, then said, "Sorry."

Harmony deflated a little. She hadn't even attempted to understand the other woman's perspective up until now. She hadn't even considered how lost and confused she would feel if she were suddenly dumped in some peasant village and told she had to blend in or risk exile or worse. "Do not concern yourself with it. I understand that this is a learning experience for you. I know it may not seem like it from the way we were forced together, but I do genuinely want to help you."

"Oh, lying really does work with you lot. I fake one sorry and suddenly we're best friends."

This time, when Harmony laughed, it was not the polite snigger she'd allowed herself in front of the Prima, it was the genuine wild hoot that she made when it was just her and Artemio. It was enough to shock Orsina out of her dark mood and into a genuine, if tentative, smile.

"Well, now that we're best friends, you're going to have to let me do your hair." Harmony had been desperately hunting for something to compliment the girl on since she'd accepted her new terrible duty. "The Prima is a genius in academia, but she has the fashion sense of a fossil, and to make matters worse, she has no idea what she's doing with a headful of curls like that. I swear, I'd kill a man for them."

Orsina smirked. "They'd probably kill him for you. They've killed enough combs before to have a taste for it."

The hooting laugh of friendship sounded again.

By the time Artemio burst in, still half cut on the morning's wine and rambling about murders, Orsina's hair had been up and down more times than a ladder, and Harmony had discovered to her disgust that she had been so lonely for the past month, even a peasant with delusions of grandeur was good company.

Both women froze in place as Artemio strode by, but he didn't seem to notice them. "Weeks that I have been hunting for any clue, any lead that might bring me closer to my quarry. This very morning I grew so desperate as to enlist the aid of the ambassador of Agrant in my task, though in truth I was rather hoping that she might attack me and give me at least some direction…" He paced back and forth in front of them. "Then just when I was beginning to think that the only solution would be to use myself as bait and tease the villains out of the shadows, I turn around and…"

He froze when he noticed Orsina for the first time. His open mouth snapped shut. Harmony started to shake and giggle from where she was sitting behind Orsina, hands still tangled in the other woman's hair. "Orsina Aceta, this is my idiot brother, Artemio. Idiot brother, this is Orsina."

He bowed stiffly. "A pleasure to make your acquaintance."

"Orsina, I believe my brother needs a moment of my time. Would you be so kind as to find a servant and ask them to send up supper for three?"

"Just for two, if you please. I cannot stay."

"And why might that be, Art? What is…"

Orsina slipped out of the room as swiftly and silently as she could. Her hair still half up and half down in a manner that any true noblewoman of Espher would have considered scandalous. She had scarcely made it two steps before a hand seized her dress from behind.

Old instincts flared. She slapped the grasping hand away and had a fist up before she realized it was Artemio. He glanced from her fist to the strip of cloth dangling from his hand. "Your blindfold."

It must have been so obvious to him that she didn't belong. But still she managed to mumble out, "I don't need one."

"You're a student?" The puzzlement was plastered all over his face. She could not fool even this one man for one minute, how was she meant to pass among the rest of the nobles. Behind Artemio, Harmony went from looking surprised to meeting Orsina's eyes and tilting up her head so she could look down her nose at everything.

Whatever else she might have been, Orsina was a quick study. She raised her chin and with all the confidence she did not feel she replied. "No, I'm just some peasant who has wandered into the House of Seven Shadows off the streets."

Harmony's face went from shocked at that admission to delighted in an instant as Artemio recoiled. "Right…" He stepped backwards into the room with all haste, repeating, "Pleasure to meet you," as he shut the door in her face.

There were bells spaced between the suites of the many non-student residents of the House, that could be used to summon a servant at will, but the idea of summoning someone to serve her sat almost as ill with Orsina as the idea of demanding that somebody else make her supper for her. True enough, Mother Vinegar had fed her more often than not, but that had been an arrangement made of simplicity. The old woman stayed near the hearth for her comfort while setting Orsina her tasks, and in the dark of night when nobody was around, Orsina might admit that the arrangement between them had been something like a family. This was different.

She wandered the halls, as lost now as she'd been when she first arrived in the House. She had a vague idea that she might find the kitchens herself and make something quick, but even as she walked, she realized how ridiculous it was. She meandered back along the same identical corridors in search of a bell or a servant, whichever came first. As it turned out, what came first was a gaggle of other students. They were walking along, chattering among themselves quite happily until Orsina came into sight.

It felt like she was on the road again with a column of cavaliers bearing down on her. If she could have flung herself over the banister to escape them as she and Kagan had done with so many ditches, then she very well might have. Instead she lifted her chin, let her wild hair fall back behind her, and strode on.

Lying was a virtue among these people. So too, Orsina had realized all too swiftly, was rudeness. The more contempt she treated these nobles with, the more they'd scrabble for her approval. It explained so much about the way the world was run that this was how the people in charge of things thought.

They looked after her as she passed, and the whispering took up almost immediately. But they were not doubting her right to be there. They were not questioning her lineage or demanding she be sent away. They were jealous of her poise, of her outrageous hairstyle, even of the air of mystery that enveloped her as a new student. Glances were cast back at her, but Orsina very deliberately did not turn from her course.

She could not look back, or all would be lost.

Dinner was a simple affair of antipasto by the fireside. Finer food than Orsina had ever tasted in her life, yet she found that it could not hold her attention. Not when Harmony was right there in front of her.

Neither of the women had ever had a friend their own age before, beyond Harmony's somewhat unhealthy attachment to her brother. Every time Orsina had the other woman written off as just another snob, Harmony would let something slip, something that would have been atrociously rude in normal company but was perfectly acceptable between the two of them. Likewise, every time Harmony thought to herself that she couldn't believe she was doomed to spend her days educating some common boor, Orsina showed a little sparkle of wit that drew out an unwitting burst of laughter.

In all honesty, Orsina's ignorance was the part of her Harmony found the most appealing. There were things she just did not know. Things Harmony had grown up living and breathing were alien to a peasant. Even the things Harmony would have thought were patently obvious to anyone with eyes sometimes slipped into the other woman's blind spots.

Which was why, even though she should have expected it eventually, Harmony was taken aback when she was asked bluntly, "But why are you here?"

It stunned her so much she found herself answering before she'd even picked apart the question. "There weren't any marriage proposals, and there wasn't a chance to make friends back home in the south. There was only me. From the moment we were old enough to understand that Art was gifted, I knew this was my duty. My destiny."

Orsina's puzzled expression said more than words. Harmony groaned, "You're really going to make me say it?"

Apparently, Orsina didn't even understand the question she was asking. Of course she didn't. She was a peasant. What would a peasant know about the court and crown. Harmony took a deep breath and settled back in her chair, pondering how to tell as little of the story as possible.

"My family are not beloved here in the capital. It has been generations, but there are still those who call the Cerva usurpers and say that our claim to the throne is the more… righteous. As such, it is considered political suicide to be seen in our company. A marriage proposal, an offer of younger sons as cavaliers or courtiers, even a friendship might be interpreted as sedition. The truth is, this is why the Prima chose me to educate you—because she knows I have nobody to tell about your little deception, even if it weren't in my own best interests to help you and earn her favor."

Orsina gawked at her throughout all this without even moving to interrupt. Harmony had tears prickling at her eyes by the time she was through. "I'm so sorry. But I still don't get it. Your brother is here to study, like me. But you can't… you aren't like me. So why are you here?"

Harmony's head fell into her hands, and she let out a heaving laugh as she finally understood the question. "You aren't asking why I have been chosen as Artemio's impresario. You don't know what an impresario is."

"A what?"

"You don't know anything at all, do you?" There was an edge of mockery in her bitterness. Disbelief blending with disgust. "Not even about what you are?"

The tone put Orsina's hackles up. "I know things. Just not this stuff."

"When you do your little shade thing, it makes you older. It drains your remaining days."

"Yes, I know that," Orsina grumbled and stretched her back, pushing against the bones of her corset. "I know that much all too well."

Harmony ignored the odd interruption, filing it as more peasant strangeness. "An impresario is there to help lighten the load. We're bonded to you, so you can drain our life instead of your own." She lifted her wine from the table between them, like a toast. "A second glass to drink from."

"Wait, you're just giving up your life for your brother?" Orsina looked genuinely aggrieved at the prospect.

"I may as well share. I wasn't using it anyway," Harmony quipped.

"But it's your life, and you're just going to let him use it up like oil in a lantern?" Orsina leaned closer, taking Harmony's empty hand between both of hers. Genuinely concerned. It was almost more than Harmony could take. This girl she barely knew, feeling for her so deeply. Feeling pangs of pain for her, not out of obligation or duty or some hope of repayment, but because she actually cared. "That isn't right. I know you've got your politics stuff going on to stop you finding a husband or whatever you wanted to do with yourself, but there is so much worth living for."

She couldn't cope with the intensity of the moment. The rawness of conversation without artifice. She tried to wall herself off. "I can't say that I've noticed much."

Orsina looked so stricken when she made that silly quip that Harmony immediately wished she could swallow the words back down. She did the next best thing. She repaid Orsina's empathy with her own sincerity. "Artemio is a good man. I know he didn't make much of an impression when you met him, but he cares for me as deeply as any brother could. He wouldn't squander what I'm giving him. He wouldn't waste it. I trust him with my life." She squeezed Orsina's hand and smirked. "Besides, somebody has to take care of the idiot. He clearly can't do it himself."

It was just enough to break the tension. Orsina settled back into her seat, nibbling at her cheese and bread like she was scared it might be taken away from her.

"One thing at a time. One bite at a time, then put it back on your plate."

Orsina dropped her snack back onto the plate with a scoff. "Seriously?"

"A lady would not care to be compared to a squirrel," Harmony said, taking a delicate sip of her wine and setting the glass back down. "Nor for a reputation as a glutton to follow her."

"Reputation? That's why you lot have all the food you could ever eat and you're half starved all the same?" She lifted her cheese back up and took a delicate bite before placing it back down and scowling. "What a waste. You could feed a family of ten with what we've got here, bit of barley or lentils to stretch out the dried meat into something more substantial…"

Harmony couldn't say why, or what shade of dreadful rudeness took over her, but she found herself blurting out, "Who are you, really?"

"Orsina's my real name."

"Oh no doubt, but who are you? Whose bastard?" Orsina flinched at the word. "I'm sorry, I do not mean to wound you with my questions, but we're such fast friends already, and I've already spilled all of my family woes, and…"

"Nobody's. I'm nobody's bastard. I'm nobody's secret child. My parents were farmers. We lived in a little village with some other farmers. No lords. No kings. Nothing. I'm nobody."

It was Harmony's turn to feel affronted on behalf of her new friend. To have been lied to like that was terrible. "That cannot be."

"Even the name the Prima gave me is a joke." Orsina let out a little bitter laugh at that joke. "It's only because I studied under Mother Vinegar before she sent me here. Otherwise she'd probably have called me Orsina Selvaggia."

"Aceta Madre?" Harmony was struck by that odd detail. "Like in the children's story?"

"No, Aceta Madre." Orsina rolled her eyes. "The grumpy old crone who lives in the woods, complains non-stop, and snores like a prize hog."

All of this was getting Harmony off track, and she tried to circle the conversation back around. "So there was no local lord who liked to come and visit with your mother? No... rumors?"

Orsina's temper frayed. "Why do all you nobles care so much about who somebody's parents are? Doesn't it matter who I am?"

It was another of the many questions of the day that challenged something fundamental enough in Harmony's world that she'd never given it much consideration. "I..."

"Are you lot obsessively trying to breed for glossier manes or something?"

The image was enough to make Harmony snort and honk all over again. Eventually settling herself enough to try and work out an answer, she said, "Some part of it is history. Knowing the person you are speaking to by knowing where they came from. Some politics. Knowing the son of a political ally is liable to carry on the banner when his father died."

Orsina was listening intently. For all of her irritation with the personal questions that admittedly would have made anyone enraged, it seemed she genuinely wanted to hear Harmony's explanation of just about anything.

"A great deal of the obsession is about the inheritance of title, land, and property. Kingdoms have been forged or broken on the back of an unexpected inheritance. It is why marriage matters so much. It is a way of allying families in perpetuity. Then... there is the gift of binding. Like my 'shiny mane,' it is hereditary. So a noble family with many shade binders might expect many more in coming generations, and a family with fewer might expect their power to wilt as the centuries roll on."

Orsina spoke softly. "Money and power."

"What else is there?" Harmony snapped back, not quite meaning it, but not quite not meaning it either.

Conversation lulled for a long moment as the gulf between them seemed to widen, the two worlds they inhabited so different that it seemed almost impossible to bridge the gap. Harmony tried again to lighten the mood. "I'm sure you shall have plenty of both soon enough. If you're talented enough to have caught the Prima's eye despite your... circumstances, it shan't take long before the proposals start piling up."

Orsina seemed even more concerned about that. Everything Harmony wanted quite desperately and was denied to her was Orsina's for the taking, yet it seemed as though she didn't even want it.

"With marriage, you'll gain the protection of a family. You'll have their influence to aid you in your goals. It will be quite a step up for someone of such humble beginnings."

"So marriage is about... money and power?"

Once again Harmony caught herself quoting her own mother verbatim. "Love is for the poets."

"Maybe we should take up poetry instead of marriage, then." Orsina smiled. That same grin she'd given Harmony the first time she'd earned a laugh from her.

This time it brought a flush to Harmony's cheeks that she had to move past brusquely. She took another sip of wine and pretended to check on the fire. "I'm sure we'd make quite the pair of poets. The peasant and the hermit. Writing about the love we'll never know."

Orsina was sullen again when she turned back, so in a flash, Harmony reached for the things that brought her comfort. "Have you any lessons tomorrow?"

"Not yet. I think the Prima wants to check if your work has stuck before I'm allowed out in front of other people." Orsina's mood still seemed grim.

"Then tomorrow, I shall take you to my favorite place in the House of Seven Shadows." Harmony clapped with excitement. "The gymnasium."

Every crumb of new knowledge seemed to be enough to tease Orsina back out of her shell. Like she had a hunger to learn things that overpowered all other sense. "The what?"

"It is a space set aside for us to exercise our bodies rather than our minds. A private place, mostly, where we can talk safely without worrying about anyone peeping at us or listening in."

"Exercise? Like… work?" Orsina gawked at her again. "You lot do work for fun?"

Harmony laughed away the question, then said with a grin of her own, "Many times today you've looked like you wanted to hit me. Tomorrow I shall give you the chance."

15

ANSWERS IN THE BLOOD

Gemmazione, Regola Dei Cerva 112

I t took considerably longer than it should have to extricate the Prima from her duties, and in the end, Artemio had resorted to slapping his writ from the kings into the face of her secretary and forcing his way into her office and the presumably important meeting she was embroiled in with the other lecturers.

"Terribly sorry to interrupt you, Prima, but I require an expert opinion on something."

The Prima did not look impressed, but for all that she was not impressed, she knew who Artemio represented and why this son of a lesser house now dared to barge into her sanctum without her leave. A line appeared between her brows and she said, "Give me just a moment."

Then Artemio had stood in the corner awkwardly as his teachers and social superiors milled around, shaking hands and congratulating each other for another successful meeting of minds that would result in absolutely nothing changing. It was all Artemio could do to contain his sneer. Once all of that was over and done with, the last of the Prima's visitors walked by, scowling at him for his presumption, rudeness, and low station.

Just when it seemed the Prima was finally ready to depart, she walked away from the door and opened out a cupboard that turned out to contain a wardrobe. Casting a glance to the pattering on her window, she swept a waterproof cape around her shoulders and retrieved a waxed parasol from yet another cupboard, which she then proceeded to thrust into his arms. "My dear boy, am I to assume that you are taking me to the scene of a murder?"

His barely contained excitement threatened to bubble up and over. "That is correct, Prima."

"What a delight," she replied flatly.

"It seems that the eldest son of Lord Sabbia has expired in rather an explosive fashion that is consistent with the assassinations I am investigating." He offered her his arm, and they walked out of her office together. "It occurred to me your keen insights might be best applied in determining whether there was some arcane workings afoot if I could get you in close proximity to the focal point of such a work sooner rather than later."

She arched an eyebrow and glanced askance. "You do not trust in your own ability?"

"I trust in your experience more, Prima." It was barely flattery, mostly just the truth. He had no way of knowing when he might have another chance at a fresh assassination. If he'd had any other ideas to identify the method or the killers he'd have thrown all of them at it. As it stood, he had himself and the Prima, so that was what he used.

The Sabbia family were far from the wealthiest in Espher, and their estate within the city amounted to little more than a townhouse on the periphery of the south quarter with a rather bedraggled-looking olive tree growing in its equally cramped gardens. Terra-cotta and white stucco rather than stone, a newer construction. At least it was on one of the main thoroughfares so the Prima's coachman had no trouble getting them there swiftly.

Making it from the carriage to the house was another matter entirely. A murder was the closest thing that this stretch of the city had to entertainment at this time of night, and it seemed to be drawing in bodies from all the surrounding neighborhoods too. The crowd was packed in tight, and for all of the power she commanded, both political and arcane, the Prima was an older woman in no fit state to be elbowing through.

It seemed to Artemio that he'd had a good run so far, but the anonymity of his investigations to date were at an end. If he wanted in, he was going to be seen. It took him a moment to compose himself, to accept that he must face death head-on now, instead of sneaking around the periphery and hoping to avoid the Last King's gaze.

Stepping down off the carriage, he offered the Prima a hand so she could get herself situated comfortably on very edge of the pavement where there was enough room for her to squeeze in before turning back to the crowd and clapping his hands. The merchants, peasants, and assorted other hangers-on ignored him completely. He tried again, clapping and shouting. "Out of the way!"

Still it elicited no response. The Prima was watching him. The flush of shame began creeping up his neck, heading for his cheeks. He could feel it prickling as it rose. Fine.

It took only a blink of the eyes for him to reach out to the forge spirit and draw it inside him. The next time he clapped his hands, when they parted there was a ball of flame roiling between them. The back end of the crowd began to take notice, scattering in fear if they got a good look at the expression of pure rage on his face or gawking at him as another sideshow to the big event of the murder.

His fingers flexed and the fire snaked out. It would have been such a simple thing to burn a line straight through them all, right to the door. A clear, clean path. It cost him much more to send the streamer of fire along, squirming between the bodies, writhing all the way to the guardsmen at the door and then rippling out, sending the crowd scattering, screaming and tripping over one another to get away from the fire as it spread. Artemio released his shade and the flames leapt up for an instant before dying away. There was shocked silence from the crowd, none of them willing to step back into the place where impossible fire had appeared just a moment before. He offered the Prima his arm and flicked up the parasol to protect her from what was left of the rain. They headed inside.

The guards would have parted before them even if Artemio hadn't waved his writ at them. They could recognize authority almost instinctively. The family of the deceased were gathered in the parlor, both men and women weeping openly, but with that same distant glazed look in their eyes that Artemio had come to associate with knowing nothing. "Did anyone see anything? Hear anything?"

Heads shook.

"My poor baby."

Tears fell.

"Not a sound. No clue it had happened until…"

Useless, every one of them.

A maidservant stood by the stairs, blood barely visible around the soles of her polished shoes. Artemio laid a hand on her shoulder. "Take me to the room where it happened."

The boy's bedchambers were at the very top of the townhouse, inaccessible from anywhere except this central stairwell and his dressing room, which was, in turn, inaccessible from anywhere but the locked room ahead. A cursory search with those senses normal people lacked revealed the influence of no shade upon the door or lock. Something the Prima verified with her own study. She declared she could sense no shades whatsoever in the building. That had the potential to be an issue.

Within the room things were much as Artemio had predicted from his observations in the other bloodstained bedchambers he'd had the joy of visiting over the past few weeks. The only difference was that it was not his mind's eye piecing together the parts of the body now, it was his actual eyes seeing it all. His nose, picking up the charnel notes of ruptured bowels, rich iron-tinted blood, and the other essential salts that made up a man. The maid's footprints were there, pressed down into the squelching carpet and clearly marking her course to discovering the fate of her master. Other servants' footprints too, dithering in and out over the course of the day. Doing their duties, and disrupting the wet fragments of bone and flesh in entirely predictable patterns. Artemio accounted for them and crept in closer.

At the center of it all lay the remains of this noble scion, his blood, organs, and fluids spread out from the bed like a butterfly's spreading wings. Up the walls, from the bed's canopy—everywhere the blood had splattered it now dripped down. Pattering to the wet coverlet in odd droplets still, even after so many hours. Completely chill when it touched Artemio's skin.

He closed his eyes and reached for the victim's shade. The body was found at dawn, which meant they had until long after sundown before the spirit departed. Except there was, as the Prima had already warned, no trace of the shade. No chance to capture whatever final loop of memory it was trapped in.

He spoke it aloud, though it pained him. "The shade is gone."

The Prima was barely in the door, but she had both of her hands up and clasped over her mouth. Artemio was so accustomed to her being in complete control of every situation that it had not crossed his mind that the sight of all the gore of a murder might trouble her. He closed the distance fast and slapped a hand over her eyes. "Breathe through your mouth. Slow and steady."

She was seething beneath his hand, hissing, "Unhand me at once," but he waited until he was certain she was breathing steady once more before he stepped clear of her.

Her eyes were closed when his hand came away, and they remained closed as she carefully regulated her breathing and her tone. "I cannot sense the shade, nor any sign of shadework done here."

That was good, she was focusing on the things she could control. Artemio tried to keep the conversation afloat. "I could find no trace at the other sites myself, but I had taken that to be indicative of the time passed, rather than a sign that a shade was not employed. I mean… it seems unlikely anyone could have brought a wild animal in here unnoticed to inflict this kind of damage."

"My dear boy, there are few animals in this world that could create such a mess of a man, and I sincerely doubt any of them might fit through that doorway." She blinked her eyes open for a moment, then slammed them shut again. Puffing breaths out through her mouth. "Perhaps some sort of wyvern-beast?"

It was safe to give her a look of contemptuous disbelief with her eyes shut. "You really think it could be an animal?"

"Come now, Artemio, I know you have taken the course of lectures on basic logic at the House." She peeked at him, then realized that by maintaining her gaze only on his face she could avoid the rest of the room. Her undivided attention was a little unsettling. "You did rather well in it as I recall, there was some talk of making you teach it. Regardless, we have eliminated the influence of shades, so now you must eliminate all other alternatives until the truth is left to you."

"There are no scratches or claw marks. No feathers, scales, or fur. It seems unlikely any beast capable of this could focus its attentions so tightly. The mattress would be shredded. The carpets torn. The drapes at least. No, it is not an animal." He ticked each point off on his fingers as he paced the room. He could recall where the footprints were before he trampled them just fine. It wasn't as if they were giving him anything. Not with servants having thoroughly disrupted the scene already, entering and opening the curtains. He paused by the windows to check for any sign that an assailant had breached them, but there was nothing.

As though she were losing patience with him, the Prima nudged him on. "So what options are left to us?"

"I had considered some sort of alchemical concoction, but they have distinct aromas, and once more the destruction would not be so contained." He paced back to the bed. To the desolation that had been left of a man there. He examined it inch by inch as he spoke. Finding one area where the blood had dried already in a perfect circle, exciting him for only a moment before he knocked on the brass bed warmer where it was tucked under the covers, now chill to the touch. "There would be burns and stains if such a philter had been unleashed, and there is nothing."

"Which leaves us with?"

"Something unknown. Which is of course why I came to you, my

Prima." He turned to her with as broad a smile as he could muster in the presence of such carnage. "You have a more expansive knowledge of foreign magic than I or anyone else in Covotana. Who could do something like this?"

"Now, I know you like to flatter me, my dear boy, but to say I have a more expansive knowledge of foreign gifts is akin to saying that a white cape is brown simply because it has a speckle of mud upon its hem." She sighed. "That my studies into the subject constitute the greatest exploration of the subject is a testament to the limitations of our knowledge, not a proclamation of my grandeur."

It had been a slim hope to begin with, but Artemio pressed on with it nonetheless. "So you cannot think of any foreign power who might be capable of such a thing?"

"Why is it that you are so intent on this being the work of foreign magic?" The Prima stroked at her chin, mocking his pose and making him drop his hands to his sides.

"Quite simply, Prima, I am seeking those who would most benefit from the chaos these killings are fomenting."

Swallowing hard, she looked around the room once more. He kept his eyes on her, more interested in the reactions she did not mean to share than what she was looking at specifically. She swallowed hard, then said, "I cannot think of anything from my studies that could compare to this, but that does not mean it was not simply outside of those translations I have mustered. You would be best to discuss it with those who practice such arts."

He looked at her speculatively. "Someone like the Arazi in the kings' dungeons?"

"Do you think many would object if you were to put the question to the imprisoned spy?"

Artemio froze in his renewed pacing and almost toppled, he felt so off balance. There was so much he did not know. So many pieces to this puzzle that remained outside of his reach. Hidden from his view. "How is it exactly that you all know about that, while I did not?"

She would have tittered if her eyes were not locked now on a piece of flesh that had been flung almost the full distance of the chamber to lie by the edge of the rugs. There was the shiny inner curve of a skull on Artemio's side of the piece, so he dreaded to think what was on hers. "Because people speak to me, my dear boy. Because I am a well-known face in the courts, and it is equally well known that my favor can be won with information of this very sort."

He began to pace the room again, taking in all of the pieces, working them back to their source, which was of course the bed. Overlaying the room with his mental image of the arcs the gruesome remnants had taken. Some intersected, suggesting the victim had not been destroyed in a single burst, but rather split apart in phases. That or the angles were severely skewed by mid-air deflections. The latter made no sense to Artemio's carefully ordered mind, so he discounted it for now. Mid-air collisions would also have suggested something other than a single burst. "Perhaps his Majesty should have placed this task at your feet rather than mine."

The Prima managed a thin-lipped smile. "Alas, with all of my many duties, I would have been forced to decline and pass along a suggestion of one of my more able students with a mind for this sort of puzzle-solving."

That put his pacing to a halt. He had been wondering about his own involvement in all of this, and now it lined up. "So I have you to thank?"

"My dear boy, I could not stand the thought of you withering away to nothing in some backwater the way your father has." She came closer and cupped his face in her hands. It was profoundly unsettling. The humanity of that contact. It made Artemio's skin crawl. "To think that I would never see your mother again, simply because she made the wrong choice of husband, it was quite intolerable, and now with her passing... let me just say that it is my hope you can leverage this position to your lasting advancement once more, and that your good works might bring the Volpe family back in from the cold. You are from such a promising line, it would be such a waste to see your natural gifts squandered away over mere politicking."

"I suppose I should thank you." He tried to smile as he pulled his head back from the cradle of her palms. "But it is difficult to see this task of mine as anything but a punishment when it seems that it is an endless labor."

"I am quite certain we shall see you succeed in time. And when you do, both of us shall find ourselves squarely in the king's favor." She glanced away from Artemio to take in the blood and sighed. "Unlike certain other students of mine who shall now amount to nothing more than a footnote in the histories written of your feat."

Another piece clicking into place. "Wait, what? He was a student?"

"You didn't know? He departed a few years before you began your studies, but I had hoped you might familiarize yourself with the working shade binders in the city when there is such a limited pool of us."

The first of them to have been killed in all of these assassinations, Artemio couldn't help but feel it was personal. A trial run to ensure shade binders could die as readily as anyone else to this… method. With a dry mouth, Artemio asked, "If he were a shade binder and he tried to call upon his shades as he died, might that explain his spirit being consumed? Could we call upon them and learn what they observed?"

The Prima tutted. "My dear boy, I have already told you there were no shades called within this room. At least not within the last few days. Whatever struck him down did so before he could so much as think of defending himself."

Turning back to the room, Artemio let out a long-held sigh. "Every day I seek answers, and I'm left with more and more questions."

"Such a shame that it was him." The Prima pretended she had not heard Artemio's bellyaching. "I'd heard he'd arranged a good marriage into the Aquila family that might have seen his family's standing in the courts much restored."

Another piece of the puzzle snapped together, and Artemio began frantically searching through the pieces for the rest of the skull. Crying back over his shoulder, "He was engaged to Rosina Aquila?"

"The very same!" the Prima answered, a line forming between her

brows as she tried to work out what he was doing, scurrying around the
room. "Do you know her well?"

It was as though Artemio had not heard the question, so intent was he
upon his task. In the end, he found what he was looking for down between
the bed and a side cabinet, the front-piece to match the hair that had lain
before the Prima. Not the whole of the man's face, but enough of it that
it was recognizable to him. The fiancé from the Spring Ball. He let it fall
from his numb and bloody fingers before turning back to the Prima with
an edge of hysteria in his voice.

"Well, that is just glorious. I've become my own best suspect."

16

TOGETHER IN THE DARK

Gemmazione, Regola Dei Cerva 112

Kagan's eyes had been swollen shut for the first week. That had been better.

He could tell himself the slop he was eating every few days when they pushed it under his door was some sort of soup. That the tickling across his feet was just the straw, not rats. That the smell was just the corner he'd marked to do his business, not the rot of some corpse abandoned in another cell.

Sight made everything worse.

The torches flickered outside the barred window in the cell door, shadowed when a jailer strolled by. He had flinched each time he heard them shuffling by while he was blind, and now with sight, he got to experience that terror through two senses.

The pain of the beating had faded by the time his eyes opened up. Dragon-bonded Arazi were made of sterner stuff than mere human beings. Pain faded faster than bruises, and both faded in the time it would have taken a man who'd suffered that same beating just to stir from the dark depths of healing sleep.

What hurt him more was the confinement—and the dread. It was said there was no torture worse to a dragon than to confine it. To block out the sight of the sky it called home and hobble its wings. That much was true, and enough of the dragon had passed to Kagan through their bond that he could feel the weight of the castle up above him. The arched stone, the bricks, the dirt, all of it between him and the clean free air he longed to breathe.

The only escape from this hell had been sleep.

In his dreams, he had always flown. Spread wide his wings and taken flight, knowing that those dreams were not entirely his own, nor entirely his bond-partner's. Even though they had been so far from each other, separated by so much, they had still shared those dreams. Now he did not dream at all. Or if he did, it was of being buried alive, startling him back out of sleep the moment he found he could not draw breath.

In itself, that would have been bad enough, but he found his courage faltering in the face of torture. He had nothing to hide. There was no secret of his people that might be brought to bear against them now in his memory. He had been gone far too long for that. Everything might have been different in the land he once called home, and he would never know it.

If there was nothing he needed to keep secret, then there would be no need for torture to loosen his tongue, surely. If he told them anything they asked, there would be no need for... whatever it was he kept hearing the other prisoners screaming about in the room at the end of the corridor. Whatever they asked, he would answer truly. There was no need for deception. Even if they asked about Orsina and the witch of the woods, he had no reason not to spill all their secrets too. It wasn't as though anything he said down here might touch them, up there.

The only thing that could keep his mouth shut was his pride, and there was scarce pride left in him. What hadn't been stripped from him with his dragon and title had withered in the long years living like a savage in the woods and died a final death somewhere in the ditches he'd cowered in so little men on their little horses couldn't see him and kill him. Pride was a luxury for the powerful.

Even the strength of his arms and the surety of his aim were not his own. He'd been bonded to his dragon so young that every muscle of his body could have been rightly accounted to its influence rather than his own efforts. Everything that he was came from her, and now she was gone. He was alone in this dark place, without even the memory of wind beneath her wings to lift his heart. It had been too long. It had all been too long ago, and he had lingered on and on, even knowing it was just making things worse. He should have spit himself on the first spear he'd made after his exile. At least that would have ended their suffering.

Yet when the candlelight flickered beyond the cell's barred window, hope sparked within him all the same. Even knowing he should have died and put an end to the pain long ago, still treacherous instinct made him hunger for life. Even if all that life held was more of this misery. With a grunt of effort, he turned his head up to meet his jailer's judging stare. The eyes that peered back were blue as the open sky, framed by a spill of red hair, bright as dragon fire. Hope flared again at this omen. This was no guardsman.

The door of his cell was dragged open, haltingly, jamming on the filth and straw stuck beneath it, and blue-eyes came inside. There was no guard at the slim boy's heels. No chains on Kagan's wrists or ankles. He could kill him with a twist of his hands and be past him and free. Were the guards mad? He started to drag himself upright when a gust of wind slammed him back down with enough force to drive the air from his lungs.

"Now that is settled, perhaps we can have a conversation rather than a scuffle? I am Artemio Volpe, a pleasure to make your acquaintance. Et cetera."

Kagan eyed the boy again and saw the shadows dancing behind him, thrown up vast and looming against the walls of the tiny cell by the candlelight. "What do you want, necromancer?"

"Ah, good." Artemio glanced around the room for somewhere to sit, then thought better of it. "You understand the situation."

There was still one truth Kagan had clung to through his confinement. "I haven't done anything."

"I have no idea what crime you are accused of, so pleading your case to me is something of a wasted effort." Artemio sighed. "I have other questions for you. Questions that only Arazi can answer."

It hurt to shrug his shoulders as his scales scratched up the stones of the wall behind him, but Kagan did it all the same. "Bad luck for you then. I don't have any Arazi answers. Haven't been home since before you were squirted out."

Artemio looked somewhat disgusted at that description of his birth, but he waved the concern away. "The questions are of a more metaphysical nature."

"Do I look like a philosopher?" Kagan snorted.

For a moment, Artemio looked surprised that the brute knew the word *philosopher*, but then he reassessed. "You look like you could use a friend who could speak in your favor to the courts."

"You'd be that friend, would you?" Kagan's growling laugh was bitter.

"I'd do what I could for you. I can't promise much, because I don't know what you did, but if your information helps me, I'll ask them for all the clemency that can be offered."

Some men would have taken that honesty as a blow, but Kagan liked it. It meant that blue-eyes could be trusted to tell him the ugly truth, even when it hurt his chances at getting what he wanted. It was more than he'd expect from a noble, let alone one talking to someone so obviously helpless to take vengeance on them if they reneged. Still, he wasn't going to ignore the obvious gap in the promise. "And if it doesn't help?"

Artemio sank down to his haunches. The tails of his coat spreading over the filth of the cell floor. "So long as you tell me the truth, I shall do all I can."

"All right. I'm not promising I'll know the answers, but you can ask."

Artemio recited, word-perfect from his own lessons. "Arazi magic is empathetic. You form a bond with your dragons akin to the relationship between the Shadebound and their impresario."

He was looking down at Kagan with expectation. Kagan coughed and it tasted rusty. "Was there a question in there?"

"Is that the extent of your magic?"

"No. Before we're bonded, we can feel everything that's alive, animals, bugs, some folk even swore they heard trees humming. There's a few folk with the gift who don't bond. We use them as scouts. All of us hold on to some of that sense, but most of it goes into our bond."

"So you can sense anything living around you, even now?"

"All the dead rock around us makes it harder, but you, I feel you." He closed his eyes and let the wave of emotion wash over him. "Fuzzy from the booze. None of the static you get with liars. Confidence masking fear. Like a beast being hunted."

Artemio's face had gone pale and still. All expression drained away in an instant. His hand rested upon the hilt of his rapier in silent threat. "I would prefer if you did not do that again."

Kagan shrugged his shoulders once more. Sparks flying from the wall where his scales scraped. "You asked."

"What else can you do?" Those blue eyes narrowed down to slits as he grumbled, "Beyond probing at a man's heart for weakness?"

"You asked what I could do…"

Artemio cut him off with a glare. "And you demonstrated quite adequately. Now tell me what else you can do."

Kagan sank back as he tried to put it into words. Something so fundamental to his being, to the lives of all his people, that it had never been voiced before. "Our true power is in the bond. The bond is everything for us. We share everything with our dragon. All we feel, our lives, our strength, even our dreams blend together. We think a thought and do not know from which of us it first came. We move together like one living thing. Not man and beast, but one and the same." Kagan's breath was strained with pain as he spoke of it. Isolation in this cell had been painful, but it was not worse than he was already suffering day after day. He could speak to others, share fragments of what he was through sounds, but he would never be truly known. Not ever again. There was a beauty he would never witness again. The simplicity of it lost forever. "We become more than human. More than dragon. We become Arazi. The two in one."

Artemio reached out tentatively, almost reverentially, to press a finger to the ridge of scales on Kagan's brow. Brushing over them carefully, marveling at the way they blended into skin. Kagan shuddered at the ticklish contact and both men drew back abruptly. Artemio cleared his throat and glanced away. "That's where you got the scales."

"Among other things." He flexed his shoulders, and through the tattered remains of his hunter's garb, Artemio could see muscles rippling under his off-color skin. Muscles that he would have sworn were not present in the human body. Kagan's gravelly voice drew him in. "I can feel the wind on my skin and know how the day's flying will be. She'll see a spear in flight and know where it will travel. She could count, understand language, think as well as any man. Better than most. When we were hurt, our wounds would close faster, with another body's strength to draw on. I'll live as long as my dragon does, and she as long as I do."

"I had always assumed that the exchange would be unequal between a man and a dragon. With one having so much more to give. That your relationship to your mount was more akin to that between beast of burden and owner." He paused, realized how deeply offended Kagan looked at the implication that dragons were mere animals, and twisted his words swiftly. "It is clear that the academic writing upon this subject was sorely lacking. Perhaps when all this is said and done, there will be a treatise to be written about Arazi dragon bonds."

"Nothing more to say about it," Kagan rumbled. "When she needs my strength, she can take it. When I need hers, it is there."

"Could you kill with this power?" Artemio shuffled back again, as though he did not trust himself to keep his hands off. "Draw strength until your... partner died?"

"That isn't how it works." Kagan let out a snort at this man's ignorance. "The bond is trust. Perfect trust. You couldn't kill them any more than you could kill yourself when you're bonded."

Artemio leapt on the opening with a sort of grim desperation, as though he knew it was pointless but he had to commit nonetheless. "People kill themselves all the time."

"People aren't Arazi. Even if you hated yourself, you wouldn't hate your bondmate. You couldn't." Kagan's eyes seemed to be on something beyond the dark wall of the cell behind Artemio's back. Something long distant but still painful enough to drain his voice of its strength and timbre. "Even if they did the worst thing they could to you, even if they ruined your whole life on a whim, you could never hate them enough to wish any harm on them."

Artemio snapped his fingers. "Could you force this bond on someone? Connect people or beasts and then kill one to kill the other from a distance."

Kagan drew himself back to the now. Grim as it was, it was still better than the place where his mind had gone wandering. "The bond comes from within. It isn't something that can be… done. It's something you are. Nobody can force it. There were stories back when I was young, the kind told in whispers, not around campfires. People tricked into making a bond, coerced like an unwilling bride, but they were just stories. I'd never heard of it really being done. Not much point really. Once the bond is made, there's no going back, and it changes the both of you. Like it or not. Aligns you."

"I had hoped that with your… focus upon it, you might have had better control. But it seems that the connection is just as it is between Shade-bound and impresario. A partnership, despite the difference in your choice of partner." Artemio flopped down into the filth again with a sigh and not a care for the mess it made of his fancy clothes. "There goes that theory."

For a long moment, the silence persisted, until Kagan felt he was obliged to break it. "You want to tell me what this is about?"

Those blue eyes snapped back into focus, and Artemio smirked as some fresh idea sprang fully formed into his mind. "Dragons. Serpents. The bond can be with any of the dragon-kin, not just the Greater Dragons?"

Kagan nodded. "Right."

"So is there some smaller type that could tear a person apart? A wyvern or winged serpent. Something that could navigate within a building like this?"

He'd hunted most of them through the years since his exile. Those rare ones that still ran free and far enough from home to cross borders. There was a good market for them. Both as pets and as parts. "Most of them would rip you up soon as look at you. Harder to think of one that wouldn't."

"And they could be controlled through the bond." Artemio was back up on his knees. Hands clasped together in excitement. "Commanded from a distance to do exactly as you intend."

"No."

Like he had been frozen, Artemio stayed fixed in place, his expression unmoving. "No?"

Kagan let out a rumbling sigh of his own. "The wyvern, flying serpents, cockatrice, they're dumb. More lizard than dragon. Like wild animals if you leave them alone. They're smarter when they're bonded, but not much smarter. Not smart enough to follow instructions better than a dog."

"Another theory gone." Artemio slumped once more. Kagan looked at him properly now. Not just those odd blue eyes.

Kagan tried again. "What is this about?"

"Murders. Locked rooms. Mysterious and messy. I'm tasked with deciphering the perpetrator."

Kagan laughed. Harsh in the quiet of the dungeon. "And what, you thought we flew a dragon in to do it without anyone noticing?"

"I'm eliminating options," Artemio snapped back.

"By the burned." The chuckling rumbled on despite Kagan's best efforts to hold it back. His ribs ached with every laugh. "You must have gone through a lot of them before getting to sneaky dragons."

"Excellent. The captured barbarian spy is mocking me as a fool." Artemio raised his hands and pressed the heels of his palms into his eyes. Groaning out, "The perfect end to a perfect day."

"If my people wanted yours dead, they'd storm your borders and burn your cities down. They wouldn't smuggle a wyvern in to kill somebody."

Artemio's face remained covered as he mumbled. "Noted."

Kagan shifted slightly, pulling away from the wall. Not even reaching out for Artemio, not yet. He had moved through forests full of crackling leaves without his footsteps making a sound. A simple lean forward in silence was nothing, even if his body still screamed at him with every motion.

His knuckles were swollen and bruised from where they'd been trampled or he'd punched armored men, yet he could spread his clawed fingers easy enough now. Now that freedom was just a simple reach and twist away. This one would snap like a twig, then Kagan would have a sword. He did not know how many guards were between him and the sky, but they would not be enough. Not now.

His hands were an inch from touching Artemio when the burning started. Wisps of smoke rising from the palms of his hands. Pain creeping in a moment later.

"I thought we had an understanding."

Kagan pressed in closer, flames licking up from his hands now, blooming up between his fingers. His voice was a growl. "You think fire can stop me? My kind are forged in fire."

Still, he could not come any farther. All his vaunted strength was worthless against the invisible force emanating from Artemio. The flames leapt up all around the tiny Espheran. Not red-hot, but blue. Hot enough that even Kagan could not bear them. As Artemio tore his hands from his eyes, the fire exploded out in a wave, blasting the reptilian bulk of Kagan back against the wall.

Those eyes of his were blue flames now. He rose, languid and boneless, to stand over the man who would have seen him dead. Kagan was sootblackened, his skin crisped and cracking everywhere it had faced Artemio. It was enough. The lesson was learned.

"I shall speak of the aid you gave me in my quest when you are brought to trial." The fire in his eyes flickered out. The last light in the room dying with it. The candle by his feet was now no more than a smear of wax across the floor. "My word has worth, at least to me."

Kagan struggled to part his lips. The burns sought to seal them, and it brought fresh, terrible pain when he tore them open to groan, "Thank. You."

If Artemio heard him, he gave no sign. All Kagan heard in response was the door slamming shut once more, returning him to solitude and misery.

THE CONVERSATION OF NOBILITY

Gemmazione, Regola Dei Cerva 112

Harmony was entirely disappointed by Orsina. All of her life, as a pampered lady of leisure, she had been informed that the lower classes were violent, vicious thugs, just desperate to lay hands upon their betters. Yet here Orsina was, gasping for breath, the wooden stave in her hands swaying hopelessly from side to side.

Not once had she made it past Harmony's guard, while her own bare arms and legs were already striped with bruises, and she looked to be barely holding back tears.

"Come on, hit me."

She tried, but it was so clumsy and obvious that Harmony didn't even need to raise her own stave to block it, just step around. "You can do better than that!"

"I can't!" Orsina tossed the stick aside in disgust, as she'd been longing to since they'd begun.

Harmony surged forward to scoop it up, to press it back into her hands. The girl would not accept it. "Of course you can. "

Orsina pushed her open palms against the stave being foisted upon her instead of grasping it, and it tumbled to the sand between them once more. "No. I can't. You move. Or you hit me. Or... I can't."

"Just try again!"

"I've been trying all morning. I can't hit you. You win. Okay?" The tears hung in her eyes now. The kinship she thought she'd felt with this other girl chipped away by every whack and tap. "Whatever you're trying to prove. You proved it. You are better than me."

For the first time it seemed that one of her blows had struck home. The air was driven from Harmony's lungs in her surprise. She was so accustomed to this place as a sanctuary where she could let loose all the frustrations the rest of the world piled upon her that it did not cross her mind that it might mean anything less to anyone else.

She had to replay the hour they had spent since dawn, seeing things not through the rose-tinted memories of snatched moments crossing blades in the yard with her father's more rebellious retainers.

"I... I owe you an apology. It did not occur to me that this would not be... fun to you. I had thought this might be a place where our differences would matter less, when it seems that the opposite is true."

There were benches set back from the sand where observers might situate themselves during training sessions and exhibitions. Orsina slumped over to them, still damp-eyed but no longer so full of frustration. The painful silence stretched on until Orsina's bluntness broke it apart once more. "How many years have you been learning to hit folk?"

It had never been put to Harmony like that before. The true meaning of all her training and art. The causing of harm and pain. At first it made her back stiffen, to see her joy made so starkly about the misery of others. Yet she had driven poor Orsina far from comfort this morning, and it only seemed fair to accept a step beyond her own view of things in turn. "All the years of my life, for as long as I can recall. First for the joy of doing a thing it was not entirely right for a lady to be doing, then because it would be my duty to protect Artemio, a duty I took to heart."

"Farmers don't learn to hit folk, witches neither, I suppose." She leaned her head on Harmony's shoulder, and the tenderness of it, the forgiveness enclosed in so casual a gesture, almost brought tears to Harmony's eyes too. "I do remember being taught not to hit folk... even when they deserved it."

Harmony sniffed, to keep her own emotions from overrunning her composure. "A notion I'm afraid we may have to disabuse you of. While our fair gender might protect us from the depravities of duels and the like, I'm afraid that your own role here in the House of Seven Shadows shall place you in combat soon enough. For all that they behave like civilized folk and academics, the truth is that the military might of Espher is in her Shadebound, and if war should come, as rumors suggest it soon must, then you will be called upon to turn the tide."

Orsina jerked around to look at her, so close that their noses almost brushed. "So I'm signed up for soldiering too? Every time I blink there's a new job piled on my back."

Harmony wilted back with a sigh. "I am sorry to be the perpetual bearer of bad news."

"I'm just glad someone told me before I got my marching orders."

Harmony nodded back to the packed sand. "So at least you now understand why you must learn to defend yourself?"

Orsina stared out at the humiliations of the morning replaying in her mind. Her lower lip quivering. "I could run away if they try to make me fight."

"And make all our work for nothing?" Harmony had not even considered the possibility, and it now set her mind reeling.

To flee instead of standing her ground, it was a contemptible idea. To back down and let enemies know that you were afraid? Yet here this peasant was, framing it as though cowardice was the moral choice.

"Is it so terrible not to want to hurt anyone?"

"When would the running end, Orsina? How far would you flee, always knowing that if you had stood your ground you might have turned the tide? That your homeland had fallen to the savages of foreign lands when you could have prevented it? At what distant shore would you finally find there was nowhere else to run and see that all who might have stood at your side now lie dead in your wake?"

Harmony did not know where the words came from. She could feel some echo of her father in them, with his talk of patriotism and pride interspersed through his own sense of personal ownership over all of Espher. She had never swallowed that line of logic herself. To her, duty was a more personal thing, forged from the chains of kinship to her brother and those few others who'd shown her kindness and friendship through the years. Espher was her home, but her attachment to it went little further than that.

The other girl sat there, like she was chewing the words over. Already, Harmony knew they would not be enough. How could any commoner feel the same attachment to the land they merely occupied, rather than owned? Was it any wonder that so many of them flitted from place to place if they were not commanded to stay at their stations? Blades of grass grew roots no deeper than the surface soil. She could not hope to appeal to her in such grandiose terms. A rapid change in direction was necessary. "Haven't you ever wished you could keep yourself safe? Without having to rely on someone else to protect you?"

Orsina glanced up at her with a heat in her eyes. "I've wanted to be able to whack you with a stick after you chased me around out there for an hour."

Harmony laughed. "Then let us begin with that and leave quibbles of philosophy until such time as we must face them. What do you say we start over?"

"All right." Orsina got to her feet. "But the next time you smack my arse, I'm going to call a shade up to bully you right back."

Harmony chuckled. "Noted."

She cast her memory back, all the way to the beginning of her own training with the sword. Mimicking the movements she'd seen in the yard in front of her mirror. Fighting with hanging drapes and imaginary foes.

"Stop thinking about it like you're trying to hit somebody, think of it like… like a dance." She glanced across at Orsina's incredulous look and quickly corrected herself. "No, like a conversation!"

Orsina had scooped up her discarded stave and was swinging it back and forth like a club. "What kind of conversations do you have?"

"Just watch. And learn." She spun to face Orsina, stave in high guard, knees bent and balance perfect. She thrust her stave at Orsina, slowly enough that even a blind mule could have seen it coming and reacted. "Hello, Orsina, my dear."

Orsina batted it away successfully, though with none of the ease Harmony might have hoped such an exchange might have brought her. Self-consciously, she answered back to the conversation, "Hi."

"Yes. Good. Now greetings have been handled, the conversation can get started. Shall we swap pleasantries?"

She waited patiently for a moment before Orsina realized that meant it was her turn, then, when the clumsy swipe came, she caught it near the tip and turned it away. "Oh, perfectly well, darling, thank you for asking."

She cut in at Orsina's leg, making her stumble back out of reach. "And how are you?"

"Just." She swung the stave wildly at Harmony's head.

"Fine." Then again at her legs.

"Thanks." A thrust at her center that Harmony had to turn aside with her own "sword."

None of the attacks had any precision or skill behind them, but it seemed this game had granted Orsina some small measure of confidence at least.

So it went the rest of that morning, back and forth. Snippets of conversation interspersed with the clatter of wood on wood. A comment about the weather in the midst of a different subject turned out to be a feint that took Orsina off guard and left her open to a soft pat on the hip.

"What was that?"

"What?" Harmony replied with a little blush. "It wasn't your... rump?"

"The... that thing where it looked like you were swiping, when you were poking, what was that?"

The same natural curiosity that had driven Orsina forward in their conversations the previous day sprang to the fore again, and Harmony had to suppress a smile, knowing now with absolute certainty that she'd caught her. She came around beside the girl and showed her the feint, then set aside her own stave to guide Orsina through the motions. Movement by movement. Positioning her feet, turning her shoulders, adjusting her wrist until finally every part of it was perfect and Orsina's grin was wide enough that the top of her head was at risk of toppling off.

The day went on like that from there, the clumsy sparring interspersed with those little lessons. Orsina was not by any means proficient with a sword by the end of the day and had not come close to actually landing a blow, but there could be no denying that progress had been made. She was slick with sweat when Harmony linked arms with her to make their walk back to the House proper, the men's clothes the two of them had borrowed from Artemio filthy and marked all over with the lines the staves had smeared. Yet there was still a smile upon her face and a bounce in her step. Harmony could scarce believe it. Even she was on the verge of exhaustion after the full day's training, while this girl seemed as though she might go on for another ten rounds.

"How can it be that you are not tired?"

"What do you mean?"

Harmony clung tighter to her arm, as if she needed help to carry her own weight. "All day we've been at it, and I swear you could go on."

Orsina pulled away with a laugh. "It was fun. We were dancing. It isn't like walking from dusk until dawn."

"Was that a common feature of your days before you came to the House?" Harmony teased.

"Long way from the Selvaggia to here." Orsina shrugged her shoulders. "Even longer if you've no mule or cart."

Harmony actually stopped in her tracks as she realized that Orsina was not exaggerating. She had vague memories of the forest on her father's maps, so distant from the rest of the kingdom that it scarcely even had detail. The distances involved boggled her mind. "That is rather a long stroll."

They both fell silent as they passed through the rear door by the lecture hall, and Harmony had to slip her blindfold back into place. She took a hold of Orsina's arm once more, trusting in her to guide her back to her suite. Orsina chuckled to her. "The blind leading the blind."

"You don't remember the way?"

"This place is like the deep woods, all twists and turns that make no sense. At least there you could climb a tree and see where you were. This place is just…"

She fell silent, and Harmony could only assume it was because they were passing someone by. She spoke out loudly, "I do believe they built the House to be as deliberately convoluted as possible, so as to dissuade any of the students from ever finding their way out into the real world beyond the walls where they might discover how little use all of their dusty days of reading are truly worth."

There was a disgruntled sound from whoever they were passing followed by a giggle from Orsina. Silence persisted for a time as Orsina turned her attention inwards, to her memory. Harmony felt stairs, then the flex of wooden boards underfoot. Perhaps they were going to find their way without intervention. For her part, she could not bear to bring any doubt into Orsina's mind. Confidence was the only armor she could sheathe the girl in before throwing her out among the nobles of Espher, the only mask their contempt could never penetrate. Without her own unassailable certainty of her own excellence, Harmony had no idea how she might make it through a day of the askance glances and sneers from those who were supposed to be her peers. Orsina needed to be sure of herself, sure of everything she said and did. Sure enough that it would not even cross the mind of those who met her that she did not belong.

They made it to Harmony's chambers in only twice the time it would normally have taken her, making a detour that was presumably meant to bring Orsina back towards the familiar territory surrounding her own room so she could retrace the previous day's steps. Except that when she removed her blindfold, there was only darkness. "Orsina. I think we may have taken a wrong turn."

"Someone's at your door. I don't know her, but she didn't look right. Angry. Like she'd been crying."

There seemed to be genuine concern on Orsina's face, though Harmony had no idea what sort of situation she feared was unfolding here. It was unusual, certainly, and the timing of this visit, coinciding with Orsina's arrival, was certainly cause for suspicion, but not hiding in cupboards. "She must be one of the students. If you saw her eyes, she cannot have worn a blindfold."

"No. No blindfold. But…"

"The correct manner to approach such things is directly." Harmony could see the doubt all over Orsina's face. They were never going to manage their deception if the girl would not even meet with others without all this fear. "You and I shall simply walk up to my door, greet her, invite her in for supper with us, and thereafter decipher the purpose and meaning of her visit. You have been carrying yourself well thus far, all I'd suggest is that you remain quiet if you are uncertain how to proceed rather than putting your foot in it."

She resituated the mask over her face and held out her arm once more, like she was at the ball again.

"When you're ready."

The tension in Orsina's arm was palpable. Muscle straining beneath the shirtsleeve like a string of the harp, just waiting to be plucked. Yet despite her dread, she led Harmony out of the closet and back along the corridor. The support pillars for the ringed balconies of the upper levels passed by, each one a presence in the air for but a moment before it was gone behind them. Between them and the creak of the floorboards, Harmony felt quite certain of herself. They were close to the rooms that she now begrudgingly called home when she felt Orsina stiffen at her side. That was no use at all. She would have to work on the girl's comportment before anything else. Some rough edges were to be expected on a lady from the country, but this paralysis in the face of polite company was ridiculous.

"Harmony Volpe?" The other woman's voice did sound tear-strained.

With nothing before her eyes but darkness, Harmony tried to smile, "How can I be of assistance to you, miss?"

Darkness and silence were her only answer. Stretching out into a long, awkward silence until the very moment that she heard Orsina cry out in dismay.

That was when the force struck her in the chest like the kick of a horse. Even blind and surprised, her instincts served her well. She curled in on herself, trying to absorb the blow, to catch whoever had struck and to find her balance. It did not work. She had been hit with such force that her feet were no longer in contact with the floorboards.

There was another brief, bright flare of pain as her lower back struck the balustrade, but even that was not sufficient to halt her journey. The wood splintered, and she ploughed on through. Flipping out into the open air of the atrium and beginning her plummet down to her death.

Her chambers were on the third story of the building. The flagstones below would leave her shattered. She braced herself for the pain. For the darkness to swallow up all her other senses.

She struck water and sank like a stone into a well. The chill water enveloped her, dragging her down and down. The air had been dragged from her as she fell in a warbling cry, and now her lungs burned for air. Down and down she went. Drowning deep, still tumbling in the water as bubbles tickled up past her grasping fingers.

As abruptly as the vast pool of water had appeared, it vanished. Harmony fell once more, one final jarring foot before she struck the slick flagstones. She managed only half a gasp before the water hanging above her in a great cold mass lost its cohesion and splashed down over her. Drenching her anew.

She could not comprehend what had just happened. She struggled to gasp in air, and her cold numbed fingers fumbled at her blindfold as she desperately tried to make sense of it. All of a sudden, hands were upon her and she kicked out, flailing and screaming with none of the nuance she knew she deployed upon the fencer's field. There were voice raised all around her beyond the grasping hands, but between her confusion and the roar of the wind whipping by overhead, she could not know whether they were friend or foe. They snatched for her wrists, but once she had stopped trying to free herself of the constraints of her blindfold, they seemed to stop. Cutting through the roar, she could hear a boy's voice. "Get her outside, quickly."

It did nothing to alleviate her fear.

At the top of her lungs, she bellowed, "Orsina!"

There was no answer. Whatever was happening up above them, Harmony had no way of knowing. Her friend might be alive or dead, and she had no way of knowing which. The word *friend* had come to her thoughts all too easily there. Two days together and already the closest to her heart except the brother she'd known a lifetime. It was tragic in so many ways.

Her feet slipped as she scrambled to her feet. She had no idea where she had fallen. No grasp on the world around her beyond the heaving of her lungs and the chill water still sluicing off her. With arms stretched out ahead of her, she tried to run, to reach. Any pillar would be scratched with its number, she could find herself once more in the map in her mind, find the stairs, find Orsina. She was caught around the waist before she could reach anything, hoisted off her feet, screaming all the way.

"Orsina!"

Far beneath them all, a roar was building. So deep and low that it set the walls of the House shaking. The flagstones shuddered beneath their feet. The air filled up with steam as all the water was boiled off, fragrant with the scent of moss and rot.

"Out! Everyone out!"

Another voice, perhaps the Prima or one of the tutors. Authority was in it, enough that even Harmony found herself halted in her straining and struggles. She heard the pounding of feet. Felt the air chill as they went from the overheating main hall of the House and beyond into the sun-kissed afternoon air.

Driving an elbow down into the joint of her abductor's neck and shoulder, she dropped him and found her footing. They were out now, and she had time enough to think, pulling her blindfold away and instantly feeling revulsion as she saw the mildew blossoming across it. That same stain was upon all of her borrowed clothes, and she could see it around the legs and skirts of those brave students who had come to her aid, even knowing she was a pariah.

She felt a pang of sympathy as her rescuer found his way back up to his knees and looked up at her with teary eyes. She winced, as she choked out a brief, "Thanks."

Back to the House she sprinted. If Orsina was still in there, still fighting her battles for her, then she needed to help. It was a simple enough thing for Harmony to elbow her way through the flow of fleeing students, but she hit upon the Prima's stare like it was an iron bar.

"Do nothing foolish, my dear."

Despite that glare, and the painful knowledge that she lived so close to her brother only through the Prima's continued goodwill, Harmony still stepped forward. "You don't understand, Prima. Orsina is still in there, someone attacked us, she…"

"It is you who does not yet understand. The girl has called upon one of the Great Shades, and those that dwell within our walls are disrupted, their forces cast out of balance." With the last of the students running by, the Prima risked a glance back. "Until equilibrium is restored, it shall not be safe for any to walk these halls, let alone those who cannot even look upon them without courting madness."

Still Harmony moved forward, only for the doors of the House to slam shut in her face, seemingly of their own volition. "But Orsina…"

"Shall survive, or not, by her own luck or virtues." At least it seemed to pain the woman to say it. "There is naught any of us can do to intervene."

18

THE BITTEN THREADS

Gemmazione, Regola Dei Cerva 112

Artemio returned to the one peaceful place he had ever dwelled in all of his years to find it in chaos. Before he had even decanted himself from his hired carriage, all of those senses that made him Shadebound were screaming, and the moment he saw the full volume of the students and faculty of the House of Seven Shadows spreading out through its gardens, he knew that some great catastrophe had unfolded in his absence.

Harmony looked like she had been at the heart of that catastrophe when he caught sight of her, wrapped up in someone's cloak and shivering though the day was mild. He ran to her and she leapt up into his arms without a thought for what a show of weakness they were making. She was still drenched beneath that top layer, and the water oozed out through the cloth as he held her. Yet still he would not let her go. "What happened?"

"There was a student waiting outside my chambers. She attacked me. Orsina, she saved my life, but…"

Judging by her grim expression alone, he came to the inevitable conclusion. "She was slain?"

The Prima interrupted. "We cannot say. Someone invoked one of the Great Shades of the House, but…"

"That explains all of this at least."

With a hint of irritation on her face, the Prima pressed on. "I can assure you, we are doing all that we can to restore calm."

"Of course, Prima." He bowed to her with all graciousness, then set off towards the House.

She called after him, "Where are you going, my dear boy?"

He glanced back over his shoulder. Grim determination set in every line of his features. "I have no fear of the shades within, Prima, and if this Orsina of yours truly risked herself for my sister, then I mean to see that she is well."

It was difficult to maintain her air of dignity and command while trailing up the path after him, but the Prima did what she could. "The House is closed."

"Then I mean to open it."

She spoke up then. Loud enough that all could hear it. So that all could hold him to her word. "I command that it remain closed."

He stopped in his tracks. Turning to look first to the bedraggled Harmony with tears welling in her eyes, then to his stern-faced mentor. Rumors had surely already outpaced him about his new role in the court. There was no question that this attempt upon his sister, foiled though it may have been, was not merely the work of one of the noble houses jostling for station. Only the investigation could have spurred on such wild action. That meant the mysterious student who had meant his sister harm was assuredly one of the threads that would lead him to the greater tapestry of the conspiracy. "With all respect to your station, Prima, I serve a higher power."

The Prima set her shoulders and a shade carried her whisper to his ears on a zephyr of chill wind. "I could make you stop."

He did not deign to respond to that, turning instead, with Bisnonno Fiore already leaping out ahead of him to slam the doors of the ancient house wide open once more. The Prima did not stop him.

A thick and sickly perfumed fog washed out from within the building to envelop him, but he did not pause or slow. He might not have known the place blind as well as his sister, but he knew it well enough to clear the threshold without the benefit of his eyes.

Some shades he found it easier to form sympathies with. Experience helped, of course, and certain emotional connections made it quite easy for him to align his mind and become a willing vessel. Of the Great Shades within the House, The Fire Below had always been the one he had found the most straightforward to master. It was a primal force, an elemental spirit, as much as it was a shade, and with his own forge spirit to serve as an intermediary cajoling it into serving him, the task should have been quite simple. Yet now he could not even seem to catch its attention, so great was the agitation set upon it by the events that had unfolded here.

The fog was likely its doing, the fountain at the center of the courtyard made gaseous. Yet it did not explain away the stagnant odor, nor the chill winds that still whipped through the place, coiling that fog into contorted swirls that for but a moment seemed sneering faces.

He strode on through those faces as they mocked and roared in their silent revelry, all the feeble shades gathered in the House leaping at this chance to gain traction and notice. He paid them no heed, his mind was on other matters. His sister's chambers were where the would-be assassin had struck. Whatever had unfolded, he would begin to reconstruct from the evidence he viewed there.

Keeping his eyes unfocused and his body moving, he was almost to the stairwell when his foot came down upon on a hand. It was for the best that there was nobody else within the building, because the noise that he made upon realizing what was underfoot was not entirely dignified.

Still, for all that he had made a sound like a dog with its tail trodden, his actions were not so clumsy. He eased his sole off the fingers and crouched down to see what lay beneath the cloud of fog. From the hands he could tell little, from the black dress, all restrained finery, he could tell a little more. Yet there was still doubt in his mind as he straddled the twisted remains, legs and limbs contorted by the impact. Only when he pushed the curls away from the dead girl's face could he be entirely certain. Rosina Aquila. All of her lauded beauty gone pale and still, streaked with blood.

He cursed under his breath. She had lost her fiancé and, grief-stricken, sought out a way to find some revenge. This was worse than he could have anticipated. Not only did this newfound thread of evidence—the assassination attempt on his sister—lead to no new tangle for him to unpick, it had cut one of his existent avenues of investigation abruptly short. Whatever he might have managed to learn from Rosina about those who had put her and her fiancé up to the attempt on him at the ball was now gone. At least this had been a public enough display of madness that he could not be accused of masterminding it in a fit of vengeance on his own part. There could be few better alibis than spending the duration of the crime in the dungeons beneath the palace.

Tentative, and uncomfortable to be touching even a dead woman so intimately, he searched through her clothes for anything that might have been considered incriminating. Sadly, no noble house had placed a letter of confession within her bodice before setting her off after him.

From the broken bones he could feel shifting beneath her cooling skin, she had fallen the distance from one of the upper floors, of that much he was certain. Yet there was no sign of the girl he had met in passing the other night. Orsina had not been thrown down with her assailant. He felt some small spark of hope that she might still live. If she did, then not only would it be a comfort to Harmony, she may be able to provide him with the insight to make this event fit with all the rest. To discern some pattern from the dying words of the one who would have taken Harmony from him.

That thought brought him to a halt before he could step away from the broken corpse of Rosina Aquila. She had known him well enough, better than most within these halls, and in that knowing had been awareness of his weakness, his love for Harmony. The death of a sibling would strike anyone hard, but Artemio could not have lived without her. She had been his beacon through the long, turbulent, dark years of his youth, guiding him through to humanity on the far side of the festering storm that had threatened. He would have become like his father, just as his father had wanted, if it were not for Harmony. That was a debt that could never be repaid.

He did not kick at the corpse. He did not spit upon the grieving girl who had sought to take everything from him, not once but twice. He did not, because Harmony would not have wanted him to be the kind of person that would.

Stalking up the stairs, he let his senses stretch out. Beyond the raging of The Fire Below, there were five other Great Shades bound within the House of Seven Shadows, and not a one of them was in their appointed place. In the tower where Gufo di Archivio usually took roost, there was an echoing silence. In the volcanic cavern that had been appointed to Guscio Cavo there was no sign of that dry old suit of armor long gone to rust. Instead, it seemed that Raffica had taken up residence, coiled up in the hollowed-out room like some great serpent, just waiting to strike at the first fool to open the door. Here and there he caught echoes of the other two, one lingering around the student chambers, the other the libraries.

He did not envy anyone who tried to find things within those shelves in the coming days. Ossatura was a methodical shade, but the logic it pursued so relentlessly was not one that was recognizable or truly knowable to those who still remained on this side of the veil between life and death. With time, connections could be discerned, and indeed that was much of its value as an oracle—teaching students how to decipher the often densely complex language and symbolism that shades employed to make their natures known. Needless to say, it did not improve upon worldly filing systems.

So lost in his thoughts, mentally sniffing around for the Great Shades, Artemio came wandering out onto the third-story balcony where the fog was thinning and the damage that had been wrought was visible.

The balustrade on the opposite side of the hall was gone, ripped away by some great impact and dangling now by twisted metalwork to touch the level below. The stagnant water that was everywhere in the hall had been splashed about here quite liberally, along with no small amount of mud and spidery pondweeds. He had no clue as to what it could mean. He knew of no shade that called the swamp its domain, and certainly not one

Rosina might have encountered, living her entire life within the city. To his knowledge, her shades had been a carefully cultivated stable inherited from a grandparent. It strained even his prodigious talents of recollection to identify which specific element she had favored, but it most assuredly had not been this.

There were burn marks up the walls. Deep-charred lines that showed no finesse or precision. Perhaps they had been Rosina's, if she had been lost to her grief, but he was dubious. The purpose of rote training was to ensure that behaviors were automatic. That the motions they had been trained to go through were the ones they would go through when under duress.

Which left the possibility that Orsina had an elemental spirit of fire harnessed already, before she had even undertaken her first day of tutorship in the House of Seven Shadows. It was not entirely unheard of, but it did not strike him as likely. Particularly if the swamp shade was also hers. He had bound one shade before he had arrived, but he had also had the finest tutors money could buy. Even then, he had barely dared to call upon Fiore until months into more serious academic tutelage, when he could be entirely certain they were correctly partitioned from each other in his mind and Fiore could not make an attempt to overpower him.

There were echoes of all the shades that had been called here. Still lingering in the air, twisting the fog into their shapes. Something huge, amorphous, and amphibian lurked on the periphery of his perception, distant enough that he could not truly put words to it, but potent enough that it rivaled his awareness of the Great Shades of the House. His skin felt clammy as he came too close to its influence. It was small wonder the shades were agitated if this monstrosity had been called upon.

He had to set it aside, it was voluminous and overpowering, blinding him to everything else. He had to look at the details, not the overwhelming chaos of the fight. Careful of where he stepped and slipped, he paced around to the place where it had all begun. There was the place where Harmony had been struck. The place where Orsina had stood, watched Harmony fall, called this great monstrous specter to catch her. Tearing water from the fountain and making it into something it was not, a pool deep enough to catch a falling body and place it unbroken upon the stone below.

Whatever else had followed, he would always bear a debt of gratitude to this girl for that one act. For coming under attack and thinking not first of how to protect herself, but how to preserve Harmony.

From there, the chaos of a battle meshed and mangled his perceptions. Rosina had struck out with her shades and driven the girl back. There was a tang in the air, not just of the drawn blood but of ozone. Lightning. Rosina's elemental shade at work, without a doubt. They were a rare and storied breed, shades of the storm. Unlikely to occur and even less likely to be captured in a contract. It was a shame it had been lost.

Then came the waters once more, catching and grounding the lightning before it struck home. The telltale marks of its fizzling dispersal cobwebbing out on the floorboards. Perhaps this Orsina was a duelist savant, but it seemed all the more likely to Artemio that this was all flailing reflex rather than reasoned strategy. That pond shade was the bludgeon she had to hand, so it became her answer to every obstacle.

It seemed likely that Rosina had come to the same conclusion soon after, switching to one of the myriad other tactics that would not be stopped by a simple splash of water. Ice crusted on the underside of the roof above the doorway to Harmony's chambers, swiftly melting away in the intense heat that The Fire Below had been pumping out in its riled state, but still visible.

Cold came easily to shades, whose very nature was that of sapping and taking. To be ridden by a shade at all brought a chill to the flesh and flaked frost about the eyes. It was a simple matter to extend that chill, to weaponize it, as Rosina had.

Here and there on the floorboards he marked the triangular incisions where knives of ice had formed from the water being cast up as a shield to stab at Orsina. The splash of blood on the wall showed where one had struck home. The thumbprint on the doorframe where that blood had trickled down to her hand.

Calling up a power like a Great Shade was far easier than putting it down again. The strength it drew from the one who bound it empowered it and made it all the more rebellious. The more frequently a shade was called in swift succession, the more powerful it became, until it might make an attempt to drink down all that remained of the one who bound it. Partitioning and rotation were the key to ensuring that each shade was always weak enough to obey without question but strong enough to be of use.

Artemio could not see now whether she had tried to pull down the wall of water when the darts of ice began bursting out of it, or if her response had been sluggish and surprised. Either one might have been true. Regardless, she was too slow, she was wounded. She bled.

Bright red spots hung among the mildewed pools. Just a few of them, the initial burst when skin was parted abruptly. Nothing like a killing blow or the gruesome displays he had seen in the homes of the assassination victims.

She had been giving ground all the way, backing up from Rosina once she was certain Harmony was safe. Unwilling to press the advantage of surprise for some reason Artemio couldn't grasp. She backed away until the wall of water fell, until the darts of chill air were just resounding slaps instead of lethal blows and then... Fire?

Here was where the blackened marks leapt up, striating wood and stone in perfect lines, spaced evenly and expanding out. From the geometry of them, he could see the focal point each outburst had originated from. The place where Orsina's retreat had halted and she had begun her wild rush back towards Rosina.

The fire had eaten whatever attacks Rosina had tried to unleash in those last moments. Flares of it pulsing out from Orsina to some rhythm Artemio still could not fully discern. Her heartbeat? The pounding of her steps? Pressing his fingertips into the bubbled stone of the wall, he let his senses race back along the line to the point of emanation and felt for the shade responsible, but each time that search leapt sideways to The Fire Below. As though it were the shade that she had called upon.

Patently ridiculous, of course. Yet that was the lie his senses told him.

He followed along the striped black lines until he came level to the torn-away balustrade where first Harmony, then Rosina, had been flung. He reached out to find the shade that had dealt this killing blow and launched the girl to her death, but while one of Rosina's shades clung in a distant echo after it had struck at Harmony and started off the lethal chain of events, there was no sign another was called to repeat the motion.

Rosina was taken by surprise, of course. She had not expected one of the students to leap to Harmony's aid, and when she did, there was no way she could anticipate two elemental shades being at her would-be victim's disposal when they were so notoriously difficult to partition.

In his mind, Artemio could clearly see the trajectory that her body had followed, pushed from the ledge to soar down and strike the stone below. The droplets of blood curving around and heading straight at the gap. The scuff marks of Rosina's heels across the wet boards, then the abrupt drop off. Rosina was not slapped off the ledge by a blow or a masterful shade-strike. She had been shoved bodily off. All of her defenses ready for another elemental assault, and all she received was a push. It was almost genius in its simplicity. Something that would never have crossed even Artemio's devious little mind.

A few more spots of blood where Orsina had lingered for a moment, looking down upon what she had wrought, then the bleeding was stanched somehow, and he could track her by it no more. He cast about then, looking for the next piece of the puzzle, only to realize that the door to Harmony's chambers hung open and he would invariably find his answers inside.

He burst in to see this strange girl, this Orsina, who he had only laid eyes on once before, in a state of unseemly undress. He clapped a hand over his eyes and strangled a yelp. "My apologies."

Her voice came soft and ragged with pain. "My arm's out, not my teats."

"I did not mean to intrude when you are…" He trailed off, cheeks flushed and brain still trying to work its way around the word *teats*. It was not a term he heard bandied about among the nobility. Even those coarse younger men who bragged of their conquests.

"Just open the wine, would you?"

With no small effort, he lowered the hand from his face and opened his eyes. She was settled in the chair by the fire facing away from him, but while it was true that Orsina's chest was mostly covered, the tatters of her shirt—his shirt, really—hung loose down her back, exposing what he'd assumed would be a smooth curve of the same tan skin that covered her face, but was rather a ragged raised pattern of pinkish scars.

There was a bottle of red dangling limply from that exposed arm's fingers. The cork marked with her fingerprints in blood. Despite her injuries, she had dragged out a kettle and set it over the embers of the fireplace and uncovered a sewing kit on the mantelpiece that Harmony had dallied with for a time when the fashion for young ladies was the art of embroidery.

With a spasmodic flick, she lost her grip on the wine and it rolled across to his feet.

"Madam, is this really the time to be drinking?"

Another faint ragged laugh. "You want me to stitch myself up sober?"

He opened the wine, yanking the cork out with his teeth before pacing over to her, doing his best to keep his eyes averted. He held it out to her while she fussed, trying to thread a needle, and finally noticed him there. "Put half the bottle on to boil and see if you can't find me some clean rags."

He moved over to do it, slightly put out at being ordered around by this nobody. "Might I inquire why we are boiling wine?"

"Because there's swamp water in these cuts, and I don't fancy losing my arm to rot." She scoffed. She was paler than he remembered her being. Presumably an effect of all that lost blood, but she looked different too. He could have sworn that in their last meeting she'd been in her teenage years, but now she looked to be of age with him. Since she was wearing his clothing, it was less immediately apparent, but now he was around the front side of her, there was no denying that the trousers hung almost an inch too high at her ankles.

His brows drew down as worry niggled at him. "Just how much did you spend?"

"Beg your pardon?" From the faintly dazed expression on her face, he wondered how much of what was happening right now she was truly aware of. She'd managed to thread her needle at least, but now it dangled from that thread between her fingers.

"You've aged, substantially, since last we met."

"Trying not to think about that." She said it with a giggle, but it was barely contained hysteria, not humor. Was she a year older? Two? Just how much of her own life had she spent to save his sister?

The bubbling of the wine saved him from having to formulate a reply. He wrapped the handle in a cloth and brought it over to rest on the rug by her feet. Despite everything, she moved with confidence, dipping her needle into the wine, then snatching it back and feeding the rest of the thread through it. He had no inkling of why someone might do such a thing, but she seemed certain of her actions now in a way that inspired confidence. He plucked a handkerchief from Harmony's dresser and pressed it into the girl's waiting hand. She did not acknowledge him, just set to work soaking it and then pressing it, hissing into the slices that Rosina had made cleanly through the meat of her arm.

"I must offer you my most sincere thanks, Miss Orsina. If it were not for you, then my sister would be…" He was surprised to find emotion choking him as he considered what could have been. A world without Harmony was not a world he would have cared to live in. "I do not know how I can ever repay you for what you have done."

"Did you know her?" Orsina's voice sounded ever more distant and faded. She was pressing the once white cloth into the worst of the injuries, pressing it into the tunnel through her flesh in a way that made Artemio's stomach turn. Yet he did not look away. She had suffered this, the least he could do was to bear witness to the fruits of his failure. "The one who did all this?"

For a moment, he had to think on exactly how much he was willing to share with this stranger. He did not like to doubt her, not when she

had just done so very much for him, but neither could he find her sudden
arrival and befriending of his sister anything other than suspicious. Was
it mere coincidence? Coincidence that she would be in the right place at
the right time to protect Harmony and instantly win his trust? Artemio
was not a believer in coincidence, but neither did this girl strike him as
zealous enough to willingly give up not only her lifeblood but also her best
years just to be brought into his confidence. He gave as much as he dared.

"I did not know her well. Judging by her actions today, it seems nobody
knew her as well as they thought they did. She was a student alongside me
here for a time, and more recently she was involved in some conspiracy to
see me dead. A conspiracy that took the life of her fiancé. I believe she came
today seeking vengeance for that, though I was not the one to slay him."

"Why would she want to kill you?"

He paced to keep his face out of her sight as he tried to puzzle through
this latest conundrum. "To win the favor of the kings, perhaps, or some
other noble house that had some quarrel with my father. It is also possible
that she is involved in the assassinations I am investigating at the behest
of the crown, though it strikes me as unlikely they'd be so clumsy after
working in such perfect silence for so long."

"Sorry, what?" He glanced back to her sweat-glazed face and realized
with a gut-churning start that she had drawn the needle and thread through
her own flesh and was now pulling it taut. The edges of the cut were pulling
together like a darned stocking. "Why would the king want you dead?"

That was a step too far. There was no way anyone could be so completely
unaware of the world in which they lived. "You may be playing the hand
of ignorance too far, miss. Everyone knows of the enmity the royal house
of Cerva bears towards my own."

Her hands still moved, even as he glared at her with contempt. Not
once did she look up from her work. "Let's pretend that I don't."

"No matter how remote a country estate you may have dwelled upon
in your youth, I cannot believe that the Volpe name has never been spoken
even in jest."

She attempted a shrug, but it was an error. The half-pulled stitch lost its tension and a fresh wash of blood slipped down her arm. Through gritted teeth she groaned out, "Harmony said you used to be kings?"

"The Volpe family ruled Espher since time immemorial. The Cerva are but a few generations into their own dynasty. You cannot think why there might be some tension between us?"

The flesh wound on the outside of her arm was now closed, and she sat their shaking with pain as she gathered her composure to tie it off and start on the through-and-through wound.

"They're scared you'll steal the big seat back?"

He let out a huff of stifled amusement that was so like his sister's that Orsina turned around to look at the door, thinking Harmony had come back. When she looked to him, his composure had returned. "I have no interest in kingship."

She began on the next wound. Hissing between the stitches. "Have you told everyone else that?"

"Of course. Not that anyone would believe it. To say I did want the throne would have my head on the executioner's block before dawn, so of course I'd say I didn't. Even if I did." He sank down into the seat opposite her and realized he'd been carrying the bottle of wine back and forth the whole time. He took a swig straight from the neck of it.

"Ugh." He could not tell if she was letting out a groan of pain or disdain. "Sounds tricky."

He shrugged. "It is not the most comfortable position to be in."

"Want to swap?" she tried to joke as all the color left her face yet again.

His eyes were drawn back to the bloody mess Rosina had made of her. She may have acquitted herself well, unnaturally well, but that did not mean she had emerged from the ordeal unscathed. He let his suspicions fall away for now and asked with all sympathy, "Is there anything that I can do to help?"

"You can stop hogging the wine, to start."

He chuckled and looked around for a glass before recognizing they were a little beyond decorum and pressing the bottle into her shaking hand. She spilled some down her chin as she fumbled it to her mouth, and if his shirt had not already been ruined beyond all hope of recovery, the fresh purple streak down the front probably would have put paid to it.

After that first faltering sip, she drew deeply on it. Like it could wash all her pain away. Perhaps it could, if she got through enough of it. Artemio still needed answers before he could let her slip into oblivion. "How did you summon fire?"

"The old thing below the floor. It was just… there when I needed it."

He had suspected as much, but to hear her state it so plainly was still a shock to him. She should not have been able to call any of the Great Shades of the House; they were bound to the place both by decades of tradition and by the students' ardent belief that they were beyond mastery. Even with his own shade serving as intermediary, he'd never managed to achieve such a thing. Perhaps with the forge spirit it would now be possible, with like calling to like, but Orsina had no shade of fire at her beck and call.

"Such a thing should not be possible."

"It was angry. Jealous that I'd called Ginny. It wanted to prove it was better."

He had never heard of shades being spoken of in such foolish, humanizing terms. They did not feel. Emotion was changeable, and by their nature, shades were not. They were frozen. Fixed as what they were, for all eternity, so long as they were tended. He set it aside. When her education was more advanced, perhaps she would have the language required to truly explain how she had tapped its power. For now, he needed other questions answered.

She was stitched up, the loose threads hanging from her arm bitten short. And now she was trying to cover herself with what was left of his ruined shirt. Sympathy tugged at him again, alongside his sense of propriety. He dragged a blanket from the bed and draped it around her.

"At the very end, you pushed her?"

Through all she had done and endured, he had not seen the girl shed a tear, but now they came in a flood. Sobs racking her body as he clung to her shoulders to keep the patchworked blanket in place. It was like a hug, if the purpose of a hug was to still the one being embraced. There was a strength returned to her now, a passion in her voice that pain and shock had stripped from her until now, a passion that racked her as she sobbed. "I killed her. Just like that. I'd… all the things I said to Harmony about… then when I had the chance, I just… like it was nothing. I pushed her off. Oh… her eyes. She knew what was coming, and she looked me in the eyes, and I… I did it anyway."

She jerked out of his grasp, almost tumbling from her seat as she retched unproductively. Rosina had tried to murder her, and somehow this girl still felt guilt over stopping her own assassination. It was so ridiculous, Artemio almost couldn't understand it.

He reached down to do what he could, gathering her curls back from her face, in case one of the waves of nausea succeeded in bringing something forth. Her hair had been bound up neatly in one of his sister's braids before all this had begun, but a year's growth had that braided knot dangling low on the back of her neck now, and no small amount of the wild hair about her face had escaped.

"You did what you had to, to save my sister. I cannot pretend for a moment that I feel any sadness. If I had been here, I would have done the same. You… you did what I could not, and I am so very grateful to you."

She stared off into his emptied seat. Shivers running through her now the retching had stopped. "I'm a murderer."

He tilted her head up so she had to look at him. To see the sincerity in his face when he replied, "You are a hero."

"She didn't know me. I'd never even met her and…"

She had turned her face from him again as she spoke, and he had let her, but he could not allow this wallowing in self-pity to go on. Not when so much had been at stake. "And she would have slaughtered you without a second thought, so that she might kill my sister and cause me pain. Remember that. She was not trying to kill me, who she believed had wronged her. She was trying to kill a woman who had never so much as looked at her wrong. She would have killed anyone if it might have hurt me, and you stopped her."

Her gaze was fixed once more on the distant horizon of memory, emotions playing over her face in such rapid succession that even one trained by years of flinching from any display could not identify each of them. Eventually she replied with a sigh. "You make it sound like she was some rampaging animal."

"Perhaps once your studies are more advanced you will realize that she was more akin to a natural disaster unfolding. Someone with a complement of shades at her disposal and not a care what damage she did? Someone so lost to grief she would spend all the life that remained to her just to do more harm?" She met his gaze and swallowed down his sincerity. "I can think of few things more dangerous in this world."

Orsina went back into herself. Looking now to her own hands, still stained with wine and blood. They shook. He could almost see the flow of her thoughts, the monster she was imagining herself to be, or the monster she felt she was on the road to becoming. He did not know what more could be said to alleviate her guilt or her fear. He knew no platitude that might snatch the sting from what had happened. He was not one for speeches or rhetoric. He flung himself down opposite her and let his own exhaustion overtake him.

"Orsina."

The sound of her name stirred the girl from her thoughts and she met his stare.

"Did she say anything, before..."

"No."

He sank lower in his seat. "I suppose it was a faint hope that she might have made some confession..."

"I mean, she said no." She interrupted him before he could reach his own self-pity. "At the start, she said Harmony's name, then... at the end, before she went over... That was all. Just... no."

"Right. That's... right." He hoisted himself back to his feet, despite the exhaustion he could feel sinking into his bones. "Do you think you can walk?"

She reached up to him, and he took a careful grasp on her hands. She was lighter than he would have expected. Almost waifish under the blanket. Still the child she'd been before the shades had drunk her years. She nodded tentatively. "I'm sure Harmony will be glad to see you are well. And the shades of the House are still rather... riled. It may be best to step out for a time."

She tried a smile, but it didn't reach her eyes. "You'd better hold on to me. If I went through all that just to fall down the stairs and die, I'm going to be mad."

"I would not dream of letting you go." He blurted before he realized she was making a joke. Then a flush ran over his cheeks. "Come along."

19

HOLDING COURT

Gemmazione, Regola Dei Cerva 112

In the days that followed the attack within the House of Seven Shadows, attention began turning inexorably towards Orsina. Those who had seen her around the house since her arrival no longer recognized her. It was as though an entirely new person had appeared out of thin air to form the basis of all the gossip. A new student who had bested a graduate in a duel. A duel within the House no less. It was the sort of thing that crystallized into local legend. The involvement of the disgraced Volpe sister was just another twist in the tale, and when mixed with the rumors that had sprung up about young Artemio Volpe being the secret lover of the deceased following the confrontation at the Spring Ball—well, it was a toxic soup of whispers.

At first Orsina was able to ignore it, staying close to Harmony, who had graduated from looking at her like she was a chore, skipped many of the intermediate steps, and now treated her like there was nobody more beloved to her heart. But as the days rolled on and the Great Shades of the House were coaxed back into their usual containment, more and more of the students came back. Nobles who had never been denied anything in their lives now found the lack of access to this curious new creature in their midst to be a great frustration. Some hissed that she was a ward of the Volpe family, raised up from obscurity to be a bride to the family's heir. Others that she was the daughter of some exiled lordling come back to reclaim her family's domain from those who had usurped it in the generations since. Speculation dogged her steps, yet not a one of them ever considered the awful truth, that she was no one of note and her friendship with Harmony mere happenstance.

The Prima had been diligent in ignoring her. Orsina had tried time and again to see her, to explain and apologize for what had happened, but the woman was intent on keeping her distance. Finally, she received a note from one of the Prima's personal servants informing her that favoritism could not be shown, that her newfound celebrity ran entirely counter to any good sense, and that she was expressly forbidden from channeling shades until such time as her formal education was further progressed. That little scribbled note stung almost as much as her slow-healing wounds.

While she still had her own chambers somewhere in the bowels of the building, Orsina found that most nights she ended up bedding down in one of the spare rooms of Harmony's suite, warm with wine and relaxed by the sounds of other living people about her. The desolate silence of her own well-insulated chamber had been too alien to a girl more accustomed to being trod on in the night, the silence stretching out and leaving vacuous openings for her thoughts and fears to dwell in.

Artemio was there with them now, more often than not, sat away from their chatter with a book and candle, frowning all night long and glancing up only when prompted to issue his opinion. He still did not seem to know of Orsina's origins, though it struck her as odd at first that Harmony had not told him, until she realized that she meant to use her brother as a measuring stick by which the properness of Orsina's behaviors might be judged.

Sometimes he would tut and correct some error in her habits or comportment, other times he would barely glance up before returning to his studies with a grumble. He could be cajoled to join them at the card table when the evening was drawing on, but only once both of the girls had expressed their desire that he join them. She had asked Harmony if this was some matter of politeness that had escaped her, and Harmony had given her a little knowing smirk in return. "I'm his sister, so he can do as he pleases in my company and feel no pang of guilt, but you... You're a lady. He doesn't want to force his company upon you if you do not desire it."

Orsina had actually barked with laughter at that idea.

Laughter had come to her lips again not long after when the twins returned from a foraging expedition to the kitchens and Artemio could not even look at her without a blush. By then, they were quite accustomed to Orsina's blunt manners. So neither was startled when she flatly asked, "What?"

Harmony had descended into titters at once, and Artemio's face rapidly approached the same shade of red as the velvet upholstery. He opened and closed his mouth several times before retreating back to his little table and his little book. Sinking down with a huff to intently ignore them both.

The armfuls of their dinner were spread across the sideboard with all haste, but Harmony paid them no mind, still giggling away to herself as she situated herself on the chaise beside Orsina, all the better to whisper to her without fear of Artemio being embarrassed, as he had been during Orsina's many inquiries about corsetry.

"The scullery maids were talking about the two of you." She said it with such mirth that Orsina genuinely wondered if there was something inherently funny about whatever a scullery maid was. Seeing her confusion, Harmony pressed on. "The latest rumor is that the fight was borne of jealousy between lovers."

This time, she managed to remember the manners they had been so desperately drilling all day. She almost choked before she managed to strangle out, "I beg your pardon."

Tears were running down Harmony's face at the sight of Orsina so discomfited. "They think you and Artemio are an item, and that Rosina was trying to eliminate the competition."

So sprang forth the new tides of laughter until Orsina was scarcely able to catch a breath. Wheezing out, "That's insane. Me and him?" just loud enough that it called another flush to Artemio's face. He hunched down lower behind his book and pretended not to notice them, even as his ears turned crimson.

The girls continued to giggle for a few moments more, but when she'd wiped the tears from her eyes, Orsina noticed an odd expression on Harmony's face. One she couldn't quite identify. When Harmony whispered this time, it was definitely not with the intent for him to overhear them.

"Would it be so terrible?"

Orsina looked at her sideways, then glanced over to where Artemio was still furiously scribbling away at his notes. His quest for the kings, along with a few of the more salacious gruesome details, had been shared with her, so at least she could understand why he was so devoted to the work he had undertaken. There was a very good reason for him to sink his every waking hour into scouring the intelligence his predecessors and their little spies had gathered when the alternative was death.

"Is he so desperate for attention that you'd toss a commoner in his bed?"

Harmony rolled her eyes, then leaned in closer. "Listen to me, Orsina, I've been thinking about this ever since all of that business the other day. You know how I care for you, bastard or commoner or whatever you may be. I don't want to be parted from you. This would be a way to ensure that we can stay together in the future. If you were to marry Art, then our lives would be intertwined in perpetuity."

Orsina glanced up at him again, and she could see Artemio noticing the attention. His brow furrowed and he cleared his throat, pretending to be absorbed in the work.

"Did he put you up to this?"

"Art? No! He's too bashful by far. It wouldn't have even occurred to him. Planning weddings and alliances never seems to occur to men. They need calmer heads to guide them. But I want you to think about it. Seriously consider it, please. Once he's caught whoever is behind the troubles, our family will be back in the good graces of the court. All of our old allies will come back out of the woodwork like the lice they are, and I'm doubtful that anyone could make a more promising match for you."

She did not say, "Given you are a common lout," but Orsina still heard the implication.

"If his future is so bright, why do you think he would marry me? Surely he'll have his pick of all the rich and famous families' eligible maids." Orsina was still looking at him, actually considering it for the first time. He'd never treated her with anything beyond cold politeness up until this point, but there was no denying that the solution had appeal. She wouldn't have to spend her whole life keeping her humble origins a secret from the man she was wed to, or his family. Harmony would be there with her to help cover for any little mistakes she made and to run interference with anyone who questioned her too deeply. And he did strike quite a handsome profile, even if it was contorted into a frown of concentration.

"Well… perhaps other girls might be tripping over their skirts to get to him, but they don't matter. I don't like any of them. I like you." She took a hold of Orsina's hand and gave it a squeeze. The one that still ran a little cold after all the lost blood. She leaned in conspiratorially. "Besides, you have leverage at the moment. After the showing you put on the other day, you could ask Art to lop off his own leg and he'd ask which one you'd prefer gone."

"So marrying me would be like dismembering himself?" Orsina drew her hand back. She already knew that she was not beautiful the way Harmony and the other women in the school were beautiful. Her long months of travel and her rapid aging had seen to it that she could develop none of the gentle curves that were in vogue around Covotana, and while she ate as much as she could stomach at each meal, she still could not seem to acquire the pleasing softness in her features that the women all seemed to be seeking. Like her body was still running at a deficit since her rapid growth.

She was coltish and uncomfortable in her freshly grown body, unaccustomed to the shape of it and uncomfortable with everything she saw when changing from one borrowed dress to the next. She had not gathered the courage to look at her reflection in the dressing room mirror before she was garbed. She feared the stranger looking back might start sobbing. It was not that she cared whether some man might find her desirable. Rather that she feared she would never come to know or like her body again. It made her perpetually unsure of herself, and Harmony's words were like a twist of the knife.

"No. No, my darling. That is not what I meant. Only that if you wanted him, there is no way he could refuse you." She snatched up Orsina's hand again, the smile on her face tinged with something all too much like pity for Orsina's liking. "Honestly, I think that the two of you would be a fine match for each other, even if it weren't for your circumstances. Just think of the quality of the babies the two of you could bump out. With you both being so powerful, they'd probably be born fully fledged Shadebound! Knowing the Prima, it was probably in the back of her mind when she foisted you on me. She always had an eye for such pairings."

Orsina paled at the mention of babies. Until that moment, her consideration of marriage had extended as far as living under the same roof and eating dinner together. She was uncomfortably aware of the physical expressions of affection that were required for babies. Mother Vinegar had been the village midwife after all, and all the parts and their intersection had been clearly explained to her in the same matter-of-fact manner as the properties of herbs.

She looked at Artemio again, and this time it was her who flushed with embarrassment. "I'll think about it."

Harmony switched subjects rapidly to ensure that she did not embarrass anyone further, but there was a knowing smirk on her face sometimes when she thought Orsina wasn't looking. Like she had uncovered some girlish crush instead of being the one who had proposed… what she'd proposed. They ate dinner using more cutlery than Orsina had ever encountered before in her life, with brief pauses to ensure she was using them correctly, and even Artemio could find no fault in her, though he seemed to be looking for it quite intently.

The flush burned back up Orsina's cheeks as she cursed herself for not asking Harmony whether she had run her plans for their marriage

by Artemio before approaching her with them. Did he know? Was every
glance that he sent her way a flirtation or was he pondering the kind of
wife she might make?

Regardless, it seemed he found something to be satisfied with each
time he looked her way, and while there was no praise forthcoming, neither
did she have to endure any of the usual corrections. When they were done
and settled around the fireplace with the last of the wine, Artemio finally
deigned to pass comment. "You seem much improved in your comportment
since we first met. Quite acceptable for court, I should say."

It was enough to bring an uncharacteristic stillness to Harmony, but
Orsina didn't notice. She was so delighted at the praise that she giggled.
"And why would anyone want to go to court?"

He sipped his wine casually, but spoke with care. "To swear fealty to
the kings as they should have when they first arrived in the city?"

Orsina's mouth opened and shut a few times, but it was Harmony who
surged in to her rescue. "Surely they can't be angry about her failure to
visit. You know her circumstances were hardly ideal. If she'd come straight
to court to present herself, I dread to think the response she would have
received."

"I do not believe the Cerva are feeling vindictive about the matter, and
I suspect the Prima has already laid some of the groundwork within the
court to ensure our dear Orsina is not treated too harshly for her failure
to attend them." He set his glass down on the table between them with a
clunk. "But her presence will be required. Her name has reached too many
ears. She has made a spectacle of herself in defending you, dear sister. If
she is known of in court, then she must present herself in court."

Orsina gathered enough of her wits to croak out, "I'm not ready. All
those people looking at me? Judging me? I can't possibly do it."

Harmony rested a hand on her shoulder, and glancing to her brother
for encouragement, she said, "You could, though. I mean, we have covered
all of the basics, and while you're the belle of the ball here at the House,
in court I doubt you would garner a second look. So long as you kept your

head down, gave them a curtsy, and got out of there when they took their leave, I believe you'd be quite all right."

Orsina looked as troubled as she had in the same spot a few days before with blood on her hands, both figurative and literal. "They'll take one look at me, and they'll know, and then—"

"There is nothing to know." Artemio cut her off before she could wallow in her own panic for a moment longer. "You are a young lady recently arrived to the city with the intent to study at the House of Seven Shadows, and it took some time for you to settle in before you felt yourself presentable enough to approach the king. They need hear no more of your tale than those truths."

She wet her lips. "You truly think that I could…"

Both Volpe twins were nodding at her encouragingly. Artemio even leaned forward to pat her on the knee awkwardly. "I have business at court tomorrow. I might even serve as your escort some portion of the way."

She would rather have had Harmony, but beggars could not be choosers. She patted his hand before it could be withdrawn, and he had a bashful smile on his face when she glanced up.

Sleep was hard to come by that night. Too many thoughts seemed to compete for Orsina's attention, and each time she closed her eyes, she felt them parading back and forth across the darkened stage of her mind. Marriage. The court. The king. Her curtsy, still clumsy. Artemio had said she curtsied like a milkmaid the first time he saw it, and she'd almost burst out laughing at how close to the truth he'd cut. Not a milkmaid, a damp-footed farmer. A girl more at home barefoot in the woods than creaking over polished floorboards. A girl who was going to try to pass herself off to the king himself as one of his noble court.

The evening's elaborate dinner twisted in her gut. The soothing warmth of the wine turning acrid and prickling back up her throat. There was no way she could go through with this.

Every seam in the wood of the ceiling was committed to her memory. Every moment of the past days replayed itself endlessly. Her wounds were on their way to healing thanks to some herbs the servants had fetched at her request, but there was an ache that went deeper than any one of them. She wanted to go home.

Playacting at being something she wasn't ate at her spirit in a way the shades never had, and more and more often now, she found the line between truth and lie blurring. She was polite and kind to the men and women who fetched and carried whatever Harmony wanted, but more and more often now, she could not see herself as one of them. Whatever twist of fate had damned her to a lifetime living in the woods with Mother Vinegar had set her apart from everyone else and made her a pariah among the common folk, but she had never before considered that it might set her above them, not just apart. When she was kind to the servants now, it was in the same way that Harmony was kind to them, not the kinship of equals but the respect of an owner for a well-trained dog.

She had to get out. It wasn't just panic at the prospect of being caught out as a peasant in the highest court in the land. She was losing herself. Piece by piece, the mask was becoming her face, and if she did not cast it aside now, she had no clue where this path would end.

There was no lock upon the bedroom door. The key was in Harmony's chamber door. And there were no guards within the House or at the gates. She could walk right out if she so chose. Even after the attack by Rosina, there had been no consideration of locking the doors. The loss of face would be too much for the institution to endure. It was strange to think of a building having a sense of pride that could be punctured, but with it packed so densely with shades, it made a terrible sense. Every one of them was house-proud and riled up by the latest slight. Orsina didn't fancy any assassin's chances of making it in unscathed. Open doors or not.

Pangs of guilt struck her as she wrestled into a dress that was not hers but had been becoming hers day by day. It was not as though she had asked for the charity, nor did she intend to abuse it when such gifts were received. Now she thought she might be able to sell the dress off her back for enough to get a carriage out of the city. She couldn't go back to

Mother Vinegar. They would look for her on the northbound roads, but there was a whole wild world into which she might flee and make a life for herself as she was. Perhaps she would never master her gifts, perhaps her days would be sapped from her by each shade she encountered, but at least they would still be her days to lose. Her life to spend. Not this false Orsina devoured by the masquerade.

She tread softly on the boards beyond her door. The only one who might try to halt her flight was Harmony. She would miss Harmony when she was gone, but there was nothing to be done about it. There would be other friends for her somewhere.

The fire still burned in the main room of the suite, but Orsina thought nothing of it until she stepped out and saw Artemio waiting for her. "Good evening to you, Miss Orsina."

Brought up short, it took her a moment to force words out. "I was just…"

He waved her lie away before it could even be made. "You need make no explanations to me. Nor need you worry that I shall rouse Harmony to intercede with you. To my mind at least, you have more than earned whatever freedom you desire."

Her shoulders slumped. "Thanks."

Artemio nodded to a pouch on the table beside his books. "There is money for you, if you need it. Not much, I'm afraid. I do not have much in the way of ready money, but it ought to be enough to keep you in some small comfort until you reach whatever destination you have set in your mind."

"You didn't need to…" She backed away from the table, though the fat pouch would certainly make her flight much easier.

"I am aware." He cut her off before she could even begin, yet again. "This is not a gift of obligation, but if our paths are to part, I would rest easier knowing that you were not headed straight into strife."

"Why are… I…" She was at a loss for words. "Thanks again."

Leaning back in his chair, he shrugged a shoulder. "The debt I owe you can never be repaid."

Inching forward, eyes on the pouch, still half sure this was some sort of trap, Orsina barely heard herself say, "I didn't do it for you."

"Intentions matter little in the grand scheme. Without your actions, I would be bereft of the one person in the world I care for." He had to stop and take a breath to compose himself. "You chose to do great harm to yourself so that my sister might live. Your sacrifices will not be forgotten."

"It was just a year or so." She gave him a self-deprecating smile. "I'd probably have just wasted it anyway."

"I think not." He smiled back at her with surprising sincerity. "Besides, the shade's price is not the matter to which I was referring. I know that Rosina's death... I know you would never have chosen to do what you had to do, given any other circumstances."

Any hint of a smile washed off her face. "I don't want to talk about that."

He gave a little nod, almost a bow. It should have been ridiculous, but it wasn't. "Of course, my apologies."

Orsina picked up the pouch. It was more money than she had ever held in her entire life. Probably enough to buy half of Sheepshank. Certainly more than it would cost for a carriage out to some town in a distant province where she might disappear. She weighed it in her palm. "You aren't going to ask me to stay?"

"It would be my preference, certainly, and most likely the best course for you to take, but I cannot force my wishes upon you." He was very still. As though she were a deer he feared would spook if he rustled the leaves.

"Right. So... I'm going now."

She'd only made it a step before he asked, "Is there anything that might convince you to stay? I know that Harmony will be quite beside herself without you. No doubt your studies will suffer also without an institute of this caliber to guide you. I am certain you have good reasons for departing, but is there any way in which I could change your situation?"

"Not unless you know how to get me out of meeting the king."

"Is that what has you so pressed?" His smile now seemed considerably more genuine. "My dear Orsina, the king will scarcely even notice you. While this is a great event in your life, it shall not even feature as the most interesting moment of his hour. Personal attention from the king is unlikely. On a busier day, there is a distinct possibility that you shall not even be brought directly into his presence at all, but will swear your fealty to the Cerva via his secretary."

It took the wind out of her sails, and she slumped down into the seat opposite him. "You think?"

"While Harmony has been somewhat evasive about your family history, would it be fair to say that you and your family are not of any great political influence at this moment?" Her bark of laughter was answer enough. "You likely could have passed entirely unnoticed were it not for the unpleasantness that we need not speak of again. So long as you do nothing dramatic or scandalous between now and our rapid retreat from the court once you've had your disdainful nod, it is unlikely that his Majesty will even deign to focus his eyes upon you."

Rocking back in her seat, she could almost feel the dread departing. She dropped the money pouch back onto the spread of books between them. The two of them sat smiling at each other for but a moment before Orsina recalled Harmony's marriage suggestion and discomfort crept back in. "Why did you stop me?"

For a moment he seemed at a loss, until finally he seemed to settle upon the right words. "Friends do not let friends make bad decisions."

Settled back into her borrowed bed in her borrowed bedclothes in a body that still didn't feel entirely her own, Orsina was surprised at how easily sleep came to her. It seemed she had no sooner lain down than her eyes were springing open again to the dawn bells tolling.

Artemio had no hint of a late night about him, looking more presentable when he came knocking upon Harmony's door than he had since the first moment Orsina had set eyes upon him. There was no malingering cloud of wine hanging over him, nor any of the prickly irritation that seemed to fuel his usual snappish wit. Rather, he seemed subdued and composed, an entirely different man from the one she had known until now.

If last night's dress might have bought her passage from the city, this one might well have bought her the horse and carriage in perpetuity. The Prima had it delivered to her moments after dawn when Harmony had only just begun to work herself into a frenzy trying to find something suitable for court in their combined wardrobes.

There were beads stitched onto the fabric that shone like frost in the sunlight. Orsina had almost torn the thing off and fled back inside when she saw that, but Artemio was already there with a hand at her elbow. As he led her on down the path, she hissed to him, "I'm not meant to be drawing attention to myself."

"Then perhaps you might inform your snarl of that fact."

She quickly smoothed out her face, even though she was practically vibrating with tension.

He leaned in scandalously close to whisper. "In the streets of Covotana, you shall shine like a jewel, drawing all eyes. But in the palace, every woman is a jewel and you shall fit into the collection invisibly."

It was enough to shut her up. A blush burning at her cheeks from all his courtly manners. They traveled by carriage to the palace, and each time she felt her terror climbing up her throat to strangle her, he would catch her eye, or let his gloved hand brush ever so briefly upon her hers as they sat side by side.

They had gone through the process again and again before departure. With their appointment late in the morning, there was no shortage of time for repetition. Yet still he repeated his instructions like a litany. "When we arrive at the palace, I shall walk with you as far as I might, but you can trust in the ushers to see you right. The Prima has already written to the court making your intent to visit clear, so it should be a simple matter. You will be announced, so you need not speak. If you do see the king rather than his secretary, do not look boldly into his eyes as you do with my sister and I. Keep your gaze upon his chest, perform your curtsy, and then await dismissal. It should all take only a moment. Curtsy again, retreat backwards, turn, leave. I shall await you outside the court. Speak to no one unless you are forced, and then say only that I am waiting for you. My family name may offer scant protection, but it is now widely known that I am in the king's favor of late."

She couldn't even look at him as she breathed out heavily, feeling every bone of the dress pressing in around her newly filled figure. "Thank you, Artemio."

"Think nothing of it," he said, though it was patently ridiculous. She knew how desperately he must have been burning to return to his work, yet here he was riding along with her, dawdling in the halls of power he seemed to loathe, all just to offer her some small comfort. Perhaps he was simply ensuring that she did not attempt to bolt again, but if he were a jailer, he made little attempt to intimidate. If she'd expressed a change in heart, she suspected he'd likely have seen her to the city gates himself. It was a strange situation, made stranger by this sense of debt he seemed intent on using as his guiding principle.

It would have been uncouth to hang out of the carriage window and stare up at the rising spire of the palace, and Artemio insisted he would have Harmony take Orsina on a proper tour of the city once she was more fully situated. Yet her admirable restraint in behaving at least a little like a noble lady instead of a gawking peasant in the big city for the first time meant that she had no idea of how close they were to arrival until the carriage doors were hauled open by a guardsman.

As all the livery and shining steel loomed, she realized with a start just how doomed she was if this little deception went awry. A peasant trying to pass herself off as a noble was the sort of story even her mother back in Sheepshank, far from the reach of kings, would have feared to tell. There could be no happy ending to it.

Still, she held her head high as she passed first under the warming light of the sun and then on into the deep shadow of her impending doom. Artemio walked by her side, and the hand clasped to her elbow was no longer to steer her towards the gaping maw of the palace, but rather to keep the fear from dropping her to her knees.

Yet as they stepped inside and the clamor of bodies all around her pressed in, there was some part of her that was not afraid, and she reached for it. Fear was not her base nature. She had wrestled shades of legend, slain a dragon, bested a graduate Shadebound when her own training had so far consisted of naught but a bath. What could the stern stare of some man in a high chair mean when placed in comparison with all of that? That grain of arrogance was all she needed to slip into her mask of nobility and stride forth.

Everything was very carefully ordered and timed within the palace, and she was led smoothly from one place to the next with scarcely a word passing from one servant to the next. Artemio had released her elbow now they were so close to court for fear of tainting her with scandal before she had even begun, but without that contact she could not say with any certainty when he had left her. She glanced around as she was led from one chamber to the next, and while he was by her side in one, in the next he was gone.

A blur of color and sound assaulted her senses. Her life before the deception had been simple and small. The most company she'd enjoyed was that of two people and no more. Here individual courtiers had entirely vanished into the amorphous blob known as "court." There were faces here and there that she might recognize if she glanced askew, families of students at the House who she had encountered, but there were far too many for her to ever hope to pair names to those faces. How anyone could navigate this place and the tidal shifts of silk and finery, she could not even begin to comprehend. Still, she kept her chin up and her eyes locked upon the servant tasked with leading her.

When one grandiose space opened into the next, she scarcely noticed, and when the bluster and batter of noise from all corners abated, it was more of a shock than the sudden space devoid of bodies. The long stretch of room between her and the throne. The throne and room were the same white stone from which the whole castle were made, but where elsewhere the stone was smooth, here carvings strove to crenellate each exposed inch with patterns and shapes, beasts and men, stories like those on tapestries in lesser palaces. Her eyes could not stall upon any one part of them, though not a single part was hidden. She needed to maintain her focus and decorum until her name was called.

There were men and women both arrayed between her and the stretch of carpet, each waiting so patiently it made her want to shout out. She quashed that suicidal urge and pressed her face into a pleasant smile so anyone who looked upon her might think this was where she was meant to be, that she was happy to be coming and bowing and scraping before a king she'd never even heard of before this week, a king who somehow had the right to decide whether she lived or died.

Kings were like lightning, exciting to see from a distance, but nothing anyone sane would seek to be close enough to touch. Yet here she stood, knees feeling watery beneath the wide skirt and stomach skipping over itself. She stood her ground and waited.

As Artemio had promised, the king could not have looked less interested in the proceedings. He was present, certainly, but only in the physical sense. His eyes had a glazed look, and his fingers drummed upon the arm of the throne. Orsina couldn't see any good sense to making a chair out of stone when there was perfectly good wood about, but after the first four of her fellow supplicants were called out and did their fealty-swearing bobs and nods, she began to understand the necessity of it. If the chair had been comfortable, the king would have been fast asleep by now.

Step by agonizing step she moved closer and closer to the carpet running the length of the place. Soon it would be her turn to stroll down, bob up and down, and then get out as fast as her legs could carry her. The king himself may not have cared too much about any one of them, but his was not the only scrutiny she hoped to avoid. There were dozens of courtiers, not present to be announced, but just lurking. Hanging around as though they could think of nothing better to do with their time than bask in the boredom. Their stares were not glazed, and she had seen more than a few of them glancing her way before turning to whisper in the ear of another.

The longer she lingered, the more of them seemed to notice her, and before long it felt as though there were more eyes on her than on the poor girl out on the carpet. Even the servants and attendants in livery seemed to be looking her way more frequently than she'd have expected. She knew the story of the Aquila girl's death had traveled as far as the palace, but she'd hoped it might not have reached this very room.

It felt as though she had been there for an hour by the time she was the next in line to be called, and all of her dread had now contorted into a bloody-minded determination to just get through it as quickly as possible. The waiting had been the awful thing, not the thing itself.

She was waiting for her name to be called, body already tensed to move, when the shouting began. The king did not stir from his stupor, but every other head in the court seemed to snap around at the sound outside the grandiose doors by which not a one of them had entered.

Orsina waited for her name. There was a cry in some language she did not know, deep and guttural, and a thump against the wood as if whoever was out there meant to break their way in. The guards to either side of the door looked askance to each other, but neither moved. It was not as though they were the only armed men within the palace. There was no question that whoever was causing such a ruckus would be dealt with imminently.

And still Orsina waited for her name. The whole court had fallen silent, straining to catch a sound from beyond the doors. The usher who was meant to be hustling her forward to get everyone through the day was just as susceptible to a break from the monotony as the rest of them. Orsina almost lost her temper and shouted out her own name before storming down, but before that madness had any opportunity to manifest, the grand doors to the throne room burst open.

To anyone else in the court, the sight of a man towering eight feet high with serpentine scales coating his skin would have been a shock, but Orsina had spent too long with Kagan for this man to startle her. The guards from outside the doors lay scattered in his wake, tossed to the ground and struggling like upturned tortoises to regain their feet. His voice roared like crashing mountains through the halls of power.

"I speak with kings, not lapdogs."

Those startled guards on this side of the door may have known fear at the sight of such a creature, but they knew their duty well. Both stepped forward to meet this monster with their crescent-headed halberds descending, and both were cowed with just a snap of his head and a bark. He barked twice at one and once at the other, and they were so taken aback that they paused long enough for him to stride through. The king held up his hand to them before they charged, and in that one motion the whole court stilled.

"Ambassador, our meeting was scheduled for this afternoon."

The upheld hand did nothing to slow the raging giant's approach. "Arazi do not have time to waste."

Still the king showed surprising composure. He had loomed so large in Orsina's mind throughout the day that she had built him up to be a giant. But this little king on his little throne was dwarfed by the sheer bulk of the man approaching. This Arazi was not dressed in hides the way Kagan had been. Every inch of exposed skin glistened with scales, and everywhere else, boiled leather was shaped to his contours. He wore none of the draped finery of the Espher court, but his presence and the fine craftsmanship of the leatherwork he bore put them all to shame.

The king called out with a smile, "Then I am delighted to entertain you now."

He waved a hand to the gathered lesser nobility, and they began to scatter. All the rest of the line dissolved behind Orsina, but still she stood frozen. She had been so close. Could they not just acknowledge her quickly, and then let her move on with her life? Would anyone even remember that she hadn't done her little curtsy before slinking away?

"I am Hazal, the Omen, I speak for the Arazi."

Orsina meant to slink away, she really did. There was no good reason for her to stay in the throne room for a moment longer than was necessary. Every moment had a greater chance of drawing attention to her and dooming her, but when confronted with one of Kagan's people in all their glory, she found herself rapt.

The king was certainly attentive now, in stark contrast with the bored sneer he'd worn all day. "Greetings to you, Hazal, I assume introductions are not necessary on my part since you are in my kingdom and my palace?"

Though she'd chanced a glance at the king and his looming guardsmen while he spoke, Orsina found there was a hypnotic attraction to the Arazi ambassador. There was a certain stillness that overtook Kagan during the hunt, when all the humanity seemed to drain from him and only instinct remained. The first few times she'd seen it, Orsina had been unsettled, but as with all the strange parts of her life at that time, eventually she had come to accept it for what it was. This Hazal had been in the stillness since the moment she first laid eyes upon him. In anyone else she would have called it tension, but in truth, it seemed to Orsina to be the complete opposite. The only time Kagan had ever seemed truly at peace with himself was in those moments before he struck.

Hazal's voice was no longer a roar, more like a slide of gravel than stone slabs colliding. "My people send me to make a generous offer to you, king of ghosts. You shall keep your throne, you shall serve your people, and your children can still inherit your titles and lands as ever they did. All that needs to change is your fealty."

The king chortled. "I beg pardon, but it sounded like you just offered me the throne on which I already sit?"

"In exchange for your fealty as our vassal, the Arazi shall protect your people and make them strong. Turning back your enemies and adding your strength to the great conquest." Hazal had stretched out his arms wide. "All you need to do is submit."

The sneering laughter had drained out of the king as swiftly as it came, replaced with a cold dead expression that gave nothing away. In her momentary glance towards him, Orsina saw all she had feared a king could be. As inhuman as the looming serpent-man before him. "Might I ask why the Arazi think we would choose to abandon our sovereignty?"

Hazal did not seem impressed. "You are surrounded on all sides by powerful foes. You are too weak to fight them all. They circle like jackals. Waiting for the opportunity to strike."

"And in this little has changed for centuries." The king scoffed. "I might suggest that the Arazi have failed to grasp the strength of Espher."

"How you feel does not matter. Only the reality." Hazal drew himself back up to his full height. "Do you know why I am called the Omen?"

"Because you're terribly fun at parties?" Even Orsina had to be a little bit impressed that he was still quipping in the face of the looming giant.

Hazal paid him no mind. "I am the warning that comes before doom. I am the threat of things to come. Submit to me now, and none of your people need to die begging and screaming for their lives. Submit and you might live on instead of being burned from the annals of history."

If she had been asked before this day what made a king different from a common man, Orsina could not have said, but now she saw it. This foppish little man had a will as strong as tempered steel.

"I must decline."

"Then you shall lead your people to their new domain."

Hazal surged forward, hands outstretched to catch the halberd blades as they were swept into his path. The scales on his palms threw up sparks where the sharp edges caught them, but his grip must have been like iron to halt the swings before they could draw a drop of blood. The other guards poured along the carpet towards him. Yet more burst out from cubbyholes Orsina had not even spotted amidst the graven stonework. There were a dozen men barreling straight for Hazal, and the man did not even spare them a glance.

She did not know why she was running forward or why she had not fled. If she had been asked to put any part of her motivation in that moment into words, Orsina would have been at a loss. Later she might have said she caught the familiar scent of dragon venom in the air before Hazal's jaw slipped open and a great gout of flame leapt forward, or that the shade of Ginny Greenteeth was so attuned to sudden bursts of heat since its rivalry with The Fire Below flared up that the pressure on Orsina's mind gave her warning. Perhaps it was both of those things or none.

All that mattered was that when the Omen let loose his lethal breath of fire to wash over the king, it met water not air.

For just a moment there was the blinding orange light of flame, then the sudden eruption of steam set all the men stumbling back in shock. The billowing cloud shot straight up between them to wash over the ceiling, and Hazal's surprise gave the guards the moment they needed to close on him.

What came next was not a great feat of heroism on the battlefield, but butchery. The halberds swung and struck off the scales across the Arazi's skin. The force of the blows knocking him about, but no blade finding purchase. Yet still the guards came on, hacking and hacking until the natural armor gave way beneath the hail of blows and blood began to spray. Hazal's growl echoed out, not pain but rage.

Time seemed to slip back into its normal flow, and Orsina cast Ginny out of her as swiftly as she'd come on. Her eyes snapped down to check her hemlines, to see how much more of her life had been stolen away. There looked to be no change. Only weeks or months then, instead of years. The slaughter went on as the guards crowded in. Some casting aside their polearms and drawing swords so they might better navigate through the storm of violence.

The king stood perched on his throne, robes in disarray. He must have leapt back as soon as the fire burst, and now his eyes darted frantically around the room, settling for just a moment on Orsina's own frightened face. The very attention she had been so desperate to escape.

They were staring at each other wide-eyed with shock when Hazal burst free.

Blood covered him, a dozen wounds hung open in his armored flesh, gristle and muscle open to the air as he leapt out from amidst the storm of blades. With his own arms as a bludgeon, he slammed the nearest stalwart defender of the crown to the floor like he was batting a fly. When that brave knight's sword came loose from his grip, Hazal ducked another sweep of halberds at his head to snatch it.

Outside the scrum of bodies, only the king and Orsina saw him. The king could do nothing, but Orsina raised her hands like she could snatch Hazal from the air and Ginny flooded back through her.

The fog that had spread out across the ceiling spiraled back down and the blood spattered about the pristine white floors leapt up, not to strike the would-be assassin, but to hold him back. There was not enough water in the room to do that lumbering beast any real harm, but if she could buy the guards a moment to understand what was happening, they would do plenty of harm for her.

She lacked the control experience might bring her, and Ginny was not accustomed to working with anything less than a pool to draw upon. The chains that she lashed about Hazal burst like bubbles as soon as he strained against them, time and again, forming and popping in rapid succession.

There was not enough water, so Orsina pulled with all of Ginny's might to draw more in. The air turned crisp and Hazal's charge faltered. Not because her chains of pond water had stopped him, but because she had torn the blood from his seeping wounds to fuel them.

He thrust, and blood splattered up onto the throne. Royal blood that ripped away as soon as it was spilled to thump into Hazal's chest and knock him back before he could strike again. Orsina could not see what had happened. All she heard was the cry of the king, abruptly cut off.

It shattered her concentration, and, already taxed, she lost her grip on Ginny and the shade slipped away.

Sheer weight of numbers bore him back, a press of bodies dragging him down and away with no care for his raking claws. He was a titan, but even a titan would fall when enough pressure was applied. He toppled and was dragged along the carpet, trailing blood as he went.

His gaze passed over Orsina as he went by, but he was so frenzied by that point she could not have said if he'd even seen her. She staggered away as the butchery began anew.

Attendants swarmed around the throne, any hope of seeing what had happened already thwarted. The press of bodies from outside the chamber had flooded inside now, along with more servants than Orsina could have ever imagined any one person needing. There were cries going up for a doctor, for the queen, for everyone and anyone.

Artemio was at her elbow again before she had convinced her legs it was time to run.

"That could have gone better."

SONGS OF SILK AND SIN

Gemmazione, Regola Dei Cerva 112

Madrigal Cerva lived, and the one who had ensured that was neither doctor, guardsman, or noble. It had required no small part of fast talking on Artemio's part to ensure that Orsina was not dragged along into the ensuing madness of recriminations and terror, making her excuses for her and claiming she was overwrought by the awful thing she had borne witness to. She had been almost entirely speechless by the time he had recovered her from the throne room and shuttled her out to a carriage, but from others he had managed to extract the fullness of the tale.

He had scarcely needed their contributions when every step of the battle was still laid out before him. The scent of stagnant water from Orsina's now familiar shade hung in the air, some pattering down from the ceiling above in droplets.

Nobody had known that Arazi themselves could breathe fire. Artemio himself had been in the presence of one mere days before and never even considered the possibility. Moreover, he'd been in such a position with the dungeon-bound Arazi that if that man had been capable of spitting fire in his face, he had no doubt that the prisoner would have done so. The fact that the king had come within an inch of death seemed to have rattled the hornet's nest of the palace up quite nicely. The fact that it was only blind luck and some untrained girl of no importance who had saved him from his fate was considered to be less a matter for celebration than a damning indictment of the security measures in place.

They'd found the other twin sitting placidly in the solarium after his brother had been fussed over to the limits of his patience, and then all the doctors had been sent away, all the servants, everybody except for Artemio. It was just the three of them now, stewing in a sudden and unexpected silence.

While the injured twin nursed his injured pride with a glass of pale blue wine, the other spoke. "Is it fair to assume that this attempt on the royal self is related to our previous assassinations?"

"No." Artemio sighed. "It would be so much simpler if it were, but I cannot see any connection between the Arazi and our existing troubles."

The wounded king snapped, "Assassination seems a rather clear connection."

Artemio didn't really want to argue with a man who was in a foul mood and capable of having him decapitated with a nod, so he went gently. "The methodology is different."

"We thank you for the presence of your agent in our moment of need, though it would be best in future to work with us rather than independently."

"She… I…" He didn't know how to respond, so he reached for a platitude. "I am glad that she was there."

The wounded king let out a wet little simper of laughter. "As are we all."

Artemio glanced between the two men, still entirely unsure as to why he was there, but almost too worried what the answer might be to pose a question.

When it seemed that Artemio was not going to be the one to break the silence, the clean-faced king spoke. "You know that it is a cardinal crime to spill royal blood."

Artemio did not give an answer. He had heard many long rants deep into the dark of night in his childhood about the indelible stain such an act would have upon the souls of the Cerva family and all of their descendants. Every time there was misfortune in the Kingdom of Espher, it was to that blood curse that Baron Volpe had turned for his explanations.

"In itself, this is a reprobation that has served whoever sits the throne rather well, but it does mean that in certain practical issues, we find ourselves struggling." When it was obvious that Artemio was not grasping his meaning, the king sighed. "When a physician says that bloodletting will help our health and humors, he refuses to be the one who administers it. When a lesser injury might prevent a greater one, our loyal courtiers hesitate. More often than not, we have been forced to turn to each other in times where blood may be spilled and expected our twin to do the necessary."

Artemio could imagine that such a thing was an irritation, but he still had no clue what it had to do with him until the king lifted a handkerchief from the table beside him and a dagger was revealed.

"We are mismatched."

What was being asked of him struck Artemio like a hammer blow between the eyes. They meant for him to cut the king? To cut his face? "Your Majesty, I... is there nobody else who might be able to perform this duty with more surety."

The injured Madrigal replied simply, "No."

His brother added, "Nobody we could trust not to try cutting a little farther than is required."

"Nobody who would not... lose face if the story ever got out." He smiled a little at his own little joke.

Canticle Cerva caught his gaze. "Nobody but you. Besides, I'm sure your family would be delighted to learn you had bled one of the Cerva like you were lancing a boil."

Madrigal picked up where his brother had left off. "And then there is the matter of blood. It is quite acceptable for those of royal blood to spill that of other royals. There is no taboo."

The dagger shone in the midday sun. Drawing Artemio closer even as he longed to be anywhere else. It was a tremendous show of trust on the part of the Cerva kings to offer him this opportunity, even if there were ample reasons that he was the best choice. "I see."

He was startled out of his reverie when Canticle laid a hand upon his sleeve. "May I speak candidly with you, Lord Volpe."

Another great honor, far beyond anything his service had earned him. They really were taking Orsina's actions as a reflection of his own will. Yet another debt he owed the girl. "Always, your Majesty."

"It is a great shame that your sister was not of age when the time came for us to begin extending our family tree, or that you yourself were not born a girl so that we might have both had one to ourselves." He gave Artemio a wink that would have bordered upon scandalous if anyone else had seen it. "Marrying our two lines would have put an end to a great deal of turmoil behind the scenes of Espher's Teatro. Perhaps next generation another opportunity will present itself."

Artemio was utterly gobsmacked. The idea that the royal family would even consider bringing his back into the fold, back into the bloodline, it was more than anyone could have expected. It was all dependent upon his own obedience and success, of course, but the prize had never shone brighter than in that moment. "I... thank you, your Majesty."

"Now cut me."

Madrigal drew aside the silken bandages that bound his face and turned so that the damage was clear to see, and his twin matched his pose and position with practiced ease. A trickle of blood escaped the jagged wound as he irritated it, but it was little more than a teardrop's worth.

The Arazi's blade had thrust in at an awkward angle, the tip had glanced off the cheekbone and then the sharpened edge had slit along the cheek. A crooked injury, but one Artemio felt confident he could mimic. Though of course he had no need to match it perfectly, only to ensure the scar left behind was a match for his brother's.

The swelling and bruising would go down, and only the cuts would persist. Two incisions then, one at the point of impact to mimic the tear from the initial thrust, and another along the length of the cheek. He ran through it in his mind, over and over again until he was certain he could mimic it properly. Then he cast around for something the king could bite down on.

Canticle whispered, "Just do it."

So Artemio obeyed.

His estimation of the Cerva twins had always been influenced by his father's opinions and those of the few who were brave enough to call them allies. The twin kings were soft, weak, spoiled, and foppish. They cowered behind the skirts of their family's Agrantine allies and showed no drive to improve the station of Espher in the world. It was an image they seemed quite intent on projecting. Even in their first encounter with all the doom gloom and threats they brought to bear, Artemio had never quite managed to take them entirely seriously. They were rulers by birth, not by nature, in his estimation.

Now he was seeing behind the mask. As he pressed the dagger tip into Canticle's cheekbone, the man did not flinch. There was pain evident in his expression, tears gathering in his eye, but he did not pull away. Even as Artemio drew the dagger out and set it for the next cut, there was no suggestion he stop. To sit there and do nothing while someone cut into you, simply because you had rationally decided it was the wiser course to be hurt, that took a force of will that even Artemio himself could not have hoped to match.

He finished the cut with a downward twist, keeping it shallow along the length of the cheek as it had been on Madrigal, but then dipping in dangerously close to the jawbone at the end.

Artemio was so intent upon his work that he had not even noticed the blood until Madrigal brushed past him to press a handkerchief in place to stem the red wash. Canticle's cheek was slick with it, his stiff collar stained a startlingly bright, fresh cherry red, and still he did not flinch. Rather, he held as still as he could until Madrigal held up a hand mirror and they could examine themselves side by side.

With his work done, there was no more need to flatter Artemio. Madrigal nodded to him, then glanced to the door, dismissing him like a servant. "Send in the physician when you leave."

Obedient as could be, Artemio did just that.

All eyes were upon him as he departed, and he felt certain that everyone must know exactly what had come to pass in the solarium, even if Canticle had somehow made it through his entire ordeal without crying out. The physician would know at least, and he was as gossipy an old thing as had ever walked the earth.

If he was a success in his larger task, then this would be taken as a sign of the king's great faith in him. If he failed, then they had casually found a way to eliminate the only living person to have spilled royal blood. Either way, the Cerva won. It struck Artemio that this had been the case since the moment he came into their employ.

Striding off from the court until the passages he walked were silent, he found his thoughts regarding the Cerva had grown turbulent. They were more than they had pretended to be, and the things he had taken for simple factors of the situation they were all in now seemed to Artemio to be deliberate decisions upon their part.

He ducked behind a tapestry and into the servants' tunnels, then made all haste through them towards the Rose Garden.

The failures of the two dead scions of noble houses who had preceded him might not have been the unfortunate result of incompetence, but rather a series of political maneuvers. Their families had been prominent enough to warrant some attention from the court and the potential to advance themselves, but not so powerful that there would be any sort of consequences for the kings if they failed to protect them. Seeking the best person for the job had only come later when Artemio himself was produced by the Prima of the House as a candidate. Another one who could be spent without consequence.

There were servants moving about back here even when the public halls stood empty, and it was a unique experience for Artemio to be the one flinching away from their approach, ducking into cupboards or stairwells to avoid crossing their paths.

Was it his competence that had made him their inquisitor, or the political gain the kings would receive? Either he failed as all others had and a rival to the throne was eliminated, or he succeeded and the kings could show they had tamed the wild Volpe. He had considered his precarious position to have been an advantage to the kings, but now he truly wondered if it had been their sole reason for choosing him.

All of which begged the greater question of whether the kings wanted these assassinations to be halted or not.

When he reached the outer wall of the palace, he strode up the stairways to the rooftop gardens with a surety of direction none could have expected from him. The only time he had ever spent in the palace had been in the past few months, and it had been very deliberately limited to the areas farthest from the royal chambers. His grandfather's memories were fragile as bubbles of blown glass, touched too firmly and they would fragment into nothing. But so long as he gave them no concentration, merely letting his feet lead him, they were his to use.

When he had asked in the very beginning who benefited the most from having the nobility of Espher unstable, there had been one very obvious answer overlooked. When all of the noble houses were fearful, they looked to the kings for leadership and protection. Even rebellious dukes and half-feral country ladies could be brought to heel under such circumstances, and there was no denying that the Cerva had no shortage of those to be dealing with.

Before, he had been treading carefully so as not to tip his hand to the assassins and their backers, but now he had to wonder if the ones who had set him the task even wanted it completed. They had a constant and full accounting of his motions so they could strike him down if he drew too close to the truth. They had the resources to make seemingly impossible things happen, and while he could see no clear pattern to the deaths that had occurred so far, that did not mean they were random. Only that the choices that were being made were according to some rules he did not understand. Even if they were truly random, striking factions both loyal and wavering, they would have the same effect.

Until he had looked into Canticle Cerva's eyes as he cut into the man's face, Artemio would never have thought the foppish buffoons on the throne to be capable of such a deception, but now he found he was beginning to doubt the very foundations his entire quest had been built upon.

If the kings had meant for him to fail, then they could not have set him up for it more efficiently than they already had. The fragmented information left behind, the constant threat of death, enough authority to put him in the way of harm with not nearly enough to protect himself from it.

Bisnonno Fiore was standing ready when he reached for him, granting him eyes on the other side of the gilded wooden door at the top of the stairs. The chaos sweeping through the palace below had not reached these heights. Indeed, the few guards strolling around the walls were looking out over the city rather than turning their attention inwards to the doors. They were so deep into the maze of the palace that a whole army would have to fall before an enemy could make it through to this place.

With the choice of literally anyone in the kingdom to seek out the mysterious assassins, the kings had chosen him. He was confident in his intellect, but he could not believe there was not a single person more qualified. Indeed, he was only a student in the House of Seven Shadows while there were a multitude of graduate Shadebound at their beck and call. More and more this began to feel like a trap that he had only just noticed closing around him.

Still, this was all supposition and fearmongering. What he needed was evidence. If he could find enough proof that the kings were behind the assassinations themselves, then Artemio could use that information as blackmail to halt their crimes, or to at least claim his just rewards for resolving the mystery.

There was a chill that came to him when Bisnonno Fiore rode him. Not the cold of the grave, but a certain calmness of thought that he could not achieve independently. It let him consider the options available to him without the burning rage at his heart taking hold and guiding his hands. Mother was one of the victims of this plot. The idea of coming to a compromise with her killers should have appalled him. But what was the alternative? Declare war upon the Cerva? They had the whole Kingdom of Espher at their service and enemies pressing in on every side that would sweep through and leave the victor of any internal squabble as the king of naught but ashes.

Perhaps someday there would be a time when these things were not true and Artemio could avenge himself on the Cerva, but until that day, he needed the cool touch of the last true king of Espher on his fraying resolve.

When Fiore's senses confirmed that the guards were as far from the entrance as their patrol would take them, Artemio stepped out into the Rose Garden. At once his senses were overrun by the beauty. A dozen different floral delights swept over his nose. The pristine white stone of the walkways was surrounded by rich dark earth, but only glimpses of it could be seen through all of the innumerable flowers cultivated here. Fiore's memories of this place were strange and shrunken, but filled with delight. He had played here as a child, long before the throne, before his betrayal and his death. Artemio let the shade slip away; he had no time for nostalgia and he had pared back his own emotional outburst enough that he was merely stomping forward into this place of beauty instead of razing it to the ground.

What he needed before he could act upon any of his suspicions, one way or another, was proof. To find that proof, he needed to find someone who was close to the kings but who hated them with such a passion that it would not matter to them if the truth reduced the whole kingdom to cinders so long as the Cerva burned first.

When he rounded the next bend in the path, he dropped smoothly into a bow, startling the queen from sniffing at a particularly luscious bloom.

"Your Majesty."

Cadence Cerva turned to face him with surprise evident on her face. According to Fiore's reconnaissance, her ladies-in-waiting were scattered around the place in various states of drunkenness, unable to keep up with the grueling rate at which their mistress ploughed through the wine cellars the Volpes had spent centuries filling. They were alone, with no chaperone, and Artemio couldn't even begin to bring himself to worry about the potential scandal. He still had her husband's blood on his cuff. Anything he did or said would be less scandalous than that.

Her cheeks were flushed, from the sun or the wine, he could not say, but she did not seem entirely concerned by his sudden appearance. "To what do we owe the pleasure of your visit, lord…"

"Artemio Volpe." He dipped a little lower in his bow, lower than he had ever bothered for her husband. Or should he say husbands. "I am your Majesty's inquisitor."

That seemed to spark some interest at least. Cadence had started out her gilded life far from Espher, to the south. A princess of some vassal kingdom of Agrant or another. Her age, station, and temperament had made her an ideal match when the time came for the Cerva to marry, and the choice of her over all of the locally sourced desperate, single noblewomen had been quite a statement about where the loyalties of the royal family lay. She had been the Agrantine emperor's choice.

"And what are you being inquisitive about in my garden?" she asked with a smile.

"Why, the fairest rose of them all." From the fall of her face, he could see that had been the wrong answer. False flattery would have been so commonplace to any queen as to have no hope of success, but for this particular queen, chosen almost exclusively for her beauty, trapped in her gilded cage because she was such a pretty little thing, it was taken like a slap across the jaw. She took a step back from him and he was forced to dip his head down once more. "Forgive me, your Majesty. I meant no offense. My mother often said that my runaway mouth would be the death of me."

She seemed to soften a little at that, but trust wasn't forthcoming. He'd arrived here unannounced without a single guard or attendant in tow, cornered her where nobody would see them talking—it was all very suspicious. "No forgiveness is necessary, Lord Volpe. It takes more than a silvered tongue to ruffle my feathers."

Given all she had endured since her wedding and coronation, he could believe it. The people of Espher were not much taken with their new queen, and the living arrangements she had to suffer through did nothing to improve her standing. Rumor had it that both of the Cerva twins took turns playing at being her husband and she could not tell them apart, even in the sheets. The more sordid rumors spoke to the carnal appetites she must possess to demand the constant attentions of not one but two men, but most of polite society discarded such tales out of hand. The common folk did not. She was the subject of many a bawdy tavern song. To make matters worse, it seemed that all of the fornication she was assumed to be undergoing was entirely unproductive. Not a single heir had been sired by either one of the men who claimed to be her husband. Unlike the carnal aspects of the royal triangle, the matter of heirs did draw rumors out in high society. The currently circulating suggestion, recounted by the rat-maid under duress, was that the queen was known to be barren before the wedding and placed in Espher to stunt the continuation of the royal line. Though that seemed so preposterous even Artemio could not give it any credence.

"I have some questions for you, my lady. With regards to the assassinations of which I am sure your husband has spoken."

She flicked open a fan and began to flutter a breeze on herself though the midday heat had scarcely had time to begin building. Mostly she seemed to use it to hide her face from his stare. "And what would I know of any of that? Potted wallflower of the court that I am."

"You would know what is spoken behind closed doors and when." He tried to catch her eye, to convey his meaning without having to resort to spelling it out. "You would know if his Majesty had discussed matters with you relating to these assassinations that cast... suspicions in your mind."

At last she seemed a little more intrigued than concerned. "Is there something you fear you have not been told?"

"There are a great many things I have not been told, your Majesty. The question that troubles me is whether any of those untold things are liable to rear up and kill me the moment my back is turned." He gave a self-deprecating smile and she seemed to warm to him once more.

Even if her tone did not shift from nasal and distant, at least her words seemed to come more freely "And you expect me to give you answers?"

"Who might know your husband's mind as well as you?" There was a tightrope he had to walk here, letting her know that he understood how injured she had been by her husband's choices without giving any hint of disapproval towards his monarch. His position here was extremely precarious, and with just a word about this little visit, she could end his life quite easily.

Her eyes narrowed, but it was safe to assume she had taken his meaning clearly. She offered him a hand and after he bowed once more to place a kiss on her knuckles, she tightened her grip and led him along through the rosebushes until they emerged at a little fountain that was struggling to maintain any pressure after the water had been pumped so high. At least there was nothing splashing on their backs when she settled them both side by side on the rim.

"My husband is not always at his most talkative when he visits with me. Perhaps I pry too much for news. Perhaps he simply does not want to lay conversational traps for the next exchange of places."

He was briefly stunned by her candor, but a moment later he found his words once more. "Apologies, your Majesty. I had not anticipated that their safeguarding of their identities continued behind closed doors."

"There are no closed doors when you are a king. Every matter is a matter of import to the court. There are chambermaids, physicians, guards, eyes everywhere." She looked off towards the sky. "At least they are gentlemen about it. They take turns. They allow me the illusion that they might be one and the same man."

There was nothing that could be said to that, and any question he might make about the matter would be prurient. Could she tell her husband from his brother? Artemio did not want to know the answer. He'd never taken the queen into his estimations often, but in all the barbarity hidden under silk within court, he wondered if her degradation might not be the most foul. She had been candid with him, so it was the least he could do to return the favor, even if it sank him ever deeper into danger.

"I believe your husband and his brother to be capable of arranging these assassinations to keep the houses of Espher off balance. I do not know if they are the guilty parties, but any evidence you can provide me that might sway my thoughts one way or the other would be greatly appreciated."

Her lips were pursed, but she was not screaming for a guard. "As I said before, they tell me little."

"Yet even if they themselves say nothing, there is, as you so rightly observed, an entire frothing hive of courtiers and servants surrounding them. Men and women who must surely be known to you by now. People who may not have been in their favor prior to the assassinations who now seem to have their ear."

She narrowed her eyes. "Other than you?"

"Obviously."

She did not take offense at that, which was purely luck, but she did turn her gaze from him once more. "I shall have to think on it."

Artemio did not grit his teeth or make anything resembling a complaint. One did not demand of a queen, one begged. "If it pleases your Majesty, I can be reached at the House of Seven Shadows. Perhaps through the Prima?"

"If the opportunity presents itself, I should be delighted to write to you, Lord Volpe, though you may find my communiqués come through the Ambassador Modesta."

He forced a smile. "Then you have my undying appreciation."

There was a little tug at the side of her mouth, as though she had almost smiled, but it was gone as soon as it appeared. "Now perhaps it is best for you to depart."

He ducked into an awkward little bow that conveniently kept him out of sight of the patrolling guards on the wall. "As you wish, your Majesty."

"And if you should feel the need to contact me again so directly, might I suggest you do so in a less direct manner? I do have all manner of servants and courtiers myself, every one of them absolutely bereft of subterfuge due to my lack of political involvement. You may very well make their day a little brighter."

He didn't laugh, but he was finding himself won over by this woman far too swiftly. Perhaps she was not so divorced from the matters of court as she pretended. Perhaps she was the hand behind the assassins raking her kingdom. Artemio would find out soon enough. If she were the ringmaster of that particular circus, he could expect to be hauled in front of the courts for his scandalous behavior in seeking this audience sooner rather than later.

21

SHADES OF TRUTH

Gemmazione, Regola Dei Cerva 112

I t took days before Orsina truly believed she was not going to be hauled back in front of the court again. Artemio had been in such a flurry of activity that they scarcely seemed to cross paths, and his reassurances that she need not fear further contact from the kings did not entirely relax her given the manic edge to everything he said.

At least she had no time to focus on her fears. True to her word, the very moment the Prima considered her to be capable as passing for a member of the nobility, Orsina had been given a list of classes to attend and tasks to perform.

The same dread she always felt when calling on a shade followed her into the lecture hall, and she could feel sweat prickling on her back beneath the lace and layers that seemed so unsuited to a day of concentration. Yet when the mousy-looking lecturer emerged and began talking without introduction, the blandness of it all soon began to chip away at any fear Orsina felt. There were eyes upon her, once in a while. Other students intrigued by the stories they'd heard. Too many stories in too short a time. She tried to pay the watchers no heed. The lecturer's words were what she needed.

"…much debate has been had through the ages as to the fundamental nature and classifications of shades. At present, our best understanding still reflects those six great spirits bound to this house in ages past. Subdivided, they present in three essential categories, with some crossover between them. The elemental shade is possessed of powers related to the fundamental energies of the world, most commonly fire, air, earth, or water. The knowledge shade is a depository of memories constructed primarily from the source's lifetime, but often supplemented by additions from prior users and the absorption of other, lesser knowledge shades. The third and final category is often typified as a secondary form of knowledge shade, yet the interaction that it has with the one channeling it is entirely dissimilar. These are most often referred to as combat or guidance shades. Now who can tell me which of these three are the most difficult for the novice to utilize?"

Some hands were raised, but the lecturer's gaze was sweeping back and forth across the chairs, like there was one person in particular he was looking for. Orsina sank down into her seat a little, but it seemed even here her reputation preceded her.

"Lady Orsina, might you know the answer?"

Her first class, the first question, it didn't seem fair. There was no way she could know the answer. All eyes were turning towards her now. The sweat prickling her back had turned cool and clammy. "Elementals," she said with a quaver in her voice, looking around the room, "are the easiest."

There was a ripple of amusement spreading along the rows. A pause just long enough for everyone to see the lecturer's wry smile, then he replied, "Typically the elemental, as the most abstract from our usual mode of consciousness, is considered to be the most difficult to master."

She could remember childhood bullies well enough to know when she was the target of one, regardless of whether he wore a peasant's sackcloth or a courtier's silk. She sank a little deeper in her seat. More attention was not going to fix this.

A pale boy on the far side of the room piped up, making sure to meet Orsina's eye. "One might argue that a novice would find it easier to accept an abstract tool than the level of integration required for a knowledge shade."

"We speak not of your feelings, but of the practicality of the matter. If you wish to be coddled, then I might suggest the House of Seven Shadows is not the place for your education, Lord Anatra."

There were some more titters, but the bubble seemed to have burst, and the lecturer moved on. Orsina cast a glance across the room to this Lord Anatra and received a polite nod in answer. Maybe having a reputation wasn't all that bad. Maybe there would be as many people trying to lift her up as kick her back down. She glanced at the other cold faces turned her way. Maybe not.

The rest of the lecture seemed to devolve into distinguishing characteristics of the three types of shades, their potential uses, and a few more jibes about the ease with which any other shade than the elemental might be mastered. She began to struggle to pay attention. It wasn't that Orsina wasn't interested or that the topic wasn't interesting to her—indeed she was silently fascinated to hear shades being spoken of in the same terms a farmer might use to describe crop rotation. It was more that none of it seemed to have any practical application. How did knowing which label to apply to a shade make it any easier to make it do your will? How did any of this matter?

When the class finally ended, Orsina felt like she was no better off than when it began, but there had been just barely enough of interest hidden inside the bland lecture to keep her from fleeing the room like the droves of others. She made her way to the front of the room against the tide, ignoring the eyes upon her. The Anatra boy in particular seemed to be lingering, waiting for an opportunity to speak with her. She'd learned her lessons from Harmony well enough to know that she was in no way ready to conduct a private conversation with some lordling, so the tutor, despite his hostility, seemed the better option.

For the longest time, the lecturer behaved as though she were not present, but eventually he succumbed to her polite waiting. "How can I be of assistance to our resident celebrity?"

She didn't know what that meant, so she ignored it. It seemed to work well for all the rest of the nobles when confronted with something they didn't understand, so why not for her? "There were some things you mentioned in your lecture that I wanted to ask about?"

"I have no doubt, that is why it is one in a series of lectures intended to elucidate you on all matters relating to shadework, not a comprehensive introduction to the subject."

"You said that knowledge shades absorb lesser shades?"

He didn't even bother to look up from the papers that he was gathering. "Indeed, amalgamation and predation is one of the primary manners in which shades hoard the essence required to maintain themselves without a living donor. Did you have any other questions a glance at the basic reading material could answer?"

"Perhaps you might be able to tell me what your problem is?" She bit the inside of her cheek, but the words had already jumped out.

It was enough to earn her another placid glance. "Whatever could you mean?"

She let the well-gnawed bit of cheek go before she drew blood. Spitting blood on him probably wouldn't have been considered ladylike. "Nothing. Thank you for your time."

Out in the corridor, the majority of her classmates had dispersed, and not for the first time, Orsina felt a pang of jealousy. All of them knew they were meant to be here, they had been born for this, they were surrounded by friends and family. She was alone. No small part of her wanted to abandon the day's work and go scampering off to find Harmony, where she at least felt wanted, if not entirely safe. That attachment concerned her in a way she couldn't put into words yet. She might spend the rest of her life hiding behind Harmony's skirts. Fading into the background. Being nobody and nothing, just as her blood demanded.

The afternoon's lectures were somehow worse for being all the more instructive, because the calm and collected repetitions of phrases that were utterly alien to Orsina's life began to heap up. What did she know about contract law? She was a peasant farmer girl. Clauses and strictures and rules had never been a feature of her life until this moment, and the way that the House of Seven Shadows was teaching its noble pupils to interact with shades sounded more like the preparation of a densely written contract of employment than the primal struggles she had experienced herself. All around her, notes were being scribbled and heads were bobbing as each new rule of conduct was covered, and she had no part in any of it. She may as well have been sitting outside in the sunshine for all the good this lecture was doing her. Every one of the students around her had teethed on stipulations and proclamations of intent and spoke this language as readily as Espheran, and she felt as though she were trying to build a house atop a swamp. Every new block she added just made her sink a little deeper into the mire of ignorance.

The concept was clear to her from the beginning. When you bound a shade, you defined and outlined everything it would be used for and the payment it received. You established the manner in which your arrangement could be severed and the terms under which it could be altered. You negotiated back and forth with the mindless mass of a shade until such time as it agreed to your terms, and then through the lens of the contract you allowed it entry to lay an anchor within you. Yet she had no idea how to make such a compact. When she called on Ginny Greenteeth, each time there was a struggle to decide on payment. Arguments of fairness. Each side trying to gain ground. There was no bartering, there was a battle of wills.

After the first lecture, she had been on the receiving end of all manner of looks from her peers as they headed to the door. Now there was a uniformity in their contempt for her. Every one of them had an armful of notes, and she had not even brought a quill to her seat. Every one of them had absorbed every word of the lecture and committed it to heart, while she… she was none the wiser.

The morning lesson had made her want to run and hide in Harmony's room until her misery faded away. The lesson of the afternoon made her want to flee the House of Seven Shadows entirely. She was not made for this. These people were so unlike her they may as well have been a different species. It was a miracle they didn't see her for the imposter she was every moment they were in her company. She was not this accomplished a liar. She was going to get caught, and she was going to get flogged, and everyone who had tried to help her would suffer.

Instinct told her to bolt. To run. To hide. To get as far from this place as she could. Instead she forced herself to stride past the stragglers and head to a part of the building she had never dared to venture near before.

Reading had never been one of her lessons, not as a girl and not in Mother Vinegar's care, but from what little she'd gathered from the morning's lecture, it had seemed to her there was little need to fear exposure. At least half of her classmates in the morning seemed to consider taking notes beneath them and likely felt the same way about reading the writing of others. It was only in the afternoon as the language had become technical that even the most braggadocious youth had turned to vellum. Still, it mattered little now; reading would not be a requirement to make use of the knowledge the House of Seven Shadows served as the receptacle for.

The library itself was still in a state of disarray after the great upheaval that Orsina's clash with the assassin Rosina had wrought. There were few students trying to pick through the chaos, and those who were seemed to be doing so with an air of abject depression. Every index paper, scroll, book, file, essay, notation, and engraved tablet had its own place within the library, and while some could be found in those places already, they seemed to form a thin veneer of order over the deeper chaos. What had begun as a slow but steady work of refiling had now turned to a complete overhaul of the entire suite of rooms. Every single leaf of paper had to be accounted for and returned to its correct place, and it would be the work of weeks if not months.

Orsina tried to find guilt in her heart for causing such discomfort to the librarians and her fellow students, but she just could not muster any. They were inconvenienced; she had been forced to murder someone. They were not the same.

Still, she tried to avoid their gaze as well as she could. She might not have felt any pangs for them, but that didn't mean they weren't furious with her for disrupting the careful order of their lives. She slunk by, down the corridors of shelves, twisting and turning through what could have been a labyrinth had she no beacon to guide her ever onwards. She did not hear the great Owl of the tower in her mind, but all it took was the slightest easing of her raised guard to feel its presence. A steady rhythmic thumping at the edge of her perception like a great beating heart.

The stairwell up to the tower was not well marked, and it had not yet been touched by the refurbishing book addicts. There were still sheaves of loose papers in there, blowing in the wind, fluttering about like there were bats roosting above. Orsina did not hesitate to begin her ascent, but soon found progress more perilous than anticipated. She wasn't used to the delicate shoes they had her dressed up in, nor the loss of balance from having her guts cinched in by corsetry. What would have been merely tricky for her in her coltish teenaged body was now profoundly difficult. The steps were steep stone, and torn shreds of vellum and parchment were the least of her troubles. Here and there it seemed the paper had been wet and formed itself into lumps and bumps upon the steps. The higher she climbed, the less regular the steps became and the more the papers spread their way up the walls, until finally she was scrambling on hands and knees up into a tunnel of ruined old books, layered and twisted into a nest.

It came to an abrupt halt at hollow around an open window. The luxurious glass that Orsina still marveled to see elsewhere in the city was shattered from the frame, long lost to time, and the wind at such a height bit into her in the light dress she wore.

That same staccato beat of the shade's presence that had led her on surrounded her now, beating against her mind from every which way, like she'd wandered not to the doorstep of the thing, but right into the belly of the beast.

Not that it mattered. Here she was with a shade that could tell her all she needed to know with none of the arduous efforts of classes and reading and all the rest. The only question was the price. She'd lost so much already, she didn't suppose anyone would notice another year shaved off her life, if that was what it took. Likely sitting through all the classes and drivel would take longer than a year, so she was making a net gain. There was no reason to be afraid about lowering her defenses. No need to fret about the rhythmic thumping, which now sounded all too much like the beating of wings overhead.

There were no dragons here. There was no sting of fire or dark oblivion just waiting. There was only an owl. Who in their right mind was afraid of an owl? She drew in a stilted breath and then whispered out, "Hello?"

There was no change. No voice booming in, nothing but the steady beat.

It took all her courage to loosen her grip on the guard she kept raised at all times, and even now she felt her attention splitting to keep an eye on Ginny so she didn't try to barge in through the cracked door.

"Hello? Uh… Owl? Are you there?"

Gufo made no sound or sign that it heard.

Orsina knew what she had to do. She had known it from the moment the Anatra boy had spoken about the difficulty of working with knowledge shades. Mother Vinegar had taken pains to ensure she knew the dangers of letting a shade into her mind. It had been at the forefront of her education for more years than she could recall. Even her brushes with Ginny Greenteeth before the fateful day of the dragon had been in the pursuit of learning to keep shades out. When her life was at risk, she could cast aside her doubts and let Ginny in, but her life would not always be at risk. She could not rely on her own fear to open the door.

Inch by agonizing inch, she opened herself up. The beating of wings came closer and closer, until she could feel it thunder on her skin. Until she felt like it was her own body in flight, every part of her straining against the pull of the world below. Still she heard no voice in her head. The Owl did not cajole or beg, it did not pry and writhe into the gaps she had left open. It was all around her, but it would not come in. Everything she knew of shades told her it should have leapt at the opportunity, yet still there was nothing. No chill on her skin, no rush of inhuman awareness, just nothing. It had to be a trap, it had to be waiting until she had opened herself so far there would be no forcing it out. Yet still it did not come. Finally, she tore down everything she had built, every fence erected around her soul, every barrier around her mind, everything was gone, and she was as bare as she'd been as a babe, dangling the light of her life like an angler wading out into a pool of sharks. Yet still there was nothing.

"Anybody here?"

She could feel Ginny lashing back and forth in her distant pool, tasting the scent of Orsina's life on the air but unable to creep in closer unnoticed. Yet still the shade that surrounded her did nothing.

Closing her eyes and shutting her mouth, she thought at it. If it was a shade of knowledge, maybe that was the only language it spoke. To believe an owl would speak was patently foolish, she knew. Like something out of a children's story. Her thoughts echoed inside her head, around and around until finally with one last surge of effort she pushed them out. Her mind brushed against something. Something soft and feathered and huge. A shudder ran through her body, but once more she strained to evert her mind, turning her internal thoughts into an external projection. It felt wrong, like the sensation of vomit creeping up her throat, but it worked. The next time she pushed, she felt her thoughts snare in the dense cobweb of knowledge that surrounded her, and when she tried to pull them back in, she dragged all that information in with them.

Words in languages she'd never heard. Numbers she couldn't count to. The overwhelming weight of it buffeted against her. None of it coming to roost, but all of it slapping down on her to the steady beat of the wings. Again she tried to speak. "I want to know..."

The weight of all that she didn't know pressed in on her again, the sum of knowledge she would never have. Crushing down from every side. Words were not enough. Nothing was enough. There was an ocean here she would drown in the moment she let herself sink in. It was suicidal to let herself be carried away into those drowning depths, just as surely as it would have been to let Ginny Greenteeth drag her down, yet all the same she felt herself reaching for it. Everything she needed to know was here, everything that would let her catch up to her peers, to surpass them, to become everything she knew she needed to be if she wanted to get through this masquerade unscathed.

The sea parted before her. Waves lapping away before she could touch it. She reached out again, and once more the ocean leapt away. She almost cried out in frustration. "I need it..."

It was only when she stopped straining for it that she could feel the ocean lap back in to surround her once more, and only then she realized her mistake. It was not in the nature of a shade to give, only to take. Even if this shade wanted nothing from her, it would not share its knowledge without exacting a toll.

From the very beginning, Mother Vinegar had told her she had a hole in her heart. An emptiness at the center of herself she had to guard lest the monsters that went bump in the night crept inside. Even now it sat empty. Even when she called on Ginny or fed life to The Fire Below, it had remained hollow. Only twice in her life that she could remember something residing inside her there. When the old dead woman had forced herself in, and when the dragon had swallowed her down and she'd abandoned all hope of salvation.

She didn't need to drag the Owl in, any more than she had to push it away. They were both occupying the same space already. She just had to let it occupy her.

It slipped into her mind so easily it was as though they were made for each other, and in an instant she knew. She knew all the shade had remembered for its keepers through the ages and the price that it extracted for sharing what it knew. It was a spirit of knowledge, it traded in knowledge.

What was she meant to offer it? She was nobody, she had studied nothing. The swollen library of its thoughts was so vast there was nothing she could contribute. Nothing but memories of scampering through rice fields and climbing trees in some distant back end of the kingdom.

She offered it all up, all the same, and she was unsurprised that the Owl had no use for it. All the secrets she held back from everyone else, she spilled out like they were nothing. The plants, their names, their uses in medicine, most of these things were well known to the Owl, but there were encroaching flora blown down from off the steppes it had never seen and uses for some herbs and berries that it didn't know. All of this was small change, barely worth any exchange of the knowledge that Orsina was so desperate for, but it gave the shade a taste, and now that it was inside her, it began prying for more. Her private moments, alone in the dark of night when there was nobody there to see her or hear her weep. Her dread of being discovered. The sideways glances she saw Harmony sending her way. The words of conversations she replayed to herself. The memory of her mother so still by the grave. The uncertainty of everything that gnawed in her gut like a carnivorous worm set loose. Still nothing worth taking, nothing worth trading, all of her life was being sifted and judged and found to be uninteresting. Then it struck upon the pain.

It had crusted over the memory like a scar. The pain of dragon's fire ripping over her flesh, stripping away licks of skin, twisting all that was beneath. Ruining her. The Owl cracked right through it, filing away the sensations of the venom on her skin before the flames caught up to it, the scent of it, the roar as the alchemical concoction the dragon regurgitated caught alight. This was all new. This was all valuable. The sensation of the rugged texture of the dragon's teeth as they scraped by, striated with age, glassy on the back side where flames had caught prematurely.

Orsina was lost in her memories, frantic and flailing and terrified. Reliving it all again, but slowed to a crawl, moment by moment, so the chaos of sensations could be dissected and weighed. The ridged roof of the dragon's mouth. The protruding spike of blackened bone where the spark was made. The open venom glands at the back of the mouth on each side, reeking of their noxious contents and puckered from use. The undulating darkness of the throat, drawing her down whole, sucking at her wounds, throbbing in anticipation. Slick with drool and venom.

She ripped the Owl from the hollow inside her and cast it out. Tears streamed down her face and she could taste her own death in her mouth. And still the shade wasn't sated, it pressed in on her again, battering off the wards she'd flung up. Desperate for those last glimpses of something it had never seen before. Something it didn't know.

The contracts the House of Seven Shadows proscribed to its students ensured they could not be double-crossed or tricked by the shades that served them. They ensured there was a fair and equal exchange of life for services. They entirely eliminated the ability to haggle. Orsina was shaken by what she had felt in those last moments, buffeted about by the beating of invisible wings, and she was smiling. Trickery was a two-way street.

Gufo wanted the rest of her memories. It had been cut off from the flow of completely new knowledge abruptly, and now it was going absolutely berserk trying to get back in again. It wanted what she had, not like she wanted what it had, but with the desperation of a creature whose sole solace and purpose was the consumption of knowledge. She had something it didn't just want—it needed, and that meant she had it over a barrel.

She made a laundry list of all the things she felt like she needed to know, then added in everything else she felt like she might plausibly ever want to know, then finally presented it to the Owl as her price for the remainder of the memories about the dragon. It was hard to communicate all she wanted without words, or even with her limited knowledge of the things she needed to know hamstringing her ability to describe them. Even so, it felt like she was demanding the whole world on a silver platter.

In the abstract, all the negotiation and contract nonsense from the class before had meant nothing to Orsina, but now that she was face-to-face with a shade, it felt more like second nature. She was trading not only for the knowledge she'd held back, but for what the shade had already stripped from her mind. It considered that to be a free sample; she considered it to be a part and parcel of their arrangement that it had not yet compensated her for. In the end, she compromised by agreeing that it was entitled to all it had taken from her. She could feel the smugness radiating in from the Owl until it realized that her price still had not shifted down to compensate for the reduced quantity of memories being negotiated over.

They went back and forth and back and forth, but ultimately Orsina had nothing to lose at this point and everything to gain. She held out, ready to slip back down the page-lacquered stairs and go about her evening, but the Owl could not let her go, not when it hungered for what she had so badly. So it kept coming back with counteroffer after counteroffer, begging and wheedling in a manner that should have been entirely beneath its dignity but apparently was not when it ran the risk of missing out on a truly unique meal. Orsina was exhausted by the time it was done, trembling with the effort of holding her soul open so she could hear the shade and the tension of having to be ready to snap it shut before anything else could be savaged from her. Yet despite her exhaustion and all the time it had taken, she had still won. Every one of her demands was to be met, every single one.

When the tide washed over her again, she opened her soul wide and drank it down. She felt Gufo slip into her mind like a rack of needles, and she cried out in pain, but she did not flinch away. She knew how to read. She knew how to read three languages and speak them too. She knew how contracts were made with shades and how they could be written to accommodate the specific needs of both parties. She knew what "the specific needs of both parties" meant. All of the language and history and structure that underlay an education in the House were now hers to use as she saw fit. All the lessons she would learn were laid out to her here and now.

She paced the library studying for her exams, scribbling notes. She sat in the lecture hall, nodding attentively as the Prima demonstrated how to chill the air and make ice. She crouched in a ditch by the side of a dusty road, feeding scraps of soul-stuff to the shade of a little frog that would one day be cultivated into an elemental. She was everyone who had ever left a memory in the House of Seven Shadows, and they were all her in that one blinding moment.

When she woke, it was morning, and she was different.

Dew dampened her hair, and print clung to her face as she pulled herself awake. Her dress was likely beyond repair, and her heart would have been broken if she had ever felt like it actually belonged to her rather than being the latest in a long list of disguises others demanded she wore. Of the Owl there was no sign, though she sincerely doubted it would have abandoned its roost so readily just because she was there. With a little push against her own defenses, she could still feel the rhythmic thumping of wings, but now there was no pressure to them. She and Gufo were done with their business. It had taken all it wanted from her, and she had what she needed from it. Was it as clean a deal as she could have forged now, knowing all she did of contracts and their construction? Perhaps not, but she doubted a more educated supplicant could have done a better job of whetting the old Owl's appetites and cutting a deal.

She felt like she should have seen the world differently now. In a way she did. The words on the paper beneath her were no longer irrational squiggles, they were a sentence. A sentence in a rather drab book about carriage maintenance and repair. No wonder it had been shucked from its cover and condemned to be a bit of a bird's nest.

Joints aching, she crab walked her way down until she was certain the stairs would keep her upright, then she forced her way to her feet and kept up the momentum. There were a few slips and spills, a few times when she had to fling out her hands, catch herself, and read a few words from a bit of the paper stuck up on the wall like it had been spackled there, but once she reached the library itself, she might have passed for a normal student again were she not drenched and bedraggled from her night of sleeping rough in a shade's nest.

Still, it was early enough that there were only servants in the halls, blindfolded and unaware of the state of her. She made her way safely to her own chambers, not daring to risk Harmony's ire by turning up there. It had been some time since she had returned here, though her understanding was that Harmony had been stopping in for some reason or another.

As it turned out, the reason was heaped upon the table by Orsina's door. Letters, sealed with wax. A dozen of them or more, not to mention the latest note that had been pushed under her door some time through the night when she was absent. A dinner invitation from the young Lord Anatra.

She was so startled at the contents that she scarcely realized that reading it was a revolutionary act in itself. So much of the communications of
the upper echelons of society were bound up in these scribbled little letters,
and now she could understand it all. She could talk to them in their own
language. She could cite precedent. Who knew that was a thing she would
ever even want to do, let alone be something she was capable of achieving?

The other letters had been opened, presumably by Harmony, and discarded due to their content. Every one was an introduction, an invitation
to some long-distant social event, an inquiry after some family member
or another who the noble in question believed might have married into
the Aceta line. Whether they were genuine traps or merely attempts at
ingratiation, Orsina found herself relieved that she had not had to worry
about how they would be dealt with. Presumably answering none of them
was considered to be rude, but that fit well with the mask of arrogance
she had been advised to cultivate. If she had been entertaining the idea of
marrying into a noble family with any seriousness, then Harmony's actions would have been a betrayal, but for now at least such thoughts did
not factor largely into her concerns.

The formal invitation to the palace was still lying there too. It had arrived sometime after Artemio's warning to the same effect. She wondered
what would have happened if she had been left alone to try to deal with all
of this herself. If she could have tricked some maid into reading her mail
to her aloud while she fiddled with her hair and pretended that she were
too strapped for time. Would she have answered them all?

She set it all aside for now. She had no time to dither when the bells
were already tolling the hour across the city. Most of the clothes she had
left behind in these chambers were of such complexity to put on that she'd
avoided dealing with them until now, so of course she would first have to
dress herself in the midst of a panicked scramble and hope she could pass
for as pristine as the House demanded.

In her desperation, she was about to call on a maid when Harmony
burst through the door like a whirlwind in crinolines. She took in the state

of Orsina and darted right past her to snatch up the washcloth from the basin. "Are you all right, darling?"

It took Orsina a moment to parse the question. She hadn't been all right in so long that it seemed like a distant horizon at this point in her journey. She supposed what Harmony was really asking was "can you pass," and with a little work she was quite certain she would.

She nodded even as the wet cloth slopped into her face and the scrubbing and tugging began. "I must tell you that I am quite furious you never came home last night, I am certain you have your reasons, but with things the way they are, I was almost entirely beside myself with worry."

Orsina tried to reach up and catch the girl's hands, to let her know that she meant no harm, but Harmony was already turning away, scrambling through the gowns and dresses to find something workable. Orsina ended up talking to her own feet. "Sorry."

Harmony worked as she spoke, hauling off the old dress and tossing it in the general direction of the fireplace. "No time for that now, there are so many things happening all at once. I was so worried they'd happened to you."

"I was…" Orsina was cut off by a yank on her corset ribbons. She had no idea how Harmony could be getting her ready so quickly. It went beyond practice and into an almost preternatural haste.

She caught the younger woman by the chin and then attacked her hair with a ferocity that looked all too familiar to someone who had stood across from her on the training yard. "No time. Just come back to me when your classes are through, I beg you. There will be scant enough chance to explain things before we leave, but I'm not abandoning you here without so much as a word."

Only scraps of this made it to Orsina through the frantic combing and twisting going on above her eyeline. "Abandoning… you're leaving?"

Somehow when she looked at herself in the silvered glass, Orsina was stunned to see she was presentable. Decent looking, even. Better than she could have done herself with an hour's run-up. Harmony was already pushing her to the door when she tripped over and caught herself on Orsina's back. "We'll talk later. You must go. Quickly. The Prima is waiting." Orsina almost choked. "The Prima?"

She was given one last mighty shove towards the door and had no choice but to drag it open and depart, with Harmony, eyes crinkled shut, calling after her, "Questions later! Run now!

It was uncouth to be seen running, but there were only blindfolded servants to dodge with the majority of her peers already having filed into the classrooms and lectures. If the Prima was in attendance, then they would not have wanted to be late. Orsina did not want to be late either, but as she skidded to a halt outside the lecture hall and stepped inside, it became immediately apparent that she was—and that the Prima had stopped abruptly in the midst of saying something at the sight of her.

There was a seat left empty by an aisle, so she made for it with all haste and her shoulders hunched, as though appearing smaller might make a blind bit of difference to the shame that was already mounting up atop her.

It didn't. The whole room hung sullen and silent until she finally found the courage to look up into the Prima's eyes.

"I suppose you have some reason for your tardiness? Perhaps you have already learned all that you need to know of practical shade manipulation?"

"I'm sorry Prima. I…" She scrambled for an explanation that wouldn't give too much of her desperation away. "Was up late studying."

There were open guffaws from some of her fellow students, a great deal of eye-rolling from those who said nothing, and a general feeling of seething contempt. She did not allow tears to pool in her eyes when the Prima looked up at her with disappointment. She was a noblewoman, an arrogant noblewoman, not a cowering peasant. She met the stare. Not defiantly, because she didn't have courage enough for that yet, but steadily enough all the same.

"Then perhaps your extracurricular studies may have informed you of the manner in which combatant shades are best deployed." It was a cruel jibe meant to put her in her place, just like the sneering lecturer the day before had meant to. It was also an open enough question that no matter how she answered, if she could even fathom an answer, the Prima might claim she was wrong.

Still, she found her lips moving along with the words of the question, and the answers she had imprinted on her mind the night before rose to the surface. "Philosophically, simply calling upon a combat shade can already be considered a failure of planning. The moment that it becomes necessary, you have already lost all of your other options."

Quiet fell over the room, and Orsina could swear she heard someone scribbling notes.

"So your reading included the Baronet Ragna's *Treatise on the Military Applications of the Necromantic Arts.* The material is a little dry and obscure, but the point is valid. As Shadebound, your duty is greater than that of the common foot soldier, your presence constitutes as prominent an effect upon the field of battle as a river or mountain. Direct martial conflict with opposing forces is likely to provide your commander with the least value you could offer."

In her lecturing, the Prima had turned her gaze towards the other students, and Orsina finally felt as though she might be safe to breathe again. It was a brief moment of delusion before the Prima's gaze snapped back to her. "However, this is a practical class, rather than one of philosophy. So perhaps you might answer the question that I posed to you? The manner in which combatant shades are best deployed."

Orsina didn't even know how they were used, let alone the best use of them. Her accumulated information from the Owl had been entirely abstract knowledge, not practical experience. She knew all the intricacies of negotiating a contract with a combat shade, but none of what it truly meant to use one. So in a snap, she fell back on her own wits. If elementals took your spirit to work and knowledge shades took your mind, then that left only… "The combat shade takes your body, it steers it for you, makes you move the way it would have moved."

The Prima fixed her with a glare. "Yes, thank you for a clumsily worded and basic instruction on what a combat shade is. Now perhaps…"

"The only way to use it successfully is to trust in it," Orsina began, tentative at first, then with more certainty as the truth resonated with what she had learned. "To give yourself over to it entirely and let it rule your every action. You must give up yourself, abandon making choices for yourself, and let the shade command."

There was a smile on the Prima's face when she turned away. Barely more than a smirk really, but enough for Orsina and anyone else looking to recognize it. "So we come to the crux of the matter. Trust. How can any one of us truly trust in a shade? How can anyone, knowing the nature of them, hand over command of themselves to a hostile force that wishes us harm?"

This was a thought that had dominated Orsina's thoughts ever since she'd given herself over willingly to Ginny Greenteeth. She knew the shade wanted to devour her, to drink down every last drop of her life, yet still she kept reaching to her every time she felt threatened. Like a knife where the handle was a blade too. It was obvious by now that she needed Ginny, and that trading with her ad hoc was getting her better deals than a contract, but short of brute-forcing the shade out of her each time it overreached, what could be done? She looked to the Prima with hope that there might be some answer, but it seemed the woman's question had not been rhetorical. She was looking around the lecture hall for raised hands. A dark-haired girl Orsina had never met was one of the few to raise hers.

"You can ensure that your compact is airtight."

"That is certainly some comfort." The Prima's lips were thinned, not impressed. "But it doesn't address the fundamental issue of trust. Rather it highlights its absence, no?"

A tanned boy with rather prominent teeth piped up. "You can ensure that your shade has the same goals as you?"

"Very good, Lord Coniglio, if you happen to have inherited the shade of a family member then certainly you can assume they will attempt to work in the best interests of their house. But of course there is a great rarity of hereditary shades at the best of times, and when the specificity of them being expert combatants comes in, that narrows things down even more dramatically. Few of us are so lucky."

There was another murmur spreading around the room. It seemed that Coniglio had given something away that he was not meant to. Orsina knew from a few barked remarks she'd received from Artemio that sharing the specifics of the shades you had personally contracted was considered to be a foolish idea from a tactical standpoint. But it was interesting to see that it was considered a social faux pas to discuss your tamed shades too. No wonder everyone was so reluctant to voice an opinion when it might be twisted and interpreted in such a manner.

"Before you are set loose upon the world as a House-certified Shade-bound, you will contract a combat shade of your own. It need not be a singularly talented ancestor, nor even a particularly apt combatant. The purpose of the exercise is rather for you to demonstrate your mastery of the shade and your ability to trust in it entirely, despite its nature. Some of you may be considering this task and viewing it as a distant and impossible goal. To you I say, first of all, that you are still early in your tenure in this institution of learning, and secondly, that there are a great many ways to ensure trust between shade and master we have not yet begun to delve into. Matters we can discuss later. For now, let us simply attend to the practical. Let us see if you can channel a combat shade."

With a clap of her hands, Guscio Cavo arrived. Or better to say it was revealed, since it had been present from the very beginning of the lesson, only hidden from sight by Orsina's own protective walls. She wondered if the other students had known it was there—those more advanced than her, or those who had not yet assembled sufficient protections to keep the voices of the Great Shades at bay.

The shade looked like nothing more or less than a suit of cavalier's armor, devoid of any of the heraldry, gilding, or pomp, and built to a scale far greater than any one person could truly wear. It loomed out of the deep shadows behind the Prima like the monster in some storybook, and all that ran through Orsina's mind when she saw it was Kagan's admonitions about the purity of knights.

There was a structure to their progression, with each student descending to the staged area at the front of the lecture hall based upon the order in which they were seated. It placed Orsina ahead of some of her fellow students, but not the majority. To begin with, she believed there would be no chance that the whole hall would be able to make an attempt in what was left of the morning, but once students began ascending to the stage, she was soon corrected. This was not an opportunity for them to revel in their new experience, it was an experiment to see if they were capable.

At last the dim lighting of the lecture hall began to make some measure of sense. The candelabra on the raised stage in particular served not so much to illuminate the space as to cast a single stark directional light upon whoever stood in view of the room. Of the gathered students, Orsina was surprised to find that most cast only a single shadow in its light, their own shadow. A little less than half already showed a second shadow when they began, and only one or two had a complement of three shadows, surpassing Orsina's own progression.

Of course, the purpose of this exercise was for them to manifest another shadow, even if it was only for a moment, and it was to that goal that each of them silently turned for their moment in the light.

Orsina stared past them to the looming shade, wondering all the while if a success would make it suddenly blink away inside of the one using it. She supposed it wouldn't, given that Ginny Greenteeth was undeniably still skulking around at the bottom of some pond in the Selvaggia, even if she did have an anchor hooked in Orsina's gut.

Some of them succeeded in their task within the moment the Prima watched them, others failed just as swiftly. Orsina could not understand how they were managing to negotiate terms so quickly with the great looming cavalier, until she realized that all of the usual chatter and grandstanding that would have accompanied a lesson had faded to silence. She did not need to be up on the stage to speak with the shade, just as the shade did not need to give her its full attention. It was not a person, it did not have a mind or concentration that it needed to maintain. She lowered her protections and reached out for it as she would an elemental. Almost at once she realized that Guscio Cavo's armor was not purely an affectation. It was solid to the touch of her spirit in a way that no other shade she'd encountered had been. Her thoughts skittered off its chest plate like a spritz of water.

She was not surprised, not truly. She had enough experience with yesterday's Owl to know that the different types of shade had to be interacted with differently. This first probing attempt to touch on the looming armor's awareness had been tentative at best. Next she attempted the inversion she had used to draw Gufo inside her yesterday. It also failed. It was as though she could gain no traction, as though she were water and the shade a solid rock against which she was breaking.

She didn't know when her hand began to reach out towards it, she didn't mean for it to happen, but there was an undeniable logic to the idea that physically touching this thing would be the way to make it hers. Gufo needed her mind, Ginny needed her spirit, it made sense that this one would need that touch. But reaching out and touching it was not what the people on the stage were doing. Of the few who successfully manifested another shadow, there was no sign of movement at all. There was something Orsina was missing. She turned her attention inward, to all of the books and notes she had dumped into her memory in her desperation, but none of them dealt in practicalities. She was going to step up onto the stage, surrounded by her peers, under the watchful gaze of the Prima, and she was going to fail.

The longer she watched, the more successes there were. The Prima was forceful in severing the connection swiftly, in dragging her students back to themselves and moving them on, but as Orsina stared, there was no denying the number of successes were mounting. They knew something she didn't. They were touching minds with the shade and making some arrangement. Tears threatened to prickle at the corners of her eyes once more. This was not fair. She had tried so hard and done everything that could have been asked of her, and now the Prima was going to judge her as unworthy of the trust she had placed in her, the investments she had made, and the risks she had run, all so Orsina might have a place to study, so the shades did not consume her. So that she might survive despite the unfortunate twist of her birth.

As her turn grew ever closer, Orsina began to panic. She flung more and more of her life out towards the armor, like bait on the end of a line, but still she had no luck, no contact. She had to think, why couldn't she think. All the memories that had been dumped into her skull seemed to swirl around in a tempest of her confusion, bits and pieces of lore and legalese that were worthless in this moment. There were fewer and fewer people up ahead. Fewer and fewer moments until her shame was made clear to all and sundry. She could swear that everyone who stepped up now was proving successful. It made her own failure stand out ever more sharply. Why couldn't she do this? Why couldn't she think? Why couldn't she still the swirl of nonsense and gibberish pressing in on her from every direction? What had robbed her of her peace of mind so thoroughly that even though she recognized something had gone awry, she still could not right it? It must have been the Owl, it must have done something. Disordered her thoughts. Made as much a mess of her brain as the other shade had the library. She could not rely on her mind for what came next. She had to turn elsewhere.

Hauling hard on Ginny Greenteeth, she flung the shade out towards the suit of armor, half ambassador and half battering ram. The old shade washed over Guscio Cavo just as Orsina had, lapping around him but finding no way in. From the back of her mind, Orsina could hear the old swamp beast wheedling and whining, but she couldn't concentrate well enough to pick any one word out. The overall impression was of a farmer trying to sell a bow-legged horse at market before anyone noticed it had wooden teeth. The armor did not budge, the shade did not answer her, there was nothing she could do. Her feet felt leaden as she climbed up onto the stage. She could feel every eye in the auditorium turned her way. The gaze of the Prima was like a needle piercing to the heart of her. She had to do this. She had to succeed. It was now or never. She opened herself up to the shade, reached out her hand—and realized all at once how stupid she was being. A shade had no physical form to touch. The armor was no more a suit of armor than a drawing of one could be. It was just how the shade was choosing to appear, where the shade was choosing to appear. If Ginny Greenteeth could be here and in a pond half the world away, then Guscio Cavo could be in the same place as Orsina.

She felt metal surround her as the realization came. She felt the echo of the shade in the hole in her soul, in her mind. Everywhere. They shared the same space, they were one and the same. She could do this, she could do it. She glanced nervously back to see the three shadows streaming back from her across the well-trod wooden boards, then she saw a fourth, barely flickering for a moment before Guscio Cavo's voice echoed in from every direction at once.

"Peasant."

All the life and energy and power she had poured out to secure the armor in place rebounded in on her. Slapping her off her feet and down deeper into waiting darkness. The last thing she saw before the world faded away was the Prima stepping up, a swarm of shades about her, trying to hold the long-dead cavalier back as it roared in her mind. *"You are not worthy of me!"*

22
FALL OF THE BLADE

Gemmazione, Regola Dei Cerva 112

Harmony had dawdled entirely too long waiting for her pet peasant to come back from classes before finally accepting the girl had slipped loose of her apron strings. It had pained Artemio to drag his sister away from the House when Orsina still lay within its walls, but there were more pressing matters to attend to than the girl happenstance had dropped on them both. It did not matter that she was his sister's dearest friend. It did not matter that she was his sister's savior. No matter what affection he might have held for her, none of it would matter if he were not around to express it. So he made the difficult decisions that his sister would not, as had always been his lot.

When the heart rules the head, men end up dead, as his wet nurse used to sing.

There was a suite set aside for him in the palace now, where he meant to spend his nights until such time as the investigation was concluded. His connection to the inquisition was now known by all and sundry, and pretending not to be under the wings of the twin kings was liable to make him look a fool. He needed their authority to do his work, and he needed to be seen openly in their favor if he wanted their allies to consider him trustworthy. So he and Harmony traveled by carriage with a chest of clothes and belongings apiece, and he hoped despite all evidence to the contrary that he might find some time before the year's end to actually do a little bit of studying and graduate.

She would not speak to him. He had delayed almost the entire day so that she might say goodbye to her little project, and he could not afford any more time if they meant to be settled by nightfall. Already so much of the work the day could have held had slipped through his fingers, and it was only the comforting weight of his invitation to dine with Ambassador Modesta at luncheon tomorrow that kept him from entirely losing his temper.

It had been a short missive, but one laden with meaning. It seemed their mutual friend had suggested a meeting sooner rather than later would be to their mutual advantage. As though he did not have much time left for lunches. How the queen might have known the hammer was about to fall, Artemio could not say, but he was inclined to believe her word, given what he knew of her.

All of which meant they needed to be relocated and settled in to more secure accommodations as swiftly as possible, whether Harmony intended to sulk the whole way or not.

Between them on the carriage seat was the second point of contention—an entirely too well-fed rodent in a storm-lantern that now seemed much too small a cage. Given nothing to do, and all day to do it in, the rat had taken to eating as much as it possibly could, and since Artemio had been unable to discover the correct feeding schedule for rats among the library books, he had been forced to continue providing food each day when it seemed that supplies had been depleted, working on the assumption that the beast would stop eating when it was full. This had been an error.

At first Harmony had insisted she would not even look at the rat, but when they rounded a corner and it slid into her hip, her opinion on the matter rapidly changed to squeals of disgust, followed by a very fixed stare at the creature, as though it had deliberately crept over and nudged her.

The remainder of the trip was made in a furious silence, and they departed to their new quarters amidst a flurry of servants with all haste, barely even troubling to nod to all the courtiers who had suddenly developed an interest in them after years of behaving as though the pair were invisible. Ever were there more pressing matters to attend to.

They took their dinner in their chambers, parted ways early in the evening, and Artemio settled in to read more of his predecessors' final written words with a growing sense of unease. He had to fight the urge to barricade the door. He had turned the key in the lock, but that had done previous victims no good. In the end his rationality and fear warred with each other until he wedged a chair under the door handle and turned in.

The fire had burned down low, and the light was dim and red on the crossbeams above the bed as he stared up into impending insomnia. His grandfather was set at the foot of the bed to watch over him, he had done what he could to ensure his own survival through the night, yet still this did little to ease him into sleep. Normally a brief interlude with his good friend wine would have sent him off into his slumber, but tonight he did not dare lest it make him sluggish. Would every night be like this from now on? Just waiting for some impossible death to be visited upon him when he least expected it, or worse yet, would it become so normal that he could sleep through it? Like the old soldiers' tales of men who dozed through a battle. He could not say which would be worse.

Yet for all of his fretting and tossing and turning beneath the rather fine quilted blanket, at some point sleep did come. He could not pinpoint the moment the darkness before his eyes became the darkness beneath his eyelids, nor the moment the jumble of his fearful thoughts became haunted and hunted dreams, but nonetheless, he did fade away.

Pain lanced through him before his eyes were open. It was a shallow cut on the outside of his arm, barely a graze through nightclothes and skin, but it brought him out of his stupor faster than any amount of shouting could have. With consciousness came a flood of knowledge. Bisnonno Fiore was watching over all, relaying all he saw to Artemio with the distance and calm that only the grave could grant a watcher.

Still, it was not as clear or easy to understand in the moment when it was all dumped directly into his brain. Things seemed distant and misshapen, like they were being viewed through a warped looking glass. Faded and grey in the dim light of burned-down embers. His body lying still and defenseless on the bed looked tiny. The rag-cowled figures gathered all around him with hooked knives loomed larger than life. Pillars of doom and darkness hanging over him. The only one in the image who looked even vaguely true to life was Harmony. Her sword turning what should have been a killing strike against him into the scrape he'd felt.

"Wake up, you're being murdered in your sleep!"

At least the late hour had done nothing to dampen her usual wit.

Six of them against two Volpes. He'd take those odds any day.

With a pulse, Artemio set Fiore to his task, flinging his own sword across the room into his waiting hand. It was still sheathed, but it served to turn aside another hacking blow of a knife as Harmony drove the first assailant off him. All of them had knives not swords, but it was only for simplicity's sake that he'd even call them knives. One wielded something like a meat cleaver. Another some hooked tool Artemio thought he'd seen in a tanner's yard. These were not warriors or assassins or anything of the sort. They were not trained for combat.

He proved it with a deft twist of his wrist, sending his second assailant's hook soaring across the room. There were feathers on the back of the hand that his cross-stroke severed.

As he rose to his feet and the blanket fell away, he saw Harmony cut down the one who'd drawn his blood, and froze in his tracks for but a moment. It was a girl. Human as him. There was no magic at work here. No explosive or dragon-beast or any of the wild theories he'd entertained. They were just people. People who committed such grievous butchery that the victims could no longer be recognized as anything but meat.

The courage of their conviction could not be questioned, though. Even seeing themselves outmatched, they still came on. One darting in at Harmony's back and two leaping right onto Artemio, meaning to bear him down with their own weight while a third prepared a killing strike. Were he just a man, it would have done for him. But he was more.

"Behind you!"

Flames leapt along the length of his blade as he crossed it over his body. Searing into the toad-faced woman with a reeking acrid stench that caught in his throat. The other caught a lance of flame expelled from his other hand in the throat and fell without a sound to the bloodstained rug beneath the bed.

With a heave, the toad-girl's body tumbled into the path of his last assailant, knocking their wild swing wide to wedge into the bedframe. The flames he'd set in her gut roared out to consume her and scorch at that man too. The smell was overwhelming, and Artemio found he had to scramble back to avoid the black cloud of it billowing up. With a twist of his mind, he redirected the attentions of the forge spirit from the consumption of flesh to the fireplace, setting the near-dead charcoal of the night's logs ablaze once more and flooding the room with light.

Harmony had made swift work of her own foe, and now the two of them turned on the last of the six. A hunched figure that seemed less interested in fighting them and more interested in tearing everything from the shelves of their quarters, digging through cupboards, whipping aside discarded clothes, and generally making as much of a mess as possible. The curiously familiar form was so intent upon her task that she did not seem to have noticed the battle had been fought and lost by her allies in the time it took her to dig through some wardrobes. The one that poor Harmony had been lurking in all night notwithstanding.

In that moment, Artemio's mind tore back through the events before he had been stirred from his slumber. The servants' passage that had been opened behind the grand tapestry by the fireplace. The cupboard hanging open where Harmony had leapt into action with all haste. Bisnonno Fiore's inaction as he saw servants going about their business in the night, as a king might expect them to. Out of sight out of mind. Passing invisibly through a world of their betters. All of this time, the mystery of the murders had been so simple, and they had all been so blind to it.

Artemio released his shades and sheathed his sword. "You're not going to find the rat in there."

The maid froze in place, looking more like a cornered rat than she ever had before. Her shoulders still hunched up, the tip of her tail barely protruding beneath the rags in which she'd clad herself; a distinct step down from the usual finery on which she spent her ill-gotten gains.

She turned to face him, knife still in hand, and Artemio vaguely recalled some advice regarding cornering a rat that one of his father's retainers had shared. So he showed his own empty palms to her with a smile. "You aren't going to find her scurrying around this place. I'm not a fool to leave my leverage in plain sight. If you had any sense, you would already know this. You can feel your bondmate just as surely as I can smell burned meat. Just because you don't want to believe what your senses tell you, it doesn't mean anything will be different."

Harmony glanced back and forth between the maid and her brother. "You know her?"

"Yes, this is the treacherous little rat-maid I told you all about. The one with her fingers in all the pies and a dozen rich men paying for her scraps. The one who seemed quite incapable of finding anything out about the assassins plaguing our kingdom. I suppose we know why that is now…"

The maid's grip on the knife seemed to waver. "I told you to give up. I told you to quit. Why wouldn't you listen?"

Harmony piped up, "Because he's an arrogant prick?"

His head whipped around, and his mouth hung open. "Whose side are you on, dear sister?"

"Yours. She was entirely correct. You should have listened to the nice little assassin when she gave you the chance to quit." Harmony had not taken her eyes off the rat-maid this entire time. She still considered the girl a threat. Artemio should have too. For all he knew, his predecessors' blood was on her fluffy little hands.

There was a heat in his voice when he put the question to her. "All of this time, you were working against me. All of this time you were right by my side. Why did you wait until tonight?"

"Orders was to do you tonight. Before, he thought you were just going to run in circles until you gave up. Thought you were like the other fools." When she saw Artemio's brows drawing down, she quickly added, "I warned them. I told them you weren't. They wouldn't listen to me."

Even after attempting his murder, she was still trying to protect his feelings. It was a curious little paradox.

"Orders from whom, exactly?" He saw her eyes dart from side to side, and let his hand come down to rest on the hilt of his sword. "And please bear in mind, before you decide you want to lie to me again, that your life is on the line at this moment."

Her whiskers twitched and her beady eyes darted and her whole body seemed to tremor with barely contained energy, but none of it mattered a jot. There was no way out for her, except through him. She dropped her knife. "The Last King."

"I am assuming that you are not referring to Demetrio Cerva when you use those words, but rather the mythical shade who consumes all living souls upon death?" Artemio could already feel his annoyance building into a headache behind his eyes. Why couldn't she just give him the name he needed.

She curled her lip up at him. "There's only one true king."

Artemio took a deep breath and let his anger pass. This was the task allotted to him, to make sense of that which made none. It was hardly fitting for him to be enraged now that he was finally drawing out some answers. He carefully took his hand away from his sword and crossed his arms. "I've heard that before, you know. It was a servant saying it then too. I didn't quite make the connection to some old fairy tale back then either. 'There is but one true king in this world, and his crown is made of bone.' Is that the one?"

"You know nothing." Rat-girl sneered once more. "Nothing of what the real world is like. Where you have to scrabble and claw just to live. Sitting on your thrones. Wearing your finery. You don't know what it's like when the Last King is the only one you'll ever see or know. But you will…"

He cut off that ramble before it could degenerate further. Whoever had been inflicting an ideology on these peasants had done a good job embedding the rhetoric. Even this fearful little mouse seemed to have the courage of a lion now she was speaking of her Last King. "I'm sure your excuses for butchering the people in your care while they sleep are very compelling, but perhaps we might turn our attention to more pressing matters. Who is this fairy-tale specter who commands you, and where shall I find him?"

She drew herself up to her full height, which wasn't much. And squared her shoulders, which were entirely too sloped for such a gesture of defiance. "The King is no story, he's real, and you'll never find him. I'll never betray the cause."

Artemio sighed. "Oh I do wish you hadn't said that."

For all of his posturing, Artemio didn't have much stomach for torture. That was why he glanced away just before the basket hilt of Harmony's rapier crashed into the rat-girl's back and drove her to her knees.

Harmony didn't have much in the way of evil in her, but the same temper that simmered away in all the Volpes was down there beneath her façade of kindness and ladylike manners. "Answer his questions, or you'll answer to me."

Rat-girl's defiance didn't crumble under the blow. If anything, it seemed to coalesce into something more solid than before. Her ratty little face tightened over her distended skull, and she looked more beast than man. "No. I won't."

She was a peasant born, made her living as a servant, spy, and assassin. Pain was an old friend to her. Beatings and floggings and all of the rest. They would not get her to talk by hitting her. No matter how much the wrath in Artemio's gut at her betrayal bayed for her blood.

In one motion, the rat-girl scooped up her knife and thrust it at Harmony's guts. They'd thought her broken and finished. They were wrong. Neither twin had time to react.

Fiore was another matter.

The dead king's specter roared into being between his granddaughter and the jumped-up peasant that dared raise a hand against her. Ice crusted the blade and it shattered on contact with Harmony's dress-laces.

The force of the stab still carried through and doubled Harmony over, but there was no sharp edge to cut into her now. It was little more than a pointed punch that drove her dinner up her throat and out to spatter down the rat-girl's back. Good thing she was wearing rags already.

Artemio's bare heel stomped down onto the maid's tail, and he felt his own stomach lurch at the rubbery sensation of it. Her cry of pain let him know he still had her attention. Harmony took only a moment to finish spitting bile before she was on the maid, riding her down to the floorboards and beating at her with her empty hands. Slaps as often as punches. No skill or training, just anger.

The broken knife-hilt chattered across the floor, and Artemio called a halt. "Enough."

Harmony didn't really want to stop, judging by the way her fists were still clenched and drool was still oozing down her chin. "She tried to kill me."

"I've also been on the receiving end of that particular delight, as you might recall." Artemio helped her back to her feet. "You are not special."

"Rude." She gave the maid one last kick for good measure, but it wasn't clear which of them the words were directed at.

Artemio went to the bed and crouched down to retrieve the storm-lantern from its place beneath where his head had lain but minutes before. "You've already shown your loyalty to the cause is less than your feelings for this rodent. Turning your back on your little co-conspirators to seek her out."

He set the lantern down on the table and, with a sigh, put his finger over the slit for ventilation. "Now you will talk, and fast."

Rat-girl tried to spring forward only to meet Harmony's boot. Artemio watched with no small amount of distaste as Harmony wrapped an arm around the mongrel's neck and hauled her up until her twitching nose was level with the tabletop.

Within its cage, the rodent was flinging itself against the glass, trying to get back to its bondmate. It may not have understand the fear passing to it through their connection, but it experienced it all the same. It grew ever more frantic as the air within its trap began to sour. Scrabbling at the glass it had no hope of breaking.

It was hard not to feel pity for the little beast, even if it was vermin. It had not chosen to have its very life bound to the fate of some scurrilous scullery maid. All it wanted from life was to eat and sleep and make more little rats. Artemio couldn't help but feel a pang of envy for the simplicity of it.

Tears were pooling around the rat-girl's bruised eyes, but her quivering snout was set in place. "I won't."

He dragged a seat over with his foot and then settled into it with a groan. Leaping up from sleeping like that, he felt as though he'd sprained every muscle in his body. He had spent a good year or two of his life early in feeding shades during his training. It was small wonder he was feeling the pangs of age so soon. "Then you will watch your little friend here expire."

Rat-maid sobbed and raged. Her body shook, and she strained against Harmony's arms hopelessly. "You're a monster. You're all monsters. All you blue-blooded bastards, sat on top of the heap just because your great-granddaddy killed folk quicker than they could kill him. You're bred for evil. The whole lot of you."

"Perhaps you are correct, but none of that matters to little Daria here. She has no sway in the matter. Her world is much smaller, and it is constructed entirely of inevitabilities."

The minutes ticked by. The little rat's air growing denser and denser with the poison of her own lungs. The frantic scrabbling slowed to a fumble now and then. Her attention seemed to be wavering. As for the girl, her skin showed pale between the patches of fur. She seemed to wither and shrink in Harmony's arms.

Across the room, the door to the servants' passages still hung open. At any moment, another of the assassins might be coming. Perhaps a tide of them so overwhelming that two young Volpes would be pressed beyond their limits.

Artemio tried to calculate the sheer number of servants in the palace and how many of them would be loyal to the crown. He had never had to consider the loyalty of servants before, it had always seemed as certain as the rising sun. By all means, they might have spied for a stipend, but escalating to violence against their betters was so unthinkable that it drew him up short. The court heaved with nobles and courtiers, yet each of them had a staff of their own. Even the meanest household held at least a butler and maid, and the more members of the family there were, the more help they required. There were at least twice the servants to nobles in the palace alone. If only a half of them were caught up in this Last King's uprising, then Covotana would fall.

Beyond the palace walls, the scales tipped ever more in the peasantry's favor. It did not matter that they had no swords or armor when there were a hundred of them for each fighting man. The guards and men at arms were not drawn from noble stock either, which way would their loyalty swing? Beyond the city gates, the numbers turned ever against the ruling class. If this conspiracy had root across all of Espher, then the kingdom was already lost.

His stomach lurched once more as he recalled the number of nobles murdered in their country estates, his own mother among them. This uprising was not contained, except by the will of whoever led it. The Last King.

His finger hurt where it was pressed over the ventilation slit, but he did not dare move it an inch, lest it give the rat some air and the girl some hope. He looked to the dying servant and sighed. "Who is the Last King? Where do I find him?"

She spat at him, but she was so bereft of life that it came out as little more than a trickle down her lower lip.

"This can all end. All you need do is answer my questions."

She wheezed out a word that was never meant to be heard in polite company.

Artemio probably should have expected such coarse language from a creature like her, but he was still startled to hear that word spoken aloud by any lady. No matter how low her birth. Harmony drove a punch into the maid's kidneys, but she was so far gone, Artemio wasn't certain she even felt it.

This wasn't working.

He'd felt certain he had the measure of this girl. But then, he'd been certain he had her measure before. She might have been easy to startle, but she was resolute. She'd rather die than give up her master, and she was too far gone now to even fear that death.

With a jerk, he took his hand off the lantern and watched as life flooded back into both rat and girl in synchronization. Artemio could see the girl smirking, even through her daze. She thought this was a victory. That he would not dare to kill her. "This is taking too long. I am losing my patience."

Inside the lantern, fresh air had brought the rat back from the brink, and it was mewling pitifully to its partner. Tears were matting the maid's russet-furred cheeks, but as life flowed back through her, Artemio could see the spark of rebellion in her eyes reignite. She was resolute enough to watch a slow death coming. Now he had to resort to a short sharp shock.

He turned to the rat in its cage, struggling to press against the glass and get close to its beloved mistress, and he lit a fire.

The forge spirit wanted to burn hotter, it wanted to scorch every hair away from the rat in the lantern and consume the flesh and leave nothing but blackened bones behind, but Artemio held it at bay. He smelled the popped corn smell as hair began to burn, heard the squeals of distress turn to fear and agony. The maid cried out too. Desperate and struggling with all her strangulated strength against Harmony. She was too weak, too spent, and too outclassed. Even when she tried to bite into Harmony's arm, his sister just twisted it under the maid's chin out of reach. "Stop it! Stop! Please."

The fire shone bright in the dim room. Blinding bright to the maid's eyes. Her whole world had narrowed down to the rat in the lantern and Artemio's voice. "Tell me what I need to know."

She still couldn't look away from the rat and the flame. "I don't know! I don't know who he is. Please."

Artemio sighed. He was already exhausted from his fitful night of sleep and his midnight awakening. The drain on his spirit of keeping the forge fire in check was beginning to get him down. "I do not believe that will be sufficient."

"I can take you to him." The maid babbled as her hair began to smoke. "He's under the city. I know the way. Just stop it!"

Harmony rolled her eyes. "Sounds like a trap."

"It certainly does." Artemio nodded.

"It isn't! I wouldn't! I'm begging you. Please!"

He snapped the fire off with a final push of his will. The rat was scorched and wet looking on the side that had been exposed, and Artemio could not help but to feel pity for it. But if he had to be the very monster this assassin accused him of being to survive, then he would shed no tears for dead vermin.

Rising to his feet, Artemio reached out a hand. The maid tried to take it before he leaned past her to help Harmony back to her feet. To the maid, he merely said, "You will lead us directly to your Last King, and you will explain to me how you answer to a man you do not know the identity of as we go."

2 3

FIRST CLASS CITIZEN

Gemmazione, Regola Dei Cerva 112

The Prima was awaiting her wakening, but still Orsina struggled to pull herself up from the comfortable darkness. It did not hurt down here. She was not struggling and striving to be someone she was not in her dreams. In her dreams, she spread her wings and soared across the steppes, everything was her domain, everything was her prey. There was no fear or confusion, only hunger.

When the old woman had grown tired of waiting, she jabbed Orsina with a finger. Right in the ribs. That got her out of her stupor fast.

"Ow."

"Nice of you to join us."

They were in an unfamiliar room, and she was draped on an unfamiliar piece of furniture, something like the cushioned seats she'd seen in Harmony's room but stretched out like a bed. "What happened?"

The Prima was settled on a little footrest by her side with all the dignity one could muster in such a situation. She kept her knees together and her face turned down towards the fireplace. "Well, my dear, it seems that I owe you something of an apology."

"You don't need to do that." Orsina mumbled, still less than entirely aware of what was going on around her. "You've done so much already…"

"Hush my dear, I apologize to you because I did not believe you when first you arrived. All of your instructors to date have praised your gifts, praised the nobility that had to run in your blood. I, too, was taken in. I truly believed that you were merely ashamed of the circumstances of your birth, or unfortunate and abandoned. I thought the truth would out once the Great Shades pried your mind open." Her shoulders slumped, and for the briefest of moments she actually looked her age. "It seems the truth has outed in a most fearsome manner. You truly do not recall any hint of aristocratic blood in your lineage, even in those parts of your mind that you cannot reach. Guscio Cavo looked within you and found you to be all you have said you are and nothing more."

Memories were creeping back to Orsina now. Frightening memories. "He attacked me. He called me a peasant."

The Prima sighed. "Cavo is a spirit of order as much as of war. Disciplined but inflexible. It would not tolerate your touch. It would not submit to you."

"I noticed that too."

A little smile quirked the side of the woman's face, but she smoothed it back to pity in no time at all. "It was not your fault. It was simply the nature of the shade."

Orsina could not contain her shudder as the memory crept back in. This must have been how normal people saw shades, unstoppable, colossal, terrifying. "Doesn't help me though."

Silence hung over them for a time as Orsina shifted from lounging to something like sitting with a fluctuating weight in her gut making her pause every time she tried to rise. When she finally gave up on further progress, the Prima was still staring at her. Orsina shifted a little more, uncomfortable at the attention. The older woman sighed, "I must admit that this possibility had never occurred to me."

Meanwhile, Orsina's mind had turned from the past to the immediate future. "Does everyone know now? Do they all know what I am? Do I have to go?"

"No, my dear. They most certainly do not. What we hear of a shade's thoughts are for us alone. You knew of Cavo's complaint because you were connected, I learned of the complaint when I mounted him to drive him off you. But the others… they have no idea. They merely think you made a catastrophic error somewhere in your negotiations."

"They aren't totally wrong." Orsina tried to laugh, but it came out choked.

The Prima waved her hand. "None of this is my concern. The real worry to spring from all of this is that there are combatant shades known to the House, and as a rule, our graduating students make a short pilgrimage to claim one. Typically from the site of some ancient battle where the shade's legend grew. However, these shades shall all be of noble birth. Invariably. And most, if not all, will share the attitude of Cavo."

"So… I'll just never have a combat shade?" This might all be a blessing in disguise. If she had no combat shade, they couldn't make her fight, could they? She wouldn't have to be a soldier for Espher if she couldn't even swing a sword better than the average man on the street. This might be her salvation.

If the Prima saw the hint of relief in Orsina's features, she gave it no heed. "And you shall never graduate."

That was sufficient to blot out the glimmer of relief swiftly. "What… what would that mean?"

"First and foremost, it will mean that you are not bound to an impresario, permanently limiting your available power. In terms of prestige, it would mean your value would be greatly diminished in the eyes of those who matter. It would mean that rather than becoming such a roaring success that all are clamoring for you and willing to overlook any haziness in your past, you would face a degree of scrutiny. Typically a mother will do the work of trying to forge a marriage, or some patron might negotiate your adoption into a noble family as a ward. But you lack the both of these to make arrangements for you, so you would be forced to… let us just say it will complicate matters for you considerably." Orsina had never seen it before, but there was something in the slant of the Prima's shoulders that spoke to the immense burdens she bore, the many plates she kept spinning like a mummer at the summer fair, wobbling all around her. She looked tired.

So Orsina said what she thought she had to. Just as she'd been doing since she was first thrust into this strange new world. "I'll fix this."

"My dear, I do not know that there is anything to be fixed. You cannot change who you are, and it would seem that noble blood entered into your family line somewhere prior to the history you can recall, so it is not as though we might seek out an ancestor who might be inclined to favor you." Where usually the Prima spoke with a flourish, like she was reciting the lines from a play, tonight it seemed all sense of theatricality had departed. Each word was chosen slowly and carefully and doled out like Mother Vinegar might have tipped her tiny wooden spoon of foxglove milk into her heart-soothing tincture. Like she knew that a slip of the hand could spoil everything. Like she knew that too heavy a dose of this truth might kill.

Orsina's knees drew up against her chest, rucking up all the lace and layers about her legs. There had to be a way out of this. A way around it. "Might I think on this, Prima?"

"First I must have your word that you shall not attempt anything foolish, as you did with our resident Owl." The exhaustion that Orsina felt seemed to be contagious, for once more the Prima looked beyond tired, deep into the trench at the far side of sleeplessness that Orsina herself had only found on those nights on the road when the rain fell like hammers on her hood and it was better to trudge on than try to sleep.

"How did you…" She caught herself when her voice wavered. "Of course you knew."

"Expertise does tend to take longer than a single night to cultivate, my dear. Not to mention that you seemed quite dazed in my lecture. There is a reason we learn things for ourselves. The perspective of others does not always lend itself to our situation. Our understanding of matters is not the same as another's, and to force the perspective of another upon ourselves can be jarring." A hand extended out towards Orsina and patted at her wrist. Comfort or affection, from one ill used to doling such trivialities out.

"I felt like I couldn't think my own thoughts." Orsina felt it still. As she tried to put it into words. "Like the shape of them was wrong."

"Indeed, and I could have warned you that such a course of action would have led to this result if you had taken the time to consult with me, or indeed any member of the staff, before diving directly into one of the most dangerous compacts that any shade binder can undertake." The patting on Orsina's wrist now took on a distinct slapping rhythm.

"I... I didn't want to let you down."

The Prima sat back with a sigh and just looked at her for a moment. "My dear girl, I have placed my bets, and where the cards fall is not a matter of sorrow or joy. I was aware there would be risks when I took you in, just as I was aware of the potential rewards. In terms that a farmer's daughter might best understand, you need not worry about my emotions, for I assure you a lifetime in court has left that particular field fallow."

Orsina dared to risk a gentle smile. "You leave a field fallow so it blooms better the next season."

The Prima did not smile back. "Then perhaps I should have said barren."

"I like fallow better. Mean's there is hope for something new coming back."

"Now to the other matter, I must ask that you do not attempt to bind any more shades until you are sufficiently prepared to partition their access to you. You'll need to progress to a more advanced class with all immediacy, given that you already have two powerful shades in your coterie. It isn't unheard of, of course. There are some who have been in private tuition all their life to inherit their family's shades, but I must confess that in this as in all things you continue to surprise me."

Orsina stared at her blankly. "What?"

"When a binder possesses multiple shades but is not yet bound to an impresario, the increased drain upon our life force in the short term can be a devastating shock. Many have died attempting to do too much too swiftly. It is for this reason that the shades must be carefully partitioned from each other, so when one is being succored, the others cannot attempt to drink also. It will all be demonstrated for you in your lessons, you need not fear."

"No, I mean. I don't have two shades."

The Prima's finely plucked brows pulled together. "I'm not certain why you are attempting such a clumsy deception. You cast three shadows, my dear."

"But I never... I didn't..." Her mind began spinning again. Between the Owl's memories and her own confusion regarding the bond she'd forged with Ginny Greenteeth, she had no idea from where another shade could have come. She reached out tentatively, only to find her senses scrubbed raw after contact with the snooty armor shade. It had never hurt to reach out beyond herself before. She wondered if this was the kind of damage the Prima was warning her of.

For her part the Prima looked increasingly concerned. "You didn't know? You genuinely didn't know? That is... concerning. It speaks to the very lack of training we have already discussed. It suggests that there is no partitioning to speak of within your mind and spirit to keep the Greater Shades from feeding upon the energy of the lesser, or from touching on your mind without your awareness."

"What... what do I do? How do I get rid of it."

"The pact is already sealed, my dear girl. There is nothing to be done other than to find a use for this mysterious stowaway of yours. As your education progresses and you learn to construct such constraints within yourself as to allow control over each shade independently, we can hope this hidden one might be drawn up to the surface, sifted from the masking presence of the others as gold is drawn from sand."

What little conversation as could politely pass between two people of such vastly different station in life seemed to have been tapped out after that. The Prima returned to her desk, Orsina gathered her wits and some measure of strength back to her limbs, and then she set out into the dark corridors of the House of Seven Shadows.

Before all of this had happened, her mind was in flux, overwhelmed by all she had taken in. But now that her very spirit was ringing like a gong, she felt as though she were lost in her own body. It had been a feeling building up since the dragon in the forest, when she woke up a year older and she didn't know her own face. It grew worse every day she was here. Her body was different. Her life was different. Everything was changing and she just had to play along. Now her mind was different too; in her panic, she'd mangled it. She'd crammed a lifetime of learning into her empty head and now it threatened to squeeze all her own thoughts out through her ears. She couldn't stand it. She couldn't think. The damned suit of empty armor had struck her so hard she could feel her bones quaking within her. Bones that weren't hers, had been pushed inside her flesh, stretching her out of shape. Twisting her into this new Orsina. This girl who'd do anything to graduate from some school she'd never heard of. To make herself powerful, so that somebody might give her shelter from the world.

She didn't want that. She'd never wanted any of that. These were the wants of the Prima and Harmony. They were in her head, speaking in her voice. Telling her how she should live. Who she should strive to become. She needed to think. She needed to get her brain back under control. She was spiraling. She was losing herself.

Her body was a stranger's. Her mind was a stranger's. She was dressed up like some fairy-tale princess. She had a library crammed between her ears. She didn't even own her own soul anymore. There was something else inside her. Lurking in the hollow in her heart. Some stranger, some monster, that had snuck its way in while she was insensible. What shade had tied its fate to hers? When would it have had the chance when she had her walls built high and never lowered them?

Everything that she was was gone. Would anyone even recognize her now? If Mother Vinegar set eyes on her, would she be known? Kagan? Anyone?

She staggered from wall to banister as she came down the stairs from the Prima's tower. The blindfolded servants, the only ones about in the dead of night, heard her, but did not see her. Did not know her. They wouldn't dare to challenge if she was meant to be here. How dare they, they were commoners. Peasants.

She was a peasant too. She had looked at these noble scions of the most powerful families in all the land and she had thought the same way. How dare she challenge what they said was best for her? How dare she consider arguing back?

As she tried to think of the layout of the House and find her way, she kept on colliding with memories that didn't belong to her. Here there was once a door. There a runner carpet once covered the floorboards. Out in the main chamber of the house, she could look down and see the moonlight reflecting in the water. Some hint of reality creeping back in from outside all this madness.

The moon still rose. The sun still shone. The world cared nothing for the things she did or the places she went or even for the damage she dealt to herself in pursuit of someone else's dreams. It was enough to still her for a moment. To quiet the shades prying at her from all around, inside and out.

Was she still her mother's daughter, or had they made her something else? Was she still the girl who strode undaunted through a forest where grown men feared to tread? She didn't know. It certainly didn't feel like her mind was the same, nor like it would ever return to the way it had been. In her desperation, she truly feared she'd maimed herself.

Memories that weren't her own bombarded her every staggering step, but her own were the anchor that held her in place. Mother Vinegar grinding roots in a pestle. Kagan's bark of laughter when he found a gnawed-clean claw in one of his snares. The little woodland drake he was stalking had chewed right through its own flesh to be free. Scales and cracked teeth lay scattered around it. A blood trail led off into a stream, then vanished on the well-washed stones. "Let it go," he'd said. It had earned its freedom.

It had maimed itself for survival, and he had not judged it foolish, just determined. Brave beyond the limits of reason. Such things were rarely praised among the nobility of Espher, who thought more in terms of calculated odds, but among the Arazi, what she had done would have been akin to a holy act. Even a crestfallen exile like Kagan showed what scars he could with pride.

In the deep shadowed night of the unlit halls, she found her way to Harmony's chambers more by luck than any real memory of the way. She flung the door open to more desolate silence.

The fireplace was unlit, the disarray of books that usually signaled Artemio's presence was absent, and the perfumes and oils that Orsina could have sworn she'd never noticed Harmony wearing had dissipated to a dull hint. Like the scent of a candle blown out hours ago.

Her only friends in this strange new world were gone. Vanished in the night. She supposed she could go charging around, barking at servants for answers and demanding their return like a spoiled toddler upending a house in the hunt for a lost rag doll, but as she slipped into the stillness of the room, she realized what little strength she'd managed to gather on the Prima's fainting couch had now been spent. Harmony was meant to be there, to catch her when she fell. Artemio was meant to be there, in the background, tutting and clucking like a mother hen. Instead there was just this empty room again, where she'd curled around herself and patched her wounds the last time injury was done to her. It seemed this was to be the only constant in this new life—suffering alone.

With a kick of her heel, she slammed the door shut behind her. If this was to be her life, then she would survive it.

THE RED MASQUE

Gemmazione, Regola Dei Cerva 112

Arat could see in the dark perfectly, but the Volpe twins could not, so it fell to Artemio to conjure a flame. It was harder to hold that tiny flicker of light than it would have been to flood the entire tunnel with flames. Everything about him cried out for fire, and the forge spirit longed to burn it all.

These once had been pyroducts, like so many of the tunnels beneath Covotana. Lava tunnels stretching up and out from the great volcano that had formed the caldera that was now the city's outer wall. Now they were walled up behind the offcuts of the white stone that had made the city above. The original slick surface of the molten stone was disguised behind the white, and the white in turn had been disguised by centuries of effluence, mold, and moss. Gases rose from the sewage trickling along the bottom quarter of the tunnel, puffing the tiny spark of flame into a green cloud for an instant before Artemio could bring it back under control. He found himself wishing he'd taken the lantern along now that the rat had been removed from it, but they certainly weren't backtracking now.

Here and there he saw the rat-maid's eyes dart, and he tried to observe as she did. A spot where the moss had fallen away. A chipped bit of stone in the arch above. Natural landmarks of the sewers—or deliberately marked signs? He could not tell, and for all of his talents at deduction, there was simply too much unknown for him to make any sense of it all. Too much was in flux, down here in the filth, and he found his senses overwhelmed, by the stench, the sounds, and the strain of keeping the fire at bay. He knew Harmony would be doing much the same as him, observing all she could, but her attentions were forever pointed forward. Her interest was in the future, what was coming next, what would happen next, how she could intercept danger before it struck. She never thought on the past, and how things had come to be how they were. He supposed that between the two of them, they almost managed wisdom. Almost.

The rat-maid's foot slipped, and he seized her about the waist before she could splash into the filth flowing alongside them. She tremored in his grip, just as the real rat had, and she tugged herself away with more than due force. Had that been a deliberate attempt to make a noise? Was she trying to announce them to some potential ambushers? Every moment more questions arose, but beneath them all was the burning one. Who was the Last King? Who had seized this mantle from myth and made themselves a master to assassins? Despite all threats, the rat-maid had given no answers, claiming ignorance, and Artemio felt quite certain she'd have given up her own mother rather than risk her bondmate's safety again.

He could not imagine a world in which you might give yourself over body and soul to someone in a mask without even a hint as to their identity, but he supposed things were different for peasants. They did not have the education required to make wise decisions, and it was in their nature to follow. One flag likely seemed as good as any other to them. At least it provided a neat solution to the problem if this one servant was to be believed. If there was no cabal behind all of this, and only a single leader, the snake could be decapitated in a single blow.

Artemio had never made much study of sneaking. He knew that, given his upbringing, it should have been second nature to him to creep about as if he were a spider stalking prey, but he had learned early that any behavior like that was unbefitting of a gentleman and could earn him a strapping independently of the one he'd receive for whatever he'd actually been up to. So when he had gone about what his mother had called wickedness and he had called trying to live, he had always done so with his head up and shoulders back.

So it was but a few minutes along those dim-lit sewer tunnels that Harmony had to dart forward and catch him before a crumbling brick dropped him into what could be charitably described as water with a splash that would have roused the dead. "Steady now," she whispered in his ear. "You should not have started on the celebratory wine until we were done."

He pushed away from her, fumbling to keep the spark of flame under control, flaring it bigger as it threatened to die, then, suitably dazzled, crushing it back down so abruptly that the three of them were suddenly in blind dark. He had to squeeze his eyes shut against the darkness and light to find the stability required to bring everything back into balance. Then he looked about him.

The rat-maid was gone.

"Shit." Perhaps that outburst was not gentlemanly, but it was entirely necessary.

They took off at a run down the tunnel, capering and slipping in the filth and slime underfoot, all hope of stealth abandoned in the face of the far greater danger of the maid passing on some warning to her masters.

The slop of sewage and the slap of their feet on the wet stone echoed all around them, deafening them to any other sounds. Artemio sent his fire darting along ahead of them, letting it splash and rebound off the wall, popping and bursting out larger and louder with each patch of gas it struck until it was scorching the roof and bubbling the waters below.

Another necessary sacrifice, to create enough light to pick out the rat-maid's course as she twisted and turned through these tunnels, a smudge of elongated heel here, in some slime. A little moss dangling loose here, at the level of her eye, where her clawed fingers would have pried it free. At a branch, he almost ran on in pursuit of his flame before catching sight of another rat, haring its way out of the other tunnel towards them. Disturbed with a chicken bone still dangling from its mouth. There. He made the leap half-cocked, and his heels touched the vile water before he could scrabble himself back into motion.

Every delay gave the rat-mongrel more distance. If this had all been a ruse to get free of them, then that mattered little, but if she'd spoken truly and there was some meeting down in the sewers, every moment she was free brought the whole enterprise closer to its crashing annihilation—and both the Volpe twins with it.

A left turn, a right. Clawed marks on the wall where her toes had scraped and she'd hauled herself up into a crossing drain. Harmony's feet beat a steady rhythm behind him. He was gasping in the fetid air, and she likely hadn't broken a sweat.

At the end of the raised interceptor, the tunnel opened out into a stormwater drain, deep as a well and wide as a village square. Harmony caught him before he could go over, but his mind still reeled even as his feet found their place back beneath his shoulders. All of this was beneath the city, and he had never even the faintest idea. Miles and miles of tunnels that led throughout the place, hidden by their own mundanity. He had never once thought where the toilets of the city flowed or, if he had, given it a second thought. Just as he had never wondered how the servants in the palace managed to get around in all of their hundreds without a noble being forced to lay eyes upon them. Everything had been in plain sight from the very beginning, but he was simply too blind to see it.

There was a ledge around the vertical shaft, wide enough for a man to walk along it unhindered were it not so clogged with flotsam fallen from above. As it was, they had to edge their way around and hope the wet handprint that Artemio glimpsed shimmering down the right-angled tunnel to the one they entered was new and not some quirk of the environment making damp patches persist long beyond they were due to.

Looking down was obviously unthinkable, so as he nudged dead pigeons and rotten leaves aside, Artemio pondered how little it would have taken to make servants take up arms against their masters. He could not help but think of his own family as the prime example. Most of those in his father's service had been with the family through generations, as much a part of the family as any trueborn heirs. Or so his father would have said. He could not picture his nurse turning on Mother with a blade in hand. The old liver-spotted castellan closing his spidery fingers around her throat. It was as inconceivable as a pig chopping up its butcher, yet the evidence all said that it was so.

When he arrived, the handprint was unmistakably elongated into something between rat and human. They were going the right way.

The slapping of their feet began to be drowned out in the flow of water as they joined larger and larger pipes and tunnels, until there was a veritable flood of what looked to be clean water running in an underground river alongside them. Spray rose up off it, masking the rest of the tunnel with a mist, blinding Artemio to the course their quarry had taken and making the already slippery stone lethally slick. They had no choice but to carry on as best they could until abruptly the torrential waters stilled. Passing from river to a great basin in a few paces. Beneath their feet, they found battered wooden boards, and, between them, the great currents of the underwater river spun the oil clinging to the surface through a vast and complex dance, shimmering back the light of Artemio's tiny flame and the more proper torches they could see glowing beyond the walkway.

More of the same rickety construction had been undertaken on the distant shore, a stage raised up between a still lake and a baying crowd, all garbed in the same rough rag hoods the assassins had worn when they came for Artemio mere hours ago. Hundreds were massed here, and these could be only a fraction of the full army this insurrection had gathered. In every noble household there could be one or more of these killers, and beyond them in the fields that were tilled and the towns that were protected by the will and wealth of their betters, there could be nests of vipers such us these under every unturned stone. So many of them it beggared comprehension.

Artemio reached back and found his sister's hand already outstretched. This was larger than either one of them could have known, and infinitely more dangerous. The rat-maid had already vanished into the crowd. She could be spreading the word of their coming. Setting the meeting to scatter, or preparing an ambush for when they emerged. Surprise remained the only thing on their side in this foreign land beneath the soil, and Artemio would not sacrifice it on the altar of his own mortal fear. He strode forward, leading Harmony on.

"What exactly do you mean to do?"

"Grab a rag, cover our heads, get in close, take their leader hostage."

She walked in his shadow, eyes wide as he let their own torch die. All eyes seemed to be directed to the stage, but wandering through with a dancing magical flame seemed a fairly clear invite to unwanted attention. Not to mention, splitting his attention in a situation like this was a good way to cut his life short.

There was chatter all about them, subdued, but enough that their own words did not leap from the crowd. Harmony hissed into his ear, "This is the cunning for which the Volpe are famed?"

They pushed into the rear ranks of the crowd, and with swift hands and a distinct lack of care for the property of others, Harmony was able to furnish them with some truly wretched-looking shawls they draped about themselves in a vague facsimile of a disguise. It wasn't much, but they didn't need much. The swarm of bodies about them was a mixture of everyone who dwelled within Espher's borders. All tones of skin, feathers and fur alike. Artemio barely contained a hiss of disgust. Whoever was in charge of this mess must truly have been desperate to invite mongrels to take an equal standing within the organization as everyone else. It was not that he had any bias against them, simply that they were unsightly and a sure sign that the bottom of the barrel was truly being scraped, given how powerless such creatures had ever been, historically.

"I haven't exactly got all evening to come up with something better," he grumbled back. "It will work. We can unmask him, use him as a shield. We have options here."

They were stopped behind a rather bulky, shrouded figure, most likely one of the few dockworker mongrels who had bonded to the turtles found in those murky waters. The twins parted and re-formed on the other side of him.

"Or her."

It was enough to give Artemio pause. "What?"

"Who's to say the Last King isn't a woman?" He couldn't see Harmony's face beneath her hood, but there was a familiar set in her shoulders. One of contrariness. As though simply arguing enough might remove her from the uncomfortable situation she was in.

"I… I mean…" He let out an exasperated huff. "Is this really the time?"

She glanced around as faces began to turn their way, then fell into step beside him once more. "Right, yes. Later."

The crowd grew denser still as they came closer to the stage. It seemed huge now that they were on the plane below it, what had been rickety woodwork from a distance transforming in the upcast torchlight into something vast and looming. Whoever had built this had done so with an eye for drama.

"Or never, that would also be quite acceptable."

It was with the same theatrical flourish that the Last King came into sight, lunging up from a ladder on the waterside. From down here on the ground, he seemed as tall as a giant, though Artemio did some swift calculations that put him at a little over average height. He was robed in rags, the same as all of the others, a mask that could be cast aside, a crowd into which he could easily blend. The only thing that made him distinct from any of the other peasants down here in his shadow was the crown upon his head. Finery would doubtless have made for a more dramatic effect, but the myths had always been clear that the Last King was not a creature of gold, but of decay. Atop his hooded head lay a circlet of woven hawthorn, and Artemio was willing to bet that it was not droplets of water from the lake dripping down from it to patter upon the stage, but the blood of whoever had been forced to weave it.

The crowd went berserk. They flung themselves forward. Their voices rising beyond human sounds into a monstrous ecstasy. Drowning out the water, the conversation, everything that had made this strange unhallowed place beneath the earth in any way comforting. The mongrels made their bestial calls, but the purebred human stock seemed intent on showing them up with their own wailing and roaring. Artemio saw a mousy-looking woman to his right throw back her head and screech to the cavern's top. And it was a cavern now that he looked. Not another part of the sewers, but a bubble in the volcanic rock that stood as the capital's foundation. It must have been here since before the city was built, unknown to anyone on the surface. Anyone except for these deranged lunatics or the one who led them.

The King held his arms wide until silence fell. For a crowd so lost to their passions, it happened so abruptly that for a moment Artemio felt as though all the air had left the chamber. He glanced to Harmony and saw his own mounting fear reflected back from her eyes. If this crowd were turned on them, shades and blades wouldn't matter a damn. The swarm would tear them apart bare-handed.

"Our enemies are weak. They are weak, and they are blind. Beneath their noses, we have seized the throne of Espher. We have taken their power, and at last, it shall be returned to where it belongs…" The Last King was a skilled orator for being an immortal shade of death and destruction, almost as though he'd had lessons in it. His voice was not muffled by the mask as Artemio had expected, but rather it echoed and rebounded out, as though some cone were fashioned beneath that dangling hood to amplify every word. "It shall be returned to those who made Espher great, those who sweat and toil while the bloodless necromancers and their lackeys lounge."

The rhetoric didn't seem to be going anywhere. It was the usual small-minded drivel about the people of Espher being too reliant upon the magic of the Shadebound. The sort of thing all of her enemies bandied about. Artemio could barely believe that all of these locally grown men and women were giving it any credence. Admittedly, they would not have been trained in rhetoric and logic, but to see them so easily led along by some foreign agent was disheartening. Still the King boomed on. "The power belongs in our hands, in your hands. We are the ones who build the streets, grow the food, do all of those things that a nation actually needs to survive. We are the ones who should govern it."

Harmony let out a huff that drew Artemio's gaze, and he realized with dismay it was a laugh. She was the very picture of contempt. Everything this peasant speaker was claiming they were. If he had heard her laugh, so too would all those around them. He caught her sleeve and dragged her close. "Sister dearest, now is not the time to express yourself."

"Art, it is drivel," she hissed. "These people can't rule. They wouldn't know the first thing about…"

His eyes darted about as he tried to master his fear. Heads were turning their way. Even with the King there before them, holding all attention with his rambling. "We can discuss this matter later."

Throughout their soft-spoken bickering, the titan looming over them all had carried on. "…and this is how we know there is only one king who cannot be made into dirt and bones, and his name is death. No gods, no kings. No more parasites lodged like ticks upon her majesty. Only Espher, eternal!"

The crowd took up the cry, echoing it back to him. "Espher, eternal!"

If the sound Artemio and Harmony been making had drawn attention before, their silence now boomed. When the closest of the hooded ones realized they hadn't shouted out about how marvelous the country they were currently attempting to entirely undermine was, they spun on him, hand fumbling at their belt for a weapon. Artemio didn't give them the chance. Stepping in close he drove a fist into the guts of whatever creature the mildewed cloth concealed, folding them. There was one glorious instant where he thought it had worked. That he'd downed them without attracting attention, but up there, dangling from the side of the stage, he met the eyes of the rat-maid where she hung. "Enemies! Enemies among us! Treachers! Parasites! Necromancers!"

Her words spread like a ripple through the crowd. Every head turning their way. All around them bristling. The King on stage fell silent, pointing with a single finger at Artemio where he stood.

"Slay them!"

Everything that could possibly have gone wrong now had, and the time for restraint was long behind them. Now was the time for Harmony's kind of diplomacy.

Artemio drew his rapier with a flick of his thumb, and with only a backwards glance to watch its course, Harmony's hand darted out to catch it by the handle, even as she drew her own.

Without a combat shade, he was no match for her talents with the blade, and as helpful as Bisnonno Fiore had been in that regard, this was not a situation any king might have prepared for.

What luck that Artemio's talents lay elsewhere.

Flinging his arms apart, he let the fire burn. All of this time, he had been holding the forge spirit at bay. Letting out little sparks and flickers. It did not want to be a candlelight in the darkness or a torturer's flame or a line of flame parting a crowd or a lance of fire chasing back along a thread of will to an upstart at a party. It wanted to be an inferno.

So just this once, he let it.

Flames leapt out from his outstretched fingers, not in careful darts or angular streams but in a torrent, a wave of fire that washed through the crowd, never staying still long enough to eat through to flesh, but never stopping either. The greasy rags they'd garbed themselves in caught alight, their disguises began to burn away. None of this mattered much to the gathered peasants when they could feel flame licking at them through their clothes.

Even the most refined gentleman became an animal when fire was upon him, and these were not refined gentlemen. They dropped to the ground, rolling and screaming, and Artemio launched himself forward, stamping on them as he surged through the crowd, stumbling on towards the stage, towards victory.

Behind him, he could hear Harmony doing her delicate dance, the slice and thrum of her blades as they flowed from step to step. He did not need to look back to know that she had cast off her burning shroud or that she was cutting down any would-be killer still holding their ground. Such was their trust.

More and more of his life trickled away, fuel for the ever-spreading flame, but what were a few more minutes of his life cut short in the face of a prize such as this. Fiore knew. He knew what this victory would be worth. He spent himself without recompense, invisible hands on Artemio, driving him on, lifting him up, catching him as he stumbled. A great turtle mongrel fell to her knees screeching before the stage, and Artemio saw his opportunity. The arc of his leap overlay the scene, and his grandfather's hands pressed up beneath his heels to launch him forward.

With one leap, he mounted the shell on the mongrel's back, driving the lumbering giant down onto her face, then he kicked off in a plume of flame and icy winds, flying up onto the driftwood stage and the Last King who awaited him there.

Say what you would of this rebel, but there could be no denying his composure. Though the stage burned, and his ragged robes with it, he did not flinch. Even as Artemio came on with flames coiling around his fists, he stood his ground.

It was time to end this. It was just a matter of time before weight of numbers overcame the momentary advantage surprise had bought them. There was no chance of taking a prisoner and escaping in one piece. There was only now. There was only this moment. Artemio flung both arms forward and the fire leapt at the Last King. Not the wild chaos he'd sown below, but two perfect lances of boiling blue flame.

They stopped dead a foot from the Last King. Strangled away to nothing.

Artemio's charge faltered. The surety and power he'd known but a moment before crumbling in the face of this impossible sight. His feet felt leaden at all the life he'd spent. His mind sluggish as adrenaline fled.

"How?"

The Last King crossed his arms across his chest and said nothing at all. Once more Artemio reached for his shades, to try again, to try something new, but the tide had turned and his chance was burned.

The rat-maid had finished her scramble up onto the stage, but that didn't exactly fill him with trepidation. Even if they had some way to quash his Shadebound powers, Artemio felt certain a chambermaid with delusions of grandeur was still well within his capabilities. Rather it was the rest that troubled him. A dozen more of the unmasked assassins now took the stage, and every one of them must have known what would happen to them if he survived. There was no plausible deniability for them now. If he returned to the surface, they'd die.

And they had knives, while Artemio's hands were empty.

In desperation, Artemio lanced out fire at the closest of them and was delighted to find that whatever protection the King bore did not extend to his minions. The dart of fire took the top off a fishmonger's head, leaving a blackened channel where face and skull had once been.

On came the rest, unheeding of the danger, intent on bearing him down, and again Artemio lashed out, a whip-line of flame to drive them back, to give him space. It lapped over the closest of them, searing through their upraised arms, blackening to bones and sizzling away hybrids' hair, but at the far end of the stage where the King still stood stalwart, it sputtered and died.

Was the King Shadebound? Was he truly a shade, dressed in mortal robing to disguise himself and pass freely among them? Such thoughts should have been preposterous, but faced with this evidence, Artemio could not think of any other way his own powers might have been subverted. He had never heard of a foreign magic that could stop Espher's shades. Nor any device or design beyond a shade in tow that could put an end to an elemental's assault.

He cast out his senses as the peasants gathered their wits. Prying at the King, trying to find the telltale signs of a shade at work, but there was nothing. Bisnonno Fiore, the forge spirit, and an empty echo where any opposition should have been.

On came the knives and blind fervor. The burned beasts barely feigning humanity. Artemio struck at them, whipping them across their upraised arms and faces, hoping to drive them back without more murder, but it was not to be.

His hands shook as life left him. As precious moments of his years were burned away in the fulcrum of his shades and became flames in truth, his skin grew looser, the brightness of the flames dimmed, the world faded towards oblivion. He was spending too much too swiftly.

He could barely hear himself think as he bellowed out, "Harmony?!"

From up here he could not see her. He did not know if she had fought her way through or if she was already dead. There was no time.

The nearest of the peasants came on, jagged knife sweeping for his throat. They were only human, only as strong and fast as a man could be; they were not his match. Artemio dragged the flames back under his control as he fell back, made a blade of them, and slashed clean through the charred and blackened rags this man had worn when he lived.

It flared blue-hot as it struck through bone, then it was gone and he was stumbling towards the back of the stage and the dead drop into the water.

"Harmony!" he tried again, desperation creeping up his throat. He could not flee without her. He would not.

A horse-headed mongrel lumbered in with a stave in hands. Clad on either end with battered copper. Some peasant's tool Artemio did not know. The mule spun it overhead then brought it down on him.

Flames licked along the length of the staff, lapping harmlessly over the copper, but biting deep through the bound leather and into the wood. It struck him hard on the top of the head, and for an awful instant everything fell silent and dark, but then the staff snapped in two parts from the damage and the pressure.

He caught the scalding half that had been meant to spill his brains and drove it forward, wreathed in more fire, right into the horse-man's guts. The great lout folded around the blow, and another burst of flames put paid to the idea that he might ever rise from where he'd fallen. Yet for each one Artemio put down, more had mounted the stage. A veritable horde, now filling in the last thin channel between him and the Last King. The man's face was still hidden, but there was no doubt in Artemio's mind that he was gloating.

Something had shaken loose with the blow to his head. Tears flooded down Artemio's face now, parting the soot and frosting on his cheeks when Bisnonno Fiore passed through him. He lanced out flame after flame, focused and tight, blue-hot and piercing. Everyone it touched screamed and sobbed and split open bloodlessly. Wounds already cauterized. But on more and more of them came. He could not do this forever, and they could keep coming without pause. There could be a hundred of them, a thousand. He had only the shallow well of his own years to draw on, and each time the bucket came up, it felt lighter. He could almost hear Fiore's voice in his head, demanding that he leave. Demanding that he abandon his post and save himself.

"Art!" Harmony's voice cut through the roar of flames and the screams of the dying. She was here. She was alive.

"Harmony?!" The darkness fell away from the edges of Artemio's vision as his focus returned. There were a dozen men and women between him and the edge of the stage. They would not slow him.

With the same simple gesture that had parted the crowds outside of the Sabbia townhouse, he lanced out lines of flame and hauled them apart. Some stood their ground, trying to endure the flame, to block his path. For these, he spent a little more of his life, flaring the fires blue-hot and parting flesh as easily as the empty air.

When he stepped forward, he felt the shade being ripped from the back of his body, the forge spirit still standing strong and burning bright in his wake. Upholding its end of their bargain, pushing back the crowds so he could charge on. Fiore was with him still, surrounding him in chill air to push back the inferno he'd created. Lightening his steps. Driving him on.

With one wild leap from the stage's edge, he soared down to land in a crumpled heap by his sister's side. Flinging himself into a roll to avoid snapping both legs like twigs, but barreling into the legs of the gathered crowd before his momentum could be spent. They tumbled on top of him, an awful crush of sweating, stinking humanity. They smelled of the sewers, of flophouses, of manure and desperation and manual labor's salty crust. Artemio wrestled his way upright, through them. Digging in his hands and prying apart the places where bodies met.

He burst free into the air to see Harmony's booted heel pass an inch from his face, slamming the last of the heap in the ribs and rolling him aside. Her rapier was snapped in two, his was slick with blood.

She'd garbed herself in his clothes for the night's work, and while they'd been well suited to this expedition, they were beyond repair. Bloodied and tattered. Yet she had not a scratch upon her. "All right?"

She clubbed a charging peasant in the face with the hilt of her broken sword, flicking out the intact blade to knock an ill-held club from a dog-girl's bristly hands. All with a smile on her face. "I'm so glad you invited me to this party, dear brother. I would have hated to miss it. Truly, the event of the season."

"Oh don't pretend you're having a bad time." He managed to haul himself loose of the fallen before any of them made their way back to their feet and recalled the forge spirit to douse them in flames. There were wrinkles on his hands when he saw them in the light of that grim pyre. How much had he aged in this one clash? Or was it simply that his eyes were now failing him too.

She kicked at those who were down, and slashed at those still fleeing her reach. A red line split the back of one woman's dress, baring whip scars running the same direction. "Still," Harmony panted, "perhaps it is time we made our departure?"

The exits were rapidly being blocked by the swarming peasantry. They had dawdled too long to make a clean escape. "The stage."

"The stage?" She thrust past him into a knife-wielding stranger he'd never have seen coming. As she whipped back into her ready position, a shower of blood struck his back. "Do you plan to sing your way out of trouble?"

"I presume a bawdy tavern song would improve everyone's temperament." He forced out a laugh as they started another run at the smoldering structure. Harmony fell into step beside him. His flames and her blade keeping the stragglers who had not fled them well at bay.

When faced with the death of their ringleader, the rebels had all flocked to the stage to protect him. Such devotion. Artemio could scant believe it. The result of this was a mass of bodies around the bottom of the stage and very few of them with the wherewithal to actually mount the thing.

An idea was beginning to push its way up out of the swampy waters of Artemio's exhaustion. Less a coherent plan and more an image composed of fractal memories he was trying desperately to pull together into something more substantial.

"Stop."

"No. No stopping." She leapt and kicked into the gut of a great lumbering mongrel who looked to have the head of a cow. Some country buffoon dragged into all of this. Artemio needed to stop memorizing them. Stop working out the details. He did not have the time for analysis. Harmony hamstrung the towering man as she darted past him, and they let him fall on his friends. "Stopping is the opposite of a good plan. Stopping leads to catching, and catching leads to us being overwhelmed in a tide of unwashed heathens laboring under the delusion that the ability to sweep a street entitles you to command all who walk it."

"Just wait, one moment. Just... one..."

He could see the fury rising on her face, but by then it was too late, she had stopped.

Along the base of the stage, the timbers were blackened and burning. Artemio's first wildfire wash had struck it and passed by without dealing much in the way of damage. Yet still, fire clung there, just needing to be stoked a little hotter to bring the whole thing down.

This was going to hurt.

The forge spirit leapt forward, more than delighted to do what it did best, but for Artemio, things were less joyous. If he went on aging himself so rapidly, there could be no doubt that it would end in collapse. Harmony could not fight and carry him, so if he faltered here, they would both fall. What luck, then, that he was a student of history. He knew the ways the Shadebound of old had made their sacrifices to the things they knew as gods. He knew the way his debt could be paid without it costing their lives.

Reaching out with the same mastery of his spirit that allowed him to feed and restrain the shades in his service, he made a ring and tightened it around the smallest finger on his empty left hand. It ached as the binding of spirit cut into it, and it burned with an awful coldness when that ring tightened right through the flesh and bone until the whole thing was severed from the remainder of his spirit. All the life divided from the rest of him. All the years that were left to that one small part of him, now dangling loose. With one last pulse of will, he tossed it into the waiting maw of the forge spirit.

The stage burst into flames. An explosion of sudden heat and destruction so violent it knocked them both back onto their heels and tossed the closest clustered peasants to their knees. Blue-hot and dazzling bright, it burned. But not all of it. Even in this, Artemio had maintained his control.

The front supports of the stage burned away to ash, the crossbeams buckled with a shriek, and the whole rickety structure tumbled forward. The stage had been meant to hold one orator, not a whole crowd of body-guards and buffoons rushing to the aid of their King. Even without half the structure broken or burned, it could not have held them all for long. Artemio had simply helped things along.

As it fell, more and more bodies tumbled into the heap at the stage's base, and as they struck, more and more of those trying to flee from the impending death by a thousand splinters were pinned in place by the weight of bodies. Their numbers had been turned against them.

In all of the chaos, Artemio tried as he might to catch sight of the Last King, but already that man had secreted himself away in some place of safety. Or for all Artemio knew, he'd simply cast aside his crown and vanished into the crowd. All were garbed the same, all were fleeing the same. If he were but another peasant, then of course he'd vanish among them without a trace. But what peasant could bind a shade?

When the stage fell, dozens were crushed beneath it, and twice as many were floored by the tumbling debris—or the tumbling fools who had fallen from its height. A clear path was open to the water of the still lake ahead, and there, at the far end of the ladder that had once run up the length of the stage's rear, was their escape. A rowboat, not even tied up, just drifting in slow circles. Harmony saw it too, and dropped her broken hilt and seized her brother by the scruff of his ragged shawl. "Move."

Together they ran once more, leaping as best they could through the fallen, Harmony's blade darting out when there was a hint of resistance. They could have made better time if she hadn't been dispensing her own twisted version of mercy, but that would have left even more enemies at their heels, and of those they had more than enough. Already those who'd fled to guard the exits were rushing back in, to help those who were injured and to chase those who'd done the injury.

Artemio wondered how many of the little businesses about town, come the dawn, would be closed due to unexpected injuries and illness.

"How much time have you spent, Art?" Harmony's eyes kept darting to him, even as she fought.

For her to even ask so bluntly, there must have been fresh lines on his face, or new grey in his hair. "Dear sister, I'd spend a hundred years if it meant we'd live to see the end of the night."

The battle-joy on her face faltered for only a moment as she realized how close they must both have been to death. Walking on the knife's edge. Then a peasant swung what looked like a copper warming pan at her and the hesitation was gone.

Once they mounted the rocking wood of the shattered stage, the going became both easier and infinitely more difficult. There were no enemies trying to halt them here, but the ground beneath their feet was beyond unstable and into the realm of the comical. Like the touring fairground funhouse they'd both attended as babes, before Father took the reins on their upbringing. They rocked from side to side, counterbalancing each other, or launching the other from the seesaw end of another timber. Up and down they went, seeking equilibrium and a few steps of balance where they could, but finding little. It should have been some comfort to them that any pursuer would be similarly encumbered, but the truth was they had no pursuit.

When the outer crowds returned to the rescue of the friends and kin from the fallen stage, none pursued them onto the still-collapsing heap. Rather, they drew lengths of corded leather from their scorched sleeves, snatched up what debris they could find, and begin slinging it after the twins.

For once, fortune seemed to be favoring the Volpes. The erratic motion of the rocking timbers and the chaotic path they were forced to pursue to avoid areas of collapse made them trickier targets, but not impossible ones. A soaring rock clipped Artemio's shoulder, bruising to the bone and setting him off balance. He stumbled, caught a jagged length of upturned wood in his hip for his trouble, and then took off once more, bleeding profusely down one leg.

The next few shots went wild, but the last struck Harmony square between the shoulders. She went down hard, face slamming clean through a smoldering board. Artemio's heart stopped for the moment she lay there, still and silent, then he heard her sweet voice cussing like a sailor and he could breathe again. He leapt to her side and promptly caught a soaring rock to the top of his scalp, sending a fresh wash of blood down to burst through the clotted mess that already covered his hair. Lucky it was already red, really.

When he blinked away the stars, he was on his knees beside his sister, hauling her up, pulling the long splinter of wood that had embedded itself into her cheek clear and hoping that it hadn't taken any of her teeth out. Her smile had been charming, once upon a time. He still held on to some faint hope that he might see it again, and that it might be unmarred.

She cursed his name as he hauled the wood out, called him all manner of awful things, and strongly suggested many rude and untrue things about his mother, who was of course also her mother. It mattered little. They were just the noises she was making to project the pain out from her body because she had no time to feel it.

The two of them pulled each other up, each taking a turn to climb the other a distance before switching. On their feet, there was a spinning moment of disorientation until another stone exploded a heap of wood beside them into splinters, then they were off once more, bounding over the bare rock that now took up more and more of the space before finally reaching the boat.

Artemio leapt onto the rower's bench and had barely taken hold of the oars before Harmony's boot caught him in the back and threw him into the stern.

"What in damnation's name?"

She slipped into place on the bench and started stroking with all of her strength. In between heaves, she barked out, "I row, you fight. Not like a sword will do us any good on the water."

Artemio managed to right himself without overturning the boat, then immediately ducked again to miss another slung shot. Kneeling in the water in the bottom of the dinghy, he managed to gasp out, "You're hurt."

She spat out a mouthful of blood. Not over the side, as he'd hoped, but at her feet. Where he was kneeling. Her voice came out more growl than words. "We're both hurt. We'll both get even more hurt if you keep arguing. Especially you. Because I'll hurt you."

That was enough like her usual self that his worries evaporated away. If she was well enough to threaten him with grievous bodily harm, then she was most assuredly well enough to row a little boat out of the cave.

He flung a few lances of flame back at the huge heap of wood they'd left in their wake. It was a pyre just waiting to be ignited, so he did what came natural to him. It barely cost him any more of his life. The forge spirit was well sated after the massive meal he'd already given to it, not to mention that it truly loved to burn things more than anything else. It was less like he commanded it to unleash fire upon the world and more that he let it slip loose to do what it desired the most.

Fire spread, smoke rose, and the baying crowds of rebels faded from sight as Harmony drew back on the oars once more. Exhaustion caught Artemio at last. A soft, full-body ache that he knew he could sink down into and be relieved of all his worries and cares. But it wasn't done. He was still on the very edge of death, even if it did not feel like it.

His mouth felt like it were stuffed with wool as he mumbled to his sister, "Sword."

"What good will a sword do you?" She took in his glazed eyes. His fading strength. She rolled her eyes. "Just settle down."

He would not settle. He reached out with a shaking hand. "Harm. I need it."

With a grunt of disgust, she released an oar and flung it in his direction from the seat beside her. It clattered to a halt next to him. It was slick with blood, but another swift pulse of flame wiped it clean as it could be, and a second pulse heated it so the wounds it dealt would be sealed.

Then, finally, Artemio set his hand on the side of the boat, and he looked at what he'd done.

The smallest finger on his left hand was sickly pale, almost blue with how bloodless it was. All of it except for the nail and the tip, which were already beginning to blacken with decay. A whole lifetime's worth of time applied to it in an instant. No wonder it was already dead and rotting like it had been in the grave a year. That blackness was a poison that would spread throughout his whole body if he let it. He curled all the other fingers down until they were out of the way and only the dead one remained.

One deep breath, and then the next. Lining the side of the rapier with the demarcation on his finger and the wood below. He'd have to cut below the dead tissue, into the little stump of meat that still lived, otherwise the rot would spread from there. There was no bringing the dead finger back. Not even an inch. But if he did not cut low enough, whatever remained would putrefy.

Harmony realized what he was doing an instant before he did it, crying out, reaching for him. She was too slow. The blade cut in, living blood burst out, bright and red, then it sizzled to black as it touched the heated metal. There was no pain in Artemio's life that he could compare to that moment. But he had done it. He would live.

The severed finger toppled off the boat's side into the water. Artemio toppled back into the shallow puddle at the bottom of the boat. Harmony was screaming at him, shouting all manner of insults, kicking at him, doing whatever she could to keep him awake, to make him talk. The explanation was going to be too long. The conversation too draining. He didn't want to do it. They were alive. He'd made it so they'd both live. Everything else would have to wait.

THE COMING DAWN

Gemmazione, Regola Dei Cerva 112

rsina did not think a day would ever come that She willingly walked into the palace of Covotana, but it seemed her new desire for survival at any cost meant she was now willing to plunge her hand into a hornet's nest if it meant getting what she needed. The discomfort and the fear would pass, but what she had come for would remain.

Walking the streets of the city in the dress of a noblewoman was an ongoing series of revelations. The first of which was that her mind seemed to have returned to her in her sleep. It was not the same as it had been, it was as though she were thinking through layers of thin vellum that overlaid all of her own ideas with those that had belonged to others. There was some distortion, and sometimes her own thoughts were harder to make out clearly, but more often than not, these overlaid structures actually served to help her, to give her own thinking a scaffold to build upon. She did not need to pay heed to any thoughts but her own, but neither did she ignore them when more often than not they helped her.

The second revelation was that she was safe. Even back in her own village, far from the beating heart of the kingdom, it would not have been thought proper for a young woman of marriageable age to go wandering around without any sort of chaperone to protect her from unwanted advances, but here in this thriving city where she could see more men on a single street than she'd ever encountered in the whole of Sheepshank, there was no danger to her at all. Perhaps if she'd been a commoner still, then her experience would have been different, but it seemed that wealth and station mattered infinitely more in the world than what happened to be between her legs. At least out here in the streets.

She couldn't imagine the punishment a common man might receive for laying hands upon a noblewoman, but presumably it was a gruesome enough threat that most of these men did not dare to even look her in the eyes after taking note of her dress.

Dressing herself that morning had been a struggle. A noblewoman's clothes were not meant to be assembled by a single person. If anything, just Orsina and Harmony had already been pushing the bare minimum number of hands that were required, and so on this morning, after donning a shift that she'd stolen from the shared wardrobe that Harmony had left behind for her to cover the worst of her scars, she'd been forced to call in one of the servant girls to assist her. She'd never felt more of a fool than standing there as a girl who was likely a good few years older than her dithered about, tweaking and tying where she needed.

There could be no denying the results however. She looked truly wonderful. Which was good, because it would help her to remain invisible in the eyes of the court, if Artemio's tales were to be believed. If anything he'd said was to be believed.

She tried not to make assumptions about to where the Volpe twins had vanished. She tried not to second-guess her friendships. Yet with their final meeting missed, it was difficult not to believe all the worst things her anxious heart whispered in the night. She did not want to need them, she did not want to rely on any of the nobles who would look upon her as nothing but filth if they knew the truth of her blood, but neither could she make it through all of the twists and turns of this maze of manners without a guide.

By the time she reached the palace and strolled across the vaulting bridges over the beautiful, blue waters, it was midmorning. Without cash or carriage, the city seemed to grow imperceptibly broader with each step.

There were guards barring the way when she reached the palace doors, but she was a noblewoman, so they had no reason to stop her passage. After all of the walking required to reach the city, this was not enough to tire her or draw forth an unsightly sweat, so they had no reason to think she was not simply taking in the pleasant weather while it lasted. She asked where she might find Artemio Volpe, and within a few minutes a servant was offering a gloved hand to lead her through the many chambers of the palace to her goal.

Never in all of her life had things gone so smoothly for Orsina. As though all the world were rearranging itself around her to suit her whims. This was the real magic the nobility of Espher wielded, not necromancy, but mastery of all around them. Now that she'd tasted it, she wondered if she could ever go back to a world where every single moment was a struggle.

They led her past tapestries worth more than her childhood home. Past paintings that showed landscapes mysteriously devoid of the people who worked them. The only people in art were the ones who had the wealth to commission a painter. The only residents of this fantasy Espher were those who ruled it.

Orsina wondered if this fantasy was the world the nobles truly lived in. A world of invisible servants making everything easy for them, so when they were forced to look down upon the peasants, they wondered at how inferior they were, to struggle so when life was so easy.

The austere silence of the palace began to fracture as she drew closer to her journey's end. There were shouts echoing through these hallowed halls. Hissing whispers in every niche in the white stone. Noblemen braying and bellowing to one another like goats in the field. Orsina had to push herself forward against the dense wall of noise and to still the urge to squeeze at the white-gloved hand in hers for comfort. The voices did not seem to be raised in anger, only to be heard over the raucousness. If anything, the majority of them sounded smugly amused with their own statements, whatever they may have been.

Eventually, the servant led her carefully up onto a finely carved and polished wooden balcony overlooking the source of all the furor, and for the first time in her life, she saw the Teatro. The noble court where lords laid out the laws of the land and advised the king in governance sounded like a tavern in full swing.

There were other ladies reclining about this balcony and no small number of lesser nobles too. For a moment or so, Orsina was hopeful that she might spot Harmony among their number, but her friend was nowhere to be seen. A few women from the House recognized her and gave her withering glances or confused looks, depending upon their particular feelings towards her. For now, neither much mattered to Orsina. The servant who'd led her this far was now gone back to his duties, and any hope of questioning him was lost. She knew what she was seeking, and she would not be turned from her course. Stepping forward to the balustrade, she leaned out over the rising chaos clamoring below.

Every nobleman of Espher, to her eyes, seemed to be gathered down below in all of their matching suits. If there were some way to differentiate them at this distance, she did not know it. The red hair of the Volpes was her only guide in seeking Artemio out, but it seemed entirely fruitless in the sea of olive skin and black hair. She would have fit in perfectly down there if she had a man's suit, but Artemio, he was notable in his absence.

A sudden trumpeting from up by the empty throne at the end of the chamber brought all the chatter to an abrupt end. Then some wizened old gentleman in a frankly ridiculous robe lined with fur stepped forward to read from a scroll. "Next order of business. The Arazi menace."

It was enough to silence the gathered men for almost a whole breath before they burst out into another round of bellowing. For a moment, Orsina wondered how anything actually got done, when a thump from the far end of the chamber drew silence forth once more. It was a woman, dressed strangely in black clothing, with all of her hair clipped away until it was only a fine dark sheen upon her scalp. She did not wear slippers or heels, but boots, and it was the stamp of those boots that had silenced the nobles and drawn their attention.

"The God Emperor has declared the Arazi heretics and deviants for their foul bond with the serpents of the earth. He offers up aid in this time of Espher's need."

It was infinitely more effective than the tooting of the horn. Deathly silence spread as her words echoed over them. The Owl shade echoed in her memory, regurgitating pellets of peripheral knowledge to her. The Agrantine Empire. Their theocracy. Their emperor. She had not taken in any knowledge of these things, but from footnotes and implications, she could build a picture. There was little tone in the dry academic texts that had been dumped wholesale into her mind, but still her presiding image of Agrant was that of a hunting cat, lurking just beyond the city walls, searching for a way in to the penned cattle.

If they were invited in, there would be no getting them out without bloodshed. Some grey-bearded councilor rose from his place on the velvet benches below and replied as politely as was possible that Agrant could travel freely through Espher over his dead body, and that seemed to be the consensus. His exact wording made it seem more like the impending invasion of dragons was a small matter that could be dealt with effortlessly by the standing army, rather than an existential threat, but Orsina had the impression that among men such as these, every problem was made to sound small, so that any praise a solution garnered would be similarly lackluster—and any blame more easily deflected.

The shaven woman seemed to slip back out of sight as seamlessly as she had appeared, fading back into the crowd as though she had anticipated this turn of events, as though she had known any help she offered would be rejected as simply another step in the dance.

Orsina could not understand how it was that decisions were being made in the king's absence, but she supposed small problems might be solved by lesser nobles, with only the largest troubles being brought before the head of state. She personally would have thought that a rampaging army of dragons would qualify as a major crisis, but what did she know? She was just a peasant, after all.

She could not follow all the arguments back and forth that burst out beneath her, in part because there seemed to be six of them ongoing at any one time, and in part because nobody ever seemed to say what they meant. Every noble in the Teatro seemed to be putting on a show for their peers, showing how wittily they could work their way around the points others were making, not by saying they opposed them or why, but by framing them as abstracts and poking holes in the logic. It was frankly exhausting to listen to, and by the end of the first few minutes, Orsina was already looking for a way out of the room so she didn't have to endure any more. The nobles about her were tittering, as though the whole thing was entertainment. Of course they were. They had never felt the touch of dragon's fire, and should an army come, it would not be them taking to the field to face it.

Like a lead weight in her gut, it struck Orsina that should an army of fire-breathing monsters come tearing over the horizon, it would fall to her fellow Shadebound to face it. To her. She had not powdered her face that morning, as Harmony would have doubtless suggested, and that was for the best. All the sweat she had not shed in her slow stroll to the palace was coming now. Prickling up cold on her brow.

Could she face a dragon again? Could she stand her ground, knowing what their fire felt like on her skin, knowing the way they moved, not like beasts but like a storm, tearing through all they touched, buffeting down all that they did not? Fear ignited a fire beneath her rib cage. What should have been terror burned into anger. The same passion that had driven her to the tower of the Owl and here today. Determination to survive wreathed in the fury at what she was being forced to do just to live.

When all of her internal turmoil had passed, the conversation had also turned. She learned in snippets that the Arazi ambassador she had restrained was now dead. There were oblique references to questioning him, but nothing to suggest he gave any answers before he met the headsman's sword.

Still there was no sign of Artemio or Harmony. Caught up in all the drama of court, Orsina had almost forgotten why she had first come here.

She returned to her fruitless searching as the king himself appeared at the end of the chamber and once more the scattered arguments fell to silence.

Orsina half expected to see Artemio in the man's shadow, dogging his steps, but still there was no sign of him. For the length of a breath the silence went on, then the king was settled into the throne on the dais and the official business of the Teatro seemed to begin.

From the opposite end of the chamber emerged a jailer in the black hood of an executioner, dragging a prisoner along at the end of a chain. The man who followed was tall but bent by the weight of chains, broad in the shoulder, but malnourished from his time in captivity. Orsina did not know him, until he forced his head up from where it rested on his chest and Kagan stared out.

There were whispers among the gathered nobles, and those in the front seats seemed to lose their courage as Kagan passed them by, scrambling up and away to trip over their peers. It seemed that word of the ambassador's fire-breathing had not been suppressed. Once again, Orsina felt her heart leap to her throat, and she strained to hear what was being said on the floor below.

"...caught within this very city, spying upon our defenses for his kin. Is there anyone who will speak for the accused?"

All of the day's mutters were dying down. All of the raucous bantering that had characterized this room up until this very moment now completely vanished in the face of a real question. Nobody was going to speak. It struck Orsina, almost as swiftly as the realization that Kagan's life was now in the balance. Sweet, kind Kagan who had cared for her as a child, who had taught her the ways of the woods and protected her from the beasts of the wild places. He was going to die for this preposterous idea that he was a spy.

If she spoke, all eyes would be upon her. The whole court would know her. The king, who had so far overlooked her, would know her face and her name. Her life would be in danger. Still, she opened her mouth and tried to shout out.

Instead she made a strangled little noise as the doors to the chamber slammed open once more and Artemio strode in.

He was a wreck. There were bruises and cuts all over his face, one of his hands was swathed in bandages, and his perpetually pristine suit dangled limp and awkward off hunched shoulders. Between him and Kagan, it was difficult to say who looked the most diminished since the last time Orsina had seen them. Still, he walked up the length of the Teatro to the same desolate silence as had greeted Kagan, and he spoke clearly enough, though drawing a deep breath seemed to pain him.

"I shall speak for him. This dragon-lord gave me true and honest answers that assisted me in my duties to the kingdom, and in return, I promised I would request whatever clemency your Majesty might offer."

The king did not look at him, and he did not look at the king. It was as though their eyes passed one another by. The greybeard spoke up in the king's stead. Perhaps he was the royal mouthpiece. "You speak to his character?"

"He was always entirely honest with me, and it is my understanding that even under duress he has not made a confession of guilt. If he speaks the truth and he does not confess guilt, that suggests that he is not guilty, does it not?" Artemio attempted a smile, but it turned to a flinch midway. What had happened to him in the few hours they'd been parted?

"Yet for whatever masquerade of good character he might have shown, he still cannot provide an answer as to why he was within Espher's borders." Greybeard seemed quite startled to find that the king had spoken for himself. Artemio looked equally surprised.

"I cannot speak to that, your Majesty. Only to what I myself have observed."

"And what say you, serpent spawn?"

Kagan said nothing. Even here and now with his life in the balance, he did not speak. He did not endanger her new life. Orsina could feel tears welling up in her eyes, gratitude turned bitter. Kagan could not have known that she had allies in the court, the Prima and all of the rest, who would protect her from scrutiny. He could not have known that his position was so much more precarious than her own. He was trying to do what he had always done. He was trying to keep her safe.

"Who accused him of being a spy?"

She heard the voice ring out, impetuous and proud, and it took the longest time for her to realize it was her own.

There was a great deal of murmuring from down on the floor below, and Artemio's head snapped around, though it clearly caused him pain. But the king's mouthpiece dutifully examined his papers and answered. "He was found roaming the streets of the city by night by the guard."

"This man is no spy, your Majesty. He has been living in Espher for longer than you or I have been alive. He… he was the huntsman on my family's lands."

Artemio was the one to snap back his answer. Irritation with her vying with irritation at his own suffering as he lifted his voice. "And why would a dragon-lord live as a huntsman, precisely?"

Casting about for an answer, Orsina realized the truth was all she needed. "Ask him his name."

The greybeard piped up once more, reading form his papers. "Kagan."

There was a loose thread in this tapestry, and like she'd known he would, Artemio pounced on it. "Kagan the what? The Arazi are not considered to have reached maturity without earning a deed-name."

Artemio fell to one knee beside Kagan, flinching with every motion, and he laid a hand on the other man's shoulder, drawing him from whatever stupor he had sunk into rather than facing the reality about him. "What is your name?"

The Arazi's voice rumbled deep enough to set the front rows of preening lordlings scampering back once more. "Kagan."

Artemio didn't even try at cleverness. "Your full name?"

There was no way around it, and the poor man was so broken down after so long in the dungeons that he did not even try to resist announcing his great shame. Still, his voice cracked as he huffed out, "Kagan the Exile."

It set off another round of murmurs throughout the Teatro. The grey-bearded man looked askance to the king, and the king looked up to see Orsina standing up on the balcony. He blinked at the sight of her, then asked plainly, "Do you vouch for this man?"

There was a trick in here. A trap. Orsina knew it, but she had no way of getting around it. "I do."

"Then that is all that I require." With a flamboyant flick of his wrist, the king brought it all to an end. "Rise, Kagan the Exile, a free man."

The hooded jailer was so taken aback by the sudden change in his charge's fortunes that he dropped the ring of keys when he meant to undo the chains, and Artemio was forced to press them into the jailer's hands as he rose stiffly to his feet. Between the three of them, they had Kagan unbound in but a moment. Still, the giant of a man seemed lost and blind to what was happening about him. Punch-drunk, as Mother Vinegar called it.

The king rose up from his throne, and a deathly silence rang out. Ending whatever furious whispers had started up in the stands. "It is with great sorrow that we find ourselves indebted to you, Kagan the Exile. You should not have been treated as a stranger, but as kin. Espher is a land open to all, and knowing that I have so wronged one of my citizens troubles me greatly."

Once more Orsina had the sense of a trap snapping shut, but she could do nothing but stand and watch. The king glanced her way. "If your mistress would be so kind as to free you from her service, I have an opening in my own household, and it would bring me great joy to grant you a title as the Master of Hounds."

Once more the whispers became raucous. Such a thing was absurd, some serpent-man granted a place in the king's own household, a place of such high honor as his personal huntsman? It made no sense, but for all that the wrongness of it pressed in on Orsina from her borrowed memories, she could not look the king in the eye and say no. She just couldn't. She had already been shown great favor today, she couldn't throw it back in the man's face.

Kagan turned to look up at her with a blank stare, recognition only now creeping onto his face. She gave the king her best curtsy, which Harmony would have doubtless called abominable, and she dipped her head in obedience. She had saved Kagan from the executioner, and the king was offering him a great gift. It was not her place to stand in the way of her friend's success, even if something felt off about the whole matter.

Artemio dipped into a low bow towards the king as Kagan was led off by servants, then he stormed off back down the length of the hall beneath the piercing stares of all his peers. Every nobleman in Espher seemed to be there, scowling down at him. Orsina wondered how he could bear the weight of it all.

She only wondered for a moment before she realized that her chance to catch him and learn what was going on was swiftly departing. He did not run—she doubted he could, given the state he seemed to be in—but nonetheless, he was out the doors faster than she could think.

Kagan was vanishing one way, Artemio the other. Her oldest and dearest friend in all the world being delivered into what he'd called a nest of vipers with none of his wits about him, or her new friend's brother, who had only ever been polite and frosty towards her, but could provide her with the solution she needed to survive and thrive. There was a crossroads here, another trap closing, she could feel the tension of it quake through her. She had to decide which to follow after.

She turned and headed down the stairs, brushing past servants and noblewomen alike in her dash. She tripped twice over her skirt and would have gone tumbling were it not for the brass handrail embedded in the white stone of the palace stairwells. At the bottom she turned from the gathered crowds and set off with all haste. She brushed past more and more bodies as she went, an even blend of nobles and servants that gradually tipped in the favor of the common man as she made her way through to drabber and dimmer passages where it seemed clear she was not meant to be. Catching one likely servant by the wrist, she demanded to know where Artemio Volpe was being roomed, and it seemed she had carried enough of her haughtiness over from the Teatro that they did not dare to argue.

With her haphazard directions, she set off once more, twisting out from behind a tapestry into a dark room she might have called a cellar were it not for the fact she had not descended. There were barrels aplenty that she had to weave through to reach the dim outline of a door. The next room was a dazzling contrast, an open skylight bringing all the midday sun down into what she'd have called a kitchen were it not for the absence of any means of preparing food. Wine and cheese, oil and bread, all were being assembled here by fretful servants, flowers brought in from the gardens to garnish them. A whole room, devoted to assembling the little snacking platters the nobility of Espher seemed to graze upon endlessly while they spoke among themselves.

She could not spare it a moment's thought right now, the ridiculousness of such a thing, instead she turned to the first door she felt certain was not another storeroom and she set out, striding through open courtyards and closed corridors so rapidly she felt as though the world were spinning her through night and day too quickly. She rounded a corner, still following the servant's instruction, and struck Artemio head-on. Their skulls clattering together and both falling back with a cry.

Flames leapt up about Artemio's hands and before either one had a chance to think, Orsina had enclosed his wrists in her grasp and flooded Ginny Greenteeth's chill water out to douse them. By the time it was done, he was gaping at her wild-eyed. He still bled from some of his wounds. Bruises were only now beginning to blossom where he'd been struck. It was only now, with his hands before her, that Orsina could see the real damage done to him.

"What the hell happened to you?"

For a moment she saw emotions chasing across his face before he could lock them down. Confusion and fear, anger and relief. "What are you doing here?"

"I came looking for you," she blurted out. "I mean, Harmony." A blush crept up her cheeks. "Both of you."

He plucked his arms from her grasp, took a look along the corridor to be sure they were currently alone, then he let his weight fall against the wall. It took him a moment before he could get his next words out, and Orsina wondered if there might have been a wound hidden somewhere inside him, sapping his strength. He grumbled, "And why would you do a thing like that?"

"Well, it is a good thing I did, since you look like you literally can't survive a day without me." Without a second thought, she slipped an arm about his shoulders and took on some of his weight. She may have been slightly built, but she'd had a life of manual labor to make what little muscle she bore as dense as mahogany wood. Together they set off in the direction he'd been headed. Perhaps they'd pass for lovers if they were not studied too closely. She didn't know where they were going, but hoped he might mention it before they ran out of corridor to walk.

Once they were in a rhythm, he asked again, "What do you want, Orsina?"

The almost casual use of her name after so long with him dipping and ducking and calling her miss gave her almost as much of a startle as the state in which she'd found him. In his exhaustion, he drew out the truth of the matter, because she felt like too much obfuscation might end in him blanking out the conversation entirely.

"I need help."

As they rounded a corner, he let out a groan. "And do I strike you as a person in any position to offer that assistance to you in this moment."

They limped on a little farther as Orsina tried to come up with an answer, before finally settling on, "You're all that I've got."

He let out a sigh that seemed to drain his entire body of its mass, then he picked up the pace, dragging her along behind him where before she'd borne his weight. "Come along then, swift as you like. We've plans to make."

There were twists and turns as they delved deeper into the palace, more of the drab servants' tunnels, hidden from the sight of the palace's owners, like they were passing through a mousehole each time they ducked behind a tapestry. Orsina managed to catch her breath well enough to say, "Can I ask what happened to you?"

Artemio seemed to consider her for a moment. "You can ask, but I'm not certain I trust you enough to answer."

Orsina felt like she'd been slapped in the face. After everything that had happened, how could he say such a thing? Her mouth fought her as she mumbled, "You don't trust me?"

He cast her a scowl that softened at the look of dismay on her face. But he still did not tell her what had happened to him. Rather he drew her closer into his confidence as they walked. "At this juncture, I trust nobody. The enemy had a Shadebound among them, and they were mostly commoners. Thus the logical conclusion would be for the Shadebound to be a commoner also, except of course that such a thing does not exist, or at least did not exist until such time as we encountered you, conveniently, right at the height of the murderous spree."

Orsina may have been quick on the uptake, but this kind of paranoia escaped her usual ability to follow things through. It was like his thinking had been twisted by too much time in this maze of confusion. Still, she felt genuinely hurt to hear that her most trusted friends in this world thought so little of her. "You think I'm your enemy?"

"I think that you are suspiciously convenient, showing up at just the right juncture, and falling right into my lap, to convince me that a Shadebound need not be of noble lineage." An edge had begun to creep into his voice. Not the pain that dogged his every step or the anger at being deceived. A hunger, like he was coming closer and closer to the truth of things, and his appetite had been whetted.

"I've never been anywhere near your lap," she said too loudly. Dropping her voice with an anxious glance about. "And nobody sent me. I came to Covotana because I had to."

"Because your powers just so happened to emerge at this exact moment in history. Because your Arazi huntsman just happened to be heading this way." His eyes were narrowed, and Orsina didn't know how to pry them open again, how to make him see who she really was. "There is entirely too much convenience at work here."

"Kagan was… he was the only one who could bring me. He was the only one I had."

Artemio turned on her, and the rapid twist of his torso drew out a pained gasp. "Then how is it that you have not spoken of him?"

"Because… I had to come because… I had to use my shade. I nearly died, then I used it. I used it, then I couldn't control it." Her voice trailed off to a whisper. "It nearly ate me up."

He didn't look even a little impressed. "And you did not speak of your exile friend because?"

"Because I thought he'd left. I thought he'd gone the first night he brought me here, back to his life in the woods. Back to someplace he could be safe and peaceful. I never spoke about him because I thought he was gone and he was never coming back. Because I thought my whole life was over, and there was just this…" She cast her hands about her with despair written in every line of her face. As if the luxury of the palace was the worst punishment she could conceive of. "I didn't talk about him, because I thought that if I didn't say anything, people would just leave him alone, like he wants."

He had to stop and catch his breath again. "None of us get what we want. All we get is to serve to the limit of our abilities, then break upon the rocks of failure."

"Are you…" She did not mean to reach for him, she did not mean to lift him up from the wall, she didn't mean to feel the muscles shifting beneath his shirt, or the tremors passing through him as he fought off the pain. "Did you… fail?"

He closed his eyes. There were wrinkles around them that Orsina did not recall from the day before. Strands of grey amidst the red of his hair. More than anything else, he looked older because he looked so very exhausted with life. "Not yet, but I am… I'm close."

She wet her lips. "And Harmony?"

"She's resting." He finally accepted her arm about his back, falling into step with her. Accepting her help. "I'm meant to be too, but I promised your Kagan I'd speak for him."

"And you keep your promises, even when you're falling to pieces."

He laughed, but it set off a rattle in his chest that Orsina did not like to hear. "That I do."

"Take me back to wherever you're holed up, let's see what the hurt is and what we can be doing to fix it." She could hear Mother Vinegar in her voice. The command and contempt she used to make grown men strip to the nude and rub on whatever foul mixture she prescribed them.

Orsina was practically carrying him by this point, but still he made an attempt to regain some control over the situation. "And how do I know that this is not some conniving attempt to poison us?"

She smiled to him then, but it was not the charming, open expression of the country bumpkin he'd come to associate with her. It was a smirk. "I already told you, I need your help."

26

THE HOLLOW NORTH

Caldo, Regola Dei Cerva 112

Kagan could not ride a horse. They felt wrong beneath his legs, too narrow, too soft. He rode too far forward, flung over its neck, bearing too much weight down on it, as if afraid of low branches or the whipping wind. The hunting party had three destriers large enough to bear him, and each day he was switched to another as they began to suffer under his misplaced weight. He tried to sit back, prim and proper and upright like the soldiers all about him, but by the end of each day he was slung low all over again.

Still, it was as close to flight as he had come in many a year, and if the price was the discomfort of a few horses pressing in on his empathy as he rode, then he'd suffer it. For a time after he'd left the dungeons and the tortures and suffering inflicted all about him, Kagan had felt nothing. His empathy was numbed to the point of withering, but now, with the wind brushing over his face, he could feel again.

Strength had taken time to return. Almost a week of rest and supping on the finest food Covotana could offer before he was even introduced to the people he would be commanding into perpetuity.

At a glance, they seemed unlikely huntsmen, mostly noble bastards and third sons fallen on hard times, but gradually he came to recognize the value in them as they talked and as he watched the way they moved. They did not have his natural grace in the woods, but they had a poacher's wit to them. Eyes ever darting, feet softly placed so they could feel what was beneath them before they put down their weight. It was strange to watch them about in the courtyards of Covotana, passing over the gardener's carefully raked stones without leaving footprints and pinching snacks from the servant's trays when they glanced away without disrupting the balance. In the city, their skills were turned to play. They were like jesters for the folk who lacked these talents and they seemed to revel in the attention.

Out here on the open roads of Espher, they had avoided attention with the same diligence. It did not matter that this was land ruled by their liege, or that the peasants they passed by so carefully would have readily leapt aside at their approach were they showing their colors. They did their jobs well. Far too well for mere huntsmen.

It was known that Kagan had lived and hunted in the north, by the foot of the steppes where the most dangerous of prey came down to ravage the outlying villages. It was known because he'd shared tales of his work once he'd finally clawed his way back up to some semblance of sanity. Words still did not come easily to him, but they came. Just as his memories crept back now and again, the long nights in the dark, stone pressing down above him. The voice of that little girl he'd known calling out and offering him salvation. After he finally understood what was happening, he had asked after Orsina. Asked after the lordling who'd come and spoken up for him too. Neither one was anywhere to be found. Both were meant to be students at the school for necromancers, but both had departed, last sighted at the hearing that bought him his freedom. They were out of the city, supposedly. Though Kagan could not have guessed where.

There were a great many questions still hanging over him from that day before Espher's king, and no hint of gossip from the servants did much to sate his curiosity. Volpe, last of the old king's line. Orsina, some country lady he'd taken under his wing. Not a ward, not a proposal yet, but there were rumors. Endless rumors. He'd never have guessed Orsina had the talent for talk that might have won her some near-royal brat's favor. If anything, he'd expected her to be outcast within a week given the way she'd always talked to him, but if she was willing to flex that newfound influence to save him, then he was delighted to have misjudged her.

They made camp under the stars each night, though he would have expected men like these to seek the comfort of a roadhouse or inn, and while the hunters he was meant to lead set about raising tents, he declined one. Preferring nothing between him and the open sky. As the stars watched over him, he felt life creeping back into his body. Arazi were made of sterner stuff than unbonded humans, so the chill of the night didn't trouble him, not that there was much chill now that high summer was coming on. Were he home, beyond the steppes, Kagan would have stripped down to just his leathers, letting the sun warm his skin everywhere scales shone through, but he was not, and he did what he could not to draw notice, even from the men who were meant to obey his commands.

There did not seem to be much in the way of discipline among these men. Each was a puffed-up noble or hanger-on quite certain of their own superiority, and he had expected them to chafe at having a stranger, a foreigner, set above them. Yet all of them seemed oddly content to follow the few commands he felt the need to give. Perhaps when they came upon the edge of the Selvaggia, and his expertise was required more and more often, they would learn to respect him instead of obeying with a pantomime of deference. It mattered little either way, so long as they obeyed, and he could do his duty.

It sat strange on him, this new duty. An ill-fitting cloak cast over shoulders too long bare. Little was asked of him as the king's huntsman, even this little outing was more of an exercise than a true hunt. It seemed that the Cerva had little hunger for blood nor interest in menageries. It begged the question of why they'd keep huntsmen in their household, but given all that Kagan had now seen, he imagined the answer would be tradition. There seemed a thousand little titles and jobs to be doled out as rewards or punishments in Espher, and the fact that his role was mostly vestigial suited him well. Peace in the city, and the hunt when outside it. That was a life he could find comfort in. It would never be the same as the freedom he'd once known, but it was tolerable.

The journey that had taken a season on foot with the girl in tow took five days, and the pace felt leisurely.

As the Selvaggia rose on the distant horizon, Kagan felt an ache in his chest he had not expected. They would skirt it, heading eastward away from the parts he preferred to roam, but he was still surprised by how much this patch of nothing and trees felt like home to him. Another place he'd never thought to see again.

That night, he made the men set their camp farther back from the trees, and he set a watch for the first time since they'd left Covotana. Not a one of the men seemed to believe it was needed, but he supposed they had not lived here and risked all they had to pass safely beneath the moss-laden boughs. At the periphery of his senses, like an itch that he could not scratch, Kagan felt beasts stirring within the forest.

He could not say if they were dragon-kin, but there was an intelligence there, a depth of emotion the native beasts lacked. Something down from the steppes. Bloodied and hungering for more. Not a full-blooded dragon, not by any stretch. Two running free down here in one lifetime would have pushed even his credulity past its limit.

All night, as the soft men settled to drink and chatter among themselves about the fire, Kagan sat in watch. They had looked askance to him as they made their campfire, wondering if he meant to snatch even this comfort from them, but he did not object. There were plenty of things in the woods that feared flame and plenty more he could not see without some light brighter than the crescent of the moon. Things he did not want to come upon him in the night.

Though Kagan had set a watch, he did not trust in human eyes, so he kept company with whichever hunter had drawn the short straw. Some attempted to speak with him in soft whispers, others kept entirely to their duties. Neither drew much response from him. One particularly foppish stalker whose name Kagan still could not recall began regaling him with the stories of his time poaching in the Cerva lands. The bright plumage of the birds there and what they'd fetch from the hatmakers of Covotana. Kagan could scarcely believe any man, even one born in so degenerate a place as Espher, would so readily admit to such treasonous acts as stealing game from the crown's lands, yet this man wore his crimes like a badge of pride. Even bragging that he'd never have been brought into the king's service if not for his talent with a snare and a spate of bad luck.

On and on his stories went, grating at Kagan's nerves until with a start he realized this fool was trying to ingratiate himself. These were the bragging stories that had won this man his friends, and he was trying to win Kagan over. Just that realization was enough to shake the Arazi for a moment. How long had it been since anyone felt the need to ingratiate themselves to him, since he had political power enough for it to be worthwhile? It was distraction enough that he did not see the motion by the tree line until it was already too late to call out.

His own armament had vanished somewhere in the depths of the dungeons of Covotana, and there was no craftsman in Espher's capital who made spears balanced for throwing. Given time, he could have made his own again, but they had not been near a forest in all their journey, nor a smithy.

What he had was a recurve bow. It had been so long since he'd used one that it sat clumsy in his hands, and the tension of the string on his finger almost hurt. But when his elbow rose behind his head, the tailfeathers came level to his eye, and the wood began to hum with tension, he remembered.

The first shot hit the wyvern low, under the eye, at the side of its jaw. It must have hurt, but it didn't slow the beast a step. The second hit off the beak, doing no harm. It was only when the third arrow struck it in the eye that the wild charge from the shadows became a stumble and tumble to a halt.

His previously vociferous companion only just managed to mumble out, "I didn't even see it."

Kagan was already stalking forward, a fresh arrow drawn in case of twitching. "That's why I waited up."

The supposed hunter did not move forward with him as he should have, to secure the prey. Instead, he stayed safe and distant with his back to the fire. Raising his voice to be heard over the distance. "I didn't know they moved that fast."

Some of the others began to stir at the raised voices, but Kagan had eyes only for the wyvern. Arrow point still leveled at it, steps slow and careful. There was no sign of movement, no sign of breath being drawn. Still he did not loosen his draw, turning instead to cover the tree line while he crouched by the beast's side and took it in.

There was such beauty in this fallen monster that it caught in Kagan's throat. Feathers and scales blended seamlessly in a rich deep blue that made it almost invisible in the moonlight. Behind the beak, two solid plates of bone extended beneath the bared scales, protection for the brain from the gruesome impacts that a strike with the beak would unleash. Where wings should have sprouted from its shoulders, there were vestigial humps the wyvern could have drawn back along its ribs to pass through tight spaces or speed its course, or expanded out from its body to appear larger and startle off predators. It was full-grown, despite standing only a little taller than Kagan at the shoulders, one of the lesser breeds that his people had not even troubled to tame for the most part. Even flightless wyvern were rare this far south. Kagan had seen only a handful since he'd come down to these lowlands, and even those had been the wounded and the dying, fleeing from predation by the healthy and hungry, in desperate search of respite. Between this and the aslinda-dragon he'd crossed paths with the previous year, it was becoming abundantly clear that something was truly awry on the steppes. The only dragon-kin found there were the outcasts and the ferals, and to see even those few stragglers driven off, it made Kagan wonder what could be disrupting things so badly.

Little in the way of sleep followed for the rest of that night, so Kagan and his merry band set about stripping the feathers and scales they could carry. By rights the kill was his, but it was good practice to have the men at your back holding sharp objects indebted to you, so he shared the prize. The meat they strung out to dry, but Kagan doubted they'd pass back this way to claim it before another predator found its way up to the ropes strung from branch to branch.

With dawn, they set off north once more. His instruction from on high had been to skirt the steppes, seeking out signs of any troublesome beasts. In essence, he was set to tour the essentially abandoned border territories and report if they'd been overrun by wolves in the absence of governance. It seemed a good use of his talents, so he had obeyed.

Yet as the Selvaggia spread wilder and wilder and the ground beneath the horses' hooves became ever more rocky, there seemed to be no intent among his companions of turning aside. On they went to the north, until plateaus began to jut up and they found themselves passing through shallow valleys between them. Shade covered them until midday had the sun peering straight down at them out of the strip of blue sky overhead, and only then did their pace begin to slow. Kagan was looking around for a natural ramp, having no desire to abandon the horses down here for a hard climb. "We need to get higher if we want to see anything."

"Ah well, that would also allow us to be seen, would it not?" the fop piped up.

Kagan gave him a blank stare. "Do you fear the beasts of the steppes so much you don't even dare to look at them? Is this the courage of the men of Espher?"

Another spoke up. "It's a hot day, maybe we go up when the sun's down to take a peek, eh?"

"Perhaps we'll find a better spot, farther in," said another, one who'd stayed blessedly silent until now. It seemed the full dozen men at Kagan's side had an opinion on where they should be going next. Almost like they'd already discussed it without him.

"What's going on?" He eased his hand away from his weapons as he turned to face them, letting all his fingers show on the reins.

"Whatever do you mean, sir?" Fop was sweating. Kagan hadn't expected a liar like that to be so easily rattled. "We're just making suggestions for an easier passage."

Kagan drew up his horse entirely and turned it crosswise to the path. If it came to fighting, it would make a solid shield against their first volley. "Look, I'm here now, I'll do whatever we need to do, just tell me what is going on. I'm not like you, I've no patience for secrets."

Looks were exchanged among the men, and gradually, as he watched, the fops and fools who'd been flouncing around Covotana seemed to fade into seasoned men of the land. Their prim upright seating became a slouch, ready to drop low. The fop became the poacher he'd bragged of being right before Kagan's eyes. All pretentions melted.

"We're scouting for an army coming south. Dragon-lords. Weren't sure how you'd take that."

Kagan let out a sigh. "Wish you'd the sense to tell me sooner."

"So you could have turned tail?" Eyes were narrowed all about him.

"So we could have done this right."

That was enough to knock the wind out of their wings. "What?"

"You don't bring animals to hunt dragons. You don't move in packs. You check which way the wind is flowing. You... If they're within ten miles, we're already fucked."

Their arrogance may have been a mask over their true nature as scouts for the Espher army, but there was a seed of truth in it. One of the quiet ones was rolling his eyes. "What are you—"

"What is the point of bringing me if you aren't going to listen? We need to pull back. We need to find someplace secure for the horses, then we need to talk about how dragons hunt and how Arazi can sense you from miles off, even if you don't make a sound or come in sight." Kagan could not help himself now that he knew what was happening. His eyes kept turning up to the blue strip of sky above them, just waiting for a shadow to pass, and a flame to follow. "Turn us around. Now."

"You're just trying to get us away before we spot them," one of the quiet ones called back to his fellows. "This is all a farce."

"I'm an exile, you half-wit. Wherever a dragon's shadow is cast, the land belongs to the Arazi. They could have claimed all the steppes by now. The worst they'll do is kill you. If they catch me on Arazi land, it will make your little dungeon back in Covotana look like a country estate orgy. We need to move."

For a long languorous moment, none of them did. Nobody spoke and nobody moved, until the poacher reared his horse up to spin her in the tight confines of the gully. "If he wanted us gone, he could have let the wyvern eat us. Let's go."

There seemed to be no ranks among them, no hierarchy at all, yet when the poacher spoke, they listened. Even the ones who'd been decrying him as their nemesis a moment before had changed their tune now.

All the day's slow and steady progress was abandoned, and they took off at a trot, as fast as they dared in these tight corridors of risen sandstone. It was enough to make the broad-shouldered Kagan snarl with irritation. This passage was cut wide enough for Arazi to ride three abreast, but these fools had such little control over their mounts they had to leave a margin for error wide enough to be all their graves. He had no such impediment.

Letting his emotions loose, he fed his fear down into the beast below him, threaded it through with his desire to be away. He blinkered the horse with his own focus. They needed out. They needed out into the open where they could run free. A horse understood that terror, that need not to be penned in. Beneath the tortures Espher had used to break them and make them obedient, their natures still persisted, and both mount and rider, they needed space about them to feel alive.

Kagan burst past the others as they trotted along, first at a canter then a full-on gallop as they rounded a bend and into a straight-run passage back towards the green land beyond the steppes. Still he could not stop himself from twisting around, looking back, looking up, and it seemed those who rode in his wake had been afflicted with the same habits. Every one of them rode like a true hunter now, but all were so distracted by their own impending doom that the marked improvement in their skills was unnoticeable.

When at last they burst out from amidst the high walls into the steppes' foothills, there was a palpable relief. They slowed their pace, spared their horses the spurs, and wondered for a moment that Kagan had not. How could he, when he felt that itching presence at the back of his mind, warning him, as it would be warning the Arazi in flight, that another of his kind was nearby?

At first it was just the faintest brush of the empathic sense over them, the emotions of the riders and horses both burning bright enough to catch on the periphery as they stretched in search of prey, then a tighter focus as they were felt. As they were recognized.

The only thing Kagan could offer to his followers in the way of protection was a bellow back. "Faster! They're coming!"

Huntsmen or scouts, it mattered little, they spun in circles on their horses, trying to sight something that was still over the horizon. Looking for their doom instead of fleeing it. If they saw a dragon in the sky, it was already too late for them all.

The Selvaggia had been Kagan's sanctuary for decades, and now he rode hard for it once more. Lather slicking the sides of his horse as it staggered on. There was life enough there to confuse Arazi senses, a density of beasts and the dull ache of slow-moving emotion from the woods themselves. He could feel his mount's exhaustion, feel it weakening and breaking, he felt that pain as though it were his own, but still he pushed it on. He could almost justify it to himself because he was feeling the horse's pain. He could pretend he was driving the both of them to the edge of death. There was the perfect justification in the logical human parts of his mind; they would both die if they were caught out here in the dragon's sight. Yet how could a horse understand that? Instead he fed it fear, snippets from his own memories, of being stalked, of being chased. It ran and ran until the legs beneath it broke, and even then it would have tried to go on if Kagan hadn't leapt clear.

In a broken heap it lay squealing and bucking, still trying to move, still trying to flee. He could not spare the moment to put it out of its misery, but neither could he run on still feeling its pain. His bow was crushed beneath its bulk, but there was ever a knife at his belt, and with a wash of calming feelings, Kagan stilled the beast long enough to drive the tip of the blade home behind its jaw. He felt the blood spilling, the sharp pain at his throat, the heat rushing over his hand. He felt it, and then he closed himself off to it so the waiting darkness could not swallow him down too.

With his empathy snapped shut, he could not feel the scouts racing to him or the dragon and rider. Only his eyes and ears availed him, and compared with the usual cornucopia of senses at his disposal, it was like looking at the world through the eye of a needle. At least blinkered so, he could concentrate on the path ahead of him.

Tucking his head down and letting the weight of his broad body rock forward, he ran.

The hoofbeats of his scouts drew closer, but he fled them as though they were the enemy. All energy directed forward. If the dragon-lord saw them, the forest could not save them. Under the cover of the woods and the many tangled emotions of the beasts within, there was a hope that the soaring scout might consider their empathy was confused, but with any glimpse of these men, death was sure to follow. What protection was a forest canopy from a creature that could breathe fire?

Was it hoof drumming or distant wingbeats? Would they live, or would they die? Kagan could not say, and he dared not slow, even as his lungs burned and his saddle-sore legs ached. The horsemen rode on right by him, and he would have knocked them away if they'd tried to hoist him up into their saddles. He was so intent on his desperate sprint, he didn't even notice when the blue sky gave way to filtered green light and the open plain narrowed down to twisting forest paths. Bursting into a lightning-struck clearing, he found the men scrambling down off their horses, gasping as though they'd been the ones to run.

"Strip them, swiftly. If we set them loose on the plain the rider might mistake them for the sign that drew him south."

"Abandon the horses?" The one Kagan judged to be youngest finally found his voice.

"They won't outrun a dragon in flight, but they might spare us." The men went on staring at him blankly before he barked. "Move."

Whatever else these scouts or spies may have been, at some time they were soldiers. They could feel the pressure of an order, and when they had no thoughts of their own, their bodies moved to obey. Every trace of civilization was cut from the horses, their supplies, their tack, only the shoes on their feet were left, and Kagan could only hope they were dulled enough that from the sky they wouldn't be seen.

For a moment he let his empathy leap out of his skull once more, feeling everything all around him, feeling the terror just lurking beneath the careful training of the horses. He poured his own heart-pounding dread in, and the banked fear overran them. They took off for the open air, where they might run free, every one following the one ahead as herd instinct took hold and they followed the leader.

Kagan turned to the men, low-laden with their own gear and looking much worse for wear. "Now spread out, arm yourselves, and think happy thoughts."

Poacher piped up. "You're joking."

Kagan ignored him as best he could. "Meet me back here in an hour if you're still alive. You've all had enough training to find your way about the woods?"

Again the poacher tried to interrupt. "Yes, but…"

"If you've got gods, pray to them. If you've a woman, think of her. Whatever you can do to still your minds and calm your feelings. They'll be how the Arazi find us."

The young one spoke softly still, despite how raggedly his breath came. "What happens if we can't?"

"The forest burns, we all die, you learn an important lesson about telling me things before it is too late." There was no point in coating the truth in sugar. Chances were they were already dead. At least if he burned to death down here they wouldn't take him alive.

At least some of the men had a hint of practicality to them. "How far do we spread?"

"Far as you can go and make it back in time. Avoid the beasts you can. Climb trees, most of the creatures out here cannot climb."

They broke apart, dumping what gear they could afford to lose and shifting what they couldn't into their bags as they went. The only one who still wanted to hang around for a chat was the poacher, who Kagan finally turned to face. The little fop asked, "Most?"

"Yes, most. Now do you need me to hold your hand? Wipe your arse for you?" Kagan growled. "Run."

Kagan took his own advice before waiting to see if the boy had obeyed. The farther they were spread out, the less of a beacon they'd be to their hunter and the more the ambient life of the forest would mask them. He pulled his empathy tight in against him, and then surprised himself by whispering out a little prayer to the Burned. It had been so long since he'd spoken his own tongue that it felt thick in his mouth, the weight of it so different from the flighty words of Espher. Yet for all that, it calmed him.

These woods were not the ones he had once stalked so bravely, but they were close enough to feel like home, and with the hallowed words spilling forth from him like a guttural hum, Kagan felt as close to calm as he ever had without a dragon beneath him. He could only pray it would be enough.

In the distance, the horses began to scream.

He could not think about it, nor the volume they had to be shrieking at to be heard through the muffling of the wood. They had to be terrified. Even with the push of fear he'd given them, they had not made a sound above a whinny. Mortal terror must sound like that screaming. If Kagan reached out to them through his empathy, then he would know just how bad things were, but he could not. He must not. He had to deny everything he was and keep his head down to avoid the low-hanging mosses of the Selvaggia.

When the screaming stopped, it was not a slow quieting as the horses fled, it was instant. One moment they screamed, the next there was a soft thump, and then silence. It took but a moment for the wave of heat to pass through the trees and wash over Kagan's scaled skin. All of summer come at once.

He shivered in anticipation.

It should have been fear, it should have been dread, to be so close to the destructive force of a dragon's breath once more, but he could not shake his memories. The rush of land beneath them, the gorge rising in his throat as they made their dive and venom poured forth. The sweet sting as the flame caught.

Dropping to his knees, Kagan scrabbled his way to a bush, forcing his way under, hiding from the sky, trying to slow his hammering heart, trying to calm his bloodlust. The bloodlust that he could not say was truly his.

He truly thought it had worked. That he might survive. Then he heard it. The beating of wings above him. The rhythmic thud and the shiver of leaves as the wind swept down through them.

27

SLAVES TO HISTORY

Caldo, Regola Dei Cerva 112

Harmony stirred to find her head nestled on Orsina's lap. She was careful not to shift, nor to stir. It was not often she was allowed such closeness, and it would be foolish to interrupt it when there was no call. Through half-open lashes, she peered up at the girl. There were all the signs of nobility in her, the aquiline nose, the oval face, even the thick tangle of hair. She could have been any noble of any house.

It complicated matters in so many ways. Arranging a marriage with Artemio to serve as her intermediary would be complex. There would be papers that needed to be forged, lineages that would have to be stitched. They were slaves to their family history, and Orsina had none.

Wild thoughts crossed Harmony's mind as she lay there upon the thighs of her dearest friend in all the world. They could flee. There was no need to go back to Covotana, not now, not ever, they could take a ship across the sea, Harmony could dress in a man's clothes and marry Orsina herself, they could live a life without expectations or demands. She could work as a sell-sword. Orsina's talents as a healer and what she'd learned at the House of Seven Shadows would have made her a profitable little workhorse.

The only one who could not fit into this dream was Art. There was no hope that he would abandon Espher. Not now, not ever, not with all of their lives in the balance and impending doom descending on all sides.

The carriage rocked as they slipped out of a rut in the road, and Orsina's hand came down from the book she was holding to cradle the top of Harmony's head for a moment, to protect her from being disturbed. She didn't even glance down, such kindness was just her nature. Harmony felt she might cry, but there was no hope that a wet lap would not disturb her current repose, so she fought it down.

The book was something Artemio had given Orsina before the three of them had departed the palace, after the long blissful week of convalescence, when each day Orsina would check on their wounds, apply her salves and her sympathies. It had taken days before the barest touch on her skin had stopped setting off a shiver that made Orsina apologize for her cold hands. Orsina did not have cold hands. Nothing about her was cold.

Harmony did not know precisely where they were going, but she knew what they were fleeing. Artemio's strength had taken a blow after so many of his years were used, and he did not mean to be caught out again.

Matters relating to his studies as one of the Shadebound had always been kept abstract to his sister. She was not meant to know how things worked any more than she was meant to know how laws were writ or ships were sailed. Tradesmen did not share their expertise, and women were meant to keep their heads as blissfully empty as possible, lest they get confused. What she had managed to piece together was that Orsina was rushing ahead of the others she studied alongside and had struck upon a blockade that coincided with whatever Art felt was holding him back.

They would no longer pass as twins. He had aged too far for them to be an even match now, skin beginning to sag from his bones. Harmony would have placed him at five years her elder now, but knowing how their family took the burden of years, he might well have lost ten. Not to mention the finger. He had not explained that little trick to Harmony, nor to Orsina, though she'd pressed him. It had seemed all too obvious to him that she meant to use the same trick, yet whatever trust they had for each other seemed oddly strained now. There had been no good time to ask what had placed the barrier there, but she could feel a chill in the air between them, like there was a shade lurking in the carriage.

Eight days had passed now since they left the capital under cover of darkness with Art perched atop the rental carriage like a mongrel driver. Every moment before they'd departed, Harmony had been waiting for the other shoe to drop, for the assassins to come swarming out of the walls and lay waste to them.

Even now, Artemio would not let them halt at an inn by night, choosing instead to camp out in the carriage and set watches like they were soldiers in the field. It maddened her, but more, it left her exhausted. It wasn't as though there was much else to do in the carriage but sleep the days away. Reading the technical texts and histories that Art felt it essential to bring along did little for her other than give her a headache, so most days, she napped and took on a portion of Orsina's watch out of thanks for the small comforts the girl gave up through the day, letting herself be used as a pillow.

Atop the carriage, moonlight changed the world. What had looked like bland countryside became a million lurking shadows. The calls of foxes sounded ethereal and monstrous in the dark. It was never truly cold now that summer had come, but still Harmony found herself shivering each time a breeze passed over her.

Sometimes she thought she saw things moving in the sky. Wisps of cloud blocking out the stars. They might have been shades. They might have been nothing at all. She had no inkling.

Orsina shifted a little, setting aside her book and looking down into Harmony's face where it lay. The attention was too much. Her eyes opened, she felt a blush spread across her chest. She tried to play it off with a yawn. "Morning."

She should have gotten up, pulled away, but instead she lay there, daring Orsina to throw her off. Instead, the girl's hand came down, and her fingers brushed the red strands of hair from Harmony's face. "Afternoon now, I think."

"Did I miss anything terribly exciting?" Full of regret, Harmony drew herself up off Orsina's lap and leaned back against the horsehair-stuffed back panel of the carriage. It itched.

Orsina stretched and yawned as though she were the one who had just woken up. "Fought a few dragons, overthrew an empire, the usual."

"Same as every other day then." Harmony smirked.

"And you managed not to drool on me, that is a nice change."

She didn't mean to, but Harmony gasped at that. "I do not drool! I'm a lady."

"Then I regret that I must inform you, my lady, that the area around your mouth sweats terribly in your sleep."

She looked away, hoping the blush might abate. "Well, it is this heat, isn't it. Summer."

Orsina prodded her in the arm. "It's cute. Like a puppy or something."

"Of all the comparisons to dogs I've suffered, this is without a doubt the nicest," she sniped back.

The carriage stopped rocking. It was so unexpected, both women fell silent for a moment before scrambling over to the windows and looking out. If they'd hoped for something dramatic, they were soon to be disappointed. It was a dull stretch of road, hemmed in on either side by a smattering of rocks and scrub grass. Their grand pilgrimage come to an end here, nowhere. Yet it seemed this was truly the end of the line. Art drove the horses off the road to a patch of grass, then the carriage rocked once more as he leapt down to the dirt.

With a flourish, he drew the door open and grinned. "Welcome to the secret battlefield you never knew was but a week's journey from Covotana. The place where the whole kingdom was once almost felled, yet which makes no appearance in any of the great histories."

Harmony clambered down with a roll of her eyes. "Are you going to be entirely insufferable the entire time we're here? Yes, we're all very impressed by your ability to read books that nobody ever reads. Bravo. Where can I go piss?"

With her ablutions managed behind one of the slightly larger boulders dotting the landscape, Harmony returned to the carriage to find herself in the midst of a history lecture she had not signed up for. "…Rossi and his army were met on the road by a cavalry charge but repelled it using the same tactic as before, densely packed units, polearms protecting the center. With the charge broken and the advantage of surprise lost, the cavaliers fell back to the main line where they discovered dissent in their own ranks. The enlisted soldiers were bucking orders, and one of their officers had been pulled from his horse when he attempted to apply lashes to one of the ringleaders. It was clear that the rebels' sentiments had spread among the common men of the Volpe army."

Desperate to stop him before he got into his flow and wouldn't shut up for an hour, Harmony cut in. "Volpe?"

He glanced aside to her. "Well, I can't very well call it the army of Espher, given that it was a civil war. Shall I say loyalist?"

Orsina's voice came softer than Harmony would have expected. Like there was a sadness to her that didn't touch her face, or perhaps just a cautiousness that had never before come to the fore. "You could say peasants and nobles."

"As I've already said, there were enlisted troops and men at arms among the Volpe army, so that distinction…"

Artemio started off down a tangent, but Harmony dragged him back on course. "What happened next?"

"The loyalists discovered that their front ranks were anything but loyal. In fact, Rossi himself had infiltrated the enlisted men and was intent upon assassinating the king. When the fighting broke out, the enlisted were overpowered by the superior training and armament of their social betters, but Rossi fought on, holding the cavaliers of Espher at bay until the rest of his army had traversed the distance and met the broken formations of their foe."

"So hold on, this isn't the first peasant rebellion?" Harmony could have kicked herself when she saw the look Artemio gave her. In the brief moments they'd managed to snatch together, he'd made it clear to her that she should not speak anything of what they'd seen in the tunnels below the city, even to Orsina, but it seemed frankly ridiculous. Who was Orsina going to tell?

"There have been many throughout history, most quashed with all necessary force before they could propagate, but very few of them have been so all-encompassing as either Rossi's Rebellion or the current... matter." He trailed off. Eyes on Orsina, trying to work out how much she had taken in, how much she had inferred from his silences. Harmony bit the inside of her cheek.

Orsina blundered on as if she hadn't heard a thing. Was she smart enough to play dumb? Harmony knew the woman had a brain in her head, but she was still a commoner, unused to the politicking twists and turns of a conversation. "I'm guessing this Rossi guy didn't kill the king, since we still have... kings."

"Once the armies met, Rossi carved through the heart of the Volpe ranks until there was only a single man standing between him and regicide. What luck, then, that the man was Saveria Gatto, the finest duelist to ever live." Art's smile spread. It was so rare to see it now, and this was not the false face he presented to those he meant to ingratiate himself upon, but the genuine, small smile that came out only when he was entertained. "If Rossi had not been some peasant farmer, this song would still be sung across the land. Gatto's legend would live on forever, instead of being relegated to backmatter notes on histories more important. He was a master of the rapier, a match for any fencer Agrant could muster. They met in spitting distance of the king, where the man who ruled all these lands cowered back from the chaos of battle."

Harmony frowned. "He didn't try to fight Rossi?"

"He was no match for him, even with Gatto by his side. To go within Rossi's reach would have sealed his fate." He turned to Orsina, backing through the empty field slowly, glancing about as though the ghosts of the past might spring up about them at any moment. "Though Rossi was peasant-born, he had trained all his life with the farm tools until he could outfight every man in his village. He was sent on tour around the villages, like a fair attraction, and none could best him. In his fury, he'd cut through every cavalier that came upon him. You must realize that such a thing is preposterous, that this must have been a giant among men?"

She didn't seem all that impressed. "So who won?"

"The king escaped, the peasant uprising was put down, it seems reasonable to believe that Rossi expired on this field. Yet there is no mention of Gatto in any histories after this date. So perhaps mutual destruction was the outcome."

That was enough to draw a snort of surprise from Harmony. "You don't know?"

"I mean to sate my curiosity in this matter shortly."

Orsina's frown deepened. "And how are you going to do that?"

"Binding Saveria Gatto's shade, of course. He may not have the widespread remembrance that would empower an elemental, but there is enough reverence for him among formal students of the blade for his shade to have retained coherence through the interposing years."

That all made sense. But Harmony could see that one thing was not adding up for Orsina.

"And what does all this have to do with me?"

"You haven't guessed? I mean for you to tame Rossi." He grinned at her, and for a moment, there was a genuine delight in his eyes. Like he'd spotted some great prize that had just come into reach. He was probably more excited about learning the true history than he was getting a shade to protect him. "He has definitely retained his form. There have been countless accounts of a whirlwind sweeping alongside this road, and while there is a tacit prohibition upon sharing tales of his uprising, there have been folk songs captured here and there. With a skill such as his, even if little else remained of the shade, we should have some success."

"And his shade…" Orsina's eyes were cast to the uneven ground. "It will accept me?"

"An attempt was once made to bind him by a talented gentleman of noble blood. He did not survive the failure. Rossi's detestation for his betters has persisted long after death. I cannot imagine any other Shadebound would be capable of retaining his services."

Harmony's eyes narrowed. Orsina might not have been used to the half answers of the nobility, but she could smell a dodged question when it hung stinking in the air. That was not a yes.

She opened her mouth to say so, when abruptly, both Shadebound cocked their heads to the side, like they were hearing something she could not. "Is that...?"

"Both of them. Make haste."

They took off running in some random direction, leaving Harmony there with her mouth half open. All of these years, trailing after Art and the excitable nature he kept hidden, only to discover that now... "Grand. Just grand. Now there's two of them."

Rocks were scattered upon the open plains, the only sign some huge battle had once been waged upon this earth. Harmony had hoped there might be rusted-out swords sticking out of bone heaps, or something, anything that marked this as any different from everywhere else.

She felt a little like their keeper, trailing along behind them and remembering the way back to the carriage, quite certain that neither of the other two would be up to the task. Artemio had been a wreck last time he bound a shade, and from what she'd managed to absorb through the snippets of conversation that made any sort of sense, this kind was going to be even more invasive. The heat had risen from Artemio's skin as they rode back to their ancestral home, but what would he leak this time? What would come pouring out of sweet Orsina when she took this rebel savage inside her heart?

Whatever they chased, even Harmony could feel it now. The chill winds whipping around, setting the grass cascading in waves about them, the pops and shudders of the earth beneath their feet, thunder without lightning, war without end.

She chased after her brother and Orsina with the beginnings of worry beginning to creep up on her. What could they see that drew them like moths to the flame. Despite the blue skies above and the blazing sun, gust after gust of chill winds swept her off track. Still the other two strode on, buffeted about but oblivious to the danger.

Ahead of them, the world twisted.

At first, Harmony's eyes could make no sense of it, but soon she realized it was the air itself, spinning so fast that it distorted her view of the land beyond. Like a great dry whirlpool drawing them all in. The thunderous bangs came from it, the winds were being cast out from it, it was the heart of this haunted place.

Then, with but a single thunderous beat, it was gone. Harmony had barely made it into sight of the damned thing before it disappeared. The others couldn't have caught the shades already, could they? Last time it had taken Artemio what felt like forever.

The two of them were spinning around like this was some dance, searching for their apparition. Like the whirling wind had infected them too, and now they had to waltz. When another chill breeze caught across Harmony's neck, it was almost a relief that their time had not been wasted. Which was about the moment when Orsina screamed, "Get down!"

Harmony took her at her word. She took a dive for the scrub grass, hoping it was softer than it looked. It wasn't.

A thunderclap boomed overhead, where her head had been but a moment before. The wind began to whip once more, not striking at her from afar but spinning around Harmony. She could see it tear by, but it did not touch her. Indeed, the air here seemed bizarrely still. Almost thick. Yet the chill could not be denied. Looking up, she could see the whirlwind rising up about her, the open circle of clear blue sky at the top showing just how unnatural this cyclone was. As she watched, the eye of the storm wavered and moved. She had to scramble to stay within it, lest she be picked up and flung, but even staring up into the spiral of it, she could not guess which way it would next leap and bound.

Twice she felt the cone of wind pluck at her and twice she had to twist and scramble on all fours like some ape to get clear before it could haul her from the ground. Between her fingers, she found bundles of torn-up grass and could not remember when she'd hauled them out.

Above her, the shades spun and clashed. Within this tempest, she caught glimpses of a darting blade, high up, beyond her reach. Not the blade itself, never the blade itself, but the light that would have caught upon it had it been real. A shimmer, then the same concussive blast that had almost taken her head before, hammering her back down onto all fours. Reminding her of her place in the dirt, beneath these ancient legends that clashed forever in the sky above.

She had been warned when she came to the House of Seven Shadows never to look at shades. She had been warned that her eyes must be bound or madness would creep in. Was this what going mad felt like? To see something that was impossible and accept the evidence of your eyes? To look at something so much greater than you could ever be and have no choice but to accept your place in the world? Art and Orsina could master these things, control them, make them their own, but the rest of mankind lived or died at their whim. Harmony didn't even know if these dueling specters recognized that she was there at all.

They showed no sign of interest in her, if they were even capable of perceiving her. She couldn't see them, maybe it went both ways. Even the slightest hint of the second shade escaped her. Shouldn't there be two sets of flashing blades? When they clashed and she was knocked, rolling end over end to the storm's edge, shouldn't she have seen the parry?

It was only when she hit the razor's edge of the wind and her sleeve parted in a red blossom of blood that she knew where the other shade's weapon was hidden. Rossi was not calling up the storm, Rossi was the storm. Distorting everything beyond, making Orsina and Art skew sideways as they ran up to save her.

They could not save her. Even though she knew in her heart she would not survive this place much longer, just as surely she knew that to try to pull her out with the powers they wielded would end in her death.

But no shades had been called. Orsina's bare hands were held up, she looked so tiny and fragile beyond the storm, twisted back and forth like she was only visible through a warped mirror. Even as winded and wounded as she was, Harmony still tried to stop her. Tried to call out to her to stop. The words and the air were snatched from her mouth, spun away from her. "Stop." "Don't." They were screamed up into the air, but never made it past the storm.

A streak of red spun by. Orsina was touching the blade-storm. She was reaching in, though a thousand tiny cuts opened up on her arms as she did. Pain should have stopped her, it should have pushed her back, but her eyes were locked on Harmony, and she strode on as if it were nothing at all. Then with a lurch, it became nothing at all. The wind stopped. The blood fell in a sheet to the ground. Orsina did not fall. Her hands were still held up. Blood running down where they'd been bared and dribbling from her elbows to mark the soil beneath her.

It was but a short time after midday, the summer sun still shone bright as it ever would, there was only a hint of shadows beneath the girl's feet, but as Harmony watched, they began to swirl about her. As the blood fell, it spiraled down in a circle about her. She had swallowed the shade down whole.

Art stood gaping in horror at the sight of it, at the procedures and planning and protection she'd abandoned in her hurry to save Harmony again. Orsina dropped to her knees, wrapped her arms about herself, as though that would help her to keep the storm inside her from escaping. She panted for breath, suddenly all too easy to hear in the utter calm of the meadow. Harmony's own voice came in a whisper.

"Orsina."

Then the invisible blade struck out again.

A fresh cut slit Orsina from mouth to ear. A second the moment after, perfectly mirroring it. Widening her pretty little smile into a bloody gaping line. Still Orsina held on. Kept her lips pursed tight, like the shade within her might escape through her mouth if she unclenched her jaw. It took

Harmony a moment to understand what she was seeing, what the scars meant. Dueling scars. The marks the greatest bravos would place on their foes, to show they could have killed them, but chose instead to shame them.

Saveria Gatto lunged for her again, a killing blow, a shimmer of steel in the sunlight. Rossi rose to block it. Water sprang from Orsina's palms, crystallizing to ice as it moved to intercept the invisible rapier, a hook of ice that caught the side of the blade and turned it aside. A second sprang to life in her other hand, snapping across to catch the blade lower, then both twisted out.

There was no way for Harmony to know what was happening. Whether the shade's blade was broken, or merely snatched from his hands by the odd little sickles Orsina was spinning in her hands. It didn't matter, so long as he was disarmed and they had a moment to think.

"Orsina, you got Rossi?"

The girl shuddered, and the ice melted away as she regained control over her body. "I have him, but I don't... He isn't under control. I need time. I need to... You need to... give me time."

Glancing from one Shadebound to the next, Harmony barely had to say, "Art?" before he replied with all she needed to know.

"We are beginning our negotiations." Sweat beaded on his forehead, running along fresh lines on his forehead that Harmony could have sworn were not there but a day before. Whatever he was doing, it was taxing him. "They'd be... easier if Orsina would move away."

Orsina turned her head to look his way, eyes wide, pupils blown until they'd swallowed all the brown. She looked sick. Drunk. Wrong. Her words came slurred. "I... I can't move yet."

"Can I move you?" Harmony closed the distance in a few strides, ignoring the warm dampness of blood where it spread down her own arm. The wound the same shade Orsina now wrestled had dealt without even noticing.

Drawing a shaky breath, Orsina whispered back to her. "You can... try."

With each inch Harmony moved towards Orsina, the wind whipped harder in her face, chill and sharp in a way that no summer breeze could be. Not the cutting cold of winter, but the cutting cold of a knife's edge tracing over her skin. "Oh, I do not like that."

Despite the unbearable weight within her, Orsina still mumbled out, "Sorry."

She reached out and lay her arms about Orsina's shoulders. "My sweet creature, it isn't you who needs to apologize, it is the clod swinging farming utensils about."

Though he couldn't spare them a glance, Artemio still managed to bark out, "Any day now, Harm."

She shot a venomous look back and then started to bodily drag Orsina away. Beneath her tattered sleeves, the slick of blood, and the wiry muscles that only a lifetime of country living could grant, Harmony could swear she felt the sharp edges of Orsina's bones. Orsina did not walk beside her so much as she lurched, her feet dragging along until Harmony felt sure she'd simply topple, then just before they both went tumbling down, a leg would jerk forward to take the strain. It would have been easier to pick her up and carry her, but stopping now might just send Orsina into a heap.

So they lurched on as Artemio did his quiet work in the middle of nowhere, talking to nothing. Nothing that had ruined Orsina's beauty. The nothing that Art still meant to keep as a pet, or that meant to keep him as its.

At some point the chill of Orsina's skin became too much to bear, and Harmony, plucking her hand from the girl's shoulder found there was frost about the fresh blood where she'd been holding her. Orsina said nothing at all, her eyes were open, but they saw nothing. All of her attention was turned to the battle raging within.

"Orsina, my darling. Are you winning?"

Sluggishly, she turned her gaze to Harmony. Tears had crusted to ice about the dark pools that her eyes had become. "He's willing. We're just… balancing the books."

All that had been eerie about the sight before her now brought the old snort of laughter from Harmony now. "Balancing the books?"

"Working out a..." Orsina shuddered. "Fair trade."

All of this time she'd been worrying for nothing. "Just like Art and his—"

"No." There was an echo to Orsina's voice. A man's voice, strained and old and deep. "If your brother can't seal the deal, his shade goes away. If I can't... he is already in me. He's... inside..."

"What happens if you can't reach a deal?" Harmony felt every bit of the cold now. Not just the chill that had crept up into her hand, or the numbness spreading from the cut on her arm, but the bone-deep cold as realization sank in. This was not a game. As invisible as the forces Orsina was juggling might be, they were still clearly lethal.

"I... will," Orsina growled, her voice almost entirely given over to the bass tones of the dead man. "I know how. I'm... I can do this."

Harmony did not mean to break her concentration, she did not mean to shout, she meant to be every bit the quiet proper lady she had trained all her life to masquerade as, but the cold would not let her. It drew her breath in short gasps. Not fear, but panic. "Orsina, what happens?"

Cupping the girl's bloody cheeks in her shaking palms, Harmony drew Orsina up to face her. All the humanity that made Orsina herself was missing from the face, the eyes, once brown, then black, were now milky white. Harmony gasped at the sight of her friend blinded, but then she looked closer. The white behind her eyes was not blindness, it was the storm that had threatened to consume her, now trapped inside Orsina and raging to be set loose.

With a deep steadying breath, Orsina answered in her own voice once more. "I... crush him."

There was a certainty there that should have set Harmony's mind at ease, but instead made her draw back. Without arms to support her Orsina slumped down to her knees. This was not the peasant girl Harmony had taken under her wing, the harmless, helpless little creature she'd nurtured like a kitten. Despite all she'd seen and heard, Harmony had never quite realized that this girl could do things like snatch a monster from the air and smother it.

The air about them seemed to still even more unnaturally as Orsina knelt there in the dirt. Then there was another of the soundless thunderclaps that had driven Harmony to her knees again and again. Coming not from the sky above or the clash of legends but from the girl. It knocked her off balance, it made her reach for the sword at her hip, it filled her with a feeling somewhere between terror and awe. She thought she knew everything about Orsina, but here she was surprising her all over again.

"Was that it?"

Orsina smiled at her, though it pulled on the wounds on her cheeks and made her flinch. "That was it."

"Did you..." Harmony didn't even know how to ask.

"I won." Orsina tried to get up and seemed almost surprised to find Harmony right there, hoisting her to her feet. "I got it."

Harmony glanced back to her brother and grinned. "You have beaten him to the punch, he'll be livid."

What started as a cough became a laugh. Then Orsina swiped at her face, looking surprised when it came away red. "Helps when you've got leverage."

All the fear that Harmony had felt for Orsina was absent when she looked back across the plain to where her Artemio still muttered endlessly to himself. She knew he could handle himself, she'd seen him master the shade down in the old smithy. But more than that, she knew him, she knew without a doubt that he'd talk his way around whatever problem presented itself. So when she wrapped herself around Orsina and started hauling her back to the carriage, it was with the certainty that he'd follow.

THE PYRE OF HOPE

Caldo, Regola Dei Cerva 112

The Selvaggia burned. The moss was dry from the summer heat, and it was as rife to burn as paper. The woods were old, and for every living branch, there were dead and dry ones aplenty. The undergrowth that had always plagued Kagan's passage was tinder. He ran and he ran with the hot air burning at his lungs and sparks raining down about him.

The dragon had passed over him, it had passed him over, curled up and cowering, then just as he felt that he might breathe again, the roar of flames had come. He had trained all of his life to control his emotions. The scouts had not.

They had broken under the shadow of the dragon. They had run. They had died.

Water flowed in narrow channels through the forest, sometimes joining together into something like a river, but more often just trickles. They were not enough of a barrier to the spreading fire. Not when there hadn't been rain up on the steppes in so long and they were barely a muddy mouthful to be had. They would not save Kagan. They might kill him, though. Just one turn of his ankle and this wild flight through the burning forest was over. The sun was long gone, blocked out by the smoke trapped beneath the canopy, a thick acrid cloud that would not rise until the leaves had seared away or the charcoaled trees had fallen. He could not breathe it, but that mattered little to one who had ridden on a dragon's back. He had soared through smoke such as this so many times he did not even have to think on holding his breath now, only on his destination.

He fled west. To go north would bring him closer to the dragon-lord's scouts and ensure certain death. To flee back east out of the woods would have put him into the open, and at risk of the very same scout who had set the world aflame spotting him. You did not set a forest alight to kill the people within it, you set it alight to drive them out. Kagan would not be driven out, he would not be picked off as he fled. He'd rather burn than give them the opportunity.

Strange as it was to him, he was lost. He knew which way was west, and he headed for it with all speed, following whatever trails were still clear, racing the flames to gulp down fresh air before it caught up to him and the air, but beyond that, he could not have said where in the great forest he was. All of the landmarks he had used to guide him were gone. Changed with the seasons or disrupted by the fire. It was like he had never been here before, though the earth beneath him was familiar and the trees twisted in patterns he thought he could recall, like the shapes of clouds he'd once passed by, now lost to memory.

Outrunning the fire was a foolish dream, if he were to be honest with himself. Though his breath would hold longer than any plain human's, it still wouldn't outlast the distance between one end of the great forest and the other. Eventually he would need to draw breath, and eventually the smoke would get him.

Leaping a fallen log and landing amidst a tangle of brambles that were still blessedly unburned, Kagan crushed down his fear. It did not matter that he felt it, but he could not let anyone else feel it. He had to run as though this were nothing at all, as if it were just a turn around the training yard. Half of his attention was on his feet, half on his heart, trying to keep all that he felt from singing out. It was the kind of divided attention he could blame all of his stumbles on. It also explained why he came bursting out beneath the open sky without even realizing it was ahead.

Blue opened up above him, threatening to swallow him whole. His head snapped back and he dragged in the clean air. The smoke billowed up in a wall behind him, reaching as high as he could see. Blocking him from the sight of anything flying over the flames.

If it were him, that was where he'd have kept his dragon hovering, riding the thermals, resting so when the time came to swoop down on prey, it was primed and ready. Maybe whoever was up there had not been so well trained, but he doubted it.

The opening he'd sprung into showed signs of new growth all over, but it had clearly been burned not so long ago. There were still fallen trees turned to black amidst the fresh grass. It was a straight line, cut across the woods. Impossibly straight. No lightning strike or forest fire could have burned a clean strip like this. It was a fire break. Someone had deliberately cut back the forest and burned the rest so that summer fires could not spread. Someone was caring for his woods, even though he was gone.

His first thought was that it was Mother Vinegar, saving his backside again, but she wouldn't have had the physical strength to do this. It was a mystery for later. He had to run. There was no guarantee the rider above wouldn't take a turn this way and spot him if he lingered too long.

The rich green of the woods on the far side beckoned to him like a lover's embrace, the cool of the shade seemed to radiate, he could already feel the relief before he'd closed the distance.

Bursting into the undergrowth, feeling thorns tug at him and the cool dark of the Selvaggia envelop him once more, Kagan could hardly believe he'd missed these discomforts. Yet here he was grinning as wide as a buffoon as he ripped through the greenery.

He had done the impossible, and he had survived, and that made him feel joy like he hadn't since he was last soaring through the air. He'd outrun a dragon in flight. He had barely made it six feet into the dark and soothing woods before the empathy he'd dragged back in to reach no farther than his skin pulsed out and detected the people surrounding him.

They had not been lying in wait, they were not tensed for battle, they

were simply waiting for the idiot who had made such a horrific noise running through the woods to come into their midst so they could close in
behind him. If it were just the humans, he would have tried his luck. He
had his knife, he had the woods he'd known for decades. The wyverns that
were bonded to them, those he would not dare to fight without preparation.

They were wingless Arazi cavalry, not so different from the wild beast
he'd felled to the east, but with all the cunning and planning that a connection to a human mind granted them. The bond was a two-way street.
The wyverns and the dragons gained as much from their riders as the
riders from their steeds.

As the Arazi slipped out from among the trees, Kagan bent over to put
his hands on his knees and catch his breath. If it came to a fight, he would
not fall without blood being spilled, but for that, he needed to breathe.

The first words in his own tongue that he'd heard in so long, and he
could not understand them. Could not hear them over the pounding of
his hearts in his ears. He growled back, "What?"

She hissed back, "Where is your mount?"

He let some small part of his anguish slip loose from beneath his
smothering control. "She fell. Trapped."

It was not easy to lie to Arazi, most never even attempted it. How
could you lie to someone who knew the truth in your heart? As it turned
out, it was mostly about feeling the right things at the right time. Was the
relief he'd felt as he broke free because of his own struggle to escape the
fire or because he recognized the firebreak as a sign that help was close
by. Was his fear because of the dragon overhead or for the one he'd left
pinned somewhere in a crash. It took an expert to discern such fine detail
from empathy, and most warriors never troubled to train beyond ensuring
their bond was secure. Kagan supposed he would not have tried to hone
the edge of his own connection if he'd been linked to an idiot beast like
those now peering out from behind the trees with their feathers flared.

Still using his panting as an excuse and his panic as a mask, Kagan
choked out. "Go. Please. Help."

If there were strings on an Arazi's heart to be plucked, then the image of a rider and dragon separated, with one hurt, was the surest way to strum them. All but the closest of the gathered scouts took off with all haste towards the burning woods. Kagan counted off the six of them, each leaping to kick off a tree, springing into the air, and their wyverns simply knowing where to be to catch them in their stirrups. It sent a pang of pain through Kagan to see. A pang that he saw them all flinch as they felt. That loss. That knowing that he would never experience such harmony again. They set off with all speed, slung low over their beasts' backs so that the burning branches could not catch them.

Kagan felt the thunder of clawed feet through the earth, he felt the heat as it struck their faces, he felt their determination to do whatever they could to save the fallen dragon, no matter the cost. He felt it grow weaker and weaker the farther they traveled, as he stood there folded over and panting for breath so he did not need to look the Arazi who had stayed behind in the eye.

Still, the woman tried to speak with him. "I do not know you. Which clan are you from?"

Kagan opened his mouth to lie, but he knew his heart would betray him. "No clan."

She blew out a snort of disbelief. "No clan and bonded to an aslinda-dragon?"

The patterns of his scales, the changes in his build, all of these things would have given him away. He could not pass for any of the lesser riders. He was a dragon-lord, through and through.

"No clan and bonded to an aslinda-dragon." He echoed it back, nodding his head slowly, keeping an eye on her feet. In Espher, men bragged of knowing a foe's next move from the look in their eyes. Arazi were more practical. If her stance changed, he'd charge her.

There were dragon-lords outside the clans, though they were few and far between. Most of them remnants of families exterminated in the interminable civil wars before the Arazi unification. Some of them warriors of great valor who had caught some greater clan's eye and been offered a bond with their brood in the hope that it would draw that hero into the fold.

Kagan was neither lonely scion nor hero. He was the only other kind of clanless dragon-lord. The only one in the world that he knew of, for no other dragon-lord had ever committed a crime so despicable in all of their history. But of course he did not announce this. She moved in closer, but her stance was still open, she was still calm. The last hints of the others faded at the periphery of his fully extended perception.

He held out his hand to her, and without hesitation she took it, pulling him back up to his full height. The knife came up, under her chin, through the tongue and soft palate to pierce her brain. Blood ran from her nose, from her mouth. She had trusted him, held herself open to him. He was a murderer now, truly.

The wyvern bucked as the blade slipped home. Then all the coiled strength in its body was unleashed in every direction at once. Every muscle spasmed, every organ failed. This was the true face of death, so often hidden by the damage that was dealt to bring it on. The body being abandoned by whatever force animated it.

Kagan did not deserve to look at either one of the bodies as he stripped them of their spears and whatever gear might serve him best in the coming flight. He had only minutes at best before the other scouts returned from their fruitless search. He did not have time for grief and sorrow, only for the hunt. That he was the prey this time around mattered little. The motion was the same. The heightened awareness of all about him, the chase, the adrenaline, and the blur of trees as he ran for his life.

No more did he flee the flames. He angled southbound now, away from the ever-present danger of whatever army lay in the steppes biding their time, hoping for more familiar territory somewhere over Espher's hazy border. There was no point in trying to hide his trail or confuse them as to which way he had gone. There could be no deception in this. They would feel him regardless. All he had on his side was time and distance. The two things their mounts could snatch from him in moments.

They were too far away for him to tell when they'd lost faith in him and come to doubt that there was a downed dragon amidst the burning woods. He was too far away to feel such small emotions as confusion, irritation, mounting suspicion, and fear. He was not too far to feel the pang of grief and betrayal when they found their kinswoman lying dead. It was an icicle through his heart. His step did not falter, though. If anything, it made him quicken. They would be coming for him now.

Wyvern calls rang through the forest, high and clacking as their beaks snapped shut and open. Shrill and trilling. Kagan was too far to hear them, but through his empathy, he felt them, felt the rage for vengeance. Their shrieks were how anger felt to him, even now.

The forest grew drier as he went farther south, the runoff from the steppes gone and only the deep pools that persisted all year round still sunk into the stones and roots. The places where once he'd picked up the trails of his prey. The one place he had always avoided, at Mother Vinegar's command. Now he knew where he was, he headed for it. There was no way he could outpace the wyverns forever, but there was no doubt he could run them in circles using what he knew of this place. The hidden channels beneath the brambles that the snowmelt had dug through loose soil. The gullies that would hide him from sight as he crossed back behind their lines. The trees that stood so tall he could climb right up past the canopy and look out all the way to the steppes themselves.

He had no chance at any of those things when the first of them came upon him.

Good distance had been made, but he had found none of his clever tricks before the leader of the pack came at him. Bursting out from amidst the trees. The wyvern leapt for him, back legs up to rake him into pieces. It was caught up in the same blood frenzy as its master. Kagan did not flee or falter, he dove under the talons and rolled back to his feet, all the spears about him clattering together like the forest was chattering its teeth.

Back on his feet, he drew back his arm to throw, and he saw the scout twisted in his seat, ready to do the very same. One of them was bonded to

a wyvern, one of them was a dragon-lord. The difference showed. Kagan
had no moment of hesitation. The javelin took the boy from his stirrups,
smashing his back off a tree as he fell. The wyvern bucked and snapped
and fell to the dirt in sympathy before Kagan had even drawn back the
next spear to put it down. One thrust to the rider's heart and the battle
was won. Then Kagan took to his heels once more.

That had been luck as much as skill, and he felt short on both com-
modities by this point. His training might have been better, but he was
not sharp. He'd spent lifetimes dawdling through these woods, playing at a
peaceful life when he was born to wage war. If he'd ever thought the Arazi
would come south, he would never have stayed here. He would have plied
his huntsman's trade abroad or joined a mercenary company and traveled
the world. Just the thought of putting yet more distance between himself
and home had galled him then, but now he wondered if this hadn't been
his suicide attempt. Waiting to die by the only hands from which he could
accept death.

The ground became sucking and damp as he neared the forbidden
pool. The strands of thorned creepers hanging low would have caught in
his hair if he had any. They'd drag the Arazi from their saddles if they were
fool enough to charge in. Kagan wondered for a few steps if he should
lie here in wait rather than risk so much, but he could not. Not with so
many still chasing him.

Eleven cavalry scouts left of the initial hunting wing. More than Kagan
would have deployed just to pick through a forest for traps. Add in the
firebreak and it seemed obvious to him they were establishing a forward
camp in the Selvaggia to strike out from and to position flanking troops.
Aslinda-dragons had always made up the minority of the Arazi forces, and
there was no way they'd risk them to a forward position like this, which
meant they intended to stage whatever battle was to be waged against
Espher in striking distance of this forest.

It presented a twofold problem. Whoever faced them would have to
meet their forces head-on here, letting the Arazi choose the field of battle,

or split their forces lest they risk the dual terrors of cavalry on the flanks or enemies behind their lines. Or Kagan could die out here, and Espher would never know there was a serpent's nest in the Selvaggia and they'd be slaughtered.

When he broke out into the mossy chill about the pool that had always been forbidden, Kagan slowed his wild flight and stopped dead. The water looked lovely, deep, and still. After the hard day's running through blazing summer heat and forest fire, Kagan could think of nothing more tempting than a dip in that water. To sink down until it closed over his head and he could let the cool sap all his aches away. All of his worries would just melt, and he could finally find some rest.

Taking a step closer, he felt as though the water were wrapped around him already. The soft brush of the pondweed over his scales, tangling around him like he was slipping into a cocoon of comfort and relief.

The spear clipped his ear as it passed. There wasn't much of an ear left to start with after all these years of them smoothing off into his head, but there was enough of a ridge there to catch the tip and tear. Pain flared, and it cut through the muggy fog that had been flooding Kagan's mind. All at once, he realized just how close he was to the water's edge. All at once, he realized why this place had been forbidden to him. His enemy had saved him.

Leaping up, Kagan caught a hold on a solid-looking branch and swung himself for the far shore, landing heavily in the bushes there and savoring the sting as their thorns cut into his flesh, pinning his mind in place inside him, keeping outside influences away.

The rider hunting him down had no such protection. Both man and wyvern barreled straight on into the water, diving as they went. The still water of the pool was thrown into turmoil in their passing. The lily pads atop bucking and rocking and silt thrown up turning the whole pond a murky brown. Kagan began to pull himself free of the thorns, readying himself to run before his hunter could break the surface once more, but he need not have hurried. After a while, the rising bubbles stopped and the water began to settle once more to its perfect green stillness.

That more than anything else convinced him this trap was not worth the risk. To see Arazi taken without even a semblance of a fight, it terrified him.

With each staggering step away from the pool, he felt the mud sucking at his feet more and more, he felt the weight of the world pressing more firmly upon his back. Why couldn't he just stay and rest awhile? He'd be safe in the pool. It would protect him from the riders. He clung to the trees as he reached them, using each one to pull himself forward. He could not stop. He would not stop. This pitcher plant would not entice him in.

Gradually the pool's hold on him loosened, and Kagan began to recognize more of the forest around him. This did not feel like a place he had never been before, this was home. He knew the way each path would weave. When to dip his head beneath a low branch and when to step over a hidden dip. This was his forest.

He made better time now that he knew the way, but it could never be enough to outpace his pursuers. With each of them that had fallen, he had felt the wave of anguish sweeping out. The other Arazi would have felt it too. They would be coming for him. Closing in from all sides. They might even be ahead for all he knew, circling back to take him in a pincer.

Here was the tree where he had hung meat out to dry, and here the hollow where he'd waited out a thunderstorm in the midst of a hunt. Here was the rabbit trail he had carried Orsina along on his back when she finally gave up her fear of touching his scales, and here was where he'd first crossed paths with Mother Vinegar in the dead of night as he lay bleeding from a wound to the leg. These things overlaid themselves on his vision like ghosts, but he had no time to remember now. Not when death was coming so fast at his heels.

There was no way to outrun them, and now that they'd felt the death of their kin, they knew just where he was. The only way to turn this battle around was to find some advantage and face them. He needed a defensible position, and all that this forest had to offer was the old hag's cottage. For all that it was ancient and crumbling, it was still stone. They could not come at him from all about, only through the doorway, one by one. The entry was too tight for the wyvern. He would be taking all their advantages away, all bar the exhaustion they lacked and he was drowning in.

Despite it all, he couldn't hold back a rumble of laughter. The look on old Mother Vinegar's face when he showed up on her doorstep would make it all worthwhile. In the back of his mind, he'd always wondered just what that old witch could really do when she was pushed and couldn't hide out in the forest and avoid all of her problems. Would he learn the truth of her now? Would he discover she was Shadebound just like the girl had been, maybe even her great-grandmother, long forgotten but a font for her strange powers?

He crossed into the black once more. The trees were cut down in a line, and beyond that space, fire had taken all. There was no regrowth here. This was not an old stain on the land like the last firebreak, it was a clearance, and the ground had been scorched by something much hotter than mere charcoal burning. He could still taste the tang of dragon venom in the air.

All about where Mother Vinegar had lived was ashes. The blackened stones of her hovel still stood, but they were all that still stood. The plants that had claimed it over centuries were gone. The turf on the roof had collapsed into dust. It was destroyed. From here it was spitting distance to Sheepshank, the closest Kagan would have come to civilization in the days before Orsina. There were no trees between here and there, just that long black streak and shining patches where sand in the overturned soil had turned to glass.

The village and its fields were gone. More ash. More toppled stone. They had brought down an aslinda-dragon from the steppes to clear this place of any witnesses to their invasion. Burning hot and fast through all opposition before pulling back out of sight.

Kagan staggered to a halt. All of his hopes burned away as surely as Orsina's parents and the old witch had been.

Such slaughter, just to hide some cavalry in a forest. The worst part was that on the off chance anyone did come, it would look to their untrained eyes like a forest fire run amok. There would be no warning in this.

The Arazi had always been brutal in their methods, but this was the first time he was seeing that from the other side. Before it had always been justified. The enemy had chosen death by opposing them. But these peasants had chosen nothing, they were simply in the wrong place. Worse even than this realization was the dull knowledge that if it had been commanded of him, he would have readily made that same flight and burned the same innocents without a second thought.

Instinct had him turn before the wyverns broke free of the woodland cover. As he'd guessed, there were some already ahead of him in the southern reach, circling back to cut him off. It didn't matter now. Now they were all out in the open, and he was going to die. He had four spears left, and there were ten of them. They began to close on him, circling around to cut off any escape back into the forest. Mobility remained their great advantage, and exhausted as he was, Kagan could not even pretend to match it.

There were tears in the eyes of the one who called out to him. Sorrow was drowning even his rage. Kagan did not know which of the dead had been his lover, but it was certain to be one or the other. "Who are you, murderer?"

There would be no more running or hiding. He was going to die this day as himself again at last. "Kagan the Exile." He beat his fist upon his chest. "This was my forest, those were my people. My friends…"

A ripple of confusion had spread out among the other Arazi as Kagan spoke. They did not know of him. Strange. He would have thought he'd have been a cautionary tale sung to children by now. Another rider, a woman with what little hair she had left harshly shaved in mimicry of the smooth scalps of the true dragon-lords, spoke. "These are Arazi lands, Exile. You know your punishment."

"I know what's coming." Kagan hefted a spear in his hand. "Do you?"

In the heat of battle, so many things happen at once it is impossible to keep track of them all. That was the purpose of training, to make a body move before the mind could perceive the threat it moved against.

Three spears were unleashed at Kagan as he leapt aside, launching his own at the weeping Arazi. The first two soared by him, wedging in the ground by the ruins of the witch's cottage. The third was not so over-cast, nor so hasty. It scraped past his leg as he twisted in the air to put all the power of his contortion into the throw. His spear hammered home, not in the chest, but in the weeper's gut. It went deep, until the leather-wrapped handle was soaking blood. Nine left.

Rolling back to his feet, Kagan ran. They were ready for him to charge, to use their bodies as shields against their kinsmen's volleys. They were not ready for him to flee. The precious moments it took them to switch their grips on their weapons bought him half the distance to the javelins sticking up out of the ground.

When they launched, they aimed ahead of him, like they'd take a bird in flight. It worked in the air, where every move was a graceful arc. Down here in the dirt, where Kagan could twist aside and run a different way, it was less effective. Another round of misses and another near miss, scraping across his back and knocking him off balance as it struck the hafts of the javelins he himself still carried. Splinters rained behind him. No time to worry now.

The stumble saved him from the next launch. One of the fools had charged after him, blocking the line of fire for their kin, but closing the distance enough to throw from close range. It would have taken him through the neck had it not been for the last blow knocking him off kilter. Instead it clipped off his shoulder, and he kept on running.

A dragon perceived the world differently from a man, and some mea-sure of the dragon was in Kagan. He could tell the angles of a spear's flight. He could tell that by running in a straight line from the charging wyvern, allowing it to close the distance, he was shielded from assault from the rest of their line.

Allowing it to close the distance. As though he had a choice at the pace the wyvern set. The beast came on so fast Kagan barely had time to put in a few paces before it was upon him, snapping at him with its beak, muscles coiling to leap and rake. Kagan was the one to leap. Ducking in past the snapping jaws and wrapping his arm about the wyvern's neck before it could jerk back. Hauling down with all the strength his body and his dragon had granted him until the whole thing toppled down on top of him.

Wyverns were top-heavy without wings or long tail to act as counterbalance. Arazi cavalry defended against this with their spears, but this rider was still reaching for the next from his saddle. Or at least he had been, until Kagan unseated him.

While Kagan was shielded under the mass of the tumbling wyvern's body, the rider was flung free. His training held, he rolled back to his feet, but all of his weapons were back on the mount, and Kagan had at least a few spears left intact. On the other hand, the wyvern had every one of its natural weapons at the ready and was raking at Kagan with its back claws even as it tried to right itself and untangle from his embrace. He hung in close. His grip on the neck lost, but his body slick against the wet underbelly of the beast, tiny scales scraping over his open wounds like emery paper.

Fingers sliding with no traction, he caught hold of one of the stunted wing stumps as it spun back to its feet, letting the momentum of the powerful creature beneath him carry him to where he needed to be. He was flung through the air in an arc to land in the saddle.

The wyvern would not bear a rider other than its bondmate. No wyvern would. But Kagan did not need its obedience, just its position.

Slaying an aslinda-dragon was the greatest crime any Arazi could commit, but to slay any bonded dragon-kin would be just as grievous in the eyes of those bonded to them. The others could not strike at him without risking the wyvern, so they would not strike. Kagan had no such compunctions.

He reached to the place by the saddle where a spear was sure to be, and muscle memory served Kagan well. He launched once, twice, three times in swift succession. A new spear rolling into place in the saddle each time. He was not aiming for killing blows, but to startle, to disrupt, to break up the flocking pattern of the wyverns so they had to rely on the judgment of the riders. The riders who were not governed by predatory instinct, but by a tangled mess of emotion they needed to pick through to make a decision. More time.

The wyvern beneath him had gathered itself enough to turn and snap, earning a spearpoint to the eye for its trouble. Its rider, who'd charged at Kagan the moment he came upright, now fell shrieking to his knees, clasping at his own blinded eye. The bond was their greatest strength—and their greatest weakness.

While he was distracted with the writhing of the wyvern beneath him, one of the riders took a shot at him, but they were so afraid to hit his mount that it soared clear overhead. Eight of them were still mounted and a threat, sixteen enemies all, to the one of him. Yet they were fettered and he was not. He returned a spear to the one who'd risked attacking him, and their mount had to fling itself flat on the ground to avoid it, thrusting out its vestigial wings as wide as it could but still nearly falling.

The rest were closing on him. It was the only sound tactic when fighting at range risked their own flight. Too much motion was going on around him to track it all, and he had no control over this wyvern to navigate through it either.

But in chaos, instinct reigned.

Injured, and feeling its own pain echoed back from its bondmate, the wyvern beneath Kagan fled to the familiar for comfort. It ran to its rider.

Kagan leapt from the stirrups to pierce the Arazi through. Weight and momentum carried him down, and it did not stop until the spearhead was buried in the ash below and the haft had snapped. What luck that there was someone waiting right there for him with another fresh spear in hand to offer him.

Rider and wyvern died as he fled, their final anguish and terror washing over the battlefield and buying Kagan another moment. Another few steps.

The ruin of the witch's hut was in reach now. It lacked its roof, but the stone mostly stood. A bottleneck to hold them back, just as he'd planned.

Just a step inside showed how little it had been touched beyond the flames. Dried herbs lay crispened on the floor. Her supplies of healing unguents were baked in their pots. Mother Vinegar had died for nothing, for being in the place where people of power needed nobody to be. All that she was, all that she had done, gone, for nothing. There would be no magic to save him, no wave of a wand to take the pain away.

Turning to face the blackened frame of the low-linteled door where he'd banged his head a dozen times through the years, he bled and he ached and he raged for all that had been lost. For his own place in the Arazi. For the old woman who'd died after lifetimes of helping others without thanks. For all of it.

When the first scout burst through the door he hit her straight-on. Their spear-hafts crossed, both twisting and pushing, each trying to line up a lethal strike.

She was young and quick, but he had done this so many times it came as easy as breathing. She made her push, spearhead leaping at his face, and he leaned in past it, raking his own blade across her chest, making her hurt instead of trying to kill. The tip rattled over her ribs.

Her grip on her own weapon loosened. Kagan roared as he drove his forehead into her face, snapping it back. Blinding her with the moment of darkness. His next thrust pierced her through the same wound in her torso, and he kicked her back out over the threshold to free up his spear once more. Ready for the next of them to come.

They had not been trained for this. Cavalry would never find themselves in close confines. They fought in the open, using lancing momentum and wide sweeps to slaughter their enemies when they were close enough. Up close, all their grace and speed counted for nothing.

Two of them tried to come on together, but the narrowed doorway stopped them in their tracks and one peeled off to find another way in. Kagan could hear claws screeching over stone as the wyverns tried to surmount the wall.

Kagan couldn't take the second one with the same ease as the first.

They'd all felt how she'd died, they'd all learned from it. This one didn't rush for a killing blow, or clash with him directly, instead he used the reach of his weapon, thrusting and feinting, trying to lure Kagan forward. Too obvious, too easy to avoid. Kagan slapped aside the thrusts that came close and ignored the rest, lacking all subtlety when emotion flowed through the air, easy to read as words on a page.

When the scout dropped to their knees, Kagan was taken completely by surprise. There was a thrust at his legs that he had to turn aside with a spin of his own spear, but it was all a grander feint than he could have guessed at.

Looking out past the distraction, he saw what was coming. The spear was already in flight, one of the others had thrown it, it was headed straight for his chest.

There was no time to dodge, no time to even think, only to cross his arms over his chest and bear the brunt as best he could. The tip pierced his wrist, smashed into the haft of his spear, and hammered it all into his breastbone. It had been a perfect shot. A killing throw.

The spear's tip broke through scale and skin to touch bone, but it went no farther.

Springing up from the ground, the other Arazi leapt to his feet to land the killing blow, giving Kagan no time to think. No time to flinch away from what had to be done.

Blood gushed out as he unpinned his arm. The spear stuck through flesh and wood remained in place, but all of it swung out and away from Kagan. Clattering off the walls, sending agonizing jolts through him. He let that pain wash out and batter against the snarling Arazi. Let him flinch in Kagan's place.

Another bought moment. He brought the shattered spear in his hand down on the Arazi, cracking and splintering it apart. Buying another moment. Then another as the wood all fell away and the full blade was left exposed. He slapped his hand down onto the wyvern rider's face. Driving the spear-tip of his kinsman into the soft flesh there. Once, twice, three times before it hooked amidst the tangle of tendon and teeth, and the next time Kagan lifted his hand, he hauled the whole man aloft.

The next thrown spear took Kagan's living shield through the back. Showering his lower body in gore. It was another perfect shot, angled low so he could not use the same method to block again. It would have gutted him if it had not been for the now dead Arazi stuck to his hand.

Reaching forward, Kagan caught his foe's spear in his off-hand as the spasms of death cost the boy his grip. Shock had washed away, leaving only the pain in its wake, burning and aching all up the length of his arm. It took two kicks to part the dead man from his palm, and each one sent a fresh jolt of agony up him. That spear had to come out. It didn't matter how he'd bleed. If he could not fight, he was dead.

The wyvern atop the house had been bonded to the one who now lay dead. It collapsed down into the room in a shower of dust and charcoaled roof-beams. Landing half on the scraps of blackened fur that still marked where the old woman had slept and half on Kagan. The spear-haft through his hand snapped under the impact of it, the head ripping the wound in his hand wide enough to see through. Bile burned at the back of his throat, but he had no time.

The other climber came down at him now, while he was still half pinned under the wyvern corpse. She landed hard on its back, crushing the full weight of both of them down onto Kagan. All air was crushed from his lungs, all strength fled him as the wound in his chest throbbed and bled.

She lifted her spear high overhead in both hands and roared out her vengeance upon him. All he had killed had been her kin. By blood or by bond, they were her people, and he had slain them. Just as Mother Vinegar had been his.

To his surprise, the spear was still in his off-hand. Still pointed to his foe and ready. As she brought her strike down with all her might, he used all that he had left to return the blow in kind, thrusting up into her gut even as his fingers went cold from all the blood he was losing.

He could not say why he hit first. If she hesitated too long. If there was less distance for his spear to travel. If he was simply faster. It didn't matter. His spear burrowed up through her guts to wedge under her rib cage, and her brutal strike pounded into his shoulder with a fraction of the power she'd meant to put behind it.

His scales were thickest about his shoulders, almost horny outcroppings compared with the smooth coating on the rest of his skin. They took the brunt of the impact. Not enough to stop the blade from cutting through to wedge in the joint, but enough to keep his arm attached.

Another would be coming for him. Another moment would pass and he'd still be here pinned in the ash waiting for death. He strained and dragged himself out with the one arm that still worked, inch by inch, back towards the open doorway where the next one would come.

Blood trailed behind him like the marking of a snail's passage. Mixing into the soil and ash until there was a black smear all the way to the doorway. He leaned on the frame to get his feet, trusting none of the other walls not to crumble away under his weight, and then he looked out.

He expected to see spears already in flight. He expected to be rushed the moment he was in the clear sunlight.

Instead all was still. A wind had whipped up the ash of this place into something like a mist, and if there were wyverns and riders still afoot, Kagan could not see them. He took one staggering step out into the dim and was almost overwhelmed by the chill. It was summer in Espher, it should never have felt so cold. For a moment he wondered if this was just death, a haziness taking his sight and the freezing embrace of death creeping inside him, but when he stumbled back into the house, it faded. The pain came back, but with it a mounting terror.

Was this the work of the thing in the pool? Some primordial monster that he had tempted out to end their lives. It did not feel the same. None of the peace he'd felt was there, dragging him down to death with the dulcet tones of his own voice. Whatever it was, the cavalry who had pursued him were making no sound and closing no distance. He had a few moments of respite.

The moments stretched on and on with silence prevailing. Kagan did not understand what had happened outside, and he dared not go and explore lest the cold already seeping into him from his wounds should start to spread once more. The fog outside still hung thick and viscous, looking less like a fallen cloud and more like the toxic product of some burning poison. When he reached out through the broken walls of this place, numbness spread along his fingertips.

Just when he thought he might go mad if he did not hear a sound beyond his own breathing, it came. The steady beat that had been the match to his own heart throughout his entire life. Somewhere up there beyond the cloud, there was a dragon in flight. He could see the shadow of it when it passed between sun and fog. He could feel it tugging at his heart. An aslinda-dragon, not one of these wyvern runts. A true beast of prey. If he was not shaking before, then he would have started now.

He sank back as deep as he could into the ruined house and held his emotions tight so they could not find him. Whatever this fog might be, a few beats of a dragon's wings could clear it and leave him entirely exposed. He had to stay still and silent if he meant to survive, even as the pounding of leathery wings made him want to leap and bound about with joy. Slowly the sound passed over him, and he began to breathe again. Then another set of wings came. Then another. His teeth chattered together as he tried and failed to keep still.

Had this been the result of the scouts' interference or a planned foray? Had he unleashed the dragon-lords upon Espher with his clumsiness? He could not say, but he could count, three dragons in all, headed due south. For the heartlands of the kingdom, and the capital.

They would have no scouts to warn of the coming beasts, and a dragon in flight would outpace any messenger the lesser towns could dispatch. There was going to be a massacre.

Finally the last wing beats abated, and Kagan unleashed his senses once more to prove to himself that another was not coming. Beneath a cracked flagstone, he found Mother Vinegar's old cat-gut line that she used to stitch his wounds. Behind a stone in the fireplace, he found the schnapps she'd always claimed not to have, the kind he knew she washed needles off with because of the way they stung and smelled when she tended his wounds. He had never done this for himself before, but he'd seen it done more often than he'd have liked. With his clumsy left hand and the haft of a broken spear between his teeth to hold down the screams, he began to stitch.

THE LAST WORD

Caldo, Regola Dei Cerva 112

Between bed rest and carriage rides, Harmony was stiff and slow. Her latest cut had been slow to heal, and even now it seemed to drag at her as she went through her routine. It was early in the morning, by the standards of Covotana, and earlier still by the standards of the students of the House of Seven Shadows.

This was the second dawn she'd woken back here, someplace that felt safe, like a home should. So it was time for her to return to her routine, to work some life back into her body so that she might fulfill her duty and keep Art safe. Dawn had risen as she made her way across the grounds, and the dew was dry by the time she reached the sand by the rear wall. She'd been right to come early. The summer's heat would make this a torture if she stayed out too long.

For a time, she could forget everything. The cavern beneath the city. The doom that was waiting for them. The problem of Orsina, and the way that her brother now stared at the girl when she was not looking. If it had been lust, that could have been cultivated into something that would serve all their needs well, but for the longest time all that Harmony had seen was focused interest. Like the common girl was a problem to be solved. It was only last night she'd finally deciphered the look in its entirety, when she saw him turning away when Orsina turned, to avoid her noticing his observation. It was suspicion.

His chain of logic was easy enough to follow from there. He thought the Last King was Shadebound, this was a peasant uprising, where had he seen a peasant Shadebound? Only here, right in plain sight, slipping into easy striking distance by infatuating his own sister. Clearing up loose ends by killing her own failed assassin to gain his admiration and trust. It was a tidy explanation that would appeal to his love of puzzles, but the real world was not a tidy place. Sometimes things happened without reason. Sometimes people existed without some place in the grand schemes of the powerful.

She froze in the midst of her routine, feeling eyes upon her, and she spun, ready to be beset by robed rebels all over again, just as she had been so many times in her dreams since their journey through the sewers.

It was Orsina. Drawn out of her slumber and down here to Harmony's sanctuary. She wore Artemio's shirt and trousers, cinched at the waist by a belt that was unfamiliar, and a pair of high boots that Harmony felt certain had not come from his wardrobe either. Last time they had been here, Orsina had looked awkward and gawky in the clothes. Now they hung on her like they'd been tailored to fit and she carried herself with an easy grace that seemed almost as alien. The smile was her old one, though, warm and open.

"Good morning."

Despite herself, despite all that had been running through her mind and that sinking feeling in her stomach that it would only make sense for her only friend in the world to be using her to get at Art, Harmony smiled right back at her. "And what has stirred the sleeper from her rest before the breakfast bell has even been rung?"

"I figured you'd be down here." Orsina shrugged, still coming closer, coming onto the sand. "Needed a chance to talk with you."

With a smile, Harmony slashed her sword through the air between them. "To talk, or to converse? I still have not finished my training for the day."

Orsina smiled too, reaching behind her back to draw out the pair of rice-sickles they'd found among the discarded weaponry of the House's armory. Old, abandoned relics, now given new life. "Can't see a good reason it can't be both."

With a little bow of their heads, they began. Harmony's blade darted out, but Orsina had not even flinched at the feint. Perhaps she was tapping into the skills of Rossi, but Harmony could see no sign. Only the firm line that had been a smile, quirking up a little at the corners. Confidence.

"Good morning, Orsina. How can I help you today?"

"Good morning, Harmony." She sprang forward, sweeping both sickles down, not so much to stab Harmony as to force her to raise her blade and catch them, bringing their faces close enough together that they could speak softly. "I wonder if you might know what I've done to offend your brother?"

Artemio. Again. As though all the world spun about him. She kicked out at Orsina, hauling up with her blade to keep her from disentangling herself. The kick made contact with the girl's hip, but it was only a brush. Orsina had simply surrendered her weapons. The jerk of the sword had flung them into the air. "Perhaps he is a little put out at the fact you mean to graduate from the house alongside him this year, having barely arrived a few months ago."

Orsina's eyes darted from Harmony to the sky and back, and then her hands darted out to snatch the spinning sickles by their handles and fend off the next thrust. "I can't apologize for being good at the thing I'm meant to be good at. That wasn't how you taught me."

It was exactly what Harmony had taught her, to hold herself up and never let others tear her down. It was just strange to hear she had taken the lesson to heart instead of merely nodding along with whatever her supposed mentor said. The pause of realization gave Orsina her opening. She leapt back in, leading with one sickle, then spinning the other up from the opposite side, forcing Harmony to flick back and forth to keep them at bay. This was proving to be a better workout than anticipated, and still the girl showed no sign of calling upon her shade to improve upon her skills. This was all Orsina. It was hard to believe.

"And have you given any thought to who you mean to make your impresario upon your graduation?" Harmony blurted out as she bounded back out of reach. The sickles combined with Orsina's shorter arms gave her the advantage so long as they kept their distance. "I know the Prima must have squirreled you away and offered up a selection of viable candidates by now."

The look that crossed Orsina's face was pure revulsion. It would have made Harmony laugh aloud if it hadn't been the distraction she'd been waiting for. Driving in at Orsina, she tested her defenses. Making her move, making her sweat, bringing her breath fast as she answered.

"She was treating it like she was arranging a marriage."

Two weapons gave her more options, but it also gave her twice the problems to contend with. Orsina had to work out where to put both of her hands while Harmony's motions were fluid and natural. She was one with her blade. Training had shriven any thought from fighting now. It gave her room enough to think, to push at the conversation as well as the weapons. "Closer than a marriage, surely. With a marriage, death might someday part you. With the bond, there is no such distinction."

"I don't want to marry a stranger." The smile had faded from Orsina's face, and while Harmony would have liked to have thought it was because her limits were being pushed, she knew that in truth it was just this troublesome topic of conversation once more.

Harmony struck with words and blade in harmony. Batting aside Orsina's defenses with a fearsome flurry of blows. Trying to drive out her sickles and leave her body open to a strike. "What has want to do with such matters? You know you must wed for position and power. Indeed, this may be a chance for you to tie two families into your protection. Select a groom from one and an impresario from another and you might even cement an alliance. If they're all clamoring for you so much that the Prima has to serve as matchmaker."

Orsina did not stand still and take the abuse. When it seemed one of her sickles was driven out too far, she spun to bring it around from the other side, ducking Harmony's halfhearted thrust at her back and coming up with the momentum to hook the next thrust aside. "How am I meant to trust somebody I've never met with my life?"

"They're all of good breeding surely, isn't that enough?" On the back foot and being pressed once more by the spinning weapons sweeping back and forth at her, Harmony tried for another verbal jab.

"Not for me."

There had not been a moment's falter. It seemed that Orsina was learning how to keep her focus. "Well, what would be your preference then? Who do you count as a friend who could be trusted with your life."

Another springing leap stole Harmony's advantage of reach. Once more both blades hooked over the top of her sword, but this time, Orsina pulled down on it hard so that the same kick would not leave her open. She was learning. It brought them nose-to-nose, both wrestling. Harmony's trained arms against Orsina's peasant-stock musculature. She looked into Harmony's eyes, and she breathed out, "You."

Feeling sweat beading on her forehead and her arms beginning to ache, Harmony twisted her sword aside, setting the sickles screeching along its length and throwing off sparks. "I am sworn to my brother already, you know this."

Still Orsina spoke softly, even now they'd sprung apart. "I know."

The heat in her cheeks had not departed. Harmony had to concentrate to keep her breathing steady. They trod dangerous ground here, whether the other woman recognized it or not. She had to choose her words with care. "Whatever affection I might bear for you, you must know that a bond such as this, it cannot be."

"I know." Her answer seemed to come even softer, even more distant. Harmony could not bear it. Could not bear the gentleness of her sorrow.

She rushed in, slashing and stabbing with disregard for her own defense. Driving the other girl back a step before she fell into a rhythm, her parries flowing from one to the next, coming closer and closer with each impact to hooking the rapier and dragging it off course. And so Harmony pressed on ever harder. Intent on barreling through this conversation and to the other side. She thought for one wondrous moment that she'd knocked a sickle from Orsina's grip, but it tumbled through the air just long enough for the girl to snatch it up again in a reverse grip, handle still grasped in her hand but the blade angled forward.

When next she parried, both hands rushed together, like a beast snapping shut its mighty jaws. The blade on top caught on Harmony's slash, dragging it down, and the other shot up past it until the tip was brushing against the ties that kept her shirt closed.

Her heart pounded beneath the tip of that blade.

Stepping back, Harmony conceded the loss. Bowing her head. Anger beginning to prickle at her. This peasant who had been nobody could not beat her, not if she wasn't so damnably distracted by the conversation.

Orsina stepped back too, a flush on her cheeks and her confident smile returning. It was real anger now. The same anger she'd imagined Art felt at the prospect of graduating alongside a girl so many years his junior who had come and surpassed even his great talents in so short a time.

She needed to pierce that smugness. Cut through all the distractions that Orsina presented. Once more, she was the aggressor, leaping forward to strike at Orsina with the same pattern of blows that had almost broken through in their last bout. "If you know that you cannot have that, then what do you want from me, Orsina?"

This time, the girl seemed to recognize the pattern. She was not pressed, and she did not struggle. She drove her sickle blades into the heart of the storm of steel and dragged it out until it spun harmlessly about her. With a huff of air, she stepped in closer, punctuating each word with a swipe that Harmony had to dance out of reach of, lest she be parted from her innards. "Friendship? Advice?"

"What should I tell you as your friend?" Harmony let out a bitter laugh. "Marry a rich and powerful man, have many magical babies and watch them rule the world in your stead. Set aside all hopes and dreams you might have had of a life of your own and give yourself over to bolstering his ambitions. It is a woman's place in the world, is it not?"

"If I was in my place, I'd be using these to plant rice." She spun the sickles, then life seemed to return to her in a rush. She moved in again with such haste that Harmony could not have countenanced it. Blades spinning about her like she was that cone of wind on the forgotten battlefield. She chased Harmony about the sand, never quite catching up to her, but never quite slipping back far enough for her friend to relax.

So Harmony did not. She slashed at her feet, at her face, places where her training had never taught her to go. She turned a blow with the guard of her sword and punched out with the hand that held it to force Orsina off balance. "Then what do you want? If you could cast aside all order and choose your own path, where would you go? What would you do?"

"I don't know." Orsina fell back under this new assault, but she did not slow, and as many strikes as she parried, she returned in kind. "I don't even know what my choices are."

"So you know what you do not want, but not what you do. You know you'd reject the path every one of us has to walk, but not where you'd go instead."

She landed another kick, not on Orsina's hip but on the inside of her knee, knocking her stance askew and buying her enough time to slap the inside of a wrist with the flat of her blade before she had to switch it back over to catch the other sickle's descent.

"I don't want to hurt anyone." Orsina sounded close to tears, though none of it showed on her placid face. "I don't want to fight…"

Harmony thrust right for Orsina's heart then, anger winning out over reason. If this had been the Orsina she first met, she'd be dead. Instead the one sickle in her hand caught the thrust, twisted it aside, and let the momentum spin her. "Then what are you doing here? Why have you got a weapon in your hand? Why have you got a killer in your soul? What was the point of it all if you're just going to run and hide?"

The momentum had flowed into a kick, and it was only when Orsina froze with her leg still raised that Harmony deigned to look down. The dropped sickle had landed with the blunted outer edge down on the top of her boot. The movement of the kick had kept it in place, until now, when it came to rest, tip-first, upon Harmony's side. With a grunt of dismay, the two of them parted, and the sickle fell harmlessly to the ground between them. "I needed to…" Orsina bent to pick up her dropped weapon with a sigh. "I needed to get stronger."

"Why?" Harmony swung for her while she was still down on one knee, and it was only some instinct that neither of them knew she had that saved Orsina from a slice across her scalp. Both sickles came up to meet the glancing blow, to hook over the sword and drive it down into the ground, leaning hard on it to keep it pinned down as she rose to her feet.

"To keep you safe." There was a flicker of shadow beneath Orsina as she leapt, one foot spinning over Harmony's blade in a graceful cartwheel and the other lashing out at her face.

"To keep me safe." Harmony barely managed to jerk her head aside, but she had to give up ground to do it. Still Orsina didn't stop. Another flicker of the shade being channeled, then another impossible springing leap, both sickles coming down to catch on either side of the rapier blade Harmony had held out to skewer her in flight. Twisting it aside, yanking it from Harmony's grip. Disarming her entirely. Harmony had never been so thoroughly bested, and she could feel the shame of it burn.

For her part, Orsina seemed to barely notice at all that she'd bested her best friend. She merely stepped back a distance, to show Harmony that she was free and safe to retrieve her fallen sword. "The whole world might turn on me in a moment if they ever found out who I really am. If this is the only way I can keep myself safe, then I need it."

Harmony silently fumed as she retrieved her weapon and assumed her position opposite the girl on the sand. She'd been treating Orsina is if the other girl were only herself, but all of this time, Orsina had been tapping into the skills of Rossi, right under her nose. Calling and dismissing him moment to moment as she needed him. It was something Harmony had never seen done. Something she didn't know could be done.

"So you'll fight for yourself, but not for anyone else?" Harmony may not have been able to best Rossi in a fight, but she could certainly distract Orsina too much to use him. "How uncharacteristically selfish of you."

When she crept back in to make her first few nervous-looking swipes, it was clear that Orsina was back in complete control of her body. That her mind was affixed on the question instead of the fight. Perfect.

"How is it selfish to not want to hurt anyone?"

The tepid assault was slapped aside, Harmony's blade darting in to press Orsina back. "And what of all of the people that the ones you let walk free will hurt?"

Both sickles swept by Harmony's face, pushing her off balance, but she was not giving up her footing this time. She twisted back and lashed out with her blade in the same motion, almost scoring a hit on Orsina before her own momentum carried her spinning out of reach.

Still the peasant was giving the fight too much attention. Harmony had to twist the knife. "If you had not fought back when that girl came for me, I'd be dead. Would that weigh less heavily on your conscience?"

That most certainly did the trick. Orsina stumbled as she found her footing, and all at once the flow of the battle changed direction. Harmony had the upper hand again. She could glance a blow off Orsina's sickles and halt their progress. She could lash out with foot and fist and drive her opponent back when she drew too close. It was as though all she had been holding back now came loose.

Harmony's blade came within an inch of Orsina's freshly scarred cheek before she mustered an answer. "That's not the same."

It was barely an answer at all. Harmony pressed her attack, turning that thrust that had gone wide into a slash that Orsina had to duck to avoid, costing her mobility when the next thrust came. She barely managed to intercept it. Still Harmony pressed. "What if it was Art? What if he was lying there sleeping and some assassin came for him with a knife, would you just watch?"

Orsina's face was always so open, even before the shade had tried to open it further. Every thought in her head seemed to be on display. It almost looked like grief when Harmony said that. She stumbled backwards towards the edge of their little arena, barely managing to keep up with the steady pattern of parries and strikes. "No. Of course not."

"The Prima, would you let her die?" Harmony thrust at Orsina's heart.

"Your fairy-tale witch?" Another thrust, coming even closer before the blunted outer edge of a sickle punched it aside.

Harmony snarled and hammered the final strike home. "Your lizard-man?"

Orsina's sickles crossed around the blade and locked it still just a few inches from where her breast heaved. She didn't sound breathless when she looked up into Harmony's eyes. She looked determined. "I'd protect them."

Harmony had to haul with all her might to get the rapier free, and even though she managed, it showered sparks onto the sand. Orsina's next swing slapped it aside, and she took a step forward. Harmony tried to throw her off again. "The people in your classes, the people from your village?"

Harmony's next parry was picture-perfect, extracted precisely from the book on swordplay that Art had dug out of the family library when she was too young to read. Angled to deflect Orsina's strike while putting her own weapon in prime position to strike back. She was doing everything right, but it didn't matter in the face of Orsina's newfound focus. The second sickle hooked her blade and dragged her open to the kick that followed. It tapped Harmony on the hip instead of taking her full-on in the gut, but it hurt, and it broke her stance. Orsina's voice came like a growl now. "I'd protect them all if I could."

With every word, Harmony rained a new blow down on Orsina, once more giving herself over entirely to offense, relying on the speed of her strikes to keep the girl off balance. "When an army marches over Espher's border intent on waging war, do you suppose they'd leave any of us intact and unharmed? You have power, real power. If you don't use it, that's as good as giving us over to the ones who'd see us all dead." She let a sickle breeze by her upturned chin, then hammered at Orsina's arm with her hilt, drawing out a yelp of pain. "You'd be better to kill us yourself. At least it would be quick."

Orsina let her guard drop, backing away from her with all haste. She looked another few words from tears. "Where is all this coming from?"

"Before, I wanted you to stay, because I thought it would keep you safe. But then I saw you out there with the shades. I saw what you can do," Harmony snarled. "Anytime, you can just reach out and change the world. All you need to do is want to." It took Harmony a moment to regain her composure. Then she asked simply, "So what do you want?"

She may not have had much advantage when it came to fighting the embodied spirit of a legendary master of combat, but when it came to talking to the lost girl before her, Harmony held all of the cards. She stepped in closer, expecting Orsina to burst back into motion, to put up a good fight despite all of her distraction, but instead her sickles still hung limply from her hands and she let out a sigh. It was going to be the easiest touch Harmony had ever scored.

Then Orsina asked, "What do you want?

It halted Harmony in her tracks. It turned the smooth thrust that would have prodded into Orsina's stomach into a stuttering motion that Orsina was able to sidestep. She opened her mouth to answer, but with a flicker of shadows about her feet, Orsina launched into motion once more.

All sign of Orsina was gone as she moved. The tempest spun behind her eyes, and the sickles in her hands did things Harmony could not have guessed were possible. Sweeping through patterns of attack and defense so seamlessly that it seemed she had more than just the two arms at her disposal. At one point a parry and strike came on with such speed that Harmony could have sworn the two sickle blades must have passed clean through each other to make it possible. She had no time to formulate a pretty answer, all of her attention was bound to this fight, to this moment. All the world faded away until nothing remained but the two of them, bodies and blades in fluid motion, dancing back and forth.

Then just as swiftly as Rossi had seized control, he slipped away, and

Orsina was herself again. Her motions still fluid and confident, but all of the implacable certainty of victory absent.

A half step and a twist was all it took to move out of the sickles' reach so they swept by her without scratching fabric. She gave her usual answer to such questions. "I want to keep my brother safe. I want to help him do all the amazing things he's sure to do."

"That's just what you were told to want." There was a hint of a smile cutting through Orsina's grief as she spun the conversation back around. Perhaps she wasn't so incompetent at this as Harmony had hoped. "A woman's place? Right?"

Each snapped phrase was accompanied by the same snap of scything blades. Knocking aside Harmony's guard. Driving her back. Driving her to her knees. Until Orsina was standing over her, sickle blades crossed beneath her neck, and she had no clue as to how they had gotten there.

Looking down on her with such sorrow and pity on her face that it had Harmony close to weeping, Orsina asked, "What do you want?"

"I want you." The words slipped out unbidden as she looked up into the girl's eyes. Watching as they widened with surprise and confusion.

"You… what?"

With a shaking hand, Harmony reached up to push the sickles down, away from her unprotected throat. She did not need to. She knew Orsina would never do anything to hurt her, as surely as she knew her own mind, but it gave her a moment to put her own thoughts into words. To place some padding between the raw heart of herself that she'd just exposed and the cold light of day.

"I want to be with you. You're my dearest friend in all the world, and I want to keep you close and safe, and I have no clue as to how that might be done." She left her sword lying in the sand and reached out to Orsina, and was almost overwhelmed with relief when there was not a moment's hesitation from the girl in sheathing her sickles and catching Harmony's hand. She was drawn up until the two of them were eye-to-eye. She could have sworn she was taller than Orsina when she'd first arrived. She wet her lips and pressed on. "I thought if you married Artemio, that might keep you near to me, but with an impresario to contend with too, I haven't a clue how to help. If I could stand for you, I would, you know I would, but Art, he has nobody else in the world. He wants nobody else in his world. It has to be me, or he'll never be whole. He'll never be a full-blooded Shadebound without someone to bond with."

Orsina stepped back from her now. Not because Harmony had so openly declared her love for her, but because it still wasn't enough. "So I just need to pick some stranger to share my soul with."

Just like that, all the tension fled Harmony. All of the suspicion and doubt about her friend's intentions had been worn away. This was all too intolerably serious. "Unless you've been hiding a secret lover beneath your skirts this whole time?"

No matter how deeply she was lost in thought, such scandalous words were enough to snatch a gasp from Orsina. "Harmony!"

"Oh, don't be like that." Harmony leaned in closer and nudged Orsina's shoulder with hers, letting out a stage-whisper. "I thought you farm girls knew all about the wonders of coupling."

Orsina's face, which had remained its usual olive tone throughout almost every moment of their brutal sparring, now flushed a bright red as she stuttered out, "I have not, nor do I intend to take a... lover."

Harmony could not help herself. She had to lean in and press a kiss to the girl's cheek. To feel the emanating heat of that skin and know that she had caused it. So close, there was no need for brash talk, just a whisper. "What a pity."

Orsina still did not pull away. Harmony tried her best not to read too much into her stillness. She was uneducated in such matters after all. It did not mean anything that she still hung within the distance of a breath. It did not mean anything that her eyes had fluttered closed as though she were gathering her courage before asking, "Why? Did you have someone in mind?"

Harmony's will broke first. She could not bare herself so completely.

She just couldn't. It was already unthinkable that she was entertaining thoughts of her friend, doubly unthinkable given Orsina's low birth. To speak them aloud, to let the girl know she meant what she had said in play, it was intolerable. "I just don't think we should close ourselves off from new experiences."

The two of them parted, the tension broken, but Orsina did not wallow in her misery anymore. Instead turning to this new lighthearted tone as an escape from the serious debate of the past few minutes. "I've had rather enough new experiences for one lifetime. Perhaps that is what I want. To retire into quiet obscurity and have nothing new happen to me for the rest of my years."

Harmony chuckled. "I do not think that either of us should ever be so lucky. These are interesting times, after all."

Orsina turned to face her with a smile, her next quip already rising. Harmony would never hear exactly what it was she meant to say, because the smile vanished and the flush drained from her as though she were being bled out. She whimpered, "No."

Behind her, Harmony heard the beating of some great skin drum. In confusion, she looked south towards the city wall to discern what festivities could be making such a noise.

The dragon hung in the air above the wall, suspended like a marionette on invisible strings. Colossal and monstrous. Scales ridged with barbed bones and wreathed in a hazy halo as heat rose off it. Hot enough that the mirage shimmer ensconced it even at midsummer.

When it stretched its jaws wide, the fire came. Not like a spray as Harmony had imagined, but like a dam had burst its banks. Pouring down into the city. Flames roaring almost loud enough to conceal the screams.

When she turned back, Orsina had abandoned her.

THE FIRE WITHIN

Caldo, Regola Dei Cerva 112

Fire spread through the city like it had a hunger. The old town resisted—white stone did not burn—but the newer parts of Covotana where the commoners and merchants made their homes, they were mere stucco and wood. Tinder for the great broiling heat that now swept with each beat of the dragon's wings to curl Orsina's hair and steal her breath away.

Orsina did not know why she was running, nor where the great speed that burst through her body was coming from. It was as though the sight of a dragon had set some dark part of her own soul aflame. Sweat that all of her training with Harmony could not have drawn poured from her skin, but she did not feel it. Only the air ripping by her skin and the heat.

She moved like the wind, leaping walls and rebounding from paved streets and terra-cotta tile roofs, things she knew her own body could not do, but a shade could allow. Fear had been her first response to the sight of the dragon, the memory of flame on her skin, the memory of the awful thing that she had to do to survive, the moment that had destroyed her life all over again just when she'd felt a hint of home.

The pain. She had shied away from it, retreated into her mind, the way she had after that awful day in the forest. It had left her body unoccupied. It had let something else take the reins. Now she flew between the streets of Covotana, with the fear inside her burning away, fuel for the fires of a rage that she herself did not know. Never had she known such wrath or loathing. It was not in her nature to seek and destroy the things that might do her harm. It was not in her nature to attack, rather than defend.

What luck, then, that the nature of the shade within her was so different. What luck that the sight of beating wings and flames filled it not with dread but with a desperate need to drive the foe who might take its territory away. Covotana was Orsina's home. Orsina was the shade's home. Shed of a body, the shade still carried within it the memory of that body, of the instincts that had driven it. The need to be master of all it surveyed. The need to survive and thrive.

Orsina mounted the roof of a grand trading house overlooking the great canals running through the city and, in a moment of clarity, reached out to Ginny Greenteeth. The shade that had stayed hidden deep in the heart of her recoiled from the swamp hag, flitting back out of Orsina's soul as fast as it had flooded her. Orsina's mind came back with the flood of cool water on her skin. Her own sweat turned to the dark pond's water by Greenteeth's presence. Water was what was needed here. Stretching out her arms and slipping her life down Ginny's waiting gullet, she caught hold of the canal. All the flow of water through it stilled as she took control, and beyond the boundaries of her reach, the canal emptied on one side and overflowed on the other as it could no longer progress.

Reaching up to the blue skies above, she lifted a wall of water. Up and up it rose, until it towered over even where Orsina stood; then she cast it out, both arms flailing as she lost her grip on it and toppled to her knees. The water passed like a wave over the city, soaking the streets, splashing over the walls and reaching only barely to the closest of the fires where the dragon's breath had touched.

They did not extinguish. Some of the water steamed off on contact with the flames, but when the water struck upon the ignited venom, all it did was dislodge some part of it from the walls. It did not go out. Rather it spread, still burning, along the water's course, slithering out through the streets and igniting anything it touched. Perhaps these lesser infernos did not burn so hot on their own, but when they found wood and plaster, barrels and carts, scattered hay or clothing flapping on the line to dry, they leapt up and burned as bright as any other. The fires caught on anything that might be fuel, and they grew into fresh plumes of smoke and fire. Spreading to destroy whatever they touched. She'd made it worse.

But worse than the destruction she'd inadvertently wrought was the attention the stunt had won her. All through the streets, the frantic citizens turned to her with desperate hope in their eyes. Here was one of the Shadebound. She would save them all. When the impossible happened, beyond the control of mere mortals, here came those they'd set above them. Orsina had no idea what to do.

They were all going to die. They had no shades to protect them and carry them off on the wind. They had no Prima to turn to and beg for guidance. All they had was their lives, and they were going to lose them.

If the people of Covotana had been the only ones to take notice of her, then perhaps things might have been different. Perhaps she would have fled and survived and none of what followed would have come to pass. But the dragon and its rider were coming for her now. The great reptile undulated through the air with each stroke of its wings, riding the thermals its own fires had created to stay level while it sped like an eel through the sky.

Orsina saw it bearing down on her, and terror seized her once more. She fed more and more life into Ginny Greenteeth, summoning up all the water she could lift and launching it in torrents at the coming dragon. It dodged her first blast with a tilt of wings, barely slowing, then it bore through the next, letting it wash over its scales and bursting free of the steam with open jaws and a shake that she could not help but read as relish for the fight to come.

Water alone was not enough. Ginny, this monstrous old thing that filled all living men with fear, was not enough to face it down. Orsina reached out again, and dragged another shade in. Rossi could do nothing against such a thing with little sickles in his hands, but mashing both of those shades together, Orsina prayed for a chance. The water about her stilled, then quickened. The wild splashes she had thrown out over the length of the city came this time as razor-edged blades of water, slashing in at the dragon like the lunge of a mantis.

The dragon let out a huff of flame and both blades puffed away into nothing.

All Orsina had learned was for nothing, all she'd mastered in the few months she'd had to remake herself meant nothing in the face of this primordial lizard, coasting on towards her as though it had not a care in the world. She tried one more time to strike at it, launching a spiral of water from below as its shadow passed over the canal. The water broke on the dragon's scales and spattered down upon the city as though it had no weight to it at all.

Then all her hope left her. The dragon was in striking reach of her now. Its mighty jaws fell open. She could see, deep down in that tunnel of darkness, the roil of motion as the venom came forth. She saw the spark as it passed out through the dragon's mouth and that spray of nothing became blue-hot flame.

It was the forest all over again. She was a little girl. Powerless and defenseless. She did not even have Kagan there to beg for salvation. She was all alone. She was going to die, alone.

She sank back into herself. All strength fleeing her as death came. Retreating into her own mind. Terror overwhelming all reason.

Within her, the hidden dragon rose.

Who was this upstart daring to bare teeth in another's domain? How dare it burn what was hers to burn? Venom and teeth and spark may have been taken from the dragon, but it was still a thing of flame. It was still a dragon in its soul.

Orsina's hands went up, and fire erupted from them.

Guttering with black smoke, the fire poured out from its soul. Orsina was just fuel for the pyre, all her days to come, the succor the dragon needed to burn brighter and hotter. First the red flames of a fresh-spawned drag-onling, then the blue heat this upstart brought against it, then finally the true flame, so hot the eye could not see it. Beyond white-hot.

It met the intruder's fire and it swept it back. The tide of flame was turned, and in an instant the confident dive of a lethal predator became the frantic flapping of a scared animal. Instinct ruled again. The rider lost whatever influence they had over the dragon's mind.

Dragons may have been territorial, but they were also hierarchical, creatures born to dominate the weak and serve the strong. It was their nature. In the face of the power of another dragon, they felt no shame in submission.

The fire burning out from Orsina left her palms raw, and when it guttered and died, she could not hold back a scream. The last time she had felt the touch of dragon's fire, she had the sweet release of unconsciousness to slip away into, but now she did not dare rest, even though she felt the weight of lost time dragging her down like an anchor. What had the dragon spent? How had it hidden its shade inside her? All these questions and not a moment for one.

The dragon circled about her in a long slow sweep, trying to get past her without coming in reach. Testing for the edge of the territory she defended.

Coiled in her gut, the dragon raged. How dare this upstart test them?

Orsina did not know when the shade leapt back into control of her body. Time seemed to pass in a stutter. Blinking her eyes and opening them to find she'd cleared another street. Flames wreathed all around her when she gasped in her next breath.

It was her nightmare. The nightmare of all Shadebound. Complete loss of herself, consumption at the shade's whim, like her first memory of a shade riding her.

Her body twisted to fit the shade's form, her neck stretching painfully longer, her back aching as wings tried to sprout where there were none. Scales scratched across the inside of her skin, just waiting to break through. Mother Vinegar had saved her the last time this happened, given her the promise that she had strength enough to push any shade out of herself that she did not want inside. When she pushed against the wild dragon, it pushed back harder.

She felt its pride wounded through their bonded minds, she felt its rage turn against her. Flames flickered out unbidden from between her parted lips as the heat within her chest rose. It did not matter that this was her body or that this shade did not fit inside the shape it had contorted itself into. It was too powerful and too well nested. She could not force it out. It was not a matter of insufficient belief in herself, or insufficient will, it was practical. They were bonded, whether by her choice or not, and the harder she pushed to get it out, the harder it pushed back and the more the darkness between moments of clarity consumed her. A glimpse of a park beneath her, of leaping for the side of a building, fingers hooked into claws, digging into the stucco as she scrambled up, empty air beneath her as she leapt. The telltale ache as her life was drained away.

She could not stop the dragon. She could not force it out or force it down. So she did all that she could do, reaching out and pulling herself atop it. If she could not be free of the dragon, then she could ride it, instead of being ground beneath its weight herself.

It resisted her at first, fighting to be the one in full control until it realized she was not trying for control. Had the two of them been lying still and calm, the dragon would have consumed her whole. She could feel that hunger in it, that desire to master her. Domination was its nature.

But here and now, it was fighting a battle on multiple fronts. Orsina saw more and more of where the shade guided her as she crept back along the length of it from the deep, dark pit in her mind where she had hidden from the fear and the pain. The dragon in the sky had swept in close to torch a stable. The horses within screeched and whinnied as the flames consumed them, enough to turn Orsina's stomach while making the dragon that controlled her salivate in anticipation of the feast to come. Neither reaction mattered. That last turn had put the rival back into Orsina's reach, and she unleashed another inferno from her cracked and bleeding palms.

In the sky, the dragon twisted to avoid the coming fire, flaring out a wing to ride the rising heat from its enemy's assault. But Orsina was not a dragon with a dragon's limitations. She did not need to hold her head steady or risk roasting through the roof of her mouth to her brain. With a flick of her wrist the beam of roiling blue fire slashed across the soaring beast's wing. The thin membrane between the dragon's wing bones blackened, bubbled, puckered, and burst apart.

Burning, it tumbled from the sky. The smooth spiral it had been moving through now twisted to terminal speed with the loss of its wing. It tumbled round and round, end over end, before it struck. Landing with the impact of a falling star and crushing through one of the bridges that stretched over the larger of Covotana's canals.

For all their beauty and power, there was a fragility to the broken dragon that surprised both Orsina and her occupant. All of the immense forces at work to let it fly or spit fire were held on a razor's edge between perfect function and total collapse. All it took was a little nudge and the whole thing could be knocked off balance.

It stirred as she closed the distance on it, and Orsina readied herself for the fight to come, but she need not have bothered. A wild dragon like hers might have stood after such a fall and fought to the death, but this one was enslaved. Bound to the heart of its rider. The rider who was little more than a red streak across the brickwork now. The motions she saw were convulsions, the dragon was dead, it just hadn't realized it yet.

For a moment, Orsina and her dragon were unified. Both felt satisfaction at besting a foe. Where they diverged was Orsina's relief that it was over. The dragon did not hunger for peace, it hungered for more.

Still, that moment of unity gave Orsina the guidance she needed, like a light in a distant window, she could feel the way back to control of her own body once more. All she needed to do was follow it. Follow the flow of the dragon's emotions, aligning her own with it until they moved as one. She could never rule it, but she could become it, just as it became her. Unification.

Another explosion rocked the city. Red-hot shards of terra-cotta showered through the air, bursting out in every direction from the point of impact. Another noble's house by the eastern wall had been struck, and all about it fires burned. Orsina had been so lost in the heat of battle that she had not even seen the second dragon's arrival. Nor the third, as it swept across the city towards the House of Seven Shadows, leaving a line of scorched roads and rooftops in its wake.

The dragon's instinct was to go at the one who was directly ahead, but Harmony was at Septombra, she and the Prima and probably Artemio too. All of them in the path of the coming fire.

At first Orsina strained against the dragon within her, trying to turn it, trying to steer it like a willful ox. It took off towards the distant dragon out of spite. She was in motion again, stomach lurching with each bounding leap, awareness flickering in and out. She had to think like the dragon. Unity of purpose. She half remembered something about that in the Owl's endless books.

The House was her home, her roost, heart of her territory, and that meant that it was the dragon's too. It couldn't ignore that pull. It couldn't, even though it wanted to because Orsina had pulled it that way.

Now that she had resurfaced, the pain was everywhere. Each bounding leap the dragon took in her body, it tried to spread its wings. But it did not have any wings, all it had was Orsina's body and the bones and skin it was contorting on her back. Blood ran freely down the back of her shirt now. Saturating it a deep scarlet. When she caught a glimpse of her hands, held up to catch onto the next rooftop, the claws protruding from her fingers took her by surprise, but almost as shocking was the fact that the burns were gone. The same telltale pale swirls marked her hands as had been upon her back since the Selvaggia, burn scars, long healed.

How much time would it have taken those burns to heal so cleanly? How many months had this dragon already devoured of Orsina's life? She fought down the swell of panic. It did not matter, it could not be changed. Fear was not in the nature of a dragon, and giving in to her fear would slip her further and further from control. Unity of purpose. They both wanted the dragons attacking the city gone. They both felt a twinge of pity for them, enslaved to the will of pathetic little apes. They would both deliver them from that slavery the only way they could.

Orsina had not crossed half the distance she would need to before she could strike out at the dragon when it was halted in mid-air. Not like it had chosen to halt or struck some invisible barrier, but like it had been frozen in amber. There was a moment of confusion for both Orsina and the dragon within as they looked at that impossible sight, then the lightning came.

A blinding flash, then sight returned and nothing had changed. A thunderous peal rolled over the city, though there wasn't a cloud in the sky. The dragon, still hanging there among the stilled smoke, was dead.

Even from here it was obvious. The lightning had not struck it, but its rider, and the death had carried on down. When whatever shade that held it released its grip, the dead dragon fell straight down, all momentum stripped from it.

Orsina had forgotten there was more than one Shadebound in the city. She had been so caught up in her excitement and terror and all of the rest, she had forgotten how small a piece she was in the greater game. Dragon-slayer or not. Septombra was filled with Shadebound, every one of them a force to be reckoned with. Working together, it was small wonder they could face down a natural disaster like the coming of a dragon.

Screams echoed up all around her. Terror and pain and pleading. She tried not to think about how many people had seen her killing another dragon. Kagan had made her swear on anything she held holy that she would never tell a soul about the last one, and now all the city had seen.

The city rocked as one of the old white stone buildings burst apart, not from dragon fire but from another of the Shadebound springing into action. The walls exploded out only a short way, revealing the silhouette of a man in the midst of it all, before they too, like the dragon, froze in place.

Surrounded by the orbiting masonry, this Shadebound leapt up at the dragon Orsina's rider had sought to clash with, launching stone after stone with more power and precision than any catapult could have mustered. Each one that missed went soaring out to destroy other, more distant parts of the city, slums, and as such of no concern to the nobility of Covotana.

The dragon and rider showed such grace in the skies it took Orsina's breath away. They flowed like the wind itself, coiling and shifting around each launched hunk of stone, not as though they were frantically twisting to escape, but like they were gliding through a course predetermined. Like they were dancing on the breeze. She knew it was not beautiful, she knew it was monstrous, but in her heart was a dragon, and it ached for the sky.

Looping around in an ever-tightening gyre, the dragon rushed in at the Shadebound who stood against it, bearing the brunt of one final slab of stone flung right into its face at the very end. Stone and dragon met, and dragon proved the stronger. A shower of gravel rained across Covotana as it opened its jaws and unleashed its fire.

Whatever remained of that once great house fell into the scorched rubble a moment later as the shade lost its anchor to the world of the living. Another black mark on the white surface of the city. On the spiral went, reversing course to arch up higher, dangling claws scraping tiles.

It was headed for the palace.

Orsina felt it in her gut, some swirling cocktail of her own suspicions and a dragon's instinct to seek the high ground. Dragons would seek the ruler, like a moth would seek a flame. They would seek the king before anything else.

She couldn't let them get him.

It wasn't anything to do with concern for the sovereignty or tactics or anything so high-minded as patriotism. The other dragons wanted something, and she would not let them have it out of pure spite. The king belonged to her. To Artemio. To her roost. She took off once more, ignoring the dragon in flight and making all speed for the palace.

She was close to the surface now, close enough that she could gain some measure of control over her body if she wanted to fight for it. She didn't. They were heading where they should, they were doing as they should, she would not waste time or energy struggling against the dragon within when she agreed with its course. The only difference with her so close to the surface was that she could think clearly enough to invoke her other shades once more. When the dragon made a wild leap from one neighborhood to the next, trying to clear a canal, she reached down with Ginny Greenteeth and hauled the water up, freezing it with the touch of Rossi into tiny platforms beneath her feet. Pushing off from them, there was no slowing of pace.

When they reached the next gap, her body moved with an expectation of that same support. Whatever else the shade of the dragon was, it was not stupid. It would not reject help just because it came from a rival for the same flesh. Accepted to some degree, the lesser functions of life seemed to be given back to her. Orsina let out the breath she'd been holding and almost gagged at the taste of venom in her mouth.

Even with all haste and all of their combined tricks, Orsina could not reach the palace before the Arazi. The first burst of flame swept up the pale stone spire, shattering stained glass that had hung in windows since before anyone living could recall, but the stone itself stood firm. It would take more than a lick of dragon fire to bring down the palace walls. It was built to survive until the world went dark.

Already Orsina could see the assault being returned in kind from the palace, guards up on the roof raining arrows down at the dragon and rider, who seemed satisfied to simply skim by before the shots could reach them and unleash more flame. The Shadebound within the palace were scattered. There was no cohesive defense being mounted, only a dozen individuals of power trying to bring that power to bear. A bar of light launched up from the lower windows of the palace, only to collide with a shimmering silver stream of moonlight coming from down by the stables. The impact set off a cacophonous boom that didn't touch the dragon at all.

Sparks and beams and flames and what looked like a flock of birds made of shadow all launched up from various places about the palace, but with the same ease as it avoided the arrows, so too did the dragon avoid these with an almost contemptuous poise. With her own dragon nestled in the egg of her skull, Orsina could feel that contempt reflected. Mobility was the Arazi's greatest gift, and these blundering apes down in the dirt could barely move, their angles of attack were entirely predictable.

Even Orsina, with no experience at all, could see that firing out from inside the palace was going to be useless. Movement was the key.

She felt her back strain as wings she had never grown tried to beat, and she reached out to her other shades to take the strain. Rossi's tempest whipped up beneath her feet, lifting her as she should have plummeted, and then, so quickly she could scarcely believe it, the palace loomed before her, in leaping distance.

The dragon within her did make that leap, but on contact with the smooth white stone of the palace walls, it kicked off once more. Rebounding into the open air.

A steady trickle of life had been feeding the shade throughout all of its domination of Orsina, but now her life was slurped down like the dragon had not drunk in a decade. Flames coiled in her open palms as the Arazi circled into sight.

It took more willpower than Orsina knew she had to clench her fists shut around those flames. To seize control of herself back from the dragon that sought to rule her. She felt it rebel against her asserting herself on her own body, but she also felt the dead serpent's restraint. It was giving her the benefit of the doubt, and she would not waste it.

Rossi leapt into her from where he had orbited, awaiting his chance, and the flames within her hands became sickle blades of blue fire. She unleashed both, tracing invisible lines across the blue sky, but a moment before gravity took hold on her and dragged her back down to the world below.

Some instinct or sense for heat gave the dragon warning. The first slash of blue flame, it twisted to avoid. The second, it had not seen. That one took it in the chest. Splitting the harness that held the rider in place, scorching deep into the dragon's chest. A plume of smoke burst up from the dragon, obscuring it and its rider from sight, but then the heat ate through to its venom glands, and, with an explosion loud enough to shatter what windows were left on this side of the palace, it exploded.

So far from the blast, Orsina was only kissed by the heat instead of flung away. She had expected her own dragon to leap in and seize control over her again, but it did not. Rather it lay still, as though she might forget it was there, silently observing her every move for weakness. In her head, reading her thoughts, ready to rule over her if she did not master herself. It was a two-way street, of course. Now she understood it as it understood her.

Ginny Greenteeth slipped in to call up a cradle of water to break Orsina's fall, easing her down onto the bridge leading into the palace. From here it barely looked like it had been touched. There was smoke drifting up from the other sides, where the flame had passed in and struck more flammable goods, but out here, all was pristine. Up until the moment Orsina turned around.

Half of the city was in flames. Just three Arazi and their dragons. That was all it had taken to destroy so much. What would happen when another three came. And another. What happened when a hundred did. They would not be called dragon-lords if they had only three at their command. Even a handful would overwhelm Covotana—and Orsina herself. She did not know how much more fight she had left in her after today. Not the will to fight, but the raw life to fuel her power. If this battle had raged on with the dragon shade in control, it would have withered her away to nothing.

Orsina's knees felt weak, her chest heaved, and all the injuries of the day fell on her, one after another. The burns and contortions. The bleeding fingertips where claws had manifested and the ache on her back where wings had tried to spring up from beneath the burns the dragon had left on her while it still lived. The dragon shade had run her raw, and now that it was time to pay the piper for all it had done, it had coiled up and slipped back into whatever hole inside of her spirit it had been lurking in. She couldn't even feel it. If she had not known it was there, then there would have been no hint.

More dragons would come. All of the Arazi, with all of their soldiers. Orsina could not guess how many people had died on this day in just the few minutes the city was under attack, but she wagered it was more than the number of Arazi. Even when she'd stopped their ambassador after hearing his words, she had not thought about them. She had thought that matters of war and state were so far above her station that she had nothing to do with them. If only that were true. Even if she was just a peasant in the field as birth should have left her, the coming of the Arazi would have changed everything. The people out there in the city made no laws and ruled no kingdoms, but they had burned and died all the same. Their lives were in ashes, all the same. Her family, however distant, would die. Her village would burn. There would be no going back.

Either she fought or she was responsible for all she could have prevented, and if the dragon-lords were not stopped, then it would be the end of everything.

31

THE DAY OF THE ORPHAN

Caldo. Regola Dei Cerva 112

I n years to come, people would ask one another, when the dragons attacked the city of Covotana, where were you? Some would inflate their
own heroics. Others would tell the truth, of how they cowered and
fled and could think of no tomorrow beyond the heat of the fire's flame.
Artemio was not so lucky as to have such a tale. Either such a tale.

While a battle for the very heart of Espher was fought in the skies
outside, he was sitting behind a desk, surrounded by the notes of two dead
men, waiting to become the third.

The secret was in here somewhere, he felt utterly certain of it. Somewhere in his notes, or in the notes of these two buffoons, the identity of
the Last King was hidden. All he had to do was find it, to think his way
around the problem or through it and out the other side. There was no
wine in his glass now. He could not trust a servant to fetch it for him
lest it come back poisoned, and wandering the dark cellars of the palace
seemed a certain way to earn a knife in his back. No matter how perfect
Saveria Gatto might have been with the sword, he would still have to be
called, and that required enough time for Artemio to be shanked in a
dozen different ways.

He was not about to disregard his survival when he'd fought so hard
and so long to ensure it. Not for wine. Not for anything. All of his life
was now narrowed down to this dank old room—and the inevitable ar-

rival of the assassins that would come calling. He had seen too much to be allowed to survive, too many details. They had no means of stopping the spread of the broad strokes of his tale, and if they had any sense at all, then they likely would have abandoned their cavern beneath the city. But if he could be removed, so could the memories that would be woven into the grander tapestry and made visible.

When there came a knock from his chamber door, Artemio froze. Harmony would have strolled right in, and assassins weren't so polite, so it begged the question: who knew he was here? Drawing in a steadying breath and brushing his fingers gently over the leather binding of his sword-hilt where the rapier stood resting beside his chair, Artemio called out, "Enter."

If it had been a dragon, a queen, or the God Emperor of the Agrantine, he could not have been more surprised than when his father passed through the door. Artemio had risen from his seat habitually to greet the visitor, and now he found himself regretting his good manners.

"Father."

"Son." Cleto Volpe gave nothing away. Stepping into the room to close the door firmly behind him before striding to take a seat on the opposite side of Artemio's desk. It was all such a non sequitur that Artemio found himself sinking down opposite Cleto, trying to work out if he had drifted off into a dream.

It was just another puzzle piece that didn't seem to fit anywhere. "To what do I owe this pleasure?"

"Does a man need an excuse to visit his son?"

"A man does not. You, on the other hand, have some ulterior motive for any social call." Artemio eyed him up and down. There was no hint of the road on him. No dust, no wrinkle to his clothes. "What else would have dragged you out of your cave in the borderlands?"

"It might surprise you to learn that I have been spending quite a bit of time in the city of late." He said it like it meant something. It was no wonder Artemio had become so fixated upon deciphering riddles and puzzles when every conversation with his own father was so laden with hidden meanings he was meant to decipher.

"Quite. I would have thought you'd still be in mourning." The perfectly pressed suit his father wore was in a deep blue, dark, but nowhere near to the black in which he should have been clad.

"We both have much to mourn, but the future is impatient." He reached out to straighten a stack of papers on Artemio's desk. As though he couldn't help himself. "Progress does not wait for our petty sorrows."

Artemio nudged the papers back to their original position. "Am I to assume you have some information on Mother's killer that you wish to impart?"

"Nothing you have not already worked out yourself, I'd imagine."

"And the servants in question?"

Cleto frowned. "The servants had no involvement."

Artemio almost leapt to his feet. Something he knew that his father did not, what a rare treat.

"Regardless, it is to other matters we must now attend." Cleto settled back into his chair. "You are my son and my heir, and in the days to come, I shall need you by my side. Just as you shall need me if you mean to survive the upheaval."

"I suspect the world in which I'm devoted and loyal to you may have passed us by, Father. I believe you beat all such high-minded principles out of me quite some time ago."

"Do not be foolish, boy. All that I did was to improve you. To make you stronger. All of the pretenders' lackeys wanted us dead. Should I have sent you out to face them unmanned and unarmed?" When such words were clearly having no effect upon Artemio's disposition, he switched tack. "Whether you like it or not, we are blood, and that means that in matters of succession, neither one of us has a say. My throne shall become yours when I pass."

"You do not have a throne, Father. You have never had a throne, nor shall you ever sit one. The twin kings rule Espher. Not you." He said it softly, with no malice. Wondering, not for the first time, if madness had taken his father. He had wanted to be king for so long, plotting and planning all by himself, that Artemio genuinely wondered if the man had finally convinced himself his dream was reality.

That suspicion shattered with his father's next words.

"There is only one king."

All the pieces of the puzzle shuffled in Artemio's mind. If he removed the personal element of his mother's death, there was nobody this peasant uprising could benefit more than a man who considered himself deposed. A man so certain of his own superiority that it would not even cross his mind that he could not simply take the throne once the nobility of Espher had been forcibly cast out by the monster he had unleashed.

"You."

"Of course it is me, you little buffoon. Are you trying to tell me that you had not worked it out? That I wasted my time coming here to placate you and keep you silent with promises of inheritance?"

Artemio called the forge spirit and cast a flickering dart of flame at his father's chest. Bisnonno Fiore caught it and snuffed it out. Cleto Volpe smiled.

Small wonder that Cleto had practically forced the old king on him as a child. Power that could never be used against him. A means to cripple a potential enemy.

It all made sense now. Everything except for Mother. "You killed her?"

The smile faded as swiftly as the fire had lit it. Cleto's brow raised. "Hmm?"

"Mother. You were the one to do it." Artemio replayed it in his mind, the patterns of the cuts. The blood. "Yours were the only footprints in the room. You... you butchered her. Made it look like the other attacks to turn suspicion away."

There was a moment where Artemio thought his father was going to falter, that he was going to show some hint of humanity, but instead the man put on his stony mask of neutrality and replied, "Sacrifices are required. Your mother, she went quite willingly, for the cause. To know that her son would someday rule Espher, she would have given much more."

"I thought you loved her. I always knew you loathed me and even Harmony, but Mother... I was so sure you loved her." Artemio felt tears pricking at the corners of his eyes. He felt like a child all over again. Lost and confused. Everything he believed about the world—a fairy tale.

"I did. More than anything in this world. But duty..."

Artemio unleashed a storm of fire. He'd rather burn the whole world down than hear Cleto's excuses. "Duty? Ambition is not duty. You care for nobody but yourself. You'd rule over a kingdom of ash sooner than live a day in a place you could not control."

The desk was aflame, the carpets and all of the papers Artemio had so meticulously gathered and studied. Smoke flooded the enclosed space, and the spreading flames drank down all the air. Yet still Cleto was untouched. Not a hair out of place. Fiore had stopped it all before it could reach him.

"Is ruling not the duty of a king?"

If he had said anything else, then perhaps Artemio could have controlled his temper. They could have spoken and settled upon some course where both of them survived. Instead, Artemio snatched up his rapier, kicked the scorched halves of the desk apart, and drove for his father's heart.

What Artemio had in youthful vigor, his father more than made up for in experience. The attack had been clumsy, well telegraphed, and the moment it took the younger Volpe to boot the furniture apart gave all the delay Cleto needed to draw his own blade.

The rapiers crossed and locked the two generations of the family together, face-to-face. "What do you think you are doing, boy?"

Artemio strained and pushed his father back a step. Beyond the scorching heat of the room around them, booms and echoes could be heard. Screams and flames. Was this the revolution come to fruition at last? Was Artemio the last loose end Cleto had to tie off? Artemio snarled, "Something I should have done long ago."

He reached out to his shades, and while Bisnonno Fiore refused the call, the other two were more than ready to spring into action. Flames wreathed his sword where Fiore could not touch them, and in the sudden flare of red-hot light, his father's eyes widened.

Saveria Gatto took the helm.

Artemio's body did not suddenly bulge with new muscles, nor did he quicken to move like the wind. He was still himself, but his every motion was guided by invisible hands.

Cleto Volpe may have been one of the finest swordsmen of his generation, he may have been the worst. Neither would have made a difference in the face of the vast gulf between his skill and that of Gatto.

Artemio's flaming blade twisted in towards his father's face, close enough to set his hair alight, and when the older man tried to flinch back from the heat, his footing was lost. The burning scraps of the investigation were spread across the floor, slippery underfoot. They were why Gatto did not risk a step forward. He merely drew back his sword, then dipped beneath Cleto's guard. Driving the tip into the Volpe patriarch's gut.

The strike was pulled at the last moment. Gatto did not pull it. Artemio certainly didn't. Only the tip punctured Cleto's waistcoat before Bisnonno Fiore forced his way inside of Artemio's body and hauled him back.

Now it was Artemio's time to slip and stumble and his father's to rise over him with blade in hand. "You dare to raise your hand against me? I'm your father! I am your king!"

Artemio's life was draining away as the man who styled himself the Last King stood there grandstanding. Both of the shades doing battle for his body were using his life to fuel their strength. In the civil war for the stretch of land known as Artemio, the only certain loser was him.

Cleto drew closer, stepping carefully over the smoldering remains of the desk and all of the work Artemio had spent months on. All for nothing. There was a coldness on his father's face he knew all too well. It was the face that still loomed up in his nightmares on his worst nights. All that was missing was the belt hanging from Cleto's hand. In its place was their family sword. An inheritance it seemed Artemio would be receiving early.

"All you had to do was what I told you to do. All you ever had to do was obey me, yet still you fight." He almost sounded saddened at the thought of killing his own son. Just as Artemio was sure he'd gone through the motions of sadness at the thought of butchering his wife's corpse. But it was not real. However well acted it might have been, there was no truth to his sorrow. Nothing mattered to Cleto except the throne. Not his wife, not his children. Nothing.

The two shades inside him clashed time and again, diminishing a little more with each exchange. Both drinking deep of his lifeblood to refill themselves.

At least he had control enough left over his body to speak, though that was small comfort. "For as long as I have known thought, I have hated you. You are the wellspring of all my misery in this world. I should have slit your throat in your sleep the first time you struck me."

"What a shame you didn't have the courage of your convictions. At least if I'd killed you back then I would have had time to raise a more worthy heir. Now I shall have to settle for your sister. Make her some match. Hope for a grandson."

Artemio strained with all his might against the shade's hold on him. "She'd sooner kill herself than serve you."

"Quite the contrary, without her loyalties divided by your presence, I expect her to be diligent in her duties. You were always the problem, Artemio. I should not have let sentiment stay my hand."

Artemio closed himself. It was the first lesson his tutor had taught him when it became apparent he would be Shadebound. To seal the hollow in his spirit and keep any parasitic shades out. He had not felt the need to do it in years, not since he'd taken in Bisnonno Fiore and inherited his protection. He was rusty.

The world seemed a dimmer and less colorful place without his other senses. Without his awareness of the shades around him, he could not tell where Fiore had gone or what he was doing. He could not temper the flames that reached up to nip at him. He could not breathe clear, chilled air when what swirled around him was hot and sooty. But he could move.

As Cleto Volpe drew back his sword to put his son to death with a single blow, Artemio flung himself forward. Surprise was on his side, as was weight. He barreled into his father, knocking both of them off their feet to land struggling on the solid flagstones beneath. Bones cracked and muscles creaked. Both men lost hold of their swords as they wrestled for supremacy. Artemio kicking out as he tumbled past his own and sending it sliding under the bed, Cleto still desperately reaching for his.

Artemio would not let him have it. He hammered at him with his fists. All hint of refinement or grace burned away in his panic to keep the weapon from his tormenter's hand. No one hit was enough to stop the man, but every one of them was enough to slow him.

With a heave and a snarl, Cleto rolled them over, and with a ferocity Artemio did not know the frigid-hearted man had in him, the blows began to rain down on the son instead.

Where his had been frantic, each of his father's punches was calculated and aimed. Striking his face, cracking his skull off the flagstones, dipping beneath his upturned chin to crush his throat and steal his breath.

As Artemio choked, his father scrambled free of him, reaching for his sword. Artemio caught his ankle and hauled him back, rolling halfway onto his own back as he overbalanced and brought the weight of the man back on top of him.

Cleto kicked him in the face, and Artemio tasted blood. He kicked again, and with a pop, Artemio's nose broke. Burning cold spread across his face even as more blood poured down into his mouth.

He had no time to bleed. No time to think. He scrambled, hooking his fingers into his father's fine coat, dragging himself up and over the tangle of flailing legs. Tearing fabric and scraping his fingers over the skin beneath as he crawled up the length of the man and seized him by the hair.

With all of his strength, he hauled Cleto's head back and hammered it down into the stone.

His strength was not enough.

Neither one of them had tired yet, but while Artemio had spent all his life with whatever strength he needed at his beck and call, now he was separated from his shades and his true power. He tried again to drive his father's face into the stone, and the old man, straining against him with all his might, didn't even let his nose make contact this time. He was getting his arms underneath himself, getting ready to buck Artemio off.

Those same grasping hands that had been tangled in hair as red as Artemio's own slipped down to close around his father's neck. The strength that wasn't enough to overpower Cleto's head was enough to cinch shut his throat. With both hands locked about it, feeling the wrinkled skin beneath his fingers shift, Artemio pulled.

All of his life his father had loomed large in Artemio's mind. So large, that it took until now, straddling over his body, hauling at it with all of his strength, that Artemio realized he was actually taller than his father. He had more bulk to his body, better reach, and it seemed that the addition of his weight surpassed Cleto's strength.

The old man made grotesque croaking sounds as he struggled for air, clawing and pawing at Artemio's hands. Trying to speak, trying to command him to stop. The arrogance. The rank arrogance of this man was almost too much to believe.

Between his legs, his father's body began to tremor, the pawing of his hands grew less and less insistent until he was barely stroking Artemio's knuckles with each pass. This would be the one and only time he was gentle with his son, when darkness was taking him.

He had come to Artemio fully certain that his son would fall into line, that he would accept his father was a mass murderer in open rebellion against the crown he had sworn his life to serve and bow before his greater wisdom.

Even the pawing at Artemio's hands had stopped now, though Artemio could still feel the pulse of life within the man's neck, could still feel the strain as he tried to pull free.

Perhaps Cleto Volpe truly had been born to be a king. Nobody else could have been so certain of obedience without even a hint of evidence it would be forthcoming.

Beyond the walls of the tiny room, the explosions and shouting had all stopped. All that was left was the utter silence. The gurgling and hacking sounds as the last few bits of air escaped from Cleto. The grunts and strains as Artemio pulled on his throat with all of his might. Sounds that turned to sobs before the deed was done. The two of them lay there on the floor of the burning room, father trying to break away from son, son holding father close. Finally, just when it seemed like it would never end, the struggle ceased.

Cleto stopped moving beneath Artemio. Artemio let his grip on the old man's throat loosen and pried his aching claw-hands away. There was blood everywhere, and with a start, Artemio realized most of it was his.

He had not made a study of medicine. He did not know how long it took for a man deprived of air to die and he most certainly did not trust his father to stay dead. Without the strength to stand or any desire to push his head up into the noxious clouds above, Artemio crawled to his family sword and cradled it in his hands. Despite all of the centuries, it still bore the old family crest on its pommel. The basket and hilt were worked silver in the design of foxes at play. He had never been allowed to touch it before. Now it was his. Now the entire House of Volpe was his.

He did not want it. The tears streamed down his cheeks as he set the tip of the sword at his father's nape. Exhaustion and pain and smoke. Not regret. He coughed out, "Why did you have to be such a monster?"

"Show me a man who says there is no monster in him…"

Later Artemio could not say for sure if his father had said the words at all or if they were just an echo in his own memory. It mattered little, in the grand scheme of things. He let his weight fall onto the pommel and barely felt a thing as the tip of the sword burrowed into his father's skull.

The body on the floor beneath him went through paroxysms as he twisted the sword clear, the spirit leaving the body, or the blade interacting with some mechanical part within the machinery of life. He could not say for sure. All he knew was that his father was dead and gone.

With a sigh, he let his guard down and the shades reappeared. Bisnonno Fiore was down on the floor with Cleto, trying to cradle the dead man with arms that could not touch to a heart that did not beat. The other two lingered just out of reach, petulant at having been cut off from their regular feed but not angry enough to test Artemio when his mood was so abundantly dark.

"Fiore. I am the last Volpe now. There can be no more rebellion. Do you understand?"

With a baleful stare, the dead king looked up at Artemio. If he could have wept, Artemio had no doubt the shade would have. It was as close to a thinking creature as any shade he had ever encountered. The memory of its life still lingering fresh.

With painful slowness, Bisnonno Fiore nodded.

"Good."

Artemio collapsed by his father's side, even as he called his shades to pat out the flames and clear the smoke. All of his research and careful study was ruined, but what need had he for it now the ringleader was dead.

All that remained was the question of what to do next. Sons of traitors did not tend to survive for long in Espher. The taint on the blood would never wash clean. As long as only he knew what had happened in this room, he had an opportunity to avoid such a fate.

All he had to do was lie to the king.

32

IN THE PLACE WHERE MINDS MEET

Caldo, Regola Dei Cerva 112

It was a strange quirk of life that Orsina felt safer facing down a dragon in flight than standing in the midst of her supposed peers. If there was anyone in the world she could share all of her secrets with, she supposed they might laugh. Yet where before she would have shied away, now she could feel a crackle of heat in her chest at the thought. Not shame at her cowardice, but the dragon's territorial nature. If only she had known it was there all of this time, it would have been the perfect teacher to make her a noble. It believed that it was the most important person in any room.

The dragon shade had fallen mostly silent in the days since the attack on the city, barely an ember within her, reminding her of who she was and what she deserved. It was nothing to do with her birth, or the lineage that had bred her. She deserved praise and admiration because she was powerful enough to level this city. Just as the other dragons had been deserving.

It was not a pattern of thought she had ever entertained before—that if the worst did happen and all the nobles of Espher turned on her, she could beat them into submission. It came as something of a shock to her sensibilities to think that the whole world had been so easily turned upside down. Her atop the heap and all of the kings and queens cast down on the dirt. Or under it, if it came to that.

So it was that when she was called forward to receive her acclaim for her part in the defense of the city, she did not flinch or look away when the king met her eyes. She gave as polite a curtsy as she could muster, glanced across to Artemio where he stood at the right hand of the king and Harmony behind him, and then rose only once both of them and the man on the throne had subtly nodded.

"Your service has not been overlooked, Lady Aceta. Without your work, the royal person would have been brought to harm, and this palace would be in ruins. Not to mention the damage that would have been suffered by our loyal subjects." He seemed to be speaking more to the room at large than to her, as if she was only a piece of the scenery in whatever play the king was performing.

She would play her part. That was what this place was all about. "You are too kind, your Majesty."

"It is not kindness to call bravery what it is. Nor to recognize the sacrifices that you and my Shadebound have made so that Espher may prosper." He leaned in closer, as if he were conveying some secret to her at a volume that could be heard from the back of the room. "Sacrifices that I assure you shall be rewarded."

It set off a murmur among the stands of nobles. While nobody could deny she had done more than anyone to defend the city, that did not mean they wanted to see some jumped-up nobody given preference over them or their children. Still the king pressed on with his proclamation. "You shall take a place in our household as our own Shadebound Royal."

It was enough of a shock to knock the politeness and pride out of Orsina for a moment. "But... I thought..." She cast about, looking for some sense to cling to. "What about Artemio?"

Nobody in the court knew what Artemio had done to win the king's absolute favor. It was rumored that he had put an end to the assassins behind the deaths of so many nobles, but details beyond that point seemed impossible to acquire. How he had stopped them, how he had even discovered who was responsible, every juicy detail of the entire endeavor seemed to be known only to the Volpes and the Cerva themselves. Elsewhere, all they had was speculation and rumor. Even Orsina didn't know what had

1

happened. Only that she had to force Artemio's broken nose back into shape before it set crooked.

A sly smile appeared upon the king's face as he took her words as the next stepping-stone in his own plans. It could not have been smoother if they had rehearsed. "Duke Volpe shall be occupied with his duties as Lord Commander of our armies."

If Orsina's new favor had drawn mutters, this drew out an uproar from the court. Once more Orsina didn't know enough about the intricate workings of court to truly understand their anguish, but she got the impression Artemio had been handed something a good number of them felt they were entitled to. For her, it sounded like the most repugnant of tasks, leading men to war, but she supposed it must have come with a great deal of honor and clout.

Addressing the grumblers, the king spoke up louder, drowning them out as none dared to shout over him. "The time has come for the Volpe line to return from the shadows of obscurity. They have a long and noble history in Espher that I would not see end without good reason. The Duke Volpe has more than proven his loyalty to me in every way that counts."

With her piece said, Orsina tried to bow out, giving another curtsy and stepping back towards the massed courtiers where she might avoid any more attention, but the king fixed her with a stare, and then glanced to the empty space at his other side. A mirror position to where Artemio was standing. The left hand of the king. Trying to contain a shudder of dread, Orsina stepped forward and then turned to face the room.

Nose-to-nose with a dragon on the warpath, she had felt less hostility than she faced from these nobles. The ember in her soul coiled and flared. How dare they look down upon her when she could make them all ash? She was so caught up in stifling the dragon rising within her that she barely even noticed the meaningful stare Harmony sent her way. Nor the progress of the court's business from her fresh appointment to more serious matters. By the time she tuned back in, they were discussing the lost scouting party that had headed north.

Orsina did not recognize the speaker, though he looked vaguely familiar. Perhaps she knew one of his children from her classes. "…finest
men the army had to offer for this sort of work. Entirely unconscionable
that they might have been taken by surprise."

Artemio replied in a bored tone. Orsina didn't grasp it to begin with.
How they could be talking about people dying and he didn't even bat an
eyelid? Had she understood the nature of him so poorly. Was he just like
all of the rest of them? "Were they not, do you think the capital could
have been taken unawares?"

"My thoughts on this matter have always been clear," replied the noble
with a hint of anger in his voice. He had Orsina's full attention now, and
she realized with a start that this, too, was all part of some grand masquerade. While Artemio pretended to be calm, he played up his own, likely
non-existent, anger to prove a point. In a snap she recognized him. Duke
Cavalla. His son was in one of her classes. The boy who would someday
become a man like this had already perfected looking down his nose at
Orsina. It seemed he took after his father. "Treachery is the only way those
men could have been slain. And the culprit is one you know!"

"Sir, I do not care for your implication." Artemio raised an eyebrow
and allowed his hand to drift down to rest on his belt where a rapier hung.
It was not one Orsina recognized from all her times borrowing from him.
It was a clear message. "Nor for your doubt of my good judgment."

Cavalla huffed and turned his head to the side, to be sure all the back
rows could hear him. "And I do not care for our capital city to be set alight
by overgrown reptiles, yet here we are."

"Despite their quality, our men are mere men. How can they be expected
to outpace and outmaneuver dragons in flight?" It was strange to hear Artemio
speaking to this crowded room, working everything through as logically as
he could with the information available to him. It was just like all of their
private talks, not a performance and not something anybody could play off.
"True, the dragons were sighted southbound, but that is not to say their
route was direct. Quite possibly scouts and dragons never crossed paths."

Still this duke played up theatrically when he turned his head back and with a tone of accusation decried, "Then perhaps, Duke Volpe, you can explain why the second foray of scouts encountered only a sole survivor?"

It took Artemio by surprise. Enough that he didn't even attempt to dissemble. The truth of it must have been hidden from him. "There was a survivor?"

"Your pet serpent, Duke Volpe," Cavalla spat with obvious relish. "The one you assured us was of good intent. How could it be that he survived while all our best men perished if he were not a servant of the enemy?"

Orsina blurted, "Wait, are you speaking about Kagan?"

"I will not sully my tongue with that treacher's name. But you, too, spoke in his favor, did you not? Telling some tale of him as your personal huntsman?" The duke leapt on her words like a starving dog with a bone. "Are you in league with the Arazi too?"

The ember in her soul flared and her shadows doubled. "I am a dragon-slayer."

Power leaked from every inch of Orsina as she stared this jumped-up little nobody down. She could tell the dragon shade was influencing her, just from that last thought about someone who was clearly an important member of the court, but she let it. Kagan was not the playing piece in some noble's little game trying to one-up Artemio and assert his dominance. He was her oldest friend, and she would not let this happen. Not if she had to fight everyone here.

Before she could strike out at Cavalla and begin the chaos, the king piped up from the periphery. "Bring him forth, let him speak for himself."

Even Artemio looked concerned, and not for the first time, Orsina wondered whose side he was actually on. Still it was the other duke who said, "Your Majesty? The last time an Arazi spy came before you…"

"I had the Lady Aceta's protection and came to no harm. As I do now." The king's tone brooked no argument. As much leeway as he might be allowing all his subjects to argue among themselves in their hunt for the best answer to present to him, that did not mean he was willing to be second-guessed.

The murmurs in the court became an uproar once again as Cavalla waved to one of the guards and they slunk out of sight. Moments passed as the uproar grew. Throughout it all, the king sat and stared placidly ahead, as if such an awful noise was part of his usual day. Perhaps it was.

Artemio and Harmony were both staring at Orsina when she turned her gaze in their direction. Both had some measure of desperation in their eyes. Both were obviously trying to convey some message to her. Here she was, thrust into the heart of the Teatro, surrounded on all sides by people who would see her dead if they knew the truth of her, and her only allies seemed to want her to fall silent, to fade into the background and allow them to control everything. She would not, and she could not. There was no way she could trust that Artemio's calculations wouldn't make Kagan an acceptable loss. There was no way she was going to let that happen.

For all of the talk of Kagan walking away from the dragon's attack unscathed, he certainly looked the worse for wear to Orsina when the guards hauled him in. There were fresh scars all over him, he looked like he had lost a quarter of his bulk to starvation, and beneath the hoods of his scaled brow, his eyes had a distant look, as though he were haunted.

With a glance to Orsina, the king carefully enunciated the Arazi name. "Kagan, can you tell us what happened?"

His bass voice still rumbled, but Kagan's words came out slurred. As though he were exhausted beyond measure. Orsina tried to work out how long it would have taken him to travel to the northern border and back. "We made it to the steppes before anyone admitted we were hunting Arazi. By the time I felt them, it was too late. A rider killed the scouts and all the horses. They've got an advance camp in the Selvaggia. Cavalry meant to take your flank if you meet them head-on."

Cavalla piped up from his place on the sidelines. "And you simply escaped the attentions of this dragon who somehow found all of our best-trained men?"

"It isn't the dragons you need to worry about, it is the riders." Kagan struggled to get each word out, like he was fighting with himself, forcing himself to say it. "We can sense you. Feel what you feel. Most don't train that skill. Enough do."

Cavalla rolled his eyes in scorn before turning to Orsina. "Is this true?"

She didn't know. Kagan had never told her how any of his powers worked, because he'd been trying to forget he had them most of the time. The few times she'd seen him using his empathy, it had been in the tracking of an animal, and where his talents as a hunter ended and something supernatural began, she had no idea.

Artemio piped up to fill the silence. "Possibly. The only Arazi I know who has spoken of such a talent is the one before us now, but I have found no sources to corroborate it." Orsina had to bite down on the inside of her cheek to stop herself screaming at him. How could he betray Kagan like this? How could he betray her? But he went on talking, and the wrath died in her throat. "With that said, it seems to me that this man has just rushed back here despite grievous injury to impart what little his scouts managed to gather before their discovery. Perhaps he might be given a little trust?"

He didn't say it to the court, or to Cavalla. He said it directly to the king. He knew there was only one person he needed to sway.

"Your Majesty, this serpent-tongued liar will tell any tall tale to save his own hide. He betrayed our scouts and left them for dead while he walked free without a mark on him. He is our enemy, and he must be treated as such." Cavalla closed his case with a curt nod.

The king looked down at Kagan, glanced at the roiling room of enraged nobles baying for blood, and sighed. "Execution seems the only viable option."

For the first time since she had taken her place by the side of the throne, Orsina spoke clear and loud enough to cut through all the ruckus. "No."

She already knew the king would not tolerate such a direct contradiction. She'd known it, but the word had boiled right up her throat and spewed out all the same. At once the rabble fell silent, with smirks on more than a few faces. Those at the rear of the hall leaned in closer to hear how she was verbally eviscerated.

The king raised an eyebrow. "Lady Aceta, unless you can provide some more compelling evidence than your mere opinion…"

Her mind felt like it was rattling in her skull as she sifted through all that the Owl had imparted to her, hunting for precedent. Hunting for some logical reason that they could not kill him beyond her desperate need for them not to. She had little power in this court. Officially, a Shadebound had no real legislative power, only influence. Her role in the king's household was brand new. She may have won his favor, but his faith would require more. She had only a single bargaining chip. So she spent it. "You cannot slay Kagan, for it would deprive your Majesty of your newly appointed Shadebound Royal."

"You would resign in protest?" The other eyebrow crept up too. Genuine surprise colored the king's features, but he was unmoved. "A tragic loss. Yet still, the laws of this land must stand. This man stands accused of the highest treason, a member of the royal household abetting our enemy. An example must be made."

Duke Cavalla nodded in agreement. Even Artemio didn't seem to have anything to say that might change things. She had to think like Artemio. She had to provide precedent. Some legal reason that the execution should be stayed. She knew so little of the laws of the land, only having brushed against them in her absorbed knowledge of how to be Shadebound. But there had to be something. Time seemed to slow as she fumbled for words that could save his life. Then all at once she struck upon them.

"He is my impresario."

The court flew into uproar once more, men rising to their feet and bellowing like cattle in dismay. She had the precedent she needed. Mattia Cerva. She had to shout to be heard over all of the bellowing. "When the impresario of Mattia Cerva stood accused of murder, his execution was stayed, for it would bring about the unjust death of an innocent. I, too, am innocent. Would you see me dead?"

Cavalla was swift to step back into the open space before the throne, his voice dripping contempt. "Madam, you are not yet a graduate of

Septombra, and you claim…"

His words died in his throat as she stepped towards him and her shadows multiplied about her. The one that she cast naturally, then a second, a third, a fourth. Each one leaping vast and monstrous behind her as she approached. Flame coiled in one hand, water spiraled in the other, and all about her Rossi's tempest began to turn. Chill wind leapt out from her, setting all the lanterns about the place fluttering and guttering until it seemed the only light left in the Teatro was that which came from her.

The guards at Kagan's arms let him go, and he swayed on his feet as she came down to meet him. The fire leapt out to swirl in a great spiral about him, the water turning to razor shards of ice in the tempest and flowing about him in the space between the blue flames. None would touch him so long as she lived.

She turned to face the king with that swirling pillar at her back, a display of such raw power that even the screeching apes in the stands had fallen silent. She didn't spare Cavalla even a glance. As Artemio had already worked out, he did not matter. Then with a confidence she did not know she possessed, Orsina said, "I am Shadebound, and he is mine."

Later, when all the dust had settled, she would realize it was her little tantrum, throwing around her power, that had convinced the king she was in fact Shadebound and not a pretender. Such an impressive display of power went beyond what the average noble in the street might have thought any Shadebound was capable of, let alone a mere student. The fact she would maintain such a display, at such a cost to her life, if she did not have a secondary source to draw upon, would have been unfathomable to the average noble, who had not the courage to part with even a single minute of their own.

The king met her eyes and finally gave an impassive nod. All of her power fell away in an instant, ice and flame slamming together as the storm departed and annihilating each other in a wash of steam that flowed up to the ceiling and out of sight as though she had meant for it to happen. In the midst of it all, Kagan did an impressive job of keeping his face calm.

"We cannot deprive one of our Shadebound of their power as they march off to war, but we must deprive your... Kagan of his freedom until such time as the fighting is done. Then we might revisit this matter with more knowledge of the circumstance."

Orsina gave up on her attempts to curtsy and instead fell to her knee before the king. "Thank you, your Majesty."

With a wry smile, the king turned his attention back to the rest of the room. "Now perhaps if the theatrics are done, we might take a brief recess before Duke Volpe lays out our plans for the coming invasion."

There was a great deal of laughter from the court. They all felt better hearing the king making a joke of the display they had just seen. They could all breathe a little easier knowing the Shadebound were leashed.

Orsina didn't give them even a moment of her attention, not with Kagan there. She made for him, only to find Artemio by her side. "I must debrief our scout, to see what other enemy movements we must account for." He snapped his fingers at the guards, and they scuttled back in to seize Kagan's arms once more.

A room was made available to them just a short distance from the Teatro itself, a bleak little stone cell with no windows that nonetheless had furnishings worth more than all of Sheepshank. She hated this palace.

The moment the door snapped shut behind them she ran to the hulking lizard-man and flung her arms around him. "Kagan, you're alive! I was so worried when they said..."

"Nothing a few years' rest won't fix," he said with a little grumble, pushing her away to arm's length and looking her up and down. "But what about you? How did you do all that? And what's this impresario nonsense?"

Artemio stepped away from the door with a tut. "I had a sneaking suspicion there was some subterfuge at play there. Given that you have not even had instruction on how to form such a bond."

Harmony burst through the door, dress hoisted up almost to her waist so she could run. She rushed over and slammed into Orsina with as much force as she'd inflicted on Kagan. The difference was that he was huge, and despite her latest growth spurt, Orsina firmly was not. Harmony gushed, "What were you thinking?! You could have brought the whole palace down on you."

Kagan reached out and separated them as best he could, plucking Harmony up by the back of her dress so he could edge Orsina from beneath her. "Who's this one?"

"My sister." Artemio stepped in and pulled her away. "So it would be best if you were to mind whatever manners you can muster about her."

Kagan turned back to Orsina with another groan. "Did you send him down to the dungeons to bother me?"

"I didn't even know you were in the dungeons when Artemio made his visit. I didn't even know he'd visited until I saw you in court... I..." She was at a loss for words. "So much has happened since we last spoke."

"Any of it good?"

Despite herself, Orsina found herself laughing. Really laughing without any worry for how she'd look or who it would offend. Tears ran down her cheeks.

Artemio spoiled the moment. "As touching a reunion as this is, I feel obliged to mention that an impresario bond is immediately apparent to trained Shadebound, and at least one of the gentlemen out in the Teatro will currently be calling on one to come and examine you and confirm the colossal lie that you just told the king."

At once, all good humor left Kagan. "Can we fight our way out?"

"I think you're under the misapprehension that I would help you to escape at the cost of my own freedom. I will not endanger my life, sister, or station for you, Arazi." Artemio looked him up and down. "Not when I've already seen how far you can be trusted and I've repaid whatever paltry debt of gratitude I owed you."

Kagan shrugged and took hold of Orsina's hand, leading her towards the door. "Fine, we don't need you."

Artemio called at their back, "Actually, I think you'll find me to be entirely vital to your ongoing survival. Given that I'm the only person in this room who knows how to form the impresario bond."

"It isn't going to work." Kagan stopped in his tracks. "I'm Arazi. I'm already bonded."

Artemio shrugged his shoulders. "I'll readily admit it is quite possible this solution is going to fail as a result of that. Then both you and Orsina will be executed, if she happens to survive that long."

Kagan's eyes narrowed as he stared the man down, sifting through his words for the threat. "Why wouldn't she?"

"Look at her," Artemio said, and with an almost painful slowness, Kagan did. "Look at how much of her life she spent with that little light show. Between this and all of her other great exertions, it is a wonder her hair isn't white."

Orsina could not see herself. She could not even see herself reflected in the dullness of Kagan's reptilian eyes. But she could read his expression well enough. He stopped in place as he recognized the changes that time had wrought on her so swiftly.

"She either bonds with you now or she'll die." With a meaningful glance to the door Artemio added, "Both of you will."

Kagan turned from the only avenue of escape and stared Artemio down. Orsina still dangling from his hand like a forgotten toy. "What does it mean? A bond between two people."

"Your spirits will be connected across any distance. You will share your life with her." He looked meaningfully at Orsina as he added, "It is not a decision to make lightly."

Orsina looked up at Kagan, looming over everyone, and a soft smile spread its way across her face. "I wouldn't want anyone else."

He looked down at her and groaned. "This isn't going to work. I am Arazi."

Harmony nudged him. "Try."

Orsina turned to Artemio, all her confidence fleeing her at this last moment. "How do I do this?"

"Watch me."

He turned to face Harmony, and before he could even ask, she had her hand held up. "I have been waiting and preparing my whole life for this moment. Do not dare spoil it by implying I might turn you down."

Artemio smiled back at her and didn't say a word, instead reaching out to take her by the hand, as though this were the opening of a dance.

With her Shadebound senses, it was simple enough for Orsina to see what happened next. His soul opened wide, and all the shades anchored within reached out and took hold of Harmony, dragging on her spirit, coaxing it out of her and into that open space. The joined hands between them were the conduit. It was like he was trying to drink her down, the way that shades fed on humans.

Just when it seemed her soul would be torn from her, some equilibrium was reached. With a shudder, the shades departed, Artemio closed, and between them both, a thread still hung. At a distance, Orsina might not have even noticed it, but having seen it made, she could recognize that umbilical connection now.

Kagan had missed it all, of course. Whatever his senses were, they differed enough that the workings of shades remained invisible to him. Still, he cocked his head when the work was done. "Why does he smell like her now?"

Orsina grinned. "Because she steals his soap?"

Both the Volpes smiled at that, not quite a laugh, but enough for Orsina to know she had not intruded too badly upon such a private moment.

Artemio met his sister's eyes. "Together."

"Forever."

Kagan didn't even spare them a glance. "Ready to get this farce over with so we can go die?"

Orsina tried again to lighten the mood. "Optimistic of you to think this isn't going to kill us outright."

"Just…" Kagan closed his eyes and held out his hand. "Do it."

Orsina opened herself. It was not easy, after so long holding everything out. It was not easy, to feel each of the shades rooted inside her reaching out to Kagan with hunger. They longed for the life within him, they wanted to rip it from him, leave him dead and empty. They hungered.

She let them reach. She could see him stiffen as the shades touched him. When he felt the chill of pond water pooling around his face, the whirling wrath of Rossi's blades passing an inch from his skin, they repulsed him.

He reflexively drew back, and a wave of heat rolled out from somewhere deep within his chest, pushing them back and protecting him from their malign influence. It answered their hunger with a territorial fury that was almost immediately answered by the dragon within Orsina. The fire leapt out from her, surrounding both of them in an instant. Kagan could see it, he could feel the heat, but neither one of them broke their hold.

Not until they had seen this through.

With a dragon woken within both of them, the two echoes of monstrous beasts leapt out and clashed. Kagan's eyes widened as he felt her dragon's breath wash invisibly over him. She wondered if he could smell the sulfurous reek of venom on the air, feel the presence of the great wings beating around them, or if all he knew of the great struggle going on above them was the pain of the fire prying at the edges of his awareness.

With a thunderous impact, both echoes of the dragons fell upon them, still scratching, clawing, and biting all the way, each one striving for dominance, each one ripping and tearing at flesh that was not there, burning with flames that were not there, clashing, parting, and clashing again. Orsina did not know how such a battle would end, if the living or dead dragon would prove the greater, and she had no intention of finding out. With a flex of her will, she drew all of her shades back inside.

To her surprise, they all came willingly, Rossi and Ginny dragging back handfuls of Kagan's soul with them, and the dragon hauling back to her with something else entirely in its grasp. It was strange to think she had mastery of them, even now. That she could command them and her hold on them was sufficient to overrule whatever decisions they sought to make for themselves. Even now she could not make herself believe what old Mother Vinegar had told her of shades—that they were mere reflections of a thing that once was, no more capable of thought or decision than your own image in a still forest pool. Still they came, and that thin thread of life connecting her and Kagan was made, interwoven with a second thread that was so tightly bound to her new impresario's that if she had not known it was there it would have been invisible.

Kagan toppled to his knees when the deed was done, gasping for air, pawing at himself to put out fires that had only burned on his soul. "What... what was that?"

Orsina didn't know how to explain it, so she just didn't. Instead turning to Artemio and Harmony where the pair of them were basking in their new shared connection. The grey in his hair was reddening once more. The wrinkles that had begun to set in about his eyes seemed to fade. His finger did not magically sprout back into place, nor did the full weight of the extra years he had struck himself with instantly depart, but he looked better than he had in all the time Orsina had known him. His smile, when he turned to her, was almost boyish.

"And now we are ready for war."

BENEATH THE WORLD

Caldo, Regola Dei Cerva 112

Exhaustion weighed down on Artemio. Even with Harmony's life flowing steadily into him, it was not enough to overcome the sheer weight of his burden. Through the day, he had led a dozen meetings with the various noblemen who were fielding armies for the crown. Every one of them intent on hoarding whatever glory they could muster while spending the least amount of coin, as if all of them were not playing the same game. It was as though they were children with no grasp of the real consequences of failure.

If the morning's complex political juggling to have Kagan confined to an Anatra guesthouse rather than a dungeon had not been enough, Artemio had then spent hours upon hours explaining stratagems and tactics to men whose best idea of either was to charge at an enemy full-pelt and trust in luck to carry them through.

The fact that the Arazi had barely tested Espher's defenses and still managed to level a fair portion of Covotana seemed to be escaping these people. They could have come in force and burned the city down to ashes, but there was something of the raider still in the Arazi heart, even if their warring tribes were unified under a single banner. They did not destroy what they did not need to. Not when it would soon become theirs. In a strange way, the barren lands where they came from had made them more civilized than the plentiful cornucopia of Espher, whose leaders would gladly salt the earth after an enemy was dead, safe in the knowledge that they had the riches of an ancient kingdom to return home to.

A full day of banging his head against a wall with nobles who until a week before wouldn't have even met his eye, all with the persistent dread still nipping at the back of his mind. His secret that he had no intention of sharing.

Complete honesty was a truly excellent mask for deception, so that was what he brought to the twin kings in their solarium the morning after he had murdered his own father. He told them it was a peasant uprising, directed and driven on to new heights of disregard for the natural order by the influence of Duke Cleto Volpe. He had found and searched his father's home in the city, the one not even Mother had known existed, tucked as it was betwixt a brothel and an alehouse down by the riverside. There he had retrieved the costuming the Last King had been garbed in, along with the accumulated paperwork gathered there. None of it had any bearing upon the insurrection. It was simply the work of running a duchy that he had brought with him from home to occupy his free time when he was not directing assassinations or planning the downfall of Espher.

It was small wonder the old man had been so enraged by their visit to him on the Cut, having been forced to snag the fastest horse from the livery stables at the south gate of the capital and race them there so he could arrive in enough time to present himself as a constant presence in the south.

He could have been in Covotana the whole time Artemio was studying. But for the time it took him to murder his own wife, there was little he would actually have been required to attend to in the south. The discipline he had instilled in his staff and underlings had seen to that. Artemio supposed he would have to deal with them at some point. Replace those he felt were terminally disloyal and just hope the rest hadn't been left with instructions to knife him in his sleep.

As for the servants here, Artemio had been keeping a watchful eye on them, but he supposed if his father had not left specific instructions

DAVID ESTES & GD PENMAN

to make another attempt upon his life should the Last King not return, then he was safe until somebody else within the rabble rose up to take on that mantle.

That could not be allowed to happen.

The Cerva twins had been intent on slaughter when they first learned of how the crimes were being committed. That the head had been cut from the serpent meant nothing to them. They meant to round up every peasant who had dared to spill noble blood and flog them to death in a public square. Failing that, a decimation of the commons might have had the same effect upon rebellious morale. Artemio had been the one to talk them down from such violence.

Morality had no part in it. If the kings admitted to the world that they were not even capable of governing serfs without their lessers biting the hand that fed them, they would become the laughingstock of the world. All the noble houses would think of them as weak. It would be a danger to the throne. Still, they could not tolerate the risk of the matter returning to haunt them if they simply left the murderous peasants to their own devices. What luck, then, that Artemio was already there, offering to handle the matter for them in a silent but efficient manner.

Without the Last King to rally around, the peasants were as likely to disperse as to raise one of their own, but the chaos that could be wrought if they did place a peasant in charge of such a secret army would have been insurmountable. For all that they were wicked, Cleto Volpe at least had goals he was driving his assassins towards. Whoever replaced him would be an unknown. Their plans, unknown. It was intolerable.

It had been simple enough to make himself a part of the escort guiding Kagan to the Anatra estate. Artemio had endeavored to stay well clear of it ever since the mess of a party he'd been forced to endure, but he had not forgotten the kindness that had been shown to him with the invite. It paid to play well with others when it came to politics, and while it may not have seemed like a great treat for them to be hosting a prisoner for him at their own expense, he was showing them the immense amount of trust he was placing in them. Given the breadth of their grounds within the city, it would also be an ideal place for the lizard-man to be hidden from sight when public sentiment during the clash to the north flared up.

For his part, Kagan had nothing to say to Artemio, and the two men were quite content to ignore each other as they were marched down the same gravel path, past the same hedgerows, flower beds, and concealed guards Artemio had noted the last time around. Artemio had no interest in any of them, he had more pressing matters to attend to.

While most nobles' eyes passed over servants like they were invisible, Artemio's attention had to be constantly drawn back to the Lady Anatra when she came out to greet him.

"My thanks to you, Lady Anatra. I'm afraid I have no estate within the city as of yet and as such am sorely lacking in quarters for guests and friends of friends."

"Well, Duke Volpe, you must know by now that any friend of a friend of yours, is a friend of ours. We shall treat your... associate with all the care and grace that befits his station."

They exchanged pleasantries while he searched faces, and finally when it seemed the entire exercise had been a waste of his scant time, he saw the one he was looking for.

"Do try not to pamper him too much, I shall want him to be fighting fit by the time I return from the front. While his Majesty may no longer have need of a huntsman, I believe his talents shall be of great benefit on my lands to the south. Once the legal matters have been resolved, of course."

The waiter from the night of the party was not averting his eyes as a servant should. He was staring directly at Artemio. With a small smile that was in some part genuine relief, Artemio gave him a nod.

Lady Anatra threw back her head and laughed as though anything Artemio had said was genuinely funny, then, as if to show how willing she was, she very deliberately strolled over to Kagan and laid a hand on his arm. "Have no fear, we shall make sure he gets plenty of food and exercise. You will not regret stabling this stallion here."

Kagan looked down at her, his implacable stare boring into her eyes. If he had hoped that she might flinch away, he was to be disappointed. It seemed she had no shame—or fear. It was amazing what a life of absolute privilege could grant.

Artemio saw them off with a smile, then walked directly to the waiter without any pause or pretense. The man's eyes widened, but he did not flinch or flee. Clear as day, Artemio declared, "Espher, eternal."

The servant's face cracked into a smile. "My lord, how might I serve you?"

In a far louder voice, Artemio called out to the guards still shadowing the Arazi. "Just going to fulfill my inquisitorial duties by finding out what vintage this boy served me on my last visit. Carry on without me."

He need not have bothered. It seemed that nobody in the entire estate had an interest in him. He put his arm around the butler's shoulders in faux joviality and led him away. "Matters have progressed beyond our expectations. My father has been forced to vanish for a time. News will soon spread of his demise. I shall be assuming the mantle to maintain the stability of the cause."

Emotions flickered over the butler's face on the periphery of Artemio's vision, but he endeavored not to react to any one of them. Showing even a hint of his own doubts would sink this ship before it was out of the dock. The butler asked, "You think our people will not notice?"

"The task can be accomplished," Artemio replied in his perfect impersonation of his father before slipping back into his own natural tone. "Besides, there are few enough who even knew his true identity among our ranks. It will just be for a time."

"If he truly feels this deception is necessary." Doubt. Already there was doubt on this man's face. He would need to be eliminated sooner rather than later. Any members of the revolution who had known who the Last King truly was would need to be excised if Artemio's plan was to work. But as it stood, this butler was the only source available of the vital intelligence that would allow Artemio to find them again.

"It should only be for a few days, but they will be pivotal days." He leaned in closer still to this servant until their faces were almost touching and then lowered his voice. "There is much afoot, and it will be vital to keep things quiet until such time as matters in the palace are more settled."

There was a significant nod from the commoner, but nothing more was forthcoming. Artemio wished he had more time to gain the man's trust, but the unfortunate truth was that the longer the two of them were in contact, the more likely it was that he'd slip up and blow his chances entirely. So he pressed on to practicality, doing his best to impersonate his father in methodology, if not voice. "When is our next meeting arranged?"

There was another sideways glance. This was something Artemio should have known. Still, he answered. "At midnight we gather at the waterworks."

"I shall attend." Artemio continued swiftly, trying to keep the focus off his own lack of knowledge. "And make my father's will known to all."

"As you wish." The answer was colder than Artemio would have liked, colder even than the greeting the butler had originally offered, but he judged they had not tipped over entirely into distrust yet.

He did what he could to get back into the man's good graces, but he feared that patting him on the back and saying, "Thank you, my friend," was too much. Perhaps it was, perhaps it wasn't, but the servant definitely seemed mollified. At least for now.

It was the last official duty of his day, though the Prima of Septombra had requested a conversation at some point, and it would be remiss of him to keep the woman who was responsible for his meteoric rise waiting.

By the time it was over, the sun was long down, his stomach was full, and Artemio found that he could not recall a single moment of it. They must have spoken of politics and her kindness, of Orsina and Harmony, and of the things she wanted from him. They must have, but his mind seemed to have absolved itself of any responsibility.

His exhaustion ran deep by the time he had reached the waiting carriage and changed from the subdued finery he had worn to court into his ragged robes. The fit was not perfect, but from a distance, it would be indistinguishable from when his father had worn it.

As it turned out, there was little difference between court and the cult of personality his father had built for himself. Doors were opened for him. The vast copper pipes of the waterworks seemed to part like curtains ahead of his footsteps as he was guided through by a crowd of cowled figures. He didn't even need to speak, not with a crown placed upon his head. The man beneath mattered nothing.

The space within the city waterworks was less impressive than the vast cavern the peasants had claimed down in the depths of the city, but it accomplished something different. It packed all of the members of this conspiracy together so densely that the heat rising from their bodies was enough to be felt, even here surrounded by the flowing chill water of the many aqueducts, fountains, and channels throughout the city. The sheer physical mass of people inside the building was enough to trip some panic reflex in the back of Artemio's mind.

He had no Harmony to save him now. She was sleeping peacefully in her chambers in the palace if his tenuous understanding of their empathic connection could be trusted. If knowledge of his actions became public, she might at least have the shield of ignorance to protect her.

It was the shot of adrenaline that he needed to bring everything back into focus. He was entirely surrounded by enemies and planning on using a childhood parlor trick to maintain control over a murderous cadre of insurgents. All of the haze that his long day's work had brought dropped away, and everything came into sharp contrast. He could hear every breath, every gurgle from the pipes about him, the creak of the boards beneath his feet as he mounted a makeshift stage and turned to face his father's slavish followers.

It took only a breath before he was ready to begin. "Blood shall be spilled."

There was an approving ripple throughout the crowd. Whatever else they might have been, they were still peasants, and there was nothing the ignorant loved more than violence.

"War has come to Espher, and soon all the parasites shall be burned from her hide."

A cheer went up at that. This kind of rhetoric was almost laughably simple. Hated people will get hurt. Prizes will be earned. There was barely any art to it at all. He was almost ashamed of his father for constructing such a dogma.

"This is not our war, but one that we can use to free Espher all the same." There was a lull in the crowd as they navigated a slightly more complicated thought, perhaps for the first time in their day. "For millennia, it has been the common man who suffered when war was waged. Our villages burned, our bodies cast into the grinder of battle. This time, the necromancers go out to fight."

Again his words met silence as they were chewed over. "I propose that we let them."

Murmurs began to spread, but Artemio did not give them a chance to gain any momentum. "Let the necromancers bleed for Espher. Let the parasites fight to defend her, and when they are spent and weak, it will be ours for the taking."

That got the cheer he was looking for and bought him the space he needed to maneuver. With both arms raised in a vague parody of the way his father had swept his about during his speech-making, Artemio pressed on. "When the time comes for us to rise up, I shall return to you. But until then, live your lives in whatever peace you can find."

It seemed to be enough. The crowd dissolved into separate conversations, and the cowled figures by the foot of the stage shuffled him through into a whole new set of meetings. The cell leaders who organized the killings were the easiest. All he had to tell them was to stand down until the battle with the Arazi was done. The spies reporting back to him were more difficult. He did not know what his father had asked them to learn, nor how to direct them. He took in all of the information they provided and filed it away, but he had no clue which way his father would have directed them next. So he plucked at the few loose threads that were left to him, satisfying his own curiosity as much as anything else.

"I want all the movements of the Sabbia over the past year, any contact with the eldest son in particular." Perhaps his father had killed the Sabbia boy to protect his heir, perhaps it had been mere coincidence, but Artemio sincerely doubted the boy attacking him so foolishly at a party had come up with the plan to assassinate him in a vacuum. He issued similar orders to investigate Rosina Aquila's family and identify how the marriage-match was made for their now dead daughter.

He wet his lips in the shadow of his cowl. "The queen passed knowledge of our movements to the inquisitor. I want to know where her information came from."

The various servants from the palace were dispatched back to their roles. The rat-maid among them. It had been difficult to express no surprise at the sight of her, but just like all the rest, she would serve his purposes now.

In the early hours of the morning, he staggered back out into the street, a second and then third wave of exhaustion overrunning him. The army marched north at dawn, and Artemio would scarcely have time to dress himself in more fitting garments before he had to be in the saddle at their head. Perhaps he could sleep in the saddle. He had heard tell of seasoned campaigners who could.

What a shame, then, that he was not so seasoned.

34

WAR DRUMS

Caldo, Regola Dei Cerva 112

Orsina and the other women rode separate from the common soldiery, but not far from the male Shadebound. They were in a curious position within the army, making a separate camp within the camp that they were actively discouraged from leaving. As though every soldier had never seen a woman before in their life and were liable to turn feral at the first sniff of perfume.

These were not students from the House of Seven Shadows like Orsina was accustomed to. They were full-grown, adult Shadebound with the full weight of years of experience upon their shoulders, impresarios to draw upon, and the backing of noble houses. Here, more than ever, Orsina was set apart. But it took only a half hour of sitting awkwardly by the night's campfire before she realized they did not look upon her as an outsider, but a superior.

The dragon within her delighted at this thought—that these powerful women, perhaps the most powerful women in all of Espher, feared her and sought to please and placate her. There were servants to set up the tents and the like, but every one of the Shadebound women seemed intent on doing something to try to ease Orsina's time in camp. Offering her cushions, bringing her water. One even fetched dinner for her, venturing out to the main Shadebound camp where the fire was for more than light and warmth.

It was almost comedic, the way they all preened to give her creature comforts when she had been sleeping in the dirt less than a year before, traveling these very same roads in reverse.

At first Orsina was bemused, thanking them politely, then horrified to realize they were trying to curry her favor. Luck and circumstance had put her in so enviable a position that these matriarchs were competing for her interest. She wondered how much of her appointment to her new position was due to the fact that she had no ties to any of these people. No existing loyalties that had to be navigated, nobody with sway over her.

In truth, she had no time for the concerns of politicking. Her thoughts were elsewhere.

She was exactly where she had never wanted to be, marching off to war at the behest of the king. Facing dragons and men and forced to kill if she wanted to survive. She let more and more of Rossi and the dragon shade into her mind to calm it. Letting their thoughts overwrite her own so she could feel anything other than sick and trepidatious.

Both of those shades hungered for conflict, and while Rossi would far rather have turned her power on the nobles around her, it was not difficult for him to transpose his wrath onto the dragon-lords. Just more nobles, setting themselves above all others, their feet literally never touching the ground where commoners had to walk. As for the dragon, this land belonged to it, and others meant to take it. The most basic of its instincts cried out for her to establish her dominance.

Atop that mountain of mixed feelings were the words Kagan had managed to bark out before being hauled away from her.

"The Selvaggia's burned. Sheepshank is gone."

She couldn't imagine a world that didn't have Mother Vinegar in it, lurking somewhere in the wings, out of sight. Her village, her parents, she had mostly made peace with never seeing any of them again. She could cry for them as and when she found the time, but the Aceta Madre was a pillar of the world. The thought she might be gone felt profoundly wrong. As though the sun had blinked out of the sky.

Dawn came after a fitful night of sleep, and then the march began anew. All around her were women sitting comfortably in the side-saddle, chattering among themselves, one even working on a cross-stitch as they went. The pace was not leisurely, but neither was it any strain to the horses. The day whiled away as they passed over days of hard travel on foot in hours. As far as the horizon, in both directions, Orsina could see soldiers of Espher marching. She had not known so many fighting men existed in the world, let alone this kingdom.

The commoners were held at a distance from her, with most of those at the head of the train surpassing her in station. As though they meant to be the first to face the enemy. The head of this great serpent, with its tail stretching all the way back to Covotana.

It was nightfall when the Arazi struck. The full body of the enemy army was still well beyond sight, as was any land that felt even a little familiar to Orsina. They soared in with the setting sun at their back, blinding Espher's scouts to their approach, and they strafed the train.

Only a single dragon was being risked. Perhaps a scout taking his chances, perhaps just a slap at their defenses to put Espher off balance. The rider made the mistake of striking at the head of the column, trying to take their command before they could reach the battlefield. The Shadebound were at the front.

As the dragon spewed forth flame, it was slammed with a dozen different projectiles, bolts of lightning, flame, ice, air, massive rocks torn from the roadside, jagged bone shards ripped from unfortunate pack animals, even the dragon's burning venom itself was caught and turned back against it. Later she would learn two nobles were injured in the attack, but not badly.

The heat washed over Orsina where she trotted alongside the line, but that was all.

The main consequence of the assault was the end of the segregation. Shadebound were stationed along the length of the train to defend against any more attempted ambushes. Orsina found herself cast to the very rear of the train, apparently by Artemio's direct command, so while the army marched on, she trotted awkwardly against the flow along the embankment of the road.

She watched as nobles gave way to cavaliers, as cavaliers gave way to men at arms, and then on past the enlisted peasantry where she belonged before finally reaching the servants and miscellaneous other hangers-on that followed any army on the march. They didn't look up at her on her horse with respect and a desire to please. They looked up at her with unabashed terror.

It had been so long since she'd been among her own people that they couldn't recognize her anymore, and worse, she found she could not see any of her in them. They were cowed, obedient, and afraid of everyone and everything. She had barely taken a step out of their position, and she already couldn't imagine living like that.

That night, a tent was set up at the rear of the train for her to sleep in. She was left entirely alone without a single distraction, and her fears grew and grew in that dark silence, until she was beckoning all her shades inside her head to share the burden.

Looking out over the peasantry with both dragon and Rossi in her head was a fascinating exercise in contrasts. The dragon looked upon them as fodder, worthy of nothing more than a swift death, while Rossi saw in each and every one of them a nobility of spirit greater than anything the noblemen of Espher had ever possessed. They had been beaten down and broken over generations, and she had the power in her hands to protect them and make things right. Neither shade was right and neither shade was wrong, and Orsina felt nothing by the time the two were done.

Another day on the road with Orsina trailing at the rear brought them in sight of the distant steppes. The Selvaggia was nowhere to be seen, nor Sheepshank, nor any of the other northern villages that Orsina had seen once or twice in her life in passing. It was as though the land beneath their feet was the same but all that lay upon it had changed.

The army began to spread as the road gave way to dirt tracks and scrubby grass. Breaking out from marching formation and being bellowed and whipped into units, then into formations. The Shadebound were not bound to formation fighting, rather they were scattered like skirmishers between the blocks of troops. Not spread out to protect the flanks like the light cavalry the cavaliers fielded, but to give them the maximum of mobility and flexibility on the battlefield. Each one was the easy match of a fielded unit in any other army. While any other lord had to field an army for the crown, Shadebound had only themselves to support. Luckily for Orsina, as she had no army to raise.

Still she found herself to the rear of the army, even as it transformed from a mass of individual bodies, all with their own fears and plans, to a single grand machine of war. She got to see it unfold and the crowd part along their designated lines, revealing what lay ahead.

The earth was scorched. The distant steppes were buried beneath leathery mounds, each one puffing out smoke. Orsina thought for one awful moment that she was looking upon the eggs of the dragons, and that they had laid a bumper crop, but then her eyes adjusted for the distance and she realized they were the stretched-hide tents of the Arazi.

Between the distant steppes and the armies of Espher were no dragons. Orsina had expected a legion of them, lined up from horizon to horizon, but there was nothing. On foot, in opposition to Espher's own pedestrian forces, there were Arazi who looked like nothing more than men in strange garb. Though here and there Orsina caught flashes of brightly colored feathers among their leather armor. Dotted in among the disorganized mass of bodies, muzzled crocorax waited to be unleashed on the prey on the far side of the battlefield.

At the flanks of this vast army swarmed the wyvern cavalry Kagan had warned them of. The forest where they were meant to have been hidden was gone, and now they were openly displayed, their numbers only concealed by the constant shifting of positions as they flocked, keeping the same distance from one another while endlessly moving. It was almost hypnotic. Drawing the eyes in from the place where nature would have dictated they turn.

On the outermost edges of the Arazi army, penning in even the cavalry, were the closest things that most of the Espheran army had ever seen to true dragons. Ironically, they were the only thing in the field Orsina had never encountered before, though they were meant to be more common than any of these other dragon-beasts combined. Thunder lizards. Each one towered as tall as a true dragon, but while they were built for flight, these were creatures of solidity. Hulking, coated in thick armored plates and scales, every one an immovable object in the path of any flanking attack.

She hoisted herself as high as she could in her stirrups, searching the skies and distant steppes for the dragons she knew had to be there, but there was no sign. Orsina felt almost giddy at the possibility they were missing. If they were off scouting somewhere, or they'd already spent their strength, then this whole battle might have become a slaughter. She'd seen enough of terror-birds and their kin to know the dangers of facing them, but with Espher's marching legion of Shadebound, they would be a paltry threat.

That was when she heard it.

At first she took it for the steady tempo of war drums in the Arazi camp, calling them to battle, but gradually the beats bled into one another until there was a constant thundering sweeping over the field of battle. So loud that the bellowed commands of nobles and the lilting battle cries of the Arazi and their beasts all faded into the background. Orsina knew what it was. There was no question of what it was. There was nothing else in all the world that sounded like it.

From beyond the horizon, the dragons rose. Too many to be counted. Too many for her mind to even comprehend. Their numbers were bulked out with lesser creatures, wyverns and flying serpents, but the true dragons ruled the skies.

She felt the old fear. Chilling and bone-deep. How could any mortal stand up to such creatures? They were a natural disaster given flesh, and she was only human.

The sky filled up with them, until they were all she could see. Until her awareness of the coming battle narrowed to just the dragons. Her sight full of roiling scale. Her ears deafened by the beat of their wings. The scent of venom drifting in the breeze.

A hand on her arm tore her back to reality. Harmony was there. She should have been with Artemio, protecting him as he commanded the army, but here she was by Orsina's side. She stepped in close to be heard over the thundering of wings, but try as she might to yell over them, neither one of them could hear the other's words. Flushed with what Orsina took to be anger, Harmony darted in close again, and their lips touched.

Orsina was so startled that she didn't kiss her back. So surprised that even the dread that had dogged her steps all these past days was forgotten. Then, as quick as the kiss had come, it was gone, and Harmony was backing away, cheeks glowing a red to match her hair. Orsina reached after her without even meaning to, and she saw the girl's face go from mortified to delighted in a step.

Her last glimpse of the woman was of that joyous smile as she ran off back towards Artemio and command. Then the army moved, and Orsina had to move with it.

The basics of the plan had been explained to her only as far as was necessary for her to do her part. The purpose of the Shadebound was to screen the ground forces from attack by the dragons, and provide whatever other material support they could the rest of the time. While most had been given free rein to move about the battlefield as they saw fit, Orsina was too afraid to leave the soldiers in her care undefended against assault from above, so she kept in step with them.

As the thunder lizards began to move forward, so too did all of the Arazi army, all in lockstep despite the apparent chaos of their forces. They had no organized units, they were spread unevenly across the field. By all logic they should have presented a weak opponent. The beasts of war they brought to bear might have tipped the scales slightly in their favor, but not enough to counterbalance Espher's discipline.

Or at least, that was how it had been explained to her on paper. Now that she saw the Arazi on the march, the illusion of disorder was shattered.

They did not need units because they could feel what the other soldiers about them felt. The beasts of war were empathically bonded to their riders and handlers and moved with the same ease as the cavalry, every part of the army moving like it was a part of some greater whole, like each body was just one small part of a living thing.

You just had to look at them carefully screening their flanks with the thunder lizards to recognize not only were they organized, they were cautious.

Dragons and war beasts were an obvious threat to any enemy, but the Shadebound could be anyone, invisible among any unit. It was no wonder the Arazi were not willing to bound headlong into Artemio's waiting trap.

Orsina assumed there was a trap waiting. Artemio had not bothered to share any details of the plan with her personally. She had barely seen the man since he saved her and Kagan.

Beneath the thunder, Orsina could make out trumpets sounding now, and the cavalry on both sides broke into a charge, the thunder lizards on the Arazi wings angling in behind them to seal off any avenue for assault.

It was the sign the dragons had been waiting for. All of the flying army surged forward as the cavalry maneuvered to cut one another off. The empty space between the armies was narrowing, but not fast enough. Their front-runners had not met before the dragons overhead dipped into a dive and unleashed a wave of flame that swept across the battlefield.

There was no protecting the cavaliers. No Shadebound among their ranks ready to shield them, the fire hit and then they were gone. Even the bones melted away to nothing in the blinding flare.

A wall of light shone between the armies, then smoke rushed up to block all sight of the enemy. All of them except for the dragons, who came bursting through the barrier and swept back over the rest of Espher's armies as though they thought the battle would be won in a single sweep.

The Shadebound of Espher raised their hands as one. An elemental shade was a requirement of graduation, and while every one of the graduates seemed to bring a different element to bear, all of them did so with the same purpose. The air between the dragons and soldiers was filled with light. Flames pushed back against flames. Spirals of wind dispersed dragon's breath harmlessly. Orsina's own great barrier of water evaporated away as fast as she could create it, but the rising steam carried the dragon's venom up and away from her. Back towards the dragons that had unleashed it.

The noise and the impact was enough to set Orsina's horse bucking and wild beneath her. She struggled to settle it with calming words or a pat on the neck, but it would not be stilled. Even through the thunderous beating of wings she could hear it screaming in terror as it threw her off and took off down the break in the ranks between the units she was to guard. She hit the ground hard, breath knocked from her, but she had not time to chase the animal, nor to do much else but scramble to her feet.

As soon as the rear ranks of Espher's army had been unsuccessfully bathed in flame, the dragons had spiraled out, flapping frantically to gain altitude as they found no thermals to ride up. It compounded their first mistake, and the Shadebound were quick to capitalize on it. Again their elemental fury was unleashed, but where there had been shields and defenses raised, now they were on the offensive, firing everything they could up into the shadowy mass of dragons overhead, blotting out the sun.

Blood rained down, but no dragons fell. Even Orsina's bolt of blue-hot dragon's fire was not enough to deal a lethal blow at this distance. By the time the dragons were back to the front ranks, they had gained enough height that the Shadebound there did not even try to swipe at them.

Mistakes had been made on both sides, but Orsina could not believe how fast it had all happened. The cavalry were gone. A solid third of Espher's army, just gone, in a single stroke. The heat from above washed over her now, drawing prickles of sweat to her forehead and a gasp from her lungs.

All of this time she had been worrying about hurting other people, and now for the first time she truly grasped that she might be the one to die out here on the battlefield. Her terror of the dragons had been abstract, pain and trauma, but the reality that this was life and death only now hammered itself home. Her life. Her death. Not just other people that she'd fail to protect and feel guilty about, not abstract people living their normal lives. This could be it for her.

She'd have expected a thought like that to scare her, to strip her of her courage to go on or take risks, but instead it hardened her resolve in a way she had not thought possible. With her back to the wall, there were no more excuses to turn away the power that had been handed to her.

To live, they had to win this battle.

A wave of chill air swept out over the armies of Espher, driving the wall of smoke out into the bare, scorched patch of earth where the enemy cavalry now had free rein to charge on and flank the foot soldiers. The Shadebound used that moment of visibility to play their next card. On the outer flanks, Shadebound with mastery over the stone beneath had been stationed, and with great sacrifice and efforts they hauled up solid walls to guard the flanks.

A charge of the thunder lizards might bring those walls down, but they wouldn't arrive until the rest of the Arazi ground troops had crossed the distance. It penned Espher's army in, but it forced the enemy army to charge head-on, unless they meant to dawdle away the whole battle running the length of the raised walls to try to assault the rear guard.

Orsina took all of this in, saw the soldiers closest by her screaming to one another, hearing not a sound they were making over the thunderous wings, and she realized that they were going to die. All of them.

Shadebound had only so much life to use up before they expired. Dragons could go on breathing fire until the sun burned out. Orsina and her kind could perform miracles, but only for a brief time. Already she could feel age creeping up on her and more life being siphoned across from Kagan to take the place of the little she'd spent. It was a strange sensation, draining her old friend's life, but she had no real control over it now. The connection was made. She could not deliberately block it.

Still the enemy army marched on, and still the cavalry swirled between the opposing forces, harrying the front lines of Espher's army but making no real headway in the face of the raised pikes. Here and there, a bolt of fire or lightning would dart out from some Shadebound on the front to strike at a rider, but a moment after, the whole flock of wyvern cavalry would swoop in, and their spears would be flung. They were targeting the Shadebound. Hardly a surprise, all things considered. They were the only thing preventing the entire battle from being a few passes by the dragons above.

As if summoned by the thought, the dragons swept down again to strafe Espher's defenders. Crossing between the two raised walls on their flanks this time, breathing venom and flame from on high, meeting raised shields of elemental power, and diving down to rake the center ranks with their hind claws.

There was little to be said for Espheran courage. The people of this land had never been famed for their grit. Yet when the claws of a dragon swept down amidst the whirling sheets of flames the Shadebound held back, there was not a single soldier in reach who did not surge in to attack.

Before it could rise again, each dragon was struck a dozen times from a dozen different directions. Not one of them flew free again once the soldiery of Espher got their weapons upon it. There was no glory in that butchery, and even once the rider was hauled from the saddle and made dead, the dragon slain by proxy, the orgy of violence against the great beast went on. Yet for all that it was pointless, the sight of it brought the rest of the army a much-needed boost to their morale. These things could be killed.

Orsina needed no convincing of the mortality of dragons.

More of them came, even as their kin lay butchered, and once more they unleashed their fire. Orsina shielded along with all the rest, but it felt more and more futile with each pass of the great beasts overhead. They had to take the fight to the Arazi. They needed to end this fast while their power still lasted instead of letting the enemy wear them down. Why couldn't Artemio see that?

She cast a glance around to where she thought he was, hoping to glimpse either him or Harmony, but the distance was too great, and while the Espheran standard whipped in the beaten wind on the raised ground he had chosen to oversee the battle, she could not see him.

Within her, the dragon's shade roiled with wrath. Both it and Rossi wanted to be out there in the field, not stuck holding up a shield for soldiers. She did her best to remind them that if she abandoned her post, then all of these men might die, but she didn't even need to wait for their influence on her thoughts before she knew how they'd answer her. She'd had them in her head enough that the form of her own thoughts was starting to conform to theirs. She could just look at what shape they'd be and know. How many more would die if she did stay here? If she did as she was told instead of what she was capable of doing? Everyone in the army was going to die if the battle was not turned around, and she could not see anyone else attempting to turn it.

The first step away from her unit was the hardest she had ever taken, but by the next one the energy of a bounding dragon getting ready to take flight was flowing through her. Rossi drew the sickles from her belt. Ginny spilled water out from beneath her feet. Each pounding step throwing up mud, then a plume of water, then finally Orsina herself. Launching her up into the air as the dragons spun for another turn.

Eye-to-eye with this tiny human, she could have sworn she saw contempt in a dragon's golden stare. The fire within her burned brighter.

She spun as she rose, a tempest thrown up about her, carrying out a lash of flame with it that took on a razor sickle's edge as it sped out into the dragons arrayed before her.

The one that was closest, the one that had looked on her with disdain, took one burning blade to the face and was blinded.

To either side of it, her flames ripped through the thin skin of another dragon's wing and bisected a wyvern entirely.

Even as she began to fall, one of the nearest dragons put on a turn of speed to snatch her from the air with its jaws, and Orsina simply faded into the background, letting Rossi take control.

One kick off the obsidian teeth bought her height, a sickle bit into flesh and hauled her up the length of the beast's face. A heel came down in the dragon's eye before she tumbled end over end along the length of the serpentine neck.

Between the dragon's wings, a rider hefted a spear and launched it for her, but Rossi had the sickles up, intersecting with each other and the haft. The absorbed momentum should have knocked her back, but she spun and flipped to launch the spear right back to the one who'd cast it, sickles snapping apart to loose it at the last moment before she fell once more.

A harrying wyvern swept in at her as the dragon above her died to its bond with its rider. The sickle blade ripped through its wing, but as it flipped and began to fall, it was the ideal platform to launch herself from.

Another dragon, this one still intently spraying venom down below. The sickle bit into its neck between scales, sliding smoothly around the throat, spilling venom out in a wash, all over the people down below. The other sickle caught in a horny ridge along the rib cage, and she kicked off once more.

Each time she thought that she was about to fall, that she would have to assert control over her body once more, there would be another dragon or wyvern or rider. She bounded and bounced among them. Sickles and Rossi and her own aching body doing all of the work and costing her only days instead of the months the dragon or Ginny would have snatched. This was working. It was actually working.

The spear skimmed past her, knocking her off target. The tip of the sickle that was meant to root in the dragon's hide instead scraped across a thick scale, and she began to fall. Rossi didn't try to grab for the original target, twisting and kicking off its leg instead as they passed, getting out into open air where the enemy could be seen.

It didn't take tactical genius to realize that the dragon-lord swooping down after them was the one who had launched a spear her way. The dragon was colossal, even compared with the ones all about it, the rider garbed in armor made more of bone than the hide and fur of the others. A leader, even among these men.

Orsina gathered blue flame about the blades of her sickles and was about to unleash blazing death when the dragon suddenly tucked in its wings. If it had spread them wide, halted its dive, then it would have been a sitting duck, but now it plunged down towards her with impossible speed, and even if it died, it would take her down with it. Weight carrying it on to splatter her across the earth.

Panic flared as the dragon's wicked jaws parted and venom began to bubble up inside, but even as she fell, hopeless and helpless, luck was still on her side. As the venom flowed out, the velocity of the dragon's dive turned it back on the creature. Not a droplet of it reached Orsina's skin.

Her own flames were carried up by the same wind that had snatched the dragon's away. Sparks trailing from her sickles to set the falling dragon alight. As it fell and it burned, it screamed. Orsina had never heard a dragon scream before. She prayed she would never hear it again. Her teeth ached as the sound swept over her, and still they fell.

With a twist of her waist, Orsina could see the open land between the armies before her, and with sight of it, an inexorable draw. Not the drag of gravity hauling her down, but something deeper, biting into her spirit. There was a pool of water down in the midst of the blackened smear that was once the Selvaggia Forest. Incongruous in how little it had changed. With another twist and a tilt of her shoulders, she angled down towards it. Perhaps it would be deep enough to break her fall. Of course it would. The water was lovely, deep, and cool. Beckoning to her even from up here in the sky, practically reaching out to welcome her into its depths. There would be no more fighting beneath the water. No more struggle. Just the cool and the calm.

Ginny drew the water up out of the pool in a great wave to catch Orsina in her descent and to slap the burning cadaver of the dragon aside.

When girl and water met, there was not a single ripple. She slipped down into the depths in one long smooth motion, and then all was still.

THE BATTLE OF SELVAGGIA

Caldo, Regola Dei Cerva 112

Harmony saw Orsina's fall, like a dying star tumbling to earth. She saw the water leap up to catch her, and she had faith that she had survived. She was less certain the girl would survive the army charging for her now.

"Art, we've got to go now!"

He was amidst a swarm of shades, his own bound servants, and all those dead souls the Shadebound of the army had sent to him to receive orders. He barked out a dozen individual orders, eyes darting about the field, launching bolts of flame into the sky in what Harmony would have called a random direction, yet which seemed to strike home in a swooping dragon more often than not, stopping their strafing run before it had begun with a puff of pain and fire. She didn't even know if he could hear her in there, yet she bellowed all the same. "Art! We need to charge, the cavalry are flanking us. They mean to take the rear. They mean to take your command post."

His hands seemed to blur through the shadowed forms gathering about him. Harmony couldn't see them, but she could see the disturbance they made in the air. Feel the chill gathered about him and see the breath misting from his lips. "I can see all that, dear sister, but if we charge, they'll take the flanks all the same."

She turned back to the battle around her with open dismay on her face. "Why aren't any of the other Shadebound fighting like Orsina, why are they just standing there?"

Two bolts of flame leapt up from Artemio's hands, striking a diving Arazi rider from the saddle and scorching another's mount. "Because they mean to survive the day. She must have spent a year of her life bounding about amidst the clouds. Impresario or no, that is too much. The shock of the sudden aging will end her, if the Arazi don't."

Eyes turning back towards the distant front lines, Harmony's lips drew tight and determination shook her. "I'm not leaving her out there to die."

Artemio feigned a sigh, but she knew he understood her feelings. "Go then. I've an army to keep me safe. But do try to remember that you are breathing for two now. If you die, I die."

"Same to you." She flashed him a smile that he didn't see. "Don't let them surround you."

"Harm, I know how to wage a war!" He let out a petulant yelp. "Let me focus. You are distracting me from my duties. Will you just get out of here?"

For a moment, her heart felt like it was swelling. He really did know how she felt, and he was risking his own life in more ways than one, just for her. She really meant it when she replied, "Love you too, Art."

Her horse was from her father's stable, the result of prized bloodlines honed over generations, bred for battle as it was fought on Espher. While others might have bucked and startled, it was stalwart and shade-blind. So when she spurred it down the battle lines and towards the opening at the front ranks, it obeyed.

She tore down the lines of soldiers in formation, past the knights and the nobles and the commoners who'd do naught but take a blow for their betters before falling. She reached the front lines as the great flock of wyverns spun again to make another pass, and she leapt over the crouched defenders gasping for respite with their shields sunk into the churned, ashen earth.

Wyverns were predators at heart. They might have been gilt in armor and ridden by men, but the instinct was buried deep in them. When they saw the woman on horseback darting out from the enemy lines, they gave chase.

In an instant, the battle turned once more. Every wyvern on the field spun away from their commanded target, their minds linked through their riders, and both combined thinking parts of the cavalry were overrun with base desire. Chase. Hunt. Kill. Feed.

There were so many bodies in motion, at such speed, that Harmony could make no sense of what her eyes told her. It was as though the whole world was twisting about her, spiraling in to meet her. She ignored it, eyes fixed on the horizon, on the water that even now lashed and splashed about, turning the ruined ground to mud and the Arazi who crept close into broken heaps.

Orsina, she had to save her. Artemio had been right enough in what he'd said. She spent her life so recklessly. Like she didn't know that it was worth a thing. Perhaps she was drunk on the bond and the new power it brought her, perhaps she simply thought herself impervious to harm. It mattered not. She was human, and she would die if Harmony did not save her.

The wyvern swept in closer as Harmony rode, spears soaring overhead as the galloping beast beneath her strained and stretched and lather built along his sides. Like Orsina, his life would be spent all too swiftly if he was ridden this hard, but Harmony just couldn't bring herself to care. Not now.

All too soon, the water seemed to rear up ahead of her, all the pond and its myriad creatures and plants torn up to hang in the air above the emptied earth. Lash after lash of the water struck out. Killing riders, wyverns, and even one dragon as it soared out from the Espher lines to face this new foe. The terror-birds set loose by their keepers could not even be encouraged to approach after the first had been flung back to the Arazi lines by Orsina's first strike.

To any untrained eye, it would look as though her shades had consumed her. That they were devouring her life and rampaging. It had happened rarely enough in written history, but the echoes of the time before the

Shadebound had rules, structure, and education still reverberated in the minds of many. Before the founding of Espher, such things were a common sight. They were at the root of people's fears of shades. This chaos would doubtless be a nightmare for the Arazi who survived the day. A legend passed down to their children, to make them fear the necromancers of the south.

Yet despite all of that, Harmony knew Orsina was still in control. For even as great sickle blades of water lashed out and parted wyverns from riders and both from life, not a drop so much as touched the woman on horseback.

The horse took a spear through its side, the barbed head almost taking Harmony's leg as it punched between the ribs of the poor chestnut beast. All she could do was leap clear before the next pinned her to the ground too. She drew her sword, turning to face her pursuers, but they had such numbers on their side that she didn't even know where to begin. She had trained against the finest swordsmen money could rent, but never against the kin of dragons or those mad enough to ride them. She almost slipped in her horse's blood as she stepped back from them, courage wavering.

Then Orsina was beside her. Humming with unimaginable power. Hair risen up to stand on end, as though she were still submerged in the pool, though now she walked free of it. "Do not be afraid, I'm with you."

It was enough to draw a laugh out of Harmony despite it all. Here was the timid mouse of a peasant that had been dropped in her lap, now standing ready to face down dragons and monsters on her behalf. Like their roles had flipped.

She grinned, even as she tried not to watch the steam that rose from Orsina's back forming in the shape of great wings. "Who's afraid?"

The girl's face split into a wicked-looking grin, but it was not hers. Harmony didn't know which of the shades that rode her was using her face in that moment, but she knew it was not Orsina.

Sickles slipped from her belt as the Arazi came on, and Harmony shook herself from her stupor. Distraction would kill her, here on the field.

She could not look at Orsina as she strode forward.

Orsina was speaking as she moved into the coming wave of wyverns, and through all the noise, Harmony could not hear it until she chased after her.

"Hello. Nice to meet you. How are you?"

Harmony burst out laughing when she realized what was happening. Like they were back on the practice yard for the first time. All the tension she'd carried across the field melted away. She knew how to do this.

Orsina's blades spun around her, blades of wind, flame, and water leaping from her to strike foes down from afar. The ones that got in close enough to avoid her elemental fury were not spared. Her body moved as though it was a doll being puppeteered by something vast and unseen. Bending and twisting in ways Harmony had never seen her move. Doing things of which no human body should be capable.

From out of that blazing cyclone of violence some few Arazi emerged alive, but not unscathed. On these, Harmony pounced. An injured man could still stab you in the back. An injured wyvern could still rake you with its claws. She put them down before they had a chance to think. There was none of the glory that Orsina was due in Harmony's actions, but they would keep the two of them alive.

The enemy battle line was almost upon them now. Curving at either side as the flanks rushed forward to envelop their first foe in a pincer movement. Time was ticking out. When that line arrived, they would die. It did not matter—Orsina's mastery of her craft or Harmony's own skill with the blade—some numbers were simply insurmountable.

Orsina exploded out from the heap of fallen cavalry in a rising star of flame. Triumph on every line of her face.

Harmony tried to warn her. She tried to cry out as the shadow fell over them, but there was no time. One moment the sky was empty and blue above them. The next it was full of dragon.

Its claws raked at Orsina as it passed, and she was slapped out of the sky. She did not strike a pool of water or even the soft earth churned by their fighting. She struck stone. Some old ruin that Harmony had over-looked entirely in the midst of everything else. The blackened and broken remains of some ancient cottage.

The crack of her skull on the stone turned Harmony's stomach. And even as she ran for the girl, she knew she would not be there quick enough. Another thunderous clap of wings had launched the dragon up into the sky, and now it spun above, coming around to drown them all in fire.

She ran and she ran until her breath felt like flame in her lungs, but it still was not fast enough. The dragon swooped down, opened its jaws, and then spat forth its venom.

The acrid spray burst apart before it reached her. The poison became a mist, obscuring Orsina from sight. It stung at Harmony's eyes as she charged in, burned at her throat, but still she ran on. Everywhere she looked, more of the same cloying poison fog swirled out over the battlefield. Filling her vision and hiding the enemy from her.

She could not be lost so long as she went on running straight ahead, so that was what she did, even as the dragon above spat fire and tried to ignite all that was beneath it. Some fog burned away. Some caught alight, like swamp gas, blazing blue before it vanished. But the fire did not touch the earth. It did not touch Harmony.

Orsina was cradled in the arms of some old woman. Harmony could just barely see the humpbacked shape of her through the fog. Some peasant hag. What the hell was she doing out here?

As she closed the distance between them, the fog cleared, the optical illusion of the woman cradling Orsina faded away. It was a trick of shadows. A shade cast on the mist. Orsina was alone, bleeding, still.

Harmony slid to her knees beside her in the ruins and mulch. Tears born of misery as much as of the burning sting of venom streaking down her cheeks. "Orsina. Wake up. You need to wake up."

"Let the brat rest. She's been doing plenty." Orsina's lips moved, but the words were not hers. The voice was not hers.

Even as Harmony watched, the girl's wounds closed up. The blood spilled on the stones did not fade, but nothing fresh flowed forth, and when she wrapped her arms around Orsina, there was nothing to feel but for the odd clicking deep inside as her bones reset themselves.

Harmony felt a disturbance in the air more than she heard any coming footsteps. The fog seemed to dampen all sound. She could scarce believe her eyes when she turned and there was a dragon landed before her.

From off its back slid one of the Arazi. A man thrice her height and built like the strongmen she saw at touring fairs. He was nothing like the one Orsina had tamed. Or rather he was, but taken to its natural end. Thick ridges of bone and scale protruded from his once human flesh. He had the shape of a man but none of its softness. Even his eyes bore vertical slits when he looked upon her and barked, "Stand aside."

Half drunk on the poison fog and shaking with grief, Harmony staggered to her feet. She drew her sword and set her stance in a single motion.

"Never."

"You don't need to die this day." He reached back and drew a heavy axe from over his shoulder, spinning it in his hands and making a few practice cuts as he advanced. "I come only for the necromancer."

"Over my dead body."

"As you wish." He leapt.

There was no way for a fragile rapier to turn such a blow aside, but Harmony could dodge with the best of them. His axe-head bit into the earth, and from that wound, yet more of the same putrid fog flowed forth. Like the land itself had been poisoned.

She darted in through the rising cloud to return a counterstrike but the thick armor plates that grew all over the lizard-man turned her rapier's tip aside. His laugh rumbled into her bones.

"Try again."

The rising axe blade swept through the space where she'd stood just a breath before, trailing fog behind it. It came close enough for her to feel the wind brush by her cheek. Entirely too close.

Without even a hint of trepidation, the Arazi strode forward, axe weaving a casual figure of eight ahead of him, still less like an attack and more like he was warming his muscles. It kept Harmony on the back foot, edging towards where Orsina lay as inevitability plodded after. She tried for a few strikes of her own, but all it took was a lean of the shoulders to sweep the spinning axe into her path.

There would be no second chance here. If sword or wielder were struck by that axe, the fight was done. Her own strikes would need to be precise, not only avoiding his guard but striking at some soft tissue too. It was an unfavorable matchup.

She'd won unfavorable matchups before.

The casual spin of the axe stopped abruptly as the towering Arazi made a brutal horizontal cut. It was what she was waiting for, but it was also a moment of adrenaline-pumping terror. Nothing so large had any right to move so swiftly, bunched muscles uncoiling like a viper's strike.

Harmony did not waver. Ducking under the sweep, she plunged in, blade-tip leading the way, angling up to strike—not at the obvious center of mass, but flitting up the length of his torso to full extension. Driving at his throat.

There was no surprise on his face when he tucked his chin down, but there certainly was a moment of alarm when, instead of deflecting from the armored plates that he grew there, the rapier-tip grazed up, ripping through the soft scales beneath his eyes and jarring on his brow ridge.

He kept the eye by luck.

Still inside of his guard, Harmony was readying another strike when his horn-clad knee jerked up to knock her from her feet. She rolled with it, throwing her weight into the tumble so that when she did come back to her feet, she was out of reach of that damnable axe.

Her breath would not come. All the air had been driven from her by that jolt, and now her starved lungs refused to draw more after the blow. She tried not to panic, stumbling back another step or two, knowing panic would only make it harder for her to breathe again, but all the logic in the world could do nothing to calm the burning in her lungs.

The dragon-lord reached up to touch the bright red blood on his face, and he grinned. All of his sharpened teeth on show. "Well done."

When he leapt, Harmony was still gasping. She lifted her sword, for all the good it might do, but it was not her he came for. In the confusion of the fight, he'd turned Harmony. He was leaping for Orsina, where she lay still.

Harmony staggered forward. She could not stop the arc of the falling axe-head, but neither could she be still when her love was about to die.

The fog about Orsina already lay so thick as to make her barely visible, but now it seemed to redouble, to deepen and curdle, to become something palpable and solid. The Arazi plunged into it all the same, vanishing from sight, but there was no muffled sound of blade biting flesh. Still Harmony staggered on, breathless. Even as she saw the dragon-lord burst free from the far side of the fog with his blade still dry.

At last, he looked discomfited. There was no falter in his step as he sprang nimbly up onto the ruined rock, but his face was contorted in confusion and anger. "What?"

The bright red blood of the blood still flowing down his face began to blacken.

Harmony had no words for the horror that unfolded before her. Scales and flesh began to slough off the Arazi's bones. His dragon, until now content to sit back smugly and watch him wage war, let out a bellow of bone-shaking terror and charged to his side. Harmony had to leap out of its path or risk her own destruction.

Orsina was safe. There was no blood on the axe. She was safe, and this was her doing somehow. Harmony felt certain of it. Just the thought let breath back within her—and with it the foul reek of decay.

Both dragon and man now rotted before her eyes. Patterns of discoloration flooding over their scales and strange bile and venom dripping from every opening. If the dragon tried to breathe fire, it was choked by the sludge pooling in its throat. If the Arazi tried to heft his axe, then the snapping of the brittle bones within his arms did not let her see its motion. Both collapsed, both reached for the other in their final moments, and neither managed to close the distance before their corpulent bodies gave away.

For a moment on the battlefield, there was nothing but stillness and silence. Then Orsina strode out of the fog.

By all rights, she should have looked like an old woman by now. All her life spent in these great acts of magic, yet Harmony could not see a grey hair or a wrinkle anywhere. She looked as young now as she had when they first met, by Harmony's estimation.

"Orsina."

Blind white eyes turned to her. It was Orsina's face, but there was nothing of her in it.

"What be you doing in my poison dell, brat?" It was not her voice. Beneath it was the challenging rumble of a dragon's roar. The human sounds were like those of an old man. Even the words and manner of speech were not her own.

Still, Harmony would not flee. She closed the distance between them, even as the other girl stared her down. "Orsina, are you all right?"

This time it was a growl carried on the wind. Harmony felt the chill of it in her bones. The earth beneath them seemed to shake with every word. An old woman's voice now. No hint of Orsina. "Dragons don't die, girl." A wheezing, crackling voice, like dried out papers being rustled. "They grow forever afore they be slain."

Harmony was almost close enough to reach Orsina now. The air seemed to nip at her skin. Sparks and flames trailing from her hair as she drew too close. Poison reeked in the clouds that hung all about them. Everything felt wrong. "What are you trying to tell me?"

"She cannot drink the ocean dry." The old woman's voice warped as she spoke. The dragon's growl coming out. "She cannot stop the coming tide."

"If you've a brain in your head you'll run," the old man whispered through Orsina's lips. "Run. I'll hold her down if I can."

All the fog about them swirled, and Harmony had to scramble back or be enveloped. It was not just the fog that had sprung up from the earth or guarded Orsina as she lay, it was all of it. Every cloud on the battlefield drew in closer. All the world spiraling into this one point.

The limp body of Orsina rose. The milky white was blown away as the tempest spun through Orsina's eyes, chased by flame and dark water, chased at last by her own brown eyes, wide and afraid for just a moment. Harmony saw the moment Orsina realized she was not being carried away on the tide of shades, she was being buoyed up on it. Her voice came faint, but in the silence, the other woman heard her.

"Harmony."

She was back. She was in control. All the terror that had plagued Harmony through her wild rush across the world departed.

She spoke with a voice like legion. Every shade within her unified in their agreement.

"Harmony. Run."

For the first time since the dragon had come to ground, Harmony could see the battlefield again. Just as all the mist had drawn in, so now did all the battle. Every dragon in the sky seemed to be swooping down towards them. Every mounted Arazi rode hard for where they stood. Even the disciplined battle ranks of their foot soldiers had fallen apart in a mad rush across the battlefield, all scrambling to get to Orsina as she rose farther and farther from their reach.

Still Harmony would not move. She stood her ground, glowering out at all the armies of the dragon-lords with her rapier held in one quaking hand. She had come this far, she would not leave Orsina now. Not even the end of all things would tear them apart.

Or so she had thought. It seemed Orsina had different plans. The fog was nothing but water in the end, and Ginny Greenteeth had mastery of that. It swept down on Harmony, knocking her from her feet, setting her tumbling end over end, falling to the ground but never quite reaching it.

She was buoyed and bounced in the torrent of steam until she couldn't tell up from down, then as swift as it had started, it was done.

She fell in the churned mud. Tramping feet almost came down on her before she could scrabble upright. Her sword was lost somewhere out on the field. She went for her belt knife before she recognized the red crest of Lord Anatra on the shields facing her and sagged with relief.

It was short-lived.

Out there in the midst of it all, Orsina still fought. At this distance, Harmony could see it all. The dragons diving down at her, only to have their flames ripped from their mouths and lashed down at their kinfolk. Great blades of ice, water, and poison fog, reaping the harvest of souls as they rushed in to take her.

Never before had the world seen such slaughter. Every motion of Orsina's one-woman war was precise and calculated, every sickle of raging death that she unleashed enough to serve her purpose then dispersing to nothing.

Yet more and more came on. All the armies of the Arazi gathered at her feet, and all the dragons in the sky spun and swung about her. The tempests she threw out downed some, but not all, never all. In the end, numbers alone would win out, and while they were legion, she was one.

Harmony did not see the exact moment it happened. The dragon that ducked a strike to brush by Orsina and knock her off her balance, the thrown spear that grazed her. Whatever made it through, it broke her concentration—and all of the immense forces she'd held at bay were unleashed.

Harmony fell. All of the front line fell. All the Arazi and Espher armies toppled before the blast. Dragons were flung to earth or launched so far into the sky that their breath was stolen. When the fog of war cleared, it was clear the battle was done.

The Arazi were in full rout.

THE LONG ROAD HOME

Caldo, Regola Dei Cerva 112

Victory did not taste as sweet as Artemio had hoped. The march home was twice as long as the ride north, made all the longer by the injured and the dead that had to be carried. The threat of attack by the Arazi had faded as their rear guard had vanished over the horizon after tasting what the Shadebound of Espher were capable of when pressed to their limits. But it seemed that all of the energy that had driven men to war was absent on their return.

Watches were still set through each night as they made camp, and the Shadebound remained dispersed along the train in case a stray dragon or two remained in the skies, but Artemio felt quite certain they would not be needed. He knew the look of a beaten dog slinking back to its master. The Arazi had been bested on the field of battle despite their obvious supremacy in numbers, and it would be a long time before they tried again, if he was any judge of character.

Raiders, savages, and privateers would not chase defeat after defeat. They'd sooner overthrow their own leaders and turn to more promising prey. If a bloodied nose was all it took to keep the Arazi from their door, then he was more than happy to have provided it to them.

Still, he felt no satisfaction. For he had his own watch to keep each night. Harmony was beside herself with grief. Overwrought at the loss of the peasant girl. But despite whatever he might have felt he owed Orsina, she was, in truth, a small price to pay for victory. He did not voice such thoughts to Harmony, of course. He was too attached to his own skin.

By day she seemed as dead and gone as Orsina surely was. Eyes sunken and staring. But by night it was as though a berserk shade possessed her. She fought him to get free of her tent. Desperate to get out, to go, to search for the girl. As if anyone could have survived that. There were scratch marks on his arms, and his jaw still ached from the first night he'd tried to restrain her without forethought. A battle he had made it through unscathed, but an evening in his sister's company was another matter entirely.

It seemed she was entirely immune to reason, at least in as far as this one subject was concerned. "She is still out there."

"Harm, even if the shades didn't kill her, she fell among the Arazi. They are not a people who take prisoners, even if it were possible to take Shadebound prisoner."

"She is alive, Art. I know she is. But the longer we leave her out there, the less chance she has." She beat at his chest, wrestling free of his grasp. "Just let me go. Let me go back. I don't need an army, I don't need you. I'll go alone. Just give me a horse, I'll find her myself. You can get back to your terribly important lording about."

He held up his empty hands and spoke softly. "Harmony, she is gone. If you go back north, I'll never see you again. You'll hunt her until you starve, or you'll find her and you'll collapse. I cannot let you go."

There was an awful fierceness in her words, a fury that would deny all reality. "She is alive."

"Then there will be ample evidence."

She blinked. "Evidence?"

"She is bound to the Arazi back in Covotana." He dared to take his eyes off her for a moment to rub at his temples where the headache of the past few days still mounted its own valiant battle. "When we arrive there and find him dead, the truth will out."

It was enough. Enough to still her wrestling and calm her clawing. A hope for her to cling to through the long ride south. If Kagan lived, then

Orsina did too. If he was dead, then at least within the walls of the palace he might have a more substantial way to contain her grief than a tent.

So much of his interest was set upon Harmony each day that he went through the motions of general-ship almost entirely by rote. He had memorized his duties early, and he did them diligently each day, but there were enough attendants and hangers-on about his camp that he likely could have delegated every part of his tasks for the day without a batted eye. Who would care, now that the war was won, if he became lax?

So it was that the army passed back through the empty countryside and fields stripped bare of their crops, rolling their eyes at the foolishness of the peasants for assuming doom was coming. There was an edge of rancor to it, this assumption that the army of Espher might fail. It seemed Artemio was not the only one who was not feeling victorious after driving the Arazi off. Men set on winning glory came away only with a story of what the Shadebound could do when set loose, and the Shadebound in turn were faced with the reality of their own limitations.

Artemio felt none of that. As for the farms, it was the logical course when you could not foresee an outcome to prepare for the worst. He stopped any harassment of the peasants with a clipped word, and they all marched on.

It was not until the city of Covotana herself came into sight that he began to suspect something was wrong. The city gates were shut and no trumpets heralded their return. Worse yet, where the green heraldry of the Cerva family should have been hanging, black cloth was unfurled.

On the march with the army, any news from home was entirely lost on Artemio, and any message sent forth to meet him had been bypassed somewhere on the southern road. Black hangings meant death, a plague in the city, or worse, a royal death.

His stomach turned at the prospect that the twin kings were dead. There was no heir. Neither had managed to father a child in all their years. It would be civil war among their cousins, chaos that many would turn to the general of Espher's armies to settle. Particularly when that general had a claim to the throne of his very own.

The army slowed, but they did not stop. Still they crept on, coming closer and closer to the white walls of the great city, until at last the walls loomed high and those soldiers atop them cut loose the banners.

Black they were, and black they remained as they fluttered open and displayed their livery to the world, shapes wrought in gold. A great eye surrounded by a sunburst.

The flag of the Agrantine Empire.

To be continued in *Bloodbound*.

Thank you for reading *The Last King: Shadebound*. **Please consider rating and reviewing the book on Amazon, as well as any of your other favorite book-discussion sites.** Thousands of books are published around the world every day, all competing to gain traction and attention from readers. If you enjoyed this book and want more like it to be published in the future, then reviews are one of the best ways you can support us.

Regardless of whether you choose to leave a review or not, thank you for taking the time to read *Shadebound*, and we will return with *Blood-bound* very soon!

All the best,
David & G. D.